ODYSSEY'S CHILD

ODYSSEY'S CHILD

John Lockton

Waterside Productions

Printed in the United States of America

First Printing, 2021

ISBN-13: 978-1-956503-55-5 print edition
ISBN-13: 978-1-956503-56-2 ebook edition

Waterside Productions
2055 Oxford Ave
Cardiff, CA 92007
www.waterside.com

For my mother, Alice,
whose tragic death caused me to write this story.

To Jill + Tom,
     A present of the
Caribbean.

TABLE OF CONTENTS

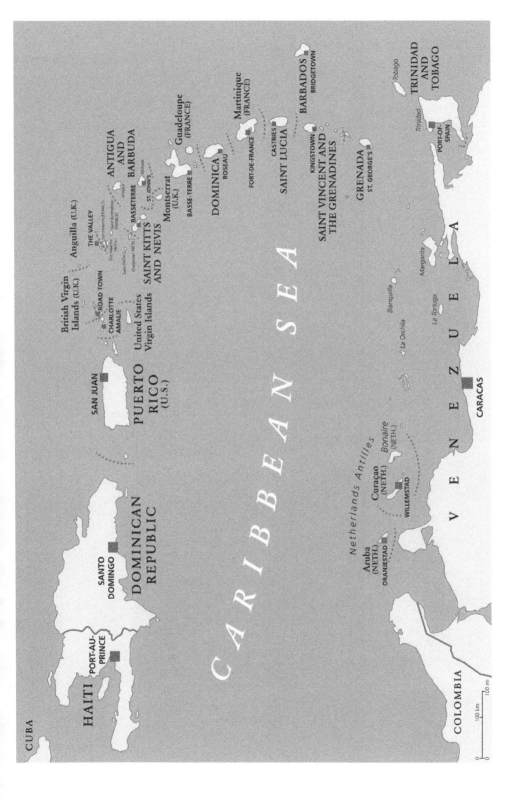

CHAPTER ONE

The kitchen was where he lost everything, February 12, 1950, almost six months to the day after his eleventh birthday. Of all the rooms in their small, one-story clapboard house he had always liked the kitchen best, bright blue and white floor tiles, Delft-style wallpaper, and small blue and white porcelain figurines his mother collected. The figurines made his mother happy, so they made him happy.

He'd gone into the kitchen hoping for a piece of pie left over from the night before, not paying much attention to his mother getting lunch, just thinking about the left-over pie. He looked up and she had stepped backward against the old refrigerator and cabinets, her hands raised up as though she was trying to grab something to keep from falling. She tottered and tried to stay upright. Her face scared him, scrunched in what he assumed was great pain. Then she fell, not exactly fell, sort of slid gently down so she was sitting on the floor, all hunched up with her shoulders propped against a cabinet and the refrigerator door. She was holding her chest.

First she just moaned. Then he heard, "How could this be happening?" She was having trouble breathing but gasped out, "Don't leave me."

He sat down next to her and put his arms around her, trying to support her as she kept slipping down against the cabinet. His voice strangled in his throat. "Mommy? Mommy what's wrong? Tell me what's wrong." He was frozen in place, so frightened he couldn't think or act, tears rolling down his face.

She took his hand and held it hard, "I love you." Then she said over and over again, "Don't leave me. I need you here. I don't want to die alone."

Everything inside him contracted. How could she be dying? Fear took his breath to shallow pants. A growing sense of loss. She couldn't die. She couldn't. What would he do without her? He couldn't live without her. He sat holding her in blind panic, bawling as though the loss had already occurred.

1

She was his life.

A long time passed with her slumped against the cabinet and with him holding her. She started crying like he was and kept saying, "Don't leave me." He begged her repeatedly, "What can I do? Please. Tell me what to do." What came back was, "Just hold me." He had to do something. Gathering his legs under him he started to get up to go for help. With her waning strength she pulled him back down. "No. Stay with me."

His mother's voice kept getting weaker. She finally said, "I'm dying." He was sobbing uncontrollably. She tried to put her arms around him, couldn't, but reached out and drew him closer. "I'm not leaving you. I'm with you forever. My love is with you forever." Her breath now came in little gasps. "Always remember I love you." Then one more time so low he could hardly hear it, "I love you."

He was still holding her when she died, telling her how much he loved her. He let her down on the floor, his tears dripping on her face as he looked down on her death.

After his mother died he ran next door. The doctor and his father got there fast. The doctor examined his mother and said she'd had a heart condition for some time. "Didn't want to tell you about it."Turning hard eyes on him the doctor asked, "How long was it between her heart attack and when you ran for help?"

"I don't know but maybe an hour or more. She didn't want me to leave. She wouldn't let me go."

The doctor cut him off, his voice shaking with fury, "I could have saved her had you gone for help. Terrible not to have gone for help. How could you let her die like that?"

After the doctor stomped out, his father turned on him, his face red with rage, fists balled to hit him, screaming, "Why didn't you do something? Why didn't you run to the neighbors? They were home. Are you so stupid you didn't even know to go to our front parlor and call the operator?" Grabbing him by the shoulders his father shook him hard, then threw him to the floor. He fell dazed, hurting, knocked flat on his back on the floor, bawling his pain and fear. His father stood over him. "Yes cry you little shit. I'm going to make you cry the rest of your life. You might as well have shot her. How does it feel to kill your own mother?"

The first kick landed on the side of his head and an arm he'd raised to protect himself. Blood trickled across his face from a gash above his eyebrow. His right eye was partially closed. Squinting, lying on his side, he could see his father was wearing his brown, going to work shoes. The shoes walked slowly around him building his dread, looking for the next place to deliver a kick. He noticed sewn seams at the toes, raised welts to make the kicking more painful. Trying to inch away he didn't get far. Another kick was delivered to his stomach, knocking his breath out. He thought he would die and retched up everything in his stomach.

"Get up. I want to look a murderer in the face."

He lay there in his vomit and blood, hoping immobility would assuage his father's anger. Now in a fetal position he put his arms around his head for protection. So the next kick landed mostly on his arms, breaking two of his fingers and badly gashing both forearms, and also leaving one ear mashed. He couldn't hear, a loud ringing sound. The final kick was again delivered to his stomach and with less force than the preceding three. Maybe his father was getting tired of it. That kick didn't hurt much, or perhaps everything hurt so much he could no longer pick any one hurt out.

He lay there for almost an hour, crying all the time, crying for his mother, crying because he was afraid of his father, and crying from the pain which had become intense. Blood was flowing freely from both his arms and his forehead. Maybe he could explain. He struggled up and staggered to find his father, locating him in his parent's bedroom. He could hardly stand everything hurt so much. Each step toward the bedroom filled him with dread and several times he started to turn back. Trembling all over he opened the bedroom door and entered. His father was lying on his back on the bed, staring at the ceiling, and didn't glance over at him when he came in.

Ethan came to the side of the bed and said in a scared, shaky voice, "I couldn't go next door. Mother begged me to stay with her. She begged me over and over again. I asked her what to do. She kept saying, 'Don't leave me, don't leave me,' maybe twenty times." He was crying so hard he had to stop talking, then in a stronger voice, "I couldn't just leave her like that."

His father continued to stare at the ceiling, then sat up abruptly and looked at him with such hate that Ethan recoiled backward as if from a blow.

"Don't give me excuses. Bunch of crap. You killed her. You could have saved her and you killed her." His father reached out from the bed and tried to hit him. He ducked and ran to hide in his bedroom. A long night howling for his mother and from the thought he might have killed her, blood seeping from his wounds to stain the bed, the bandages he'd gotten from the medicine cabinet doing little.

CHAPTER TWO

June 1951. Ethan was sure he was being kidnapped. His father dragged him toward the entrance doors of the Albany airport. He braced his feet against each passing curb. No use. The glass on the doors reflected a tall angry man and a badly frightened thirteen-year-old. He struggled against his father's tight grip, twisting and turning with all his might, his left arm already badly bruised from previous struggles. His father was too strong. Resistance was useless. Nor had his crying had any effect, though he'd cried all the way to the airport.

...

The preceding morning his father had hauled him into the kitchen and sat him down at the table for what he called, "A talk." He hated talks. Usually they ended up with a beating or other punishment.

June sunshine streamed through half-opened windows. The scent of his mother's roses filled the room, carried on a soft, warm breeze, and summer haze softened the view of distant foliage, all reminding him of how much he wanted to be anywhere but sitting where he was. First day of vacation and he'd been looking forward to spending the shining Upstate New York morning exploring nature in the neighboring woods, his favorite pastime. Always the kitchen for his father's talks. Since his mother's death a year and one half earlier Ethan hated the room. His father knew it. Which was why his father chose the kitchen for talks.

His father sat silent for a few moments, his eyes cold, his mouth a thin line, looking away. His father rarely ever looked at him. This time his father was focusing out the window. He sighed, continued to avert his gaze, and said, "With what's happened, I've decided to send you away. Mr. van Rosendahl has agreed to take you. You're leaving tomorrow at noon. He has a boat in the Caribbean. You will be down there with him for the next two months."

That was it. No explanation of why. No information on how Mr. van Rosendahl came into it. He didn't know Mr. van Rosendahl and knew his father didn't either.

His face and whole body went taunt. He jumped up from the table, hands held up in front of him to push the words away, shaking all over, looking incredulously at his father, then an open mouth howl, "No, No, No!" at an increasing volume, his vocal cords straining, rarely used since his mother died, tears bursting out so fiercely that he could hardly see as he dashed from the table into his bedroom, crawled into his closet as he often did, his refuge, shut the door to bring on the darkness. Every part of his life was darkness.

He knew exactly what was going on. His father and Mr. van Rosendahl must have thought he was really stupid not to know what was happening. They were trying to get rid of him. Somehow his father had gotten Mr. van Rosendahl to join in a plot to put him away, scheming together just like bad guys in the movies.

This was his father's revenge for having killed his mother.

He quietly opened his bedroom door and ran for the front door, determined to hide out in the woods. His father stood by the door and gave him a contemptuous smile of self-satisfaction for having anticipated his move. Grabbing his shoulder, his father said, "Don't worry about it. It's only for two months, a great opportunity."

But his eyes shifted away as they did when he was lying. He lied all the time. So probably it would be much longer. Maybe forever. He didn't trust his father at all. His father went on to say someone called Fritz Bolton, Mr. van Rosendahl's cousin's son, was going along. Probably another lie to keep him from knowing what was really intended. His father locked the front door with the big lock he had installed the last time he'd run away, and with great show pocketed the key.

Who was kidding whom? It made no sense. Why would the richest and most important man in town want to have a boy with him, a boy he didn't know? Had to be bad. In the movies when the hero ends up under the control of a stranger terrible things happened, for boys, a kidnapping.

That night his father ordered him to dig his sleeping bag out of the attic and sleep on the floor next to his bed. "Can't have you sneaking out a window and running away like the last time," which was exactly what he'd intended to do. Escape was cut off.

As he struggled to get comfortable on the hard floor, his old sleeping bag far too small, fright only increased. He feared Mr. van Rosendahl and he feared being away from home. He'd never been away from home. Now he was to go off with a person he didn't know for reasons that were lies. What was planned? It had to be more than his father was saying. No way would his father want to give him an opportunity. His father hated him. Maybe Mr. van Rosendahl was supposed to leave him at an orphanage or something in the Caribbean. Or maybe Mr. van Rosendahl had agreed to abandon him on some desert island. He'd be like Robinson Crusoe. Only he'd die there like his father wanted. He would never be allowed back home again.

. . .

The next morning his father tried to persuade him one more time that the trip would be wonderful. Ethan cried all through breakfast, couldn't hold it back. His father threatened to beat him "If he didn't end this nonsense."

He cried some more, got beaten, never said yes to the trip. Now here he was at the Albany Airport being dragged through the swinging doors to Mr. van Rosendahl.

But really, didn't he deserved whatever he got for causing his mother's death?

When they came up to Mr. van Rosendahl his fear was so great he was shaking all over. One more time he tried to pull away. Unsuccessful. But maybe there was hope. Mr. van Rosendahl looked very unhappy, his shoulders sort of hunched like something bad had happened, a dark scowl on his face, his mouth turned down. Was there a miracle? The trip called off? Mr. van Rosendahl took his father aside. His father glared at him threateningly and warned that if he moved one inch he'd get beaten right there in the airport.

Their discussion was very brief. His father frowned deeply, and looked very upset and angry. First his father strongly shook his head no to something, then after more talk he gave a small nod with his head hanging down, looking resigned to something, not looking at Mr. van Rosendahl. Mr. van Rosendahl smiled and grabbed his father's hand, shaking it vigorously. His father's hand was limp, not shaking back.

Again his father took hold of his arm. Same place. It hurt! Marched him to the departure gate. At the gate his father told him, "Fritz Bolton has broken his leg. You'll be going alone with Mr. van Rosendahl."

Ethan tried not to cry again, but it came. Now he was going to be alone with his kidnapper. The Fritz Bolton stuff was a big lie just like he expected. Everything he'd been told was a lie.

His father's goodbye at the departure gate didn't make him any happier— a bare pat on the shoulder, no hug, and no indication that his father cared that he'd be away for at least two months. All his father said to him was, "You'll be all right. Mr.van Rosendahl says he'll take care of you and make sure you have a good time." His father spoke looking at the air around him, not meeting his eyes.

Wishing him a good time didn't mean his father ever wanted him back.

His father made a final comment to Mr. van Rosendahl. "Sarah's death caused him to stop talking. They were very close. Maybe you can do something. I haven't been able to."

Mr. van Rosendahl shoved him on a bus taking them out to a plane, a firm grip on his shoulder keeping him from running away. The sign said they were flying to Idlewild Airport, New York. Mr. van Rosendahl told him that at Idlewild they'd board a Pan Am Stratocruiser for an eight hour overnight flight to San Juan.

Ethan had never been on a plane, but didn't look around when he entered the plane for Idlewild and took his seat with his head slumped down and his gaze on his lap. He didn't look up even when he was pressed against his seat at take-off, a surprising experience. And all the rattling. Was something about to fall off? He didn't care as long as Mr. van Rosendahl died in the crash. He determined not to cry any more, didn't want to give Mr. van Rosendahl the satisfaction of seeing him cry. And when Mr. van Rosendahl tried to talk to him, he put his hands over his ears. The man eventually stopped.

When they got to the Transfer Lounge at Idlewild, he decided that if he could prevent Mr. van Rosendahl from taking him on the the flight to San

Juan, maybe he could somehow get back home. He waited until almost flight time, asked to go to the bathroom, locked himself in a stall, and climbed up to stand on the toilet seat so no one could see where he was or easily grab his legs and pull him out.

The flight was called and Mr. van Rosendahl came in to find him. He banged on the closed doors of other stalls. "You in there, Ethan?" getting irritated responses in reply. When he came to Ethan's stall, and he didn't answer, Mr. van Rosendahl got down on the floor and his face appeared below the stall door. The stall door was too low for him to wiggle in.

"What are you doing? We've got to go. The flight is leaving."

He didn't move. Mr. van Rosendahl ran out and yelled loudly for an attendant, and he could hear a number of voices conversing. After about ten minutes footsteps approached. The door popped open. Mr. van Rosendahl grabbed him by the arm in the exact same place where his father had gripped him (it really hurt) and pulled him along to the departure gate. He fought as much as he could.

A policeman came over and asked Mr. van Rosendahl what was going on. He answered, "My son is just acting up."

Ethan said "no" in a strangled voice and continued to fight. The policeman frowned skeptically. Hope for a moment. But the policeman let them go.

. . .

Holy Moly, this was bad. Worse than bad. Awful. He brought to mind everything he'd heard about Mr. van Rosendahl, all the bad gossip about him at church. Every Sunday his father and his mother, Sarah, while she was alive, hauled him to ten o'clock service at Christ Church Episcopal in Schenectady. Boring. Mr. van Rosendahl never talked to him or his father at church, but he was head vestryman so there was much talk about him.

After the Sunday service Ethan would join other parishioners and mosey over to the parish hall for coffee hour. He always looked forward to the parish hall. Its interior with mullioned stained-glass windows, dark mahogany wainscoting, and a large gothic-style stone fireplace were so beautiful compared to his own modest house. But what was really beautiful was the trestle tables. Set up for coffee hour by wealthy ladies of a wealthy parish, every inch of each trestle table heaped with immense amounts of marvelous stuff to eat. His focus was the jelly doughnuts, though his father restricted consumption so as not to spoil his appetite for lunch.

Coffee hour was always gossip hour. His father sourly complained, "How can these people sit here and gossip endlessly about each other? They just came from church. What happened to love thy neighbor?" But gossip they did.

The gossip about Mr. van Rosendahl usually originated from a group of four older widowed parishioners, best friends, who seem to feel that their age and active participation in parish life entitled them to pass judgement on everybody and everything in the parish. Ethan overheard all the group's gossip at one time or another.

"George doesn't treat his wife very well. She always seems unhappy. He never talks about her or says a nice thing about her, and she is such a dear person. He's a very mean man."

And, "He's such a skin flint. Never gives much to my charity. Doesn't care about other people." Each of the women appeared to have a pet charity to which they felt Mr. van Rosendahl had not given adequately.

And a complaint heard repeatedly from the ladies and others, "He never does the Christian thing. Never gives church members a discount on cars at his dealerships."

The leader of the group was a widow with bluish hair (Ethan always stared at the hair), supported by a cane, by a clouded-eyed, wrinkled face, and by what Ethan heard was ninety years of church attendance. For no apparent reason, she announced one Sunday at coffee hour, in a voice much louder than what was necessary to reach her three cohorts, that Mr. van Rosendahl seemed to think he was better than anyone else in the church, treated others badly, only cared for himself and his comforts, was not a true Christian. She went on, "I don't even think he believes in God. He's so full of himself he thinks he knows more than God. And the mean way he treats everyone he thinks isn't as good as he is. Really evil. He's an evil man." She spouted off at regular intervals about anyone or anything, much like the venting of his mother's steam kettle. He came to think of her as the "Steam Kettle Lady," but could not avoid her gossip.

He never heard anything good said about Mr. van Rosendahl. And now Mr. van Ronsendahl was kidnaping him from home. A very bad man had him in his clutches.

. . .

When Ethan boarded the Statocruiser, a stewardess led him to his seat. He had the inside seat and George the outside of the first row of first-class. George said they were the best seats on the plane, the quietest and you were served first.

As soon as they sat down George said, "Call me George. Don't call me Mr. van Rosendahl. I'm sorry for what happened back there. I had to get you on the plane. These seats cost a bundle. I know this is all very hard for you. Here you are leaving home and not even knowing me. But when you get to know me I'm going to be the best friend you ever had. I want to be your best friend, okay?"

Ethan didn't even look at him.

George went on, "You're going to have a great time with me. I'm going to give you the best damn time you've ever had."

He talked slowly as though wanting him to understand each word, his brows knit in concentration, face close to his, eyes staring into his own in non-blinking intensity, more focus on him than from any adult since his mother died. Ethan trusted none of it. His father often lied. George probably did, too. All that George's talking nice to him meant was that he wanted something. No adult treated him well anymore unless they wanted something.

Take-off again pushed Ethan back in his seat, and the noise and vibrations were much greater than on the Albany flight. It scared him until it stopped. Now airborne, Ethan took a look around as he hadn't on the Albany flight. He'd seen a lot of airplane movies. He liked airplanes. This looked like the inside of a plane that he had seen in a movie where a spy carries a packet of secret papers to Europe.

When the seatbelt sign turned off George showed him around the plane—how the lavatories worked, the downstairs seating area for cocktails and dinner, and George got a stewardess to show him the cockpit, though she said this wasn't usually allowed. This *was* the same type of plane he had seen in the movie, but it didn't make him any happier.

What would happen if he told the nice blonde stewardess that he was being kidnapped? Probably nothing. George would say he was emotionally disturbed or something, and just missing home. The man had already lied to the cop at Idlewild.

Back in their seats, Ethan listened to non-stop talk from George. It was obviously an attempt to make him forget that he didn't want to be here and get him excited about the trip. No chance.

George started by saying they would be visiting all the Windward and Leeward Islands of the Caribbean. "The last two summers I sailed my boat with a few of my golfing buddies from the club. The boat is called *Rascal* by the way. We only visited some of the islands. This year we'll have a great adventure. Visit all the islands. You'll have some great stories to tell people back home."

Stupid statement. Back home he rarely talked and nobody listened to him when he did.

George described in great detail each of the islands they would be visiting. Each, according to George, was beautiful and fascinating. Ethan was reminded of some of the promotional shorts before the main feature where they're trying to get you to visit some place like Hawaii. All of this while George would interrupt himself with, "Isn't that great," or, "Won't that be marvelous," and similar enthusiasms. Ethan just looked at George.

Throughout George talked with an arm around his shoulders. He squirmed away as far as the seat allowed. And George threw down regular refills of Remy-Martin brandy and soda, apparently his preferred drink.

At one point George branched off from talk about islands to talk about *Rascal's* mate, Johnson, how Ethan would be very safe with Johnson aboard, how Johnson had saved the life of the prior owner of *Rascal*. According to George, the prior owner had been caught in a violent storm far out to sea, just the owner and Johnson aboard. Trying to go below deck to chart the course, the owner had pitched headfirst down the companionway and been badly injured. Johnson had single-handedly brought the boat through the storm to a safe harbor and gotten the owner to a hospital in time to save his life. George said, "Without Johnson, I wouldn't be taking this trip."

While Ethan hated everything he was hearing about the voyage, he thought he might like to meet Johnson.

George was very good looking compared to his father. Whereas his father had a receding chin and small beady eyes under sparse blond eyebrows, George had deeply set bright-blue eyes, their strength magnified by sharp contrast to bushy black eyebrows and black hair, a commanding face, large and somewhat square, thrusting chin with a small cleft, a prominent Roman nose, all capped by a pronounced widow's peak. Didn't witches and warlocks have widows' peaks? Ethan realized with a start that George's eyes were the same blue as his own.

George talked funny, sort of through his nose, like the English guys in the movies, his mouth opening very little. How did he talk so much without opening his mouth more? And he always had his big chin up in the air and looked down at him past his large nose. George posed the same way with his father at the departure gate, as if he thought he was better than anyone. And when he smiled, and he smiled at him constantly, the eyes didn't smile. The corners of his mouth turned up, no teeth showing, and that was it. George was making his mouth smile to hide from him the real George. At least his face wasn't mean like his father's.

George and his father were alike in one way. They were both starting to bald in the back. George kept patting the top of his head while talking as though checking to see what hair was still there. He'd combed his hair over from the side to cover his thinning spot, glued it down with pomade or something.

He looked a bit like Cary Grant in the movies, though heavier. People stared at George in the airports and on the planes, maybe thinking he *was* Cary Grant. Cary Grant usually played nice guys. George was a bad guy hiding behind a nice-guy face.

Dinner brought Ethan downstairs. He sat with George across from a man and his wife from Canada. The couple owned a ranch in Saskatchewan and told Ethan stories of protecting cattle in harsh winters and killing wolves. They thought he was George's son. George said nothing to deny it. Ethan wanted to object, but remained silent.

Eventually the Canadian couple asked about his mother. He burst out crying and tried to escape the table.

George grabbed him and pulled him back, saying, "Ethan's mother died not too long ago. I'm a good friend of the family, taking Ethan to the Caribbean to help him recover. He's in a bad way." Ethan struggled, but finally was forced to sit still, though he didn't eat anything.

The Canadian woman clucked over him and congratulated George. "You're doing such a wonderful thing."

Ethan felt like throwing up in the woman's lap.

As they mounted the stairway to the upper deck, George asked him what he was doing with his left hand. After his mother died he found himself regularly doing a counting exercise with his left hand—thumb touching each finger of his left hand in sequence, one, two, three, four, and then back again, four, three, two, one. He did this whenever he was nervous, which was often, faster when he was more nervous, sometimes half an hour at a time. It seemed to help. Now he was doing it very fast. He answered George's question with an empty stare.

Back in their seats, George, drink in hand, gazed at him for a long time to a point where he got embarrassed.

George asked, "Has anyone ever told you you have a beautiful face? Small ears, not like these big things of mine that stick out too much." George pulled one of his ears away from his head. "A sensible nose. No beak like mine. And a reasonable mouth. Look at my mouth. It's big enough to swallow a whale. As I recall, your mother had those same big, dark-blue eyes."

Ethan stiffened in his seat, face rigid, staring directly ahead with lips compressed.

George continued, "You probably know it already. My eyes are the same shade as yours. You could be my son. You're going to have to beat women off when you grow up. Bet the girls are already chasing you at school."

Ethan gave no indication of agreement. His mother had said much the same thing about his face. But at school none of the girls wanted to be with him, nor the boys either, though he did like to watch Betsy. He thought about her a lot. She was the prettiest girl there, and she always gave him a smile.

George slumped down in his seat and looked away. His voice went low. "I don't know whether you know it, but I have no children. I'd sure like to have a son that looked like you."

Arriving early in the morning in San Juan, they went to the Hilton Hotel to catch up on their sleep for four or five hours before taking the afternoon plane to St. Thomas. George wanted Ethan to share his room.

Ethan turned away and hung his head. He had his own room at home. George hadn't behaved like one of those kidnappers in the movies, probably an act. George had yanked him out of his home for reasons he couldn't understand. Fear in the pit of his stomach. He ran for the hotel door. Trouble with the door and George caught him. But a separate room did appear. He cried himself to sleep, dreading life.

CHAPTER THREE

The afternoon plane to St. Thomas was a four-seater *"island – hopper"* with a single pilot. Ethan found himself positioned in the co-pilot's seat. George told him that he chose the co-pilot seat for him so he could see everything. "Maybe it'll help with your homesickness."

As he entered the plane the sense of loss and abandonment welled up stronger than ever. How far he'd already come from Niskayuna. This was hopeless. Everything was hopeless. He fought against the tears. No crying in front of George.

Once airborne, Ethan did look as instructed. He couldn't help it seated where he was. Scenery like nothing he'd ever seen. Spectacular green-clad islands cradled in the deep blue Caribbean Sea, the islands surrounded by golden sand in bright bracelets, an immense concave of pure sapphire sky above, the Caribbean sky much wider and more beautiful than any at home. Then came St. Thomas and the wild green abandon of tropical foliage growing, no exploding, unbelievably lush and green around him on the way to the boat, so different from the woods in Niskayuna. And a different sun beating on his head and shoulders, much fiercer, lighting the greenery as though from an inward fire, and glittering on the sea with dancing light.

Ethan took it all in. He might as well. He was stuck with it. It just made him sad. All that light and beauty contrasted so strongly with the darkness in his life. Everything good had been taken away by his mother's death. He consciously felt sadness seeping into him, like the black rain that crept in under the cellar door in downpours. His throat felt heavy and dense with the sorrow.

Ethan's despair lifted a little when they arrived at *Rascal,* berthed in the harbor of Charlotte Amelie, and met the mate, Johnson. He had never seen a blacker human being. Startlingly black, so black he was blue-black. Johnson had a pungent cigarette dangling from his mouth. He snubbed it out, carefully placed the unsmoked butt in a shirt pocket, and came toward Ethan in a rolling walk, his feet planted well apart as though balancing on a boat's deck.

He clasped both of Ethan's hands in his own large ones. "Welcome," he said. A broad smile. A warm laugh. "You goin to be de best sailor *Rascal* ever had. My name Horatio Nelson Johnson. Name after Lord Horatio Nelson. Everybody call me Johnson. I from Antigua. Best island in de Caribbean."

Not as tall as George, but much broader. He looked very strong, lots of muscle, sinewy tendons bulging his arms. Nobody would bully him at home if he had those muscles.

Ethan liked him immediately, partly because he looked so different from the people tormenting him at home. A broad nose flaring to sharply chiseled nostrils, the broadest nose he'd ever seen, gleaming white teeth that made the rest of his face look even blacker, tightly curled hair close to the skull, square jaw, forehead wrinkled and squint lines at the corners of his eyes, kind eyes, large, so dark brown they were almost black.

The smile was amazing, the widest smile he'd ever seen. When Johnson smiled he opened his large mouth completely as though ready to gobble something big and delicious, closed his eyes to mere slits, and rolled back his full upper lip so not only teeth but gums were exposed. People in Niskayuna didn't smile in that exuberant open-mouthed way.

Johnson cocked his head and asked him, "You ever sail before dis?"

He shook his head. Johnson's voice was even deeper than George's. At first, he had difficulty understanding. The cadence was sing-song, and words were accented differently. But it was how Johnson talked to him that was really different. Johnson looked into his eyes with a constant and unflinching gaze, focused his entire attention on him, communicated more strongly than anyone he remembered ever talking to, even his mother.

"What about de ocean. You ever see de ocean before?" Again he shook his head. "You one lucky boy. De ocean and sailing' about de two best thing God make on dis Earth."

George said, "Johnson. Ethan is not going to answer you. He hardly speaks at all."

"Well, if you no talk dat give me more time to tell you thing, tell you about de ocean and sailin'. I goin to tell you everythin' I knows."

George then took Johnson aside to discuss supplies for the trip.

Ethan thought about the story George had told, how Johnson saved the man. He could believe it. Something about Johnson made him feel Johnson could overcome anything. That he could depend upon him. That if anything bad happened on the boat Johnson would get him into a safe harbor, just like he did with the man George talked about.

He feared everything about the voyage. But with Johnson aboard he felt a little better.

The discussion regarding supplies took some time, George occasionally patting his head and keeping his chin in the air, talking down to Johnson. Johnson called George "Sir" when addressing him. But he talked to George as an equal, not like some of the staff in the big houses back home who almost seemed to be bowing to the owners. Johnson had a gold cross hanging from his neck and fingered it as he talked to George.

At a certain point George raised his voice. "You got all the other supplies. Why the hell didn't you get my French coffee? I brought my French coffee press all this way down here, and by God, I'm going to use it. We need to find that coffee. It has got to be on St. Thomas somewhere. Damn. George poked Johnson in the chest with his finger. You didn't look hard enough. I found it last year. I'll find it again."

Johnson just looked at George, waiting for him to finish. It reminded Ethan of mothers in Niskayuna patiently waiting for a child to finish a tantrum.

Ethan traipsed along with George and Johnson as they searched for the coffee. George was whistling happily much of the way. How different St. Thomas was from Niskayuna, particularly the open sewers, sewers choked with broken bottles, punctured beer cans, floating excrement, and other fetid black matter that flowed slowly along the sides of the downtown streets and into the sea. The whole downtown had a sweet, putrid smell despite the strong trade wind.

They finally found the coffee in a small French-owned store at the edge of town. George bought it and Johnson bought several cartons of French Gauloise cigarettes.

George turned to Johnson, exulting, "Told you so." Johnson gazed back impassively.

Ethan thought of running away. He was fast. But then what would he do? A white boy in a black city. They would find him very quickly. No escape in the Caribbean. Trapped now with them as much as with his own despair.

He lived all his waking hours with the despair, a dark circle which started with daydreams about his mother and happy times together, then the bad memory would come and anger at himself, then the overwhelming sadness, then again daydreams, anger, and sadness. Over and over again. No way out. His mind whirled and whirled all day long, taking him deeper and deeper into black thoughts which seemed ever worse as time passed.

When they returned to *Rascal,* George changed to his sailing clothes (Brooks Brothers shirts and shorts throughout the voyage). George, his chin in the air, told Ethan he was a firm believer in dressing right whatever the surroundings. Johnson had already put on his sailing attire, pressed khaki shorts and a clean khaki shirt.

Ethan had not been told what clothes to bring, and had only one pair of shorts and these were worn from his explorations in the woods at home. He'd put them on that morning together with a much-washed tee shirt, feeling some embarrassment, just like he felt embarrassment at school because his father never bought him clothing like what the popular boys were wearing.

George looked Ethan over from his vantage point of brand-new Brooks Brother's clothing. "What clothes did you bring?"

Ethan did not answer, but opened his suitcase and showed him.

George shook his head. "Won't do on *Rascal.* If a sailor is sloppy in dress then he's sloppy in other things. I'm going to buy you the best sailing clothes I can find," and he sent Johnson out to run down appropriate attire for Ethan.

...

Clothing dealt with, Ethan stood on the dock and studied *Rascal.* He'd seen pictures of sailboats. But *Rascal* was the first he'd seen in person. Her thirty-eight feet seemed pretty big compared to boats on the Mohawk River. And very complicated. Two masts with the bigger mast forward and the smaller aft. George, standing beside him, said it was a ketch rig with main mast forward and mizzen mast aft. The ropes running up and down the masts were halyards, and those running from the ends of the booms were sheets. Everything was led to the aft seating area, which George called the cockpit. Sails wrapped around the booms. How did the sails get off the booms and up the masts to look like pictures of sailboats he had seen? A steering wheel was positioned in the cockpit between the two masts. George called it, "The helm." Entrances to below decks were through a forward hatch and a stairway (companionway) at the front of the aft cockpit.

The boat glistened in the strong sun. Bright white paint on the sides looked new, and the railings and other woodwork glowed with shining varnish. George said the varnished wood was called brightwork and that Johnson had to constantly sand and re-varnish it to keep ahead of damage from sun and salt water. The decks were teak without a mark of wear on them. What he was seeing was beautiful.

George said, "You never need to be afraid of sailing when you sail on *Rascal*. She's the safest boat around. Bad storms aren't even a problem with *Rascal*."

Bad storms? George was deliberately ignoring the most important bad thing, what he intended to do to him during the voyage. He had much more to fear from George than from bad storms!

Taking Ethan aboard, George gave him a tour of the below decks, first directing him to the port (left) bunk in the main cabin, his bunk for the voyage. George told him he would take the opposite starboard (right) bunk. Johnson would bunk in the forward cabin. Bad news. The man he dreaded would be sleeping right across from him for the duration.

Forward, George introduced him to the head with a lengthy instruction on water pumping and lever setting, and a warning not to overload the head. "Don't mess up. If you do it wrong it'll explode all over you."

Ethan imagined what it would be like if he overloaded the head, getting sick or something and vomiting into it, or having that terrible diarrhea, and then having it come back all over him. Then he pictured it happening to George, and felt his unhappiness dissipating a little.

Before going top-side, Ethan looked around one last time. He didn't think consciously about it, but felt hemmed in. George could easily close the hatches and hold him prisoner. The trap was tightening.

Ready to get underway, George instructed Ethan on safety. Then dock lines were cast off by Johnson, a graceful leap by Johnson from pier to back deck as *Rascal* motored away. Once through the boats anchored close to shore, Johnson hoisted the sails, telling Ethan what he was doing as he did it.

Ethan watched for a while, but ended up staring vacantly at the deck in front of him. He'd slipped into one of what he called his "bad times" when he withdrew from things around him, turned inside, had no desire but to be absent from everybody and everything, almost gone. He fought it as always, but the pull was very strong, to just disappear forever, to disappear inside himself, escape. If nobody can see you are you still there?

A push from above brought him out of it. They'd already cruised around Water Island and were clearing the harbor. *Rascal* heeled gently. Then another push, then a steady thrust and more pronounced heel, somewhat disconcerting as he'd not anticipated the heel. *Rascal's* bow cut through the light chop, living water gliding past her sides in quiet lapping, then gradually the motion changed to that of the sea, pitching and rolling him as he stood holding a rail. He looked up at the sails filling with wind. The rigging started to emit a low-pitched wine, *Rascal's* song. Overhead a solitary gull screeched a welcome to the open ocean.

Ethan could see the ocean stretched forever. On this clear day he was looking at the end of the world. And the space between sea and sky was vast. Unlike anything he'd seen before.

Trade-wind clouds drifted low through an azure sky, making the blue of the deep ocean seem even bluer by contrast. And the motion was now more pronounced. Waves lifted *Rascal* with relentless regularity, alive under his feet. Why this unchanging rhythm? He experimented and found that by slightly anticipating the movement he could remain upright in fairly stationary position. He practiced for some time. It was a game he played with himself, sort of like trying to stand on one foot back home or ride his bike with no hands. Gradually he got so he could stand for short periods without holding on. George congratulated him on getting "sea legs" so quickly. He didn't look at him.

While everything about the ocean was different, what surprised him most was the color variation. Light blues and aquamarines banded the shores, dark blue water around *Rascal* heaving up translucent in steep approaching waves with light shining through, shafts of purple and azure penetrating deep down when he looked over the side, and everywhere streaks of white, waves breaking white on reefs and land, white foam steaming along *Rascal's* sides and riding far astern on the bubbling wake, white beyond the point where an increasing wind was blowing tops off seas.

...

George couldn't take his eyes off Ethan standing near the bow. Ethan was staring out at the ocean, his head turning to see everything, looking totally enthralled. Slim, like his dead mother, with her fine bones. His Anglo Saxon ancestry evident in his fair skin, starting to burn in the Caribbean sun. Intelligent appearing with a high forehead and alert gaze. A thatch of thick hair that looked totally resistant to the comb, so blond it was almost white, now blown sideways in an unruly mop by errant gusts of trade-wind.

The boy appeared very immature for his age. Not in size. He was of reasonable height for his age. Immature in his open, innocent face. Vulnerable. One did not see the self-assurance that boys have entering teenage years. One did not see development of the protective maleness of maturity. George smiled to himself as he thought of his plans for the boy. He shouldn't have much trouble. The boy was so vulnerable and needy.

...

As they tacked back and forth, Ethan scrambled quickly to stand on the higher side. George asked, "Are you doing that to balance *Rascal* against tipping over?"

Ethan just looked forward at the tilt of the deck.

George laughed. "Everyone sailing the first time is afraid their sailboat will tip over. *Rascal* has a keel below balancing her with thousands of pounds of lead. She'll never tip over." George then illustrated with his hands how the weight of the keel balanced against the tipping motion. "Another thing. The tipping is a safety valve. The more we tip the less wind hits the sails." He again illustrated with his hands how the tipping of the boat relieved the wind pressure on the sails. "When *Rascal* tips she is just doing her job of protecting us from strong wind."

Ethan understood the explanation, but kept moving from side to side with the tacks, not trusting George.

Going east along the northern coast of St. Thomas, George was at the helm whistling occasionally, and pointing out what they were seeing. "That's a very dangerous reef. A boat was wrecked there last year." And, "You see those birds with big beaks flying in formation. They're pelicans. You've heard about Pelicans, right? Beaks can hold more than their bellies can." George laughed as though he invented the rhyme. "And those black birds with the forked tails flying way up there. Those are frigate birds. Wonderful birds."

Ethan just stared down at the passing water, had been doing it most of the last hour, trying by concentrated effort to keep away another of the "bad times" he felt was about ready to steal into him. The bow smashed merrily through small, inshore waves, making interesting patterns on the sea. Who cared?

When the "bad times" came at home he'd sometimes run away to his special place in the woods, a virtual cave under tree limbs. But usually he'd seek the dark of his closet. And it was in the closet that he hid to cry away from the boys' taunts and the bullying. Was there anything worse than being taunted almost every day with "mother killer?" Early on he'd run away crying with his hands over his ears. His recent strategy had been to make out that he didn't hear it, or didn't care, walking straight ahead with eyes fixed, but hear it he did.

He tried to be strong and pretend it wasn't important. He couldn't. It hurt terribly. He wanted more than anything to be liked. To have friends. He didn't have one single friend, no one who would even spend time with him. How terrible was that. He prayed the taunts would stop. They didn't. The boys liked the game they'd invented so they kept playing it. They would call him "mother killer" in Niskayuna as long as he lived.

With Johnson taking over the helm, George sat next to him and said, "Have you ever climbed a steep hill and had to hike switchbacks to get to the top?"

Ethan gave no indication he'd even heard.

"Well that's what we are doing now, only the hill is the wind. And the switchbacks are called tacks. Our anchorage is due east, directly upwind from us. We can't go straight at it as our sails would just flap around. We'd get nowhere sailing directly east. So we angle off, first to the right of the wind and then the left. Wind from the right is the starboard tack, from the left the port tack. Switching back and forth we gradually climb the wind hill. The top of the wind hill is our anchorage for today. We're about to go over to the starboard tack. Want to help?"

When would it end? This was a floating prison. I'm *not* going to do anything to help sail this boat.

Johnson called out, "Ready about. Duck, Ethan!" Then, "Hard-a-lee." Johnson spun the helm over to port and the two men scrambled about doing things. Ethan ignored it all.

When he was relieved at the helm, Johnson took George's place next to Ethan in the cockpit. He gave him his broad, open – mouthed smile, fingered his cross, and focused his intense gaze on him. "I have son name Nathan, just you age. He in school in Antigua. He de second youngest of my six boy. All in school. Two in college. One in London and one in Antigua. All good student. I bet you good student."

Ethan gave no response.

"I sail all my life. Was born on sailboat when my mother be sailin' to St. Johns, Antiqua, to have me in de hospital. I come early. Didn't make land before I born. Since then I sail on boat of every size and kind. Captain or first mate on maybe fifteen different boat. Biggest was *Anna Marie,* inter-island schooner 140 feet long. Haul timber and coffee from Guyana to Antigua and Virgin Islands. Stop at de island along de way. I have many adventure on different boat. Some good. Some bad. I have hurricane and pirate and wreck. Dat a long time ago. Before you born. Not many pirate around now and it early for hurricane."

Ethan had a flicker of interest thinking of the possibility of meeting real pirates.

Johnson continued, "I never worry bout bad things happenin' on boat. Neither should you. What I think about is de good thing from sailing. One of de most special thing God gave man is de sailboat. On a day when de wind be right, de sky bright, de sea not too rough, it de happiest place on earth."

Later still Johnson sat again next to Ethan and told him, "Every boat different. They move different in de water. They sail different. Each have it own personality. We call boat 'she.' They have different personality like women do.

"*Rascal* be good boat. Have peculiarity like all boat. She sail faster on de starboard tack than de port. I never figure out why. When big sea behind her she move back and forth a lot. And she very heavy so once she get going in a headin' she sometime hard to turn. But this all minor stuff. I sail many boat. *Rascal* bout de best. Very solid, well-built boat. You safe on *Rascal* as on any boat in de Caribbean."

Well, at least they were saying the same thing about the safety of the boat.

Standing at the helm, George burst into song. *"All day all night Maryann, Down by the sea shore sifting sand,"* and many following verses. Then, *"Brown skin girl, why don't you stay home and mind baby,"* with again many following verses. He had a good voice, and he certainly sang loudly. Was George singing happily because he had him trapped on *Rascal?* Later in the day Johnson mentioned that George regularly sang calypso songs from the helm.

That night George made a proposal as they were getting ready to sit down in the cockpit for dinner. "Every passage, every day's sail, is a real accomplishment. It's always hard work. It'll sometimes be difficult. At the end of each sail we're going to formally acknowledge what we've accomplished. Shake hands all around. Congratulate each other for survival. For a successful run." George grabbed Ethan's hand and shook it strongly. Then shook hands with Johnson.

George next announced that they would say grace each evening before dinner and Ethan was to say his prayers each night, telling Ethan, "I promised your father we would try and keep you a Christian." He pulled out a small book of graces, patted his head twice, and read one. A good prayer. Very short.

Ethan wanted to get to what was steaming in front of him. It took him about two bites to know Johnson's cooking was much better than his father's.

After dinner George said that for Ethan's benefit each evening, or at other times, he was going to tell what he called "A story of the day." It would be a story or joke about what they had been up to that day.

He sat back and began, "Do you remember that big general store in St. Thomas that we visited looking for the coffee? Well, I was in there last year and a young boy came in, maybe ten. The owner of the store leaned over to someone who was apparently a longtime customer and said, 'This is the dumbest boy in St. Thomas. Watch this.'

"The store owner pulled a dollar bill and two quarters from the cash register and offered the boy a choice. Would he like the dollar or the two quarters? The boy grabbed the two quarters and scooted out of the store. The owner threw his hands up and said to the customer, 'See what I mean. Every day he's in here and he always takes the quarters. Dumbest kid I ever met.'

"Later I ran into the same boy eating ice cream outside another store and asked him why he took the two quarters rather than the dollar. The boy said, 'If I take the dollar the game is up. The money stops.'"

George's face crinkled up, his blue eyes narrowed to slits, and he let off a loud guffaw at his own joke while slapping his right thigh vigorously. Johnson chuckled mildly. Ethan just looked at George in silence.

Ethan crawled into his narrow bunk that night, lumpy compared to his comfortable bed at home, and put a pillow over his head to smother the sound of his crying.

The next four days *Rascal* made short passages around the Virgin Islands, first a few days at various harbors on St. Thomas, and then they sailed to Necker Island and Norman Island in the British Virgin Islands (B.V.I.'s). The passages were half a day or less. George told Ethan the short passages were to get him used to the boat and to sailing. Ethan continued to cry himself to sleep, thinking of his mother, and thinking of what George might do to him.

They spent a lot of time on beaches. The only beaches he'd previously seen were some muddy areas at the side of the Mohawk River. His parents allowed him to swim there when river flow was low, but only for short periods, and close to shore. George allowed him to swim out as far as he wanted for as long as he wanted. Good news.

He loved swimming. His mother had given him swimming lessons from an early age, telling him she had great fear he might drown someday. George told him that salt water was more buoyant than fresh water and he certainly liked swimming here better. But sometimes the bad time would come, and he would dive down deep and hold his breath as long as he could, wondering if everything might be better if he never came up.

George had a small shovel on board. On one beach he went to the far end and dug a large pit, then plopped in to position himself as far away from

George as possible, warm sea water flowing in and providing some small comfort to his fear and loss, a deep-blue sea depositing small waves in front of him, and pelicans and frigate birds parading above. If he could only stay here and never see George again!

Why had all this happened to him? What had he done to deserve his mother dying and George hauling him away? He'd always been a good boy. Obeyed his parents, even obeyed his father when he was treating him badly. He thought about the boys in his class. Frank Bishop was always in trouble. You could hear Frank's parents yelling at him all the way down the block. Why didn't God punish Frank rather than him? He went over everything he'd done in his life and could find no reason. There must be some part of him that offended God, something that made him not as good as other boys. He just *wasn't* as good.

During the short sea passages George showed Ethan more about sailing. How to coil lines by circling the line over his left shoulder. How to cleat. How to use the winches. He participated only to a very limited extent, often refusing, participating only when the blackness temporarily left him. It was better than doing nothing all day. Twice he pinched fingers trying to cleat lines. And try as he might he couldn't turn the jib sheet winch. He saw George and Johnson do this with ease. He strained and strained, feeling himself growing red of face, then gave up in frustration, sure George had set him to the task to embarrass him.

The knots were another matter. George had a book illustrating the tying of sailors' knots. Ethan practiced various knots for a while each day. He liked the rough feel of the rope on his hands and the intricate designs he was creating, a little like art class but more practical. The knot George and Johnson wanted him to concentrate on was the bowline. They said it was the most important sailors' knot, used to tie the jib sheet to the jib. Said he had to learn to tie it blindfolded as he might need to help change the jib in the middle of a black night. Because Johnson asked it, not because of George's request, he practiced the bowline for some time with his eyes screwed shut and came to tie bowlines solely by touch, his first accomplishment on *Rascal*.

On the fifth day of their voyage they anchored off Norman Island, a bright green island with substantial sea cliffs.

27

George announced with great fanfare, obviously trying to stoke enthusiasm, "Ethan, that's a real pirate island. A pirate by the last name of Norman was the first owner. Have you read Stevenson's *Treasure Island?*"

Ethan nodded. He'd read it in school.

"Well, I have a surprise for you." His face lit up in a big smile and he leaned toward Ethan and pointed toward the island. "That island is the island Stevenson wrote about. That's *Treasurer Island.* And you see that barren island over there. That's Dead Man's Chest. Remember, *'Fifteen men on a dead man's chest?'* Well that's where the fifteen men were marooned."

He did not want to let on to George, but this was sort of neat, the first thing that tweaked his interest.

George went on. "According to people I talked to in St. Thomas, in about 1750 a Spanish treasure ship was taken by pirates off the Carolinas. I seem to remember it was called the *Guadalupe,* or something like that. The ship was carrying fifty-five chests of silver coins. The chests were taken off the ship by the pirates and buried on this very island. Eventually the pirates were captured by the English. That was before the pirates could return and recover their loot. So the English tortured them, found out that the silver was buried here, and dug up a lot of it. But not all. People are still digging for it. When we walk around the island you'll see hundreds of pits where people have been digging for silver, some brand new.

"There's another story," George continued. "Gold was also hidden here. That was by the pirate Blackbeard. He terrorized the Caribbean, killed a lot of people. He'd frighten people by lighting slow fuses in his long black beard and in his hat, sort of like flaming candles, then go screaming at them with his cutlass raised.

This got Ethan's attention.

Supposedly a local fisherman, Henri Creque, was caught in a storm and hid in a sea-cave on the island. At the back of the cave he found a chest of gold doubloons. The people in St. Thomas said Henri would never talk about it. But what is known is that the Creque family had been very poor, and they suddenly moved to Charlotte Amalie, bought up a number of the best shops and the largest houses in town, and started taking trips to Europe. Would you like to visit the cave?"

Ethan mouthed "Yes," barely audible, the first thing he'd said while aboard.

They got flashlights and set off in the dingy, Johnson at the oars, George singing snatches of calypso songs. The entrance to the cave was small and low. Large breaking waves were rolling directly into the mouth, and the gap between the top of each wave and the ceiling of the cave was too small to let them pass. They had to dash in during the trough between waves. Johnson waited for a lull and skillfully rode the following wave into the cave.

George broke into a sea chanty in time with Johnson's oar beats, singing in lusty voice, *"Fifteen men on a dead man's chest – Yo-Ho-Ho, and a bottle of rum; Drink and the devil had done for the rest – Yo-Ho-Ho, and a bottle of rum."*

He repeated this refrain louder and louder as they went further back in the cave, the sound echoing and reechoing off cave walls.

Thousands of bats blackened the ceiling in upside down rest. Apparently they did not like sea chanties, or at least George's sea chanty, because they all dropped simultaneously around the dingy, a mad confusion, swirling, dashing, darting around them, screaming shrilly as though trying to drown George out. Ethan cowered at the bottom of the dingy.

Finally, several hundred feet back, their flashlights picked out a hidden rock shelf that could only be seen from a particular angle. What an excellent place to stash a pirate treasure!

Rowing back to *Rascal,* George said, "You needn't have been scared of the bats. They have have this remarkable thing, ultrasonic sensors that allow them to detect and avoid objects. Never hit anyone."

George must believe him very stupid. Everyone knew that. It was just that he wasn't sure that bat ultrasonics worked when competing with a booming sea chanty echoing through a cave.

They next sailed to Jost Van Dyke Island and anchored off White Beach. George said many thought it the most beautiful beach in the world, a mile of talcum-fine sugar-white sand, deserted except for two small fishing shacks, fronted by serene azure water that progressed slowly into deep blue over a gradually sloping bottom.

Ashore he wiggled his feet in the warm sand, smooth and soft on his toes and heels. Picking some up and he let it slowly flow through his fingers, then again and again, admiring it as it fell. Why hadn't he seen how the Caribbean sand shimmer in the sunlight? He sat down and moved his arms in a wide circle, hands gently scooping glistening furrows and mounds.

The water foamed lazily over his feet when he entered, curling around his ankles, sucking sand from under his soles. It seemed to be warmer than elsewhere, maybe because it shoaled out so far under the hot sun or maybe because there was no wave action to stir up cooler bottom water. Or maybe he was just noticing the warmth of Caribbean water for the first time. A giant swimming hole just for him. Ethan swam for almost two hours, floating, stroking, floating, stroking. And when he emerged from the water he felt the warm air surround him, penetrating him. He breathed deeply, filling his lungs with the sweet Caribbean. His first real feeling of what it meant to be there.

CHAPTER FOUR

George watched Ethan swim, occasionally singing snatches of calypso to himself or whistling. At one point he called to him, "Lot different from Niskayuna," getting back a small wave, not much but at least an acknowledgement.

Ah, Niskayuna. He loved it. Made him happy thinking about it. A month ago he'd stood at the top of Niskayuna's Main Street and looked down its entire length. As always he admired the historic colonial houses, one fine example of pre-Revolutionary War architecture after another, down more than ten blocks, all behind a bulwark of stately elms, two to a house, two by two by two marching the street, and greening up in the Spring sunshine. Borders of daffodils and tulips announced the coming of his favorite time of year, May. And the brilliance of the spring sun confirmed it. He took a deep breath, breathing in the flowered smell of Spring. No doubt about it. Niskayuna was the most beautiful town in Upstate New York. Maybe the country. Modern architecture be damned.

He loved to drive through the neighboring countryside, the country roads pulling him in graceful curves to views of one perfectly set dutch-roofed farmhouse after another, the farms dating from Dutch settlement in the 1600s (some of the same families still there). White picket fences bounded the farms, put up in colonial times as a grudging accommodation to American ways, and always meandering meadow streams wending their glittering way to the historic Mohawk River, *Drums Along the Mohawk* country.

He'd even heard Madge Parsons and Betty Cramer, ladies in their dotage, exclaim to each other that they could hear the drums. They probably could. He had a distinct childhood memory (was it a dream?) of seeing from his high bedroom window the houses down the valley burning closer and closer as the Mohawks attacked under the harvest moon.

He remembered getting very happy that day in Niskayuna, a splendid day filled with thoughts of what he intended to do with Ethan that summer. Throwing his arms wide he exclaimed for everyone to hear, "Perfect. This is my town. I love it."

Nearby townspeople stared at him. He didn't give a damn. The town *was* his.

He'd glanced over at the impressive stone monument commemorating the founding of the town, 1690 by the Patroon, Killaen van Rosendahl, a Dutch lord no less, his direct ancestor. He donated the monument and considered it a monument for himself as much as for Killaen. He might not be a Patroon, but with all his financial contributions to the town, his leadership in just about everything, he was as close as he could get.

Not only was the town his. He *was* the town.

People were still glancing at him, so he said it even more loudly one more time to make sure they got it.

"This is my town."

He'd strode down Main Street, his prominent chin thrust out aggressively in emulation of his distant cousin, Franklin Delano Roosevelt, scorn for lesser people lurking in his eyes and around his lips, shaking hands with only a few leading citizens, and acknowledging the many others greeting him with only a small raise of a hand as a bishop might acknowledge his peasant flock while avoiding close contact.

When he'd received enough homage he hurried to the Schenectady dealership. He needed to fire the black janitor he'd recently hired. That fit of generosity turned out to have been a mistake. His most recent surprise inspection revealed bathrooms not cleaned to his liking, and this was the second time in a row. He called in the janitor. Fired him on the spot. No reference letter. No severance pay. The janitor cried and begged. Three young children. He'd not relented. The janitor knew the rules. He himself lived by the rules and the janitor had to live by them too.

When he exited his office all the other employs had their heads down, didn't look at him except one poor sap who couldn't help giving him a frightened look. He should be frightened. He had purposely talked loudly to the janitor so everyone could hear. He smiled to himself. The more fear the better.

Fear was one way he exercised tight control over all his businesses, his dealer-ships, his bank and hotels. He even tried to control his friends.

He never apologized for wanting to control everything. He felt it was part of him as much as his intelligence and skill at sports. A gift of his parents. With what they'd done to him he couldn't help wanting to control things. They'd had him completely submerged. No choice allowed on anything. What he wore each day (the clothes laid out for him by the servants had to be worn), what books he read in what order, where he would be every hour of every day, all tightly controlled. His parents had the servants regularly check on him like wardens in a prison.

The first thing he did after his parents' early death was to fire everyone, servants, money managers, lawyers, everyone. Now he exercised greater con-trol than they ever had, and he got such pleasure from having people under his thumb that when he thought about it the feeling was almost sexual.

From the dealership he went over to his church. Christ Church Episcopal had been founded in 1735, and he felt was unequalled anywhere in its colo-nial architecture, even in New England, one reason he attended, but more because it was the chosen church of the most important people of neighbor-ing Schenectady, Albany, and Troy. He turned the corner in the old stockade district of Schenectady and viewed the church shining white in the May sun-shine, momentarily stopping to marvel at the beauty, Spring light drawing the tall steeple upward toward God, striving to reach God.

The church was another place he controlled. Head of the vestry and larg-est financial donor, virtually nothing occurred there without his say so.

His purpose in visiting was to give Father Smallwood a topic suggestion for next Sunday's sermon. Also, to confront Father Smallwood on his last ser-mon, an example of what George had come to call Smallwood's "sin sermons."

Several times each year Father Smallwood would climb to the pulpit with his sternest face, quote copiously from St. Augustine and other Catholic theologians, then sermonize in his solemnest voice that all men are bearers of the original sin of Adam and Eve and are condemned to a life of sin from birth. Last Sunday he had looked individually at every face in the congrega-tion as though ferreting out people's secret sins and had proclaimed. "Every man has dark sins lodged in his soul at birth. Sin can be hidden from a man for decades, for half a lifetime, only to emerge when least expected to destroy him. No man can escape sin."

Throughout the sermon George felt Father Smallwood had particularly looked at him.

His admonishment of Father Smallwood went, "Original sin is a manifestation of Catholic faith. Don't preach it here. Catholics may be full of original sin. But in an Episcopal church people sin when they want to sin. All you're accomplishing is getting people upset. These people are not permeated by sin. They don't need to be lectured on sin."

Father Smallwood responded, polite as always, but he felt talking down to him, "You're mistaken. When most men sin it's not because they consciously decide to sin. They don't want to sin. The temptation to sin appears suddenly when least expected. It comes from some dark hidden place inside. They may try to resist. They're just too weak. They can't help themselves. The sin inside is stronger than they are."

George glowered at Father Smallwood, "Next you're going to want to put in a confessional." Brushing past the minister he stormed out. He always tried to be a gentleman, but it was difficult with Smallwood. Should he have Smallwood dismissed? He put that aside for future consideration.

His spirits brightened when he returned home, drove up the long driveway, rounded the bend, and there appeared the great Georgian mansion he loved so much, clothed in soft red brick, the largest house in town. Hurrying through the immense living room, not even looking at the luxurious English antique furnishing and the fine French Impressionists, quickly to his bedroom, he changed into his custom-made evening attire. Tonight was the Spring dance at the country club. He'd been looking forward to it for weeks.

He loved his club, the Mohican Golf Club, the oldest and most prestigious country club in Upstate New York, site of many PGA tournaments, where the governor of New York hung out, a sprawling clubhouse in stone and white colonial clapboard with wings stretching out on either side to welcome member and visitors alike in warm camaraderie.

Everyone at the club knew he was important. They treated him as important. And he'd been very clever in finding ways to take charge of everything. Being past president and a long time director had its advantages.

He enjoyed throwing his weight around, hiring and firing managers, approving salaries and budgets, and small things. He and his wife, Marge, must always be given the best table at club functions and be seated with the best people, and staff must always be extremely deferential. There were consequences when staff didn't perform to his liking.

That night he entered the club with Marge on his arm dressed in a brand new Dior gown flown in from Paris. Glancing at their image in the large mirror in the entryway, he smiled in approval. Marge had put on weight, but was still very attractive. Mostly he looked at himself, never missed an opportunity.

He looked pretty good for his forty-four years. Sure, his weight had crept up from his football days. A little middle-age puffiness starting to creep into the waist. He pulled in the belly reflected in the mirror. It didn't help much. Too many rich meals. He promised himself one more time to try and get in shape. He patted his comb over, an acquired habit, thrust out his chin, and he and Marge made a grand entrance into the elegantly furnished French-style club drawing room. The cocktail hour had already commenced. Conversation hushed at their entrance. There was a general turning of heads to view them.

Marge disappeared who knew where and he positioned himself at the most visible point in the room. The leading socially-prominent men in town immediately came over to talk to him. With his chin thrust out so he could look down on everybody from his six foot two height, he leaned slightly forward as he always did to dominate the conversation, and made a string of witty and intelligent remarks, more witty and intelligent than anyone else, deliberately rolling out his words with a loud voice so others around could partake of his wisdom. A couple of jerks tried to voice their opinions. He cut them off. And no one in his conversation group had the temerity to disagree with his own opinions except for one fellow, dean of Union College in Schenectady. He tried to advance a contrary opinion. George ignored him. But when he expressed the same view a second time George responded, "That's clearly a misconception of the facts. Really, before you go off pontificating like this you might try a little research in that wonderful college library of yours." The dean grew very red of face and sputtered out, "George, you're always such an arrogant bastard." George smiled and said in a quiet voice, almost to himself, "I have a right to be." The dean was not seen again that evening.

George enjoyed these small triumphs. The other person always knew they were going to lose. It was just a matter of time. Always different. Sometimes the other fellow would freeze up at his attack, stand unmoving not knowing what to do. Other times they would start laughing out of discomfort. He enjoyed every variation. And it usually ended the same way, the other person red of face, breathing hard, looking away in admission of defeat, and often running off as the dean had done.

After dinner he joined some of his buddies in the men's bar. Stories were swapped—hunting, fishing, golf, and other male activities. He considered himself a man's man. Best shot in the club, low handicap golfer, best jokes. His laugh was the conspiratorial sort one man gives another, knowing the male sex is superior. It was a laugh practiced many years in the telling and hearing of off-color jokes. And his voice went with being a man's man, deep and easily recognizable in any crowd.

One of George's bad habits, and he was aware of it, was to constantly look over the shoulder of whomever he talking to to see if there was someone more important to go corral. That night his over the shoulder reconnaissance took in Pomford Carlisle II. What was he doing here? Hadn't Pomford already resigned? Maybe he'd wheedled an invitation from some patsy.

A month ago a very expensive golf bag full of very expensive clubs had gone missing. The caddy was the one last seen with the bag. Pomford was the owner of the bag, and at the time a close friend of his. Pomford had loudly charged that the caddy had stolen the bag. Though the caddy denied it, and no hard evidence was found, the caddy was immediately dismissed. Pomford was a very important member of the club.

George knew the caddy and doubted he would steal anything. He tracked down the boy at a house in the poorest section of town. With the caddy's tearful denial of wrongdoing, George got a policeman friend of his to see what he could find out. The bag turned up in a pawnshop in a neighboring city, and the description of the party pawning the bag had matched that of Pomford's spoiled son, Pomford Carlisle III.

George confronted Pomford II and demanded the man publicly acknowledge what had happen and apologize to the caddy.

Pomford's response was, "Look. We're good friends. We've got to stick together. I'll give him a couple of hundred bucks, more than he can possibly make caddying, and we can forget about it."

George responded, his voice angry, "That's *wrong*. What about the boy's reputation? He'll always be branded a thief."

Pomford got indignant in return, refusing to apologize to a lowly caddy and refusing to expose his son.

George told the board and Pomford III was barred from the club for good. Shortly later Pomford II resigned.

As George got up and walked to the dingy he congratulated himself that whatever else he did there was one thing he always did: Protect boys.

CHAPTER FIVE

By the time they left Jost Van Dyke, Ethan knew his assignments. George said that with only three on board it was essential to have assigned roles for everything. At meals, Ethan was asked to ferry food plates up to the cockpit from the galley where Johnson was cooking. He was to help with dishwashing by scraping plates into the garbage pail. He was to help clean the cabin and head once a week. Coiling lines was his job, as was flag duty. Flag duty entailed bringing up the American flag each morning from storage below and mounting it on the stern. And at sunset taking down the flag and stowing it. He felt some small pride in being given this job.

His sailing assignment was to "tail' the main, jib, and mizzen sheets, and the main and mizzen halyards. When Johnson or George winched in a sheet or halyard, Ethan was to pull the end (tail) back to a cleat where it would be secured. This required all of his strength. When he first did tailing duty, Johnson or George would complete the cleating. By Jost Van Dyke he was starting to do the cleating himself.

Ethan usually refused to do his assigned tasks when George asked him, but did them reluctantly when Johnson asked. A lot of hard work involved in sailing *Rascal,* and he resented having to do things that helped take him farther and farther from home.

One day when asked by both George and Johnson to help with the dishes he was feeling so badly he shook his head no. At home that would have meant a beating.

George just looked at him for a moment, shrugged his shoulders, and said, "It's okay," and took care of the dishes himself.

That was a surprise.

Sailing out of Jost Van Dyke, George at the helm, Johnson sat down next to Ethan in the cockpit, held his eyes, and said in a serious voice, "Ethan. I believe in what de Bible tell us. De Bible God's word. De Bible be true. And in de Bible God make a promise about de sea. In de Book of Isaiah God say, *'Your heart shall thrill and rejoice, because the abundance of the sea shall be brought to you.'* Bible say dat to you, Ethan." He fingered his cross.

"Dat what God is going to bring you on *Rascal,* de abundance of de Caribbean Sea. I promise you. Dat my promise. Dat God's promise. George and I goin to show you everythin'. *Rascal* goin to show you everythin'.

"I love de sea. De sea my friend. Sea goin' to be you friend. It can be jumpy like some friend. But mostly it love you. It give you beauty. And joy. Food. Peace. The Bible say dat God in de sea. God's love be in de sea. You goin' to find out dat de sea love you, Ethan. You goin' to come to love de sea."

His blackness lifted a little bit.

Then George added, "The sea will take you away from your troubles at home, Ethan. You don't know it now but those troubles will grow small. You're going to have a very, very happy time with us and forget the bad things. You're going to forget the mean people. You're going to forget about the problems you're having with your father."

CHAPTER SIX

George had brought back the blackness, black thoughts about his father. His problems with his father would not go away so easily. It wasn't just his mother's death. As far back as he could remember there was no love from his father. He didn't see how that would ever change.

One of his first memories was in the living room of their house in Niskayuna. He must have been around four years old. Bright sunshine steamed into the room past pretty yellow curtains. The curtains made him happy. He'd watched his mother hang them. His mother had told him yellow was her favorite color. So yellow was his happy color. It was probably summer. The windows were open when his father strode into the room.

He rushed over to him with arms wide, seeking a hug. "Daddy. Daddy."

His father pushed him strongly away, causing him to fall down in a wail of crying. His father then walked out of the room saying over his shoulder, "Stay away from me. I'm busy." His father's face never turned to him, eyes never looked at him, never acknowledged his existence.

Later in the strep-throat time his mother, not his father, stayed at his bed for the four days until the fever broke, sleeping on a quilt on the floor. Through his delirium he heard the doctors speculating about whether he would live or die. Yet during the whole period his father only came into the room a couple times, and then only to ask when dinner would be ready. And when he had the bad concussion climbing the apple tree (he reached a new record in his climb) both parents were home, but the one who rushed him to the hospital was his mother.

Nowhere in his memory was there a hug from his father, a loving hand placed on his arm or shoulder, a kind word, or a congratulatory, "Well done." His father communicated solely through occasional instructions, usually delivered with irritation. Never games together, or teaching him to ride a bike, or to swim, or taking him to a ball game, or helping with homework, or on his model plane building projects. His mother did all of this.

Originally he thought that his father just didn't like boys. But that couldn't be. When they went to parents' nights at school, or went to church gatherings, his father always talked happily with the other boys. And when other fathers proudly introduced their sons, his father seemed delighted to meet them. But if asked to introduce him, his father showed no pride at all. He would grudgingly say something like, "This one calls himself Ethan," scowl at him, and then quickly move away as though embarrassed. It wasn't boys that his father didn't like. He just didn't like him. His father wished he'd never been born.

He thanked God one more time for his mother. Love radiated from her. She followed him with her gaze whenever they were in the same room, smiling at him. It was as though she couldn't get enough of looking at him. And whenever he said something she would listen intently, even when he said something stupid, sometimes getting down on her knees to hear him better. Never punishment and rarely a no, and she took the time to explain everything new and different, and to point out special things around them.

It didn't matter that his father didn't like him. His mother more than made up for it. And wasn't she the most beautiful mother in the world, slender and small, almost tiny, with light blond hair that glinted magically when she leaned over him, and vivid blue eyes that shone with love when she gazed at him.

From his mother came constant hugs and kisses, even when he was nine or ten. Whenever she did this, and his father was around, he looked at him with irritation or even anger. When he wasn't around she told Ethan over and over again how much she loved him. That she loved no one but him.

He wanted all her love. And gave it back in turn.

He said to his mother a number of times, "I think my father doesn't like me. I try to be a good boy and do what he says. Why doesn't he like me?"

She would reply, "He does like you. He loves you. You're the only child he has. He just doesn't know how to show his love." That wasn't true. His father had hated him from the day he was born.

Was his father his real father? He sure didn't look like his father. His mother never said anything. Still, wouldn't it be great if his father was someone else, someone like the fathers of other boys.

CHAPTER SEVEN

Johnson knew little of Ethan's background when Ethan came aboard. All he'd been told by George was that two teenagers, later one, would be joining them. Ethan was a growing concern. The boy cried himself to sleep each night. Later Johnson was awakened by Ethan's nightmares, loud cries, often for his mother. George would always rise quickly from his bunk and go to comfort the boy. Then there would be another nightmare and another comforting later the same night, or at least the next night.

Now early in the morning as *Rascal* finally turned its bow in toward Tortola, he stood on the stern deck, his usual position to observe everything going on in the boat. He smoked a Gauloises, the rich acrid smoke curling down his throat, then he released smoke through his nostrils, a moment of solitary pleasure. He frowned, fingering his gold cross, and brought his thoughts together about Ethan. His initial impression had been confirmed. Smart but introverted, totally lacking in self-confidence, without any protective layer over his incredible innocence. Johnson had never seen such innocence and vulnerability in a thirteen-year-old, seemingly totally deprived of love and even affection, a very damaged boy, his state clear in the sadness clouding his face and the agitated nervous habit he practiced with his left hand. He moped around the deck with downcast eyes, or sat for long periods with his head in his hands, his head taking on weight, hanging as though his neck couldn't support it, not even glancing at the spectacular scenery, no expression except despair.

This wouldn't happen among the blacks he knew. If someone didn't take care of a child others would step in. How could the whites allow this very nice boy to get so bad? Where were the ministers? Where were the neighbors?

He vowed to do something about it. To serve God you had to serve the needy. Ethan was definitely needy.

Born again to strong religious beliefs in his twenties, Johnson set himself the task of doing one caring act for someone each day. This was his answer to the devil. From many observations he'd come to believe the devil is very much on earth, invading most men's souls at some point in their lives, sometimes for substantial periods (and for some, most of their lives), the devil skillful in making men believe it's free will that makes them do things they shouldn't do and have thoughts they shouldn't have, hiding that it's really the devil entering men in a constant battle between God and the devil that determines how men come to live.

Many days he had to look long and hard to find the opportunity for a caring act to keep the devil at bay. But very few days were missed. He promised himself that for as long as the voyage lasted, Ethan would be the principal recipient of his daily commitment to caring.

The boy had already made some progress. He'd become more comfortable with the boat and with him, though he remained largely silent. And each new thing learned promised to gain him a small amount of self-confidence.

...

As they approached Tortola George had the distinct impression *Rascal* was alive. She was talking to him through the changeful movements of the helm under his hands, telling him of the force of waves and wind on her hull and sails, telling him what it was like to be a sailboat, a creature of air plunging through the sea, letting him know how happy she was to be sailing the beautiful Caribbean this wonderful day.

Each large trade-wind wave crashing against her port side told him of her desire to turn to starboard. Every time a gust hit the port tack sails she told him of a competing desire to turn up wind to port. The deep keel brought another message — desire to hold to forward momentum. It all came joyously together to his hands on the helm. *Rascal* was saying on this gorgeous sailing day, this hour, and this shining moment, "I am truly a living thing."

George heard it all clearly. Smiles played over his face as he felt the pleasure of control and thought of Ethan.

In the distance, parting morning mists first teased with only glimpses of the island, then suddenly lifted as though it was the duty of the morning sun to dispel all mists that sought to impede the towering vista of Tortola. *Rascal* glided through the brightening, sun-streaked water, the morning light growing in intensity. Ahead, penciled in sharp outline against the deep blue sky, were splendid, high-piling mountains, their lush green spurs over-lapping in varying contour, and then thrusting dramatically upward through the puffy trade-wind clouds.

Gradually they came into the lee of the island, out of the trade-wind. Small, tremulous zephyrs played sporadically on the sails, only tiny wind ripples on the water. Slowly they rounded the headland into the shallowing bay, the water blue, shading into aquamarine, then into gold as it reflected on the sandy bottom and depth diminished. Palm trees punctuated the shore, sometimes clumped together standing, leaning or reclining against the light, sometimes proudly alone, rising as much as one hundred feet under bonnets of green feathers. No beaches sanded the shores of the bay. Instead, sharply etched brownish rocks emerged from tangled undergrowth and deposited small cliffs at seashore. And there, perched on a dramatic promontory dominating the bay, appeared the castle—turrets, battlements, gun embrasures, even a draw bridge.

Ethan stood at the bow watching, mouth open in amazement. George called to Ethan. It was time. Ethan and Johnson attached the bottle rockets, Roman Candles, and various percussion fireworks to the ratlines at the bow. Dropping anchor beneath the castle wall, George instructed Ethan and Johnson to set them all off together. Ethan grinned from ear to ear, the first time George had seen him smile like that about anything. His father back home would never have allowed him near fireworks.

The response was immediate. Three large black men in dark green, eighteenth-century-style livery appeared on a parapet. They held English hunting horns. A long salute was blown in response to *Rascal's* explosive greeting. They were welcome.

...

The castle walls rising above them were constructed of gray stone blocks that Ethan thought must have been extremely difficult to move to the cliff-top site. While not gigantic Ethan could see the castle had everything it was supposed to have, places to throw down boiling oil and to shoot from, and the drawbridge looked really neat. Johnson brought the dingy around for George and Ethan. As they were departing Johnson whispered to Ethan, "Watch out for her. She be a witch."

And as George rowed in he leaned toward him, his face close, his voice very serious. "You'll meet a very strange woman. Don't make her angry. I'm not kidding. Don't make her angry."

Tied on one side of the long stone castle pier was what looked like a very fast speed boat, its mahogany deck shining from obvious careful upkeep. They tied up on the other side of the dock, ascended winding stone steps, and crossed the drawbridge. The three men in green jackets had converted into laborers and were working around the castle.

At the entrance Ethan stopped dead in his tracks, eyes open wide in astonishment, cupping a hand over his mouth, dumfounded. The entrance was a stone arch, maybe twelve feet tall with broad metal-studded wooden doors thrown open. But what amazed was the woman standing there.

A dwarf?

Little over four feet tall. Wide and muscular despite her short body. Large, heavily veined nose in a splotchy red face, dyed fire-engine red hair in a tangled halo, hard black eyes staring meanly at him, and most scary, a wispy gray beard.

Despite the heat, she sported a garish green and yellow kilt and corresponding bodice. In her left hand a glass of brownish liquid. In her right, a long carving knife. She had apparently been at work in the kitchen.

An angry scowl appeared as they approached. She flicked the knife back and forth, looking at him. He backed away, pressing himself against the wall of the castle, trying to hide behind George. She sure looked like a witch.

She moved around George, a waddle more than a walk, and stood right in front of him, knife still in hand. "Who the hell are you?"

George said, "This is Ethan. He doesn't talk much. Ethan. This is Moira Grayson. She's the owner of this marvelous castle."

Moira turned to George. "This your son? You never told me you had a son. You've been holding out on me."

George turned his head away and mumbled in a low voice, "No. Son of a friend."

Moira raised her eyebrows and gave George a long look.

Inside the castle on the side of the main entrance hall a full suit of armor was displayed in upright posture. Awesome. If only he could stay and examine it, go no further. No such luck. George motioned him forward. He tried to lag behind in some of the alcoves along the way. But this didn't keep him out of the baleful glance of Moira Grayson.

A very expansive room opened beyond. According to George, the great hall of the castle. The room was one of the largest he'd ever seen, and the ceiling looked twenty feet high. The darkness of the room impressed him almost as much as its size, limited light from a few mullioned windows like ones in the parish hall back home, large heavily-carved ceiling beams above, diamond-patterned paneling on ceiling and walls, a balcony suspended on one side of the room, everything constructed of wood so dark it seemed black, furniture massive in size and also of dark wood, only a few dispersed table lamps emitting limited light into the gloom. What kind of a person would want to live in this darkness in the bright Caribbean? A witch?

She spoke with an accent that sounded English and had apparently gotten a great roast of island beef and special provisions in anticipation of George's arrival. George had mentioned that she would occasionally welcome visiting yachtsmen for meals, so long as they contributed to the cost. According to Moira the makings for the dinner had been purchased in Road Town, the largest town on Tortola.

Moira said, "Bit of trouble in getting provisions these days. Scoot into Road Town on my speedboat with my three men. Fastest boat on the island. Goes fifty fucking miles an hour when it's not too rough. Time it to arrive when least expected. The men are fast runners. They spread out to purchase the supplies. Then charge back to the boat. We get the hell out of there before the police know what happened. It's a hoot. Sometimes they try and catch us in a police launch. Bunch of dumb bastards. Don't know what they're doing. We're much faster." Moira laughed uproariously.

George looked at her quizzically. "Why do you need to avoid the police?"

Moira said, almost musing, "The damn police don't like me much."

"That seems strange. Why don't they like you?"

Moira looked out one of the mullioned windows. "It's all the neighbors' fault. They spy on me with their telescopes all the time. A bunch of shitty peeping Toms. Sometimes in the evening I have a few drinks and shoot out their windows. It's what they deserve for spying." She chuckled. "There's one old biddy across the way who spied on me all the time. A real nosey bitch. One evening saw the flash from her telescope. Knew she was spying. Shot out the window above her. Glass down on her. I heard her scream from here. Haven't seen her telescope since."

George doubled over in laughter. "Marvelous. Come up to Niskayuna. I've got some nosey neighbors you can take care of."

Moira went to a cabinet and dug out a medal. "I don't think I showed you this before." She held it to her breast as she talked, holding it where Ethan assumed it must have been pinned at the proud moment of award. Her conversation was directed to George, her back to Ethan.

"This is a medal I got for bravery driving an ambulance at the Battle of the Somme. It's the highest honor the British give to non-combatants. I may have told you, I drove an ambulance through most of the First World War."

George nodded.

"The hardest part was getting the stupid British to allow me to drive an ambulance. Their rules were that an ambulance driver had to be at least five foot three. I got my family to intervene. They're connected to the royal family. I think they intervened in the hope I'd be killed. The bastards always wanted me dead." She shook her head. "Never heard from them during the war and never heard from them when I got the medal even though it was all over the papers, the shit eaters. I think the medal was a great disappointment to them. It meant I was still alive."

She continued, "The British modified an ambulance with a special seat so I could reach the pedals. Vision was terrible. Could hardly see over the dashboard. Drove that contraption in some of the bloodiest damn battles of the war.

"At the Battle of the Somme I drove through a gap in the British trenches into no-man's-land. Many British soldiers lying out there dying. Some asshole general had ordered a mass charge against the entrenched German lines. When I entered the between-trenches area machine guns and artillery were exchanging fire from each side. I just hoped everybody could see my red cross through the smoke. But the mines worried me more. The field was heavily mined.

"I drove standing up and peering ahead for turned earth, a possible mine. Or maybe a furrow from a shell. Many times I had to get out and examine the earth more closely. I don't mind telling you it was scary walking away from the red cross. Progress with the ambulance was slow. Many times I had to detour or double back to avoid a mine.

"The ambulance was supposed to hold four. I made it back with twelve wounded soldiers."

George grabbed her hands. "That's about the bravest thing I've ever heard. You never told me before. It's a real honor to know you."

"Thanks. It helped that I polished off a bottle of brandy before I started. Went out many more times. Just about finished the rest of the case." Moira then poured a very large amount of brandy into two tall glasses, one of which she handed to George.

George pointed to some plaques on the wall and asked what they were.

"Cooking awards. After the war I studied cooking. Two leading French culinary academies seemed to have liked my cooking. They gave me their highest honors. Then it became interesting.

"A young fellow in Paris was starting his first restaurant. He took a chance. Hired me as chef. I don't think he could find anyone else." She laughed. "He kept me hidden in the kitchen so no one knew a female dwarf was preparing the food. The restaurant became wildly popular. All the bohemian crowd in Paris came. Then the restaurant won one of the highest culinary awards in France. In the publicity the truth came out. It was all due to a kitchen dwarf. Well, as you can imagine, a small sensation.

"All the bohemians who'd dined there started inviting me to their soirees. I wasn't in the center of bohemian life in Paris, close enough. I knew everyone. I think they liked me at their parties because when they looked at me they all felt better about how they looked themselves.

"There was that full-of-himself Hemingway. He usually talked to me because we'd both driven ambulances. But at one party he started bragging about how brave he was with his ambulance driving. I told everybody what being brave driving ambulances was really like. Hemingway didn't say anything to anyone the rest of the night and never talked to me again." She threw back her head and released more laughter.

She sat and motioned George to a seat next to her, taking a large gulp from her brandy glass, now almost empty. Ethan was left standing some distance away behind the long banquet table.

She smiled warmly at George and pulled him close. "The bohemians sure knew how to party. You'd be at somebody's apartment. Two people would look over at each other, someone would nod or smile, then before you knew it they would be in a bedroom screwing. These were people you didn't think even knew each other. Once in a while it was even three people. You could always hear the fucking through the thin doors. Nobody cared." She winked at George and drew him still closer.

"One well-known artist, a woman, gave parties where most guests ended up buck naked. She'd get drunk, take off her clothes, offer a bottle of champagne to whomever undressed first. One evening I wore a simple shift to her party. Easy to take off. Won the prize. No one liked looking at a naked dwarf. I was never invited back.

"The more important they thought they were the more they tried to get away with. Fucking big egos. Hedonists. Didn't care about anyone but themselves. One guy, a leading French author, he was one of the worst. I won't give you his name. Had a fine house in the Latin Quarter. I watched him grab one of the women and go into a bedroom. An hour later he reappeared. Yelled at the room, 'I've worn this one out. Send me another.' Two women got into a small fight. The winner dashed into the bedroom, was half undressed by the time she got there. The author was not only famous. He was supposed to be one of the best lovers in Paris. Never gave me a chance to find out."

George laughed loudly and slapped his knee. "That's great. Send me another. I'll have to use that."

Many more similar tales.

Ethan didn't understand much of it but could tell it was about naughty people doing naughty things. George's enthusiasm for it confirmed the stories at the church about him. And wasn't a friend of a witch a bad man anyway?

George and Moira refilled their brandy glasses. George made some mention of his family. Moira replied with apparent growing anger, "My family were royalty on the Isle of Man, linked to the English royal house and ancient Scottish clan chiefs. None of that for me. Totally excluded. Paid substantial sums to stay away from the Isle of Man. You've heard of a remittance man. They made me a remittance woman."

Photographs of the vast Grayson castle anchored two of the walls. She pointed them out and grimaced. But she must have very much missed the Grayson castle. Evan could see it was the model for her Tortola castle.

After pausing she exploded. "My bastard parents locked me up. A wing of my own, sure. But no visitors allowed. Parents never visited me after I was born. May my parents rot in hell. They didn't want anyone to know they'd birthed a monster. Shipped me out in the dead of night at age seventeen. Never heard from them since except to send me checks."

Moira also repeatedly said how much she hated children, particularly boy children. Glaring at Ethan she said, "Boys always taunted me, the little bastards. In Paris they used to follow me down the street, jeering at me as an ugly dwarf, sometimes throwing pebbles. If they'd gotten close I would have killed one."

Ethan lowered himself behind the banquet table, his heart pounding.

More drinks and Moira's gun came out, a high-powered rifle. Moira waived it around, one time pointing it in Ethan's general direction with what he thought was deliberation. She was walking crookedly, Drunk? Oh no. He remembered what his father did to his mother while drunk.

Both Moira and George took shots out a window, yelling if one or the other hit what was targeted. A fishing boat appeared around the point at the entrance to the bay. Moira grabbed the rifle and fired off a quick round of shots. Grouped bullet splashes appeared close-by either side of the boat. The men dove over the side with a yell heard all the way to the castle. Moira exploded in riotous laughter, tears streaming down her face she was laughing so hard. He went cold. If she could do that what might she do to him, and laugh about it besides?

And as if to carry through on his thought Moira turned her focus to him. Throughout Ethan had been staring at her. Now she came around the banquet table and confronted him. "Why have you been staring at me? You think I'm repulsive, don't you?"

He whispered, "No."

"Yes, you do. I can tell. I'll show you what repulsive can do."

She grabbed the long carving knife from the banquet table and chased Ethan around the table, first one way, then the other, yelling, "You little bastard. I'll *get* you. I'm going to take your balls. You're going to bleed like a woman."

George didn't immediately intervene. Instead he held his arms wide, beckoning Ethan to come to his embrace for protection. Ethan kept running.

Finally George said, "Enough, Moira. Let the boy be."

Moira stopped the sport and everyone turned to the great roast, with Ethan sitting as far away from her as the banquet table allowed, trying to avoid any further staring. When he was finally able to eat, the meal was the best he'd ever had.

They had been there most of the day. In the dingy rowing back from the castle George took his hands off the oars and put them on Ethan's shoulders, trying to give him a comforting hug. He struggled, and George let him go. George said, shaking his head and frowning unhappily, his face full of concern, "I'm sorry she scared you. Shouldn't have let it go so far. She wouldn't have hurt you. I wouldn't have let her. She knows she's very ugly, hates it. When people stare at her as you did, she gets angry. It goes back to how her family treated her. Appalling. She's actually a great lady. Despite all of her physical problems, Moira is a hero of England with her ambulance driving, and she's famous in France as a chef." Later he stilled the oars again to give Ethan his full attention. Talking in a slow and reflective tone, he said, "The Caribbean's full of odd people like Moira. They came here after the war to escape the law, to escape from their families, or sometimes to escape from themselves. Away in the Caribbean they can do what they want and live as they want, nobody cares. These islands have become the safety valve for the whole world. We will meet other escapees like Moira around the Caribbean. They're not bad people. Just different people."

Ethan did not want to meet anyone like Moira ever again.

George continued, "If you were scared you should have come over to me."

Ethan looked away shaking his head. George would have embraced him just like he tried to do on the airplane from New York and just now in the dingy. He didn't want George's embrace, even to escape Moira. No way. He was proud that he hadn't turned to George's embrace.

Back on *Rascal*, Johnson pulled Ethan aside out of George's hearing. Eyes full of sympathy, Johnson said, "George tell me what happen. No you fault she scare you. Natural to be afraid. She known throughout de islands as de 'White Witch of Tortola.' People think she have de evil eye and hex dem. Think she head coven of witches. Think she worship de devil. Hide or turn der face away when she come to town. You did well to be with her and not yell or cry or anythin'."

Despite Johnson's words, Ethan lapsed into more silence, fear magnified, no longer the tentative yes and no he was starting to utter. The pace of the left hand nervous exercise accelerated. And he even wondered about Johnson. Johnson didn't stop his visit to the castle.

. . .

They anchored for the night and prepared to check in at customs in Road Town the next morning. According to George they should have done this as soon as they entered the B.V.I.s, but he hadn't because *Rascal* had been visiting smaller islands with no customs offices and the B.V.I.s were relaxed about customs anyway.

George explained, "At each island we visit we're going to have to go through a rigamarole. We can't go ashore until a customs inspector comes aboard, checks us out, and we fill out a lot of unnecessary paperwork. It always takes a damn lot of time."

Johnson said, "De' must conduct contest on each island to find de laziest men. Hire only de laziest men for customs. And de fattest. De' get fat from eating all de food de' get from boats bribing them to clear customs."

Rascal entered Road Town harbor, anchored off the customs' house, and George had Johnson raise a special pennant on *Rascal's* mizzen mast which reported they were in from a foreign port and wanted to clear customs. After almost an hour the customs inspector arrived. He was grossly fat and had trouble clearing the railing to board *Rascal*. George used the approach he'd found effective many times before. Waddling the customs inspector below decks, he talked about how much he loved Tortola, how much he was looking forward to coming ashore, asked about the inspector's family with as much interest as he could muster, and complimented the inspector on how he looked in his uniform. (A difficult compliment as the inspector's belly was visibly protruding over the top of his trousers).

Seated on a bunk, the inspector pulled out a ream of papers that were supposed to be completed, the whole process normally taking more than an hour. On the bunk directly opposite George had placed a bottle of good brandy (not the best, but good), a cartoon of cigarettes, and a large box of English toffee.

George slowly filled out the paper work, continuing to try to befriend the inspector. When he felt the turkey had been sufficiently basted in his friendship, George leaned over toward the inspector and said as one friend to another, "Really, all this paper work is unnecessary. I promise you we're not going to bring any contraband on shore. You can see we're not smugglers. This is all just a waste of your valuable time. Can't we just wrap things up so you can get back to more important things," that was probably more sleeping.

The inspector stared at the booty opposite and brought out stamps and seals to clear them into port. When he eventually waddled top side and off the boat, George expressed continuing friendship and helped carry the "gifts" the inspector had received from *Rascal*.

George later bemoaned the loss of good brandy.

Johnson said, "It de government fault. De government make de custom inspector take bribe. De' pay dem nothin. De' want dem to make up de difference in bribe. Save de governments a lot of salary money."

Still, George did not like losing the brandy.

. . .

The whole thing reminded Ethan of when he overheard his father give a couple of bottles of whiskey to a neighbor to spy on his mother while he was away on a business trip. George and his father. A disgusting pair.

Leaving Road Town harbor they headed for Peter's Island. Ethan was seated in the bow, his head in his hands, hands over his eyes, away from George and Johnson. He was trying to think through what was going on, straining to understand it all, what might happen. Boy, it sure was difficult. He wasn't used to thinking through why things were. That was adult stuff. Math problems, yes. He was good at math. People problems, no.

There was some good news. George hadn't done anything bad to him so far. And the sea, beaches, and *Rascal* were interesting, better than he'd anticipated. Also, Johnson was super though he wished he'd kept him from visiting the castle. He liked Johnson more each day. But why had George selected him to sail on *Rascal* rather than another boy? He'd seen George talking to all the other boys at the playground. He could have invited any of them. And what did George intend to do to him later in the voyage? He had no answer for any of this. Many unknowns. None of the fear had gone.

But was he feeling any better about what happened back home now that he was away? He thought about it. No. The memories were strong as ever.

A large gravel pit was in active use near his home. His mother and father had warned him never to go near it. It had real steep sides. They worried that if he fell in he'd never get out.

He often imagined himself cast into just such a pit, trapped there, abandoned at the bottom by his father and everyone else, no ladder, no one offering him a line to help him scramble up, everyone pushing him back into the pit, his father, their neighbors, the bullies at school, even his teachers and the minister at church who never reached out to him.

Would he ever escape? Maybe he'd be stuck in a miserable black pit the rest of his life. Did hope lie in being away from his father, the bullies, and town's people who knew what he did and hated him. Could that make a difference? Or maybe escape *was* in the sea. Johnson said God was in the sea. Would being on the sea help? Diminish his misery? The very size of the sea made his problems seem smaller. And it offered so many new things. Sort of inviting him. Showing him lots he'd never imagined, neat stuff. Opening a world away from his past. He felt a little less hopeless, not much, but a little. Perhaps things *could* get better here. But then there was George.

...

They dropped anchor in the secure harbor of Peter Island, B.V.I.s, staying there for two nights to explore the island, swim the deserted beaches, and plan their trip south. George tried to bring Ethan into the planning, bringing out charts and discussing with him the islands they would visit, attempting to end his silence. George described the islands he knew, and Johnson the rest.

The plan was ambitious as it covered all the islands down to Trinidad in two months and then back to the Virgin Islands, almost 1,500 miles down and back, counting planned detours.

George said, "I'm going to try and show you every part of the Caribbean I can. You're going to have a true adventure. You'll see things your classmates won't see as long as they live."

Ethan frowned and shook his head, looking at his feet with his eyes tearing. They were taking him further away than ever. He was right about never getting back.

So now they had a plan for exploration of Caribbean islands. And George thought he knew where they were going and what to expect.

As George picked up the charts to put them away, Johnson raised a hand to get his attention and said with a very serious look, "Good to have plan. But maybe not Caribbean plan. Caribbean have it own plan for people dat sail its water. Take you where it want when it want. Leave you where you no expect to be. Caribbean like to play game with boat and people on boat."

CHAPTER EIGHT

Lying in his bunk that night, hands clasped behind his head, George smiled happily. Despite what Johnson said about the unpredictability of the Caribbean he was comfortable with the plan for the voyage. But more important, his master plan was working.

It had all started when he'd noticed the tension between Ethan and his father, the alienation. He watched closely at church. If anything the tension had grown greater over the year and one-half since Ethan's mother died. From what he'd heard, Ethan's father was still blaming the boy for his mother's death.

He'd felt honestly sorry for Ethan. And of all the boys on the playground, he was the most attractive.

George thought about Ethan many times in the Spring of 1951 as he sat in his utilitarian office at the Schenectady Cadillac dealership, Rotary trophies of boy's teams he sponsored sitting across from him on the bookshelves. Was there a way he could reach out to Ethan? Was there a way he could build a relationship? Why couldn't he substitute for the boy's father? He could provide the care and parental love his father denied him. Ethan was so psychologically frail. And he really had no functioning father. Wouldn't it be easy to bring Ethan to accept him in place of his father? While Marge was against adoption maybe Ethan was the way to bring a boy into his life. Maybe if he did it right Ethan could become like the son he always wanted. This was the best opportunity he would ever have, and if he could rescue the boy it would be a marvelous act of Christian charity. He could provide everything for him— a wealthy, secure, and happy life.

An idea had come to him. Brilliant he thought then and thought now.. His cousin in Poughkeepsie, John Bolton, had told him he intended to take his wife to Europe for the summer. He would volunteer to take the Bolton's thirteen-year-old son, Fritz, with him to the Caribbean while they were in Europe. Then recruit Ethan to go along. The Boltons would probably be happier to release Fritz if another thirteen-year-old went along, and Ethan's father would probably feel more comfortable with Fritz along.

As he'd contemplated it that Spring he'd become very happy. Spending the summer in the Caribbean was going to take Ethan out of his sorrow. No doubt about it. What could be better. A great chance to get close to him. At the end of the voyage Ethan was going to look to him as his rescuer, his best friend, his angel of mercy, a father in every way but name. At the very least for the two months of the voyage it would be like having a son. Even if not a son for life, he'd have one for two months.

In late May he tracked down Ethan and his father, Fred Carpenter, in a diner near Christ Church. A little detective work had revealed that Fred regularly took Ethan to the diner after Sunday service.

George entered the diner wearing his broadest smile, the one he used in selling cars, and approached their table.

Fred gave him a weak and tentative "Hello," not surprising. Previously he'd barely acknowledged Fred's existence.

He grabbed Fred's hand in a strong handshake (it felt like shaking a wet fish) and asked if he could sit down. When Fred assented, George asked Fred to excuse Ethan, saying that he needed to talk to him about something private. Ethan was shooed away to the other end of the diner and looked nervously at them as they talked, twisting and turning his napkin.

George started by saying, "I'm coming to you as a member of the church who wants to help." He leaned forward, smiling and trying to be his most persuasive, giving a pitch he practiced several times at home. "It seems to me you have a very unhappy boy on your hands."

Fred frowned.

"I know this is none of my business but Ethan appears to be recovering from his mother's death so slowly. I've watched him in church. It makes me so sad. I can see he's still suffering terribly. It's in the eyes and that hang-dog look. I know he watched Sarah die. Awful."

Fred said nothing.

"A thought came to me the other day. There's a way I might help Ethan put his misery behind him. As you may know, I have a sailboat in the Virgin

Islands. My cousin's son, Fritz Bolton, is joining me for the summer. He's just Ethan's age, lives in Poughkeepsie. I wonder if it wouldn't be good for Ethan to join us? I'll pay Ethan's way. He'll see a lot of new things, get away from where the tragedy occurred. The whole thing should become distant in his mind. I think it would help him greatly."

Fred looked away for several moment, then turned back to George with a sigh, "It might be good for Ethan as you say. And I don't mind telling you it might be good for me. Every night I cook dinner with Ethan in the very kitchen where Sarah died. You're right. She died right in front of Ethan and he didn't try and help her. I'm being constantly reminded that he could have saved her. It's having a very bad effect on both of us. He's getting completely withdrawn. And I still have the same anger toward him. It's there just as strong as the day she died." He paused. "What I'm trying to think through is what Sarah would have wanted. Would Sarah have wanted Ethan to go off with a man she hardly knew? Fred paused for a moment and turned away thinking, then turned back. "I'm sorry, Mr. Rosenthal, but I don't think she would have wanted Ethan to go off like this."

George responded with the second argument he'd rehearsed. "Look. I know Sarah was a very devout Christian. She was in church every Sunday, right? And I know you are too."

Fred nodded.

"I intend to run this expedition as a Christian summer camp, a Christian summer camp for two boys. I already told the Boltons. That's one reason they agreed to let their son come along. They're strong Episcopalians, as you are. I've already had Father Smallwood prepare lessons from the Bible and from Episcopal literature. Being a vestryman has its privileges." He chuckled.

"We will go over them together every day. Now, I can understand that Sarah might not want Ethan to go off with someone she doesn't know. But wouldn't she think it was all right, even good for Ethan, to go to a Christian summer camp run by a vestryman in her own church?"

Fred again turned away for some time, looking at the floor and furrowing his brow. What eventually came out was, "Two months is pretty long. Any chance to cut your trip shorter?"

As an old closer of car sales George knew this meant the sale was clinched and they were just bargaining the details. He was elated but kept it to himself.

"Fritz's parents are going off to Europe for two months. I said I'd take Fritz for the whole time. I'm stuck with it."

Then Fred asked, "Is there any danger?"

George gave him a lengthy reassurance about how well built the boat was, that based on his experience of the last two summers it would not be rough, that they would only be going short distances between islands, and that he had a very competent mate aboard. He did not tell Fred that last summer they'd been caught in a vicious squall and he had jammed his hand in a winch while bringing in the jib. Very painful surgery had resulted in St. Thomas.

Finally, in a quiet, resigned voice, shrugging and looking away, Fred said, "Okay."

George got up and winked at Ethan, beaming.

A couple of days later Marge came at him. She said she'd overheard a telephone conversation with the Boltons about plans.

Blocking his exit from the room she said, "You never told me anything about any of this. You never do. I hope you're taking one of your friends along, another adult."

He was very irritated at her interference and replied gruffly, "No. The boat would be too crowded."

"George. I love you. I want you to do whatever makes you happy. But this is a big mistake. You know I have a strong intuition. My intuition tells me something horrible is going to happen. Please don't go. For my sake and your own I beg you, *please* cancel it."

George had pushed past her, quite angry.

Well, Ethan was here now and everything was going fine. So much for Marge's intuition. And he had already initiated the plans he had for Ethan aboard *Rascal*. Not much to show for it yet, but at least a start.

His intent was to gradually, gently, take Ethan under his control, bring him into loving him like a father by getting closer to him than anyone ever had, perhaps even his mother. He would be constantly helpful, listen intently to Ethan's every word, admittedly few at this juncture, congratulate him on everything he did, bring him out of his withdrawal into sharing his innermost thoughts and desires, as did some boys on the playground, then Ethan's arms around his neck in love, not calling him Dad but close enough.

He started whistling softly.

CHAPTER NINE

The next morning George said, "Do you know what snow blindness is?"

Ethan nodded.

"Well, I tell people I bought *Rascal* because of snow blindness. I was sitting there in Niskayuna the second day of a blizzard. You know how bad they get. Couldn't even get out of the house. I'd been thinking about buying a yacht in the Caribbean. A friend of mine sailed there a lot and said it was great, and I like sailing. When I was young I sailed small boats at the family compound on Lake George. A guy in New York had sent me pictures of his ketch down in the Virgin Islands. She looked great. She was sort of old. Built at City Island, New York in 1936. But she was a Sparkman & Stephens design, the best naval architects. I sat there watching the snow come down. Then going over the pictures. Then the snow. Then the pictures. I couldn't stand it. I called the fellow in New York and bought the boat right then and there. The blind part was I bought the boat sight unseen. The constant snow did it. I was sort of stir crazy from the snow and didn't do what I should have done. Should have gotten a naval survey to check out the boat before I bought it.

"When I got to the Virgin Islands I found the photos were way out of date. The boat had been used hard since the photos were taken. Sails were old. Brightwork salt stained and worn. Paint peeling. We've got new sails now, and Johnson has done a great job on the brightwork and paint. Everything I own I want to look its best. *Rascal* tells me that she's proud of how she looks.

"A lesson to you, my boy. Don't ever buy anything until you check it out thoroughly. And never ever buy anything located in a warm climate when you're sitting in a blizzard." He laughed.

"*Rascal* was the name of the boat before I bought it. I decided to keep the name to rub it in with some stupid people in Niskayuna. They think I'm a rascal." He thrust his chin out belligerently. "A rascal owning *Rascal*. Screw them. Sorry for the language, Ethan, but there are some real ignoramuses in town."

Ethan shook his head and gave George a sour look. Certainly a rascal. And he wondered what name those people in Niskayuna would use for George if they knew what he had done to him.

Johnson picked up the conversation. "Sparkman & Stephens design a very good boat. High side to keep de wave out. Wide beam so steady in de sea. Only problem is she have a blunt bow like many boat from de 30s. Slam de wave. No cut through de wave like more modern sailboat. And have a ketch rig. Wide beam, blunt bow, ketch rig sailboat go slow to windward. Dis year even harder to go to windward. Dis be heavy trade-wind year."

He turned to George. "Trade-wind vary year to year. Last two year when you here with you friends be de light trade-wind year. Lightest I remember. No strong wind. Dis year very heavy trade-wind. Heaviest trade-wind in twenty year and maybe much more."

They prepared that afternoon for the Anegada Passage. George had already noticed that the trade-wind was blowing much harder than in previous years and had some worry about the Passage. He pulled out the *"Sailing Directions for the Caribbean"* and shared it with Ethan. It referred to the Anegada Passage as the "Cape Horn of the Caribbean." Not a good place to sail in heavy wind. They couldn't go around, had to cross it to journey south.

Johnson laid out what they faced, a forty five mile beat, the wind right on the nose, from the British Virgin Islands to St. Martin and Anguilla through a nearly two mile deep trough where the Atlantic violently pours its waters into the Caribbean, the deepest and most turbulent passage by far between Atlantic and Caribbean. Strong currents. Reefs at unexpected places. Cross currents creating virtual whirlpools. Winds roaring this year. Waves piling upon waves to create monster waves with no order to allow anticipation. Tumult and danger through the whole Passage. They should expect absolute chaos.

. . .

George stared out to sea, frowned and looked around the boat that would have to carry them through. Johnson was smiling like he was looking forward to it. And Ethan gave no indication he understood anything of what he was hearing.

George turned to Ethan and said with concern, "We are in for some rough sailing. We'll come through alright. I know you're a brave boy. Just be brave."

George instructed Johnson to batten *Rascal* down completely, hatches and portholes locked closed, dingy lashed to the foredeck. Everything checked and checked again.

Everyone donned life preservers and George belted a safety harnesses around Ethan's waist. Then George and Johnson both separately instructed him that he should never *ever* move from where his belt was attached to the rigging, but that if movement was necessary as in tacking, he must un-clip and re-clip the safety harness to and from the standing rigging as fast as possible. Unclip only after a wave passes, and only then if there is a lull between waves. Move quickly to your new position. Clip in before the new wave arrives. Miss the new clip and over the side you go with little chance of *Rascal* being able to jibe around and pick you up.

George had Johnson work with him to double reef the main. A storm jib was bent on forward, a very small sail with double strong canvass. The mizzen was furled tight.

Rascal set sail from harbor at 2:00 AM, timing departure to arrive at St. Martin in daylight, running immediately into eight foot waves driven by near gale-force winds, their due east course taking them head-on into the waves and wind. Waves started breaking over the bow, smothering *Rascal* in blue water and foam, seeming intent on engulfing the whole boat. It was a very squally and storm lashed day in the Anegada Passage. The Passage seemed furious at *Rascal* for attempting its waters.

As an angry dawn broke, and they sailed farther from land, the wind increased, now blowing a full gale according to the anemometer, winds of forty five miles an hour with higher gusts, a great roaring current of air. Waves grew to ten feet, even an occasional graybeard of fifteen feet or more. And the sea went mad, coming from many different directions.

Johnson was at the helm and George found himself cowering in the cockpit, hat lost overboard, comb over blowing damply back and forth. He set his mouth in a grim line and held on hard to both railing and cockpit seat with head down to avoid the constant hard spray.

Johnson gave Ethan a big smile and an exuberant thumbs up. Everything was all right. And with Johnson calm, Ethan seemed to be calm. George studied the building waves. Johnson was overly optimistic.

With waves this size they were breaking not just at the bow but into the cockpit. Between helm duty sea water constantly swirled around George's knees where he was sitting, and often around his waist. And the wind, the increasing wind was blowing the tops off the waves. Spume hit his face so hard it hurt to look forward. He worked the tacks with his head down, largely determining the set of the jib by instinct, and even vision to the side was difficult, the air thick with wind-blown spray.

Ethan was trying dutifully to perform his assigned task of tailing and cleating, unclipping and clipping as instructed. But one sneaker wave broke over the boat when Ethan had barely re-clipped, would have thrown him out of the boat but for the support of his lifeline and Ethan's quick grab for the railing.

George yelled at him, "Stay put right where you are. Don't move. Just hold on." He seated Ethan in the stern of the cockpit, the safest place.

As sea and wind grew ever stronger, tacking became impossible. *Rascal* was stuck on a starboard tack. When she headed up into the full force of the wind to go over to port tack she was met by such power in the breaking waves that she couldn't get around. She kept getting knocked down to leeward by one raging comber after another. The double-reefed main was not producing enough thrust to propel her through the strength of the seas to go over to port tack. Johnson tried to start the engine, intending to use it to help break through to port tack. It wouldn't start. Often the case. They had to depend upon sails alone.

As though waiting purposefully for failure of the engine, disaster appeared to leeward, right where the starboard tack was taking them. Through the obscurity of spray a thundering long reef came into view, scarcely one-half mile way. The reef hurtled surf more than thirty feet into the air and spouted whirlpools at its edges, certain death to any boat that came upon it. A mariner's worst nightmare, being driven on a lee shore, George's stomach clenched with fear.

Johnson shouted at George to help him take down the main and raise the mizzen. George stared at Johnson and hesitated, not understanding the reason for the sail change, and not liking taking orders from Johnson. He looked again at the reef, now perceptively nearer, jumped up, and attacked the sails with an urgency fueled by repeated glances at the rapidly approaching reef, aiding Johnson in furling the main against the wild sail-flapping wind, and raising the mizzen. The work exhausted George, and he had to bend over to catch his breath, then sit down.

Johnson ordered a new attempt to tack to port. Gradually *Rascal* turned into the wind, finally headed directly into the wind with the sails shuddering violently and ineffectively, in irons, deciding whether to go over to port tack or throw them back toward the reef on starboard. Then driven by wind and waves at the bow, *Rascal* started falling backward, at first slowly, soon more rapidly. Johnson jammed the rudder over to port, taking advantage of Rascal's backward motion to steer the stern toward the reef and the bow to the port tack. It was working until a giant wave came out of nowhere and crashed the starboard side forward, throwing *Rascal* back over on starboard tack. Johnson, totally calm, ordered George to try again.

This time Johnson paid off further from the wind on starboard tack to gain maximum way, ending up only twenty yards from the reef, then spun the helm rapidly to bring *Rascal* into the wind. Again she paused in irons, but this time at first imperceptibly, then more quickly, *Rascal* fell off on port tack. George sheeted home the jib. They were around. The wind hitting the mizzen had given *Rascal* just enough leverage to break through the waves.

Now on port tack *Rascal* clawed her way off the reef, the closest call George had experienced sailing. He put his head over the side and threw up, hoping Ethan and Johnson weren't watching.

More hours passed. George came to believe the tumult was coming at him with a purpose. There was sinister intention in wind and waves. They were trying to take everything from him, what he knew, what he valued, what he loved, everything of who he was and everything of who he would become, to take from him his very existence.

The wild keening of the wind gave voice to the malice, sometimes shrieking a high note in the rigging, sometimes a dreadful rumble, the voice of annihilation, calling out a desire to kill him. And all the while the mast shaking, the rigging shaking, the boat shaking from the blows of the sea. The boat would go down.

Two giant waves smashed aboard from opposite sides at the same time. *Rascal* buried herself in the sea, only the two masts emerging above water. Everything else covered by cloud-gray water with *Rascal* driving along below the surface in a smother of foam.

George was totally submerged in the cockpit for over a minute. When he surfaced he gasped out the sea water, scrunched his eyes closed, and opened his mouth wide in a howl. "We're going to die! Turn around! Go back! We can't make it. Turn around now! That's an order!"

Johnson replied calmly in a quiet voice as though carrying on a conversation on a peaceful beach, "No. Too dangerous. We no die if we go forward. We might die if we go back. With de wind and wave dis strong if we turn round, put de wind behind us, we surely broach, roll de boat. Roll her two mile to de bottom. We go on."

George stared at Johnson in anger, then hunkered back down in the cockpit, holding on to the railing as though the strength of his grip would save the boat.

Over seventeen hours of exhausting work, they arrived through treacherous reefs for the dangerous landfall on St. Martin, daylight so limited that it required all of Johnson's intuition and memory skills to pilot them to safety. Weary all over. Battered from being thrown against rigging and other hard places in the heavy going.

When they finally anchored, George still had the strength to raise his bottle of brandy in celebration of survival. Repeatedly he offered a drink to Johnson and even said Ethan could have a congratulatory sip. Johnson refused and shook his head no at Ethan.

As they sat quiet and grateful, Johnson smoked his usual Gauloises and mused, "No mon an atheist after sailin de Angeda Passage on a hard tradewind year."

George turned to Ethan. "You did well. I'm proud of you. That was the roughest I've ever seen. You were very brave. The Anegada Passage was trying to kill us. I sort of panicked. You did better than I did."

This produced from Ethan the broadest grin George had seen from him.

George also congratulated Ethan for not getting seasick. "Most people would've gotten seasick. I was a little seasick. Threw up at one point."

Despite the congratulations Ethan was still monotonously doing the thumb and fingers counting exercise with his left hand. George reached over and put his arm around Ethan's shoulders, giving him several big hugs and playfully tousling his hair. Then he had everybody stand in the cockpit and all engaged in a hearty shaking of hands in celebration of survival.

. . .

During the Angeda Passage, Ethan had been mostly calm as whenever he looked over at Johnson he found him smiling like he was enjoying it. Johnson didn't even get excited with the scary submersion. It was all awesome. Wow. Was the sea angry? *Rascal* didn't mind. He and Rascal had ridden immense waves together. Survived brutal hits by the sea from all sides. And that wind was much stronger than even in those mammoth upstate New York thunderstorms. When *Rascal* was buried under the simultaneous attack of the monster waves he felt not fear but astonishment. *Rascal* was sailing along as though she didn't care that she was under water. A sailing submarine.

The passage was the most exciting thing that ever happened to him. All fear of *Rascal* was gone.

He thought further about the Angela Passage the next morning while he coiled some of the lines forward. George had called him brave. No one had ever called him brave before. Would the bullies back home have been so brave? Something new surged up inside. This was weird. He felt a little better about himself. George had been afraid. He hadn't been. Maybe George wasn't such a big, scary guy after all with his strutting around and looking down at people.

CHAPTER TEN

The quest proceeded. More islands. More adventure to pursue. From over the horizon a beckoning call. Enchantment lay ahead.

Ethan felt himself being drawn to it, like when he was on a path in the woods back home and the path pulled him along to see what lay ahead. For the first time on the voyage he found himself looking forward a little bit. Survival of the Anegada Passage had changed things.

He found he didn't resent his assignments on the boat so much. They seemed easier. Why resist anyway? It wasn't going to get him anywhere. He moved more promptly to his tailing position behind George or Johnson on whatever line was in play. At meals he stood ready for whatever he was called upon to do with plates and dishes. All the deck lines were coiled and recoiled. And instead of sitting slumped in the cockpit for long periods, he moved restlessly around the deck staring out at sea, land, and sky, sometimes smiling at what he saw, each sight brand new and different, more to be absorbed in a shorter period than ever before in his life, a different world.

Some of the islands they visited were British, some French, some Dutch. One of the French islands, St. Barths, recreated Brittany with a colony of Bretton fishing folk, women in poke bonnets and colorful costumes of Brittany, foot long French bread transported in their bicycle baskets and then transported onto *Rascal* to the delight of all aboard. The Dutch towns on Sint Maarten brought Holland— clean, neat with building fronts crenellated in the Dutch manner, and no open sewers as in St. Thomas.

On the French side of the same island (called St. Martin), George took Ethan to a restaurant in Marigot that he said was as good as any in Paris. Johnson was not invited and ate at a local restaurant across the street.

To get to the restaurants they had to cross stinking open sewers, worse if anything than those in St. Thomas. Would any food be good to eat in Marigot with this stink? The restaurant convinced him it was not only good but great to eat in Marigot. George did the ordering in French.

The first dish was a platter of snails. Ethan pushed back from the table, looked at George, and said "Ugh" with a loud voice, one of his rare utterances, and shook his head in vigorous rejection.

George speared one of the snails out of its shell, popped it into his mouth, licked his lips, smiled broadly. "Wonderful. Just like Paris. Ethan. If you eat one I'll let you off dish duty the next two days."

Ethan did not much mind dish duty. But he didn't want George to see him scared of something George wasn't afraid of. He'd showed him who was brave in the Anegada Passage.

Ethan popped one in his mouth. Held it there some time, his tongue moving over it to determine whether to spit it out, finally swallowed it smiling at George. Then for good measure he did the same with several others, finding he liked them..

Later another mystery dish arrived, a casserole with a lot of garlic and meat that tasted a lot like chicken. He ate it as he had the snails, smiling at George all the time to show him he wasn't a scaredy-cat baby afraid to eat what George ate.

They were served at the restaurant by a very pompous, very French waiter. While walking back to *Rascal* George quipped to Johnson and Ethan, "The trouble with French food is that it makes the French think too highly of themselves."

Johnson nodded. George then told Johnson proudly that Ethan had eaten both snails and frogs legs.

Johnson looked Ethan over quizzically as though assessing if he might get sick. Ethan smiled back but actually did feel like getting sick. Frogs legs?

George said to Ethan. "Do you know why the French eat snails?"

Ethan shook his head.

"It's because the French like their eating slow. Eat in a fine restaurant in Paris and you'll know what it means to eat slowly."

This got a smile from Johnson but nothing from Ethan who was still checking his stomach for possible vomiting up of frogs legs.

The next day they went to a beach inhabited by a colony of the giant iguanas of St. Martin, some over three feet in length. Johnson brought along a large sack of lettuce. Ethan was instructed to put the lettuce on a rock in front of them and stand back. The iguanas dashed madly up to the rock, fought so fiercely over the lettuce that there was blood on the sand, then dashed off with whatever they captured.

The iguanas looked like the pictures of dinosaurs Ethan had seen. He turned to George. "Dinosaurs?"

George laughed, saying he was happy to finally get a question from him. "No. These are lizards and dinosaurs weren't lizards."

This did not prevent Ethan from imagining he was feeding baby dinosaurs. And before George and Johnson could stop him he was feeding one of the fighting iguanas by hand.

"Watch out for your fingers!" George and Johnson yelled in unison.

Ethan had been watching out for his fingers and was sure the iguana appreciated being fed by hand. Later Ethan said to Johnson, "That was neat," the first time he'd spoken to Johnson. He was feeling a flicker of happiness, an emotion he'd almost forgotten existed. And he realized he hadn't had a "bad time" since the Anegada Passage.

George told one of his stories. "Last year I was on this same beach and there was a tourist reading a paperback book. One of the lizards ran up to him, grabbed the book right out of his hands, and took off down the beach. Must have thought it was something good to eat. The tourist sat there dumfounded, shaking his head in disbelief. Twenty minutes later what looked like a different lizard came up to him with the book in its mouth and dropped it at the tourist's feet. The tourist held his hands up to heaven and announced, 'A miracle.' The lizard responded, 'Not really. You had your name on the inside front cover.'"

For the first time Ethan laughed at one of George's jokes. Then he felt he shouldn't be laughing after what he did back home, and brought the corners of his mouth down to a frown.

In St. Martin, having talked a little and laughed, Ethan started getting questions from George, how he was feeling, how he liked the voyage so far, how he liked *Rascal,* how he liked sailing, and many about whether he wanted to do this or that on *Rascal* or ashore. He replied by shaking his head, but occasionally an affirmative nod. George did not give up.

"What subjects do you like at school?"

"Math," he said. He led his class in math and this was one small bright spot in his dark life.

"Great. Math is important. You can be an accountant like your father."

Ethan burst out, "I don't *want* to be an accountant. I don't *want* to do anything my father does. I hate him." Ethan screwed up his face ready to cry but held it back to avoid crying in front of George.

George put an arm around his shoulder, though he tried to pull away. "I didn't intend to upset you. With your math what you should really do is be an engineer. That's better than an accountant any day. Engineers do wonderful things— build bridges, roads, airplanes, radios, even ships. Be an engineer. I know you'll build great things. Make the world better."

Ethan had not much thought about what he would do when he grew up. But being an engineer sounded interesting. And thinking about a future away from his father put him in the best mood he'd had the entire voyage. He day-dreamed about becoming a rich and important engineer. He'd show his father. And maybe his father would come to him to borrow money or something. He'd turn him down.

CHAPTER ELEVEN

From St. Martin they sailed to the British island of Anguilla. On the way over Ethan noticed Johnson was reading. He was always reading when he wasn't at the helm or doing chores. Ethan went over. Johnson held up the book so Ethan could see the title. It was by someone called Conrad.

Johnson asked, "Have you ever read Conrad?"

Ethan shook his head.

"Do you like to read?"

Ethan nodded. Reading was one of the only escapes from the bad things in his life. Johnson disappeared below and reappeared with a well-thumbed copy of *Heart of Darkness*. "Conrad is de best and dis my favorite book." He held it up in the sun and looked at it admiringly. "De story be about a voyage in Africa, an adventure story. A bad man does scary things. Not at all like our voyage is going to be.

"Maybe later in our voyage I let you read it. I goin to have to sit down with you to help you. It have many long word and difficult sentence and big idea."

Approaching Anguilla, George told Ethan that they would lay over there for several days. "It's my favorite island," George said as they anchored in Sandy Ground harbor. "I want you to see all of it. The beaches are special. There are ten major beaches on the island. Each one is almost as beautiful as White Beach on Jost Van Dyke. I have a challenge for you. Do you think in the three days we are here you can swim all ten?"

Ethan said, "Maybe," without much enthusiasm, turning his head aside.

Transport on Anguilla was simple. All they had to do was walk up from Sandy Ground to the main dirt road that ran the length of the island. Before long a horse-drawn cart would come by, or sometimes a dilapidated truck. They didn't have to put out a thumb. The vehicle would automatically stop. If it was a farm wagon with produce the driver would rearrange things to make room, often a time-consuming task as some farm transport was piled high. If the vehicle was already carrying people they would scrunch together to make room. And when there was no room, some of the people would get off and either start walking or stand there waiting for the next ride. No transport ever passed them without offering a ride.

Once on an Anguillan vehicle the conversation was non-stop. The people talked to them as though being with them was the best thing that had happened to them in days, maybe weeks, telling them about their families, giving them information on the island, asking them about their sail and their families. How many times did Ethan hear, "Dis be de best island in de Caribbean. We de happiest people." And Ethan thought they must be. And often this was followed by, "Why you no come to my house later for a beer, or coke, and some supper."

They never accepted these invitations. Johnson said the people were very poor. If they took supper it would be taking the only food the family had for the evening.

This was a different world, a better world. At home few even talked to him. People looked at him and looked away, remembering he'd killed his mother. And he certainly hadn't been invited to anyone's house for dinner since his mother died. He daydreamed about living in a place like Anguilla, far from the unfriendly people back home, a place where nobody knew what happened, where they were happy to see him. Then he looked over at George. The real world came back. If he ever did get home what could possibly change? People would remember what he'd done forever. The daydream ended.

After two days, and eight of the ten beaches, Johnson explained what was going on. "People friendly because de' never have much slavery on Anguilla. De island too sandy for sugarcane and slavery all about workin sugarcane. Nobody here have much memory of slavery. Nobody here have much memory of de white people doing terrible thing to de black people. So de' treat you friendly like you another black person. Only better because you be visitor."

There was a festival one day. Island sloop races were featured.

George said, "See those boats out there getting ready for the race? They may not look it, but some are over forty feet long, longer than *Rascal*."

Johnson said, "I was captain on one over eighty feet."

George continued, "They're built locally on about every island in the Caribbean, right Johnson?"

Johnson nodded.

"These boat are the work-horses of the Caribbean. Most of the stuff that goes from one island to another is carried on boats like these. People too." George paused. "Ethan. What do you see different from *Rascal?*"

Ethan didn't answer.

"One mast. a short mast, and a long boom. One mast means a sloop. The short masts are because on the islands they never had the wire and steel spreaders to guy the kind of tall mast we have on *Rascal*. With short masts the only way to get enough sail area to catch the wind is to have a very long boom, so very long booms."

The island sloops sailing past, long sails stretching aft for wind, reminded Ethan of swallow wings back home, swallows of the sea. Whenever he saw island sloops, and he often saw them, stumpy masts and long booms gliding in the distance, his thoughts turned to swallows.

The race would be from one end of the long thin island of Anguilla (Anguilla the "eel") to the other end and back again, the first leg upwind to a buoy at the windward end of the island then back downwind on the second leg to finish where the race started at the leeward end of the island. Ethan, George, and Johnson joined many locals at a high observation point.

Going upwind on the first leg, each boat had as many as fifteen men sitting on, or more often, precariously stretching out from whichever was the windward side, providing ballast to keep the boat as upright as possible to catch the maximum amount of wind. At the turn came a loud whoop Ethan could clearly hear from their viewing site more than a mile away, and the ballast men hit the water with a joyous splash to swim to the beach, leaving the lightened boat for the helmsman and one sail-handler to sweep before the wind to the finish.

Ethan didn't think being a ballast man was a very good job, but George assured him it was. When they got to the festival Ethan could see why. The helmsmen and sail handlers may have been dry, but it was the wet ballast men who were given the free beer. Johnson said that the most sought-after job on Anguilla at festival time was to be a ballast man. The heaviest men on Anguilla vied for the honor.

The festival included a boxing match. Signs said it was the *All Anguilla Championship Match*. Johnson said it was limited to natives of Anguilla. The people parted and gave Ethan, George, and Johnson ring-side seats, a further display of hospitality.

It looked to Ethan that the contestants were very unevenly matched. One man was tall, heavy, and very muscular. He was introduced as the champion of the island. The other man was shorter, far lighter in weight, and while muscled, did not have the heavy muscles of the first man. He was introduced as the challenger, a returnee, the son of people who lived on the island. The parents were asked to stand. Johnson said their son had gone off island to live with an aunt from the age of fourteen.

A lot of men, and some women, were gathered at a betting stand on the other side of the ring. Johnson said, "About everybody over there be betting on de champion. Odds one hundred to one. Still de' betting. Everybody know dat when de challenger man went off island at fourteen he be sissy and afraid of things."

The fight lasted two minutes. Ethan didn't think it was a fight at all. The champion threw roundhouse punch after roundhouse punch at the challenger's head. The challenger easily ducked them all. Finally, as though tired of playing around, he came in under the roundhouses, and so quickly Ethan could hardly see them, pow, pow, pow, right, left, right to the champion's jaw. The champion fell straight back from his heels as though dead, looked dead. He didn't move for a long time, and Ethan grew very afraid for him. Even before he finally stirred fights had broken out around the betting stand. George and Johnson whisked Ethan away.

...

Walking back, Ethan thought about the fights at home. From his first memories there were always fights, always started by his father. His father would come home from his job as an accountant at the local bank, clump into the living room, look around, and frown as though he expected to see something unpleasant. His mother would give him an unenthusiastic, "Hello," not looking up from her reading, sewing, cooking, or from telling him stories.

His father would say something like, "You really don't love me at all, do you?" glowering down at her from his superior height.

His mother would reply something like, "Of course I do," or "Don't be silly." This was usually said to the room at large without looking up at his father.

"You never show me you love me. I work hard. When I come home I expect at least a kiss. You only kiss the boy. You don't even want me home."

And so on and so on with an increasingly loud voice from his father, and eventually an angry voice in return from his mother saying, "*Stop it*. Let's not argue in front of Ethan."

And always from his father at the end, "You love Ethan much more than you love me."

Sometimes the argument would be in his parents' bedroom, very noisy, waking Ethan in his room down the hall. His father would be saying, "Show me you love me." His mother's reply indistinct. But always from his father something about him, saying his mother loved him more.

As Ethan grew older his father started finding fault with everything his mother did. In each small failure he seemed to identify a deliberate slight by his mother. Maybe because he was an accountant, his father treated variances from routine as deliberate.

If he did not like what was served at dinner it was, "You know I don't like this. If you loved me you'd cook what I like." Or if dinner was slightly late, "You know I like dinner on time. I work hard and get hungry." Then he would glance at Ethan as though it was his fault.

Increasingly the fights would be physical. He would hear from their bedroom angry words from his father, followed by a slap or other blow, followed by crying from his mother, and in the morning his mother with a red cheek and occasionally a black eye. At breakfast his mother always acted as though nothing had happened, he thought to shield him from their fights.

The worst fights came from his father's jealousy. On many evenings Ethan would hear his father questioning his mother closely on where she had been all day and with whom. When they went out to dinner (not often), or to a Rotary or church social gathering, or attended a neighborhood party, they would frequently come though the front door with his father so upset that his loud voice would wake him.

"Why were you staring at that waiter? You were making eyes at him." Or, "Why did you spend so much time with Jack Larson? You were flirting with him. He knew it and I knew it." Or, "You said you were going to the bathroom and disappeared and then I saw Dave Fritch disappear in the same direction. You were both gone a long time. What was going on?" and so on. His mother's denials were as loud as his father's charges, and the arguments occurred so often that some of the babysitters refused to babysit any more.

The worst argument occurred at Christmastime the year before his mother died. His father's bank was holding a Christmas party. Though they normally drank modestly they apparently had more that evening. Ethan, and probably the whole neighborhood, heard the commotion from the street as soon as his parents parked their car. His father yelled his way to the front door, yelled some more when he came into the house. The yelling brought Ethan into the living room in his pajamas.

His father demanded, "Why did you leave me in the middle of the party and go over to sit at Allen Draney's table? He's the worst lecher at the bank. Thinks because he's a bachelor, and owns part of the bank, he can chase all the secretaries. You've known all along that Allen is after you. When I'm with you he always comes over and wants to talk. When I'm alone he ignores me. You're leading him on. It was a slutty thing to go to his table."

His father's face got redder and redder, his lips compressed, glowering at his mother, leaning forward in belligerence. Then he grabbed his mother by the shoulders and shook her violently. "You are *never* to talk to Allen Draney again! Stop encouraging him. If he comes near you, you turn your back and walk away. You're behaving like a whore. I'm telling you, if I ever see you with Allen again I'm going to do something really bad to you. Believe me. You're going to get something really bad. I'm not kidding."

His father half pushed, half threw his mother against the living room wall. She cowered against the wall trying to protect herself. Towering over her, he fisted his right hand, and tried to punch her in the face. The blow struck her with such force on the left arm which she had raised to defend herself that it knocked her violently sideways against a hard wooden bench. Her right arm crumpled beneath her as she hit the bench. Ethan heard the bone snap, and her head hit the corner of the bench with a sickening thud deeply lacerating her forehead and knocking her unconscious. Copious blood flowed from her forehead down over her face. Ethan thought she'd been killed, screamed at the top of his lungs, rushed over to hold her and tried to hit his father with his fists. His father gave him a strong shove, throwing him into a corner where he continued to scream. "Stay there," and left the room to get ice compresses and bandages. Before he returned two neighbors piled in through the front door, brought by his screams, one in his bathrobe despite the well below freezing temperature. His mother remained unconscious, breathing shallowly, and the neighbors rushed her to the hospital in one of their cars, not letting his father drive as they said he was too drunk. He later learned his mother was in a coma for the better part of a day and she returned home after four days bearing a heavy cast on her right arm and what would turn out to be a vivid scar on her forehead for the rest of her days.

Ethan imagined getting a gun and killing his father. Or maybe that long butcher knife in the kitchen. It would be difficult to get a gun. He had dreams about how he would do it.

A policeman came and talked to his mother. He could see his father was scared. His mother told the policeman she wouldn't press charges. Why? If it was to protect him from having a father in jail he was sorry. His father should go to jail.

His father never made an apology to him for hitting his mother. Instead he came at him mad as hell. "These arguments are all your fault. If your mother didn't give you all her love, if she gave me just some love, just a little love, these arguments would never happen. *You* were what made me hit your mother. It wasn't my fault. It was *yours*."

Maybe his father was right. What if he was the cause of his parents' arguments? His father said it often enough. Then one day an indistinct thought came to him. Would his mother be safer from his father if he wasn't around anymore? He puzzled this for days. Finally he reached a conclusion. Yes, if he went away it *would* protect his mother. His father wouldn't be as bad to her anymore. He was sure of it. He needed to help his mother by going away.

He tried for more than two weeks to work out a plan. Then he realized his mother had already laid out what he needed to do. On a summer night just after his tenth birthday he snuck out of his bedroom at midnight, gathered a bundle of clothes together in a laundry bag, slipped into the kitchen to add boxes of graham crackers, cereal, cookies, and potato chips, some juice and some milk, put the bag over his shoulder, and crept away from home to a place where the Mohawk River flowed gently near their house. The plan his mother had given him was Tom Sawyer and Huckleberry Finn on the Mississippi River. He slept the night in a soft grassy spot, very satisfied with himself for his brave adventure, except for swatting mosquitos and for scary noises in the woods that kept him awake most of the night.

The next morning he had potato chips and cookies for breakfast, then searched the bank and found it, the corner of a shed or old barn that had been washed down by the floods of the previous Spring. Somehow he knew it would be there waiting for him, a platform to adventures just like Huck Finn. Pushing, pulling, pushing, pulling for over an hour in the mud he finally got it launched with his bundle aboard. The platform was partly waterlogged and rode low in the water. With water slopping over the side the bundle was getting wet. Potato chips and everything else was probably in bad shape. But Huck Finn on the Mississippi wouldn't worry about that. Ethan Carpenter on the Mohawk River wouldn't either.

This good mood didn't last long. By the middle of the afternoon the river moved him to the treacherous mid-stream where roiling currents were dumping waves onto his platform from every direction. One wave, larger than the rest, wanted his bundle, took it, and almost took him. He couldn't restrain the scared crying despite trying to be brave. He wanted his mother.

Around sunset a fisherman out for the bass that boil the surface at dusk saw him, rowed out in his skiff, and rescued him.

His mother embraced him with an outpouring of hugging, kissing, and joyful tears. "You're all I have. You're the only one I love. Thank God. Thank God."

His father's face collapsed in an angry scowl, his sparse eyebrows drawn together in disgust, and mouth clamped as though tasting something bad. "You'll wish you never came back. Now I have to beat you. Maybe you should've stayed away."

This provoked one more argument between his parents. But didn't prevent a severe beating first thing the next morning.

...

After a time Johnson went ashore to find out what happened in the aftermath of the boxing match. It didn't take him long to return. "De challenger turn out to be a professional boxer from Trinidad. Promoter paid off de family, de' be very poor, paid them to say de boxer be der son. Promoter hope to clean up on de betting and get off de island before anybody wise up. De' make a stupid mistake. Everybody could see de challenger a professional. No amateur going to play around like dat and then knock out a big boxing man with three punches. De' should have had de challenger stay with it de full fight and knock out de champion in de tenth. De people caught de promoters at de dock, beat dem up, and make them give back all de money."

George asked, "What did they do to the family that the promoters bribed?"

"Nothing much. Dis Anguilla. People let dem keep some of de bribe. Rest went to de church. And de' be gathering round to help dem with food and clothin. De family very nice, church-going folk, and people ashamed de' let dem get so desperate dat de' need to take de promoter money. De' ashamed de' let thing get so bad.

"Anguilla different. People protect each other, take care of each other, forgive each other. In a family you have good people and bad people. But you love dem whether de' good or bad. Anguilla one big family."

Gosh. How different from Niskayuna. How different from what went on in his own town. His own house. Some things were sure better here.

Later that day Ethan was in the main market of Anguilla. Johnson was at a stall buying produce and Ethan walked around a corner just looking to see what was going on. He came face to face with a rotund woman with three large breasts prominently displayed in a colorful, low-cut island dress. She was selling fruit with two little children clinging shyly to her. She smiled broadly at him. He stared at her breasts. He often stared at women's breasts, couldn't help it, and this was amazing

"What you staring at, boy? Bad manners to stare." She then burst into uproarious laughter, which only made his embarrassment greater. He turned away, his face red, ashamed for staring.

Johnson responded with amusement when he heard about it. "It happen. No need to be embarrassed." Then he paused. "Woman with three breast can hex you."

Ethan shivered slightly as he thought about Moira Grayson.

In Anguilla Ethan started paying more attention to the towns they were visiting, jumbles of yellow, green, blue, and dazzling white houses of all shapes and sizes, their front yards proudly decorated with colorful plantings of hibiscus, bougainvillea and crotons, often set out in coffee jars and fuel cans arranged along the front path in welcome to the home. Did people chose the color of their homes to match their personalities? Were people in the blue houses sadder, the yellow houses happier, the green houses outdoors lovers, the white houses more saintly? And how wonderful to walk down the main street of town without having to skulk along with his head down, trying to avoid looking into faces filled with contempt. How wonderful not to have to plot a way through back streets to avoid classmates and their taunts. He'd learned in Niskayuna to be invisible. Here he didn't have to be.

In Anguilla Ethan also started paying more attention to the people, black, dark brown, rarely white, the women in gay, multi-color dress intermixing with men wearing clothes reflecting their hard life on land and sea. After his mother's death he'd stopped paying attention to people, casting his eyes downward or away, never looking anyone in the eye even when talking to someone he knew. Here he studied people with growing interest. What people felt was evident on their faces. At home everyone disguised feelings and thoughts. Not here. Were they happy? Were they sad? Was life hard? Were they worried about something? All he had to do was look.

Most people were smiling and laughing, cheerful greetings back and forth, banter and kidding on the streets and in the shops, much more spoken friendship among the people than in upstate New York where it seemed like public display of affection was frowned upon. But tiredness was visible in the eyes of many, and worry and trouble showed in deep lines on faces including young ones. Also, evidence of lack of food, a lot of people too thin, including children, clothing on some patched and threadbare. George said that the poverty on some of the islands was so great that many people were close to starvation. Yet no one Ethan saw seemed to be carrying a grudge against the world because of their poverty. Even the most poorly dressed and thinnest of body seemed to remain cheerful.

Ethan had never seen poverty at home and was at first amazed and then very troubled by what he saw on St. Thomas, Tortola, St. Martin, and now

Anguilla. Johnson told him the poverty was even worse on the English and French islands of the Southern Caribbean.

People sifted through garbage cans behind restaurants for something to eat, sat or lay in rags in numb misery in doorways, and begged from them at street corners. George usually gave the beggars something. And while there were colorful houses along main streets of towns, behind these houses, and in more rural areas, the housing was quite different—small, unpainted wooden shacks with roofs of tin cans hammered flat, often no doors or windows, outside toilets shared by many houses, no pretty plantings in front but instead children dressed in rags and sometimes naked. He peered into some of the houses and saw people living in a maze of small rooms divided by shoulder-high plywood or dirty hanging cloth. In others there weren't even dividers. Large families were living together in a fetid clump. And through it all wandered scrawny dogs, crusted with mange.

All this was terrible. He stood before a mirror in a clothing store and looked at his own body, his legs, his stomach, then posed like a strong man with his muscles flexed. They weren't much. Had he examined his body since his mother died? He wasn't fat, but certainly not thin like many he'd been seeing. Starving like that had to be just as bad as the troubles he'd faced.

As they left Anguilla, Johnson was given a large hand of bananas by a friend, more than thirty bananas on the stalk. He tied the stalk to the ceiling of the main cabin so it hung down between the starboard and port bunks, swaying freely with the motion of *Rascal*. George remarked skeptically that they looked very green and unripe, and questioned whether they would ever ripen.

Each morning George would put his chin up and say, kiddingly, in his English-like accent, "Any bananas for breakfast today Johnson?"

Johnson would always laugh back. "Bananas waiting for tomorrow."

This went on for more than two weeks, the bananas swinging back and forth in the main cabin, sometimes wildly, cudgeling them all when they ventured below decks while *Rascal* was underway.

Finally, Johnson relented and tossed the bananas overboard, saying, with mischief in his eyes, "Bananas shy. Get embarrassed when talk so much about dem. No want to change from der green dress to der yellow dress in front of you."

They joked for some days about the shy bananas that Davey Jones was now eating.

George eventual told a story. "Last year I was in a harbor-side bar in St. Thomas and a seaman charged in from a rusty tramp freighter anchored by the quay. He ordered six beers and put them down in a row in front of him. Then he took a banana from the bowl the bartender kept on the bar for banana daiquiris, cut the banana in half, jammed one half in each ear and started on the beer.

"Shortly afterwards the freighter blasted its whistle announcing departure and calling all hands on board. The bartender leaned over to the seaman and said 'Better get back on board.'

"The seaman said, 'Eh?' Another beer and a longer blast, and the bartender said in a louder voice, 'Better get back on board.' The seaman again said, 'Eh?' Finally three strong blasts from the ship and the bartender leaned over and yelled in his loudest voice, 'Better get back on board. Your ship is leaving.'

"The seaman replied as he chugged his fourth beer, 'Can't hear a word you're saying. Have a banana in my ear.'"

George apologized for the silliness of the story, saying he'd picked it up from a radio program and it was the only sailing joke he'd ever heard about bananas. But Ethan loved it. Later in the voyage, when he was talking more, every time George or Johnson asked him to do something, coil a line, help with dishes, or whatever, Evan would reply, "Can't hear you. I've got a banana in my ear." Then he would laugh for some time.

CHAPTER TWELVE

From Anguilla they sailed downwind to the Dutch island of Saba. The day dawned startlingly blue, absurdly blue, not a cloud in the sky, all 360 degrees blue from horizon to horizon, water and sky joining their blues in every possible shade, and the light so clear that even distant shores seem near. Seabirds wheeled in joyous celebration of the day.

Johnson remarked, "Conrad wrote, *'The sea has never been friendly to man.'* He never sail de Caribbean on a day when God smilin."

Ethan looked around. Johnson was right about the sea becoming his friend. It was like what happened with the woods back home. When he first visited he'd been scared. Were there animals hiding in dark places to eat him? Would he be able to find his way back? The sea was gradually introducing itself to him just as the woods did, showing in the Anegada Passage that he didn't have to fear it, and showing him on days like this that he was welcome.

They had not previously jibed *Rascal.* It had all been tacking. Johnson said the wind was too strong to jibe safely. Now with the wind behind, and somewhat abated, George decided to jibe to a new course.

George said to Ethan, "You've been doing a great job with the tacking. Now we'll do a different maneuver, the jibe. In the tack the wind is hitting one side of the bow and we turn the bow through the eye of the wind so it hits the other side of the bow. In the jibe the wind is hitting one side of the stern and we turn the stern through the eye of the wind so it hits the other side of the stern.

"The way we do it is we first bring the main in close-hauled so it's over the cockpit. We slowly turn *Rascal* until the wind hits the other side of the sail, then let the sail gradually out with the wind behind it on the new heading. You see where the sail is now?" Ethan could see the sail was set well out to starboard, almost at right angles to *Rascal's* downwind course. "If we don't bring the sail in before we jibe, the boom will crash all the way across the deck to ninety degrees out on the port side, maybe bring down the mast, or kill someone standing in the cockpit. Many sailors have been killed when jibes weren't done right."

George said, "Prepare to jibe," followed shortly by, "Jibe Ho."

Johnson cranked the main in to the center of the boat, let it gradually play out to the other side as they turned. They'd jibed around to the new course as easy as pie. *Rascal* was a super boat.

Saba was visible from a long way off, looking like the cone of a great volcano thrusting out of the sea 3,000 feet straight up, and that, Johnson said, was exactly what it was. "Called Mount Scenery. De side of de cone all cliff. Cliff down to de water. De whole island cliff. No harbor. Only one area on de lee side of de island with small pebble beach. Dat where people bring in der provision. Only can get in when de weather real good." He looked around. "Today look good. But you never know till you get der."

It was a very forbidding island. George said he'd not been there before.

They approached Saba gingerly. Johnson needed to stay on *Rascal* to keep her off the rocks and so could not row George and Ethan into the landing area. So George and Ethan embarked on the dingy with George rowing, rowing cautiously as he didn't usually do the rowing. The surf was quite high. George needed to time things perfectly to get in, wait for a break in the waves, and then row like mad to get to shore before the next wave crashed in.

George didn't time things right. An overtaking breaker swamped the dingy, turned it turtle, and carried it far up the rocky shore, away from George and Ethan who were floundering in the high surf. Fortunately, several women were by the beach, and they helped George and Ethan to shore. The women also recovered the oars rapidly floating out to sea. No damage done, but George said in embarrassment, "That sure didn't go very well."

A donkey cart was waiting on the jetty for some purpose. They never found out for what purpose. The owner agreed to take them to the nearest village, a village named "The Bottom," halfway up the volcano. He said that there was another village, "Hell's Gate," near the top of the volcano by the caldera, but inaccessible by cart.

George said, "Hell's Gate wouldn't have a chance in an eruption. These Caribbean volcanos just explode and kill everyone around. And this is an active volcano. It blew up in the 1600s."

Ethan craned his neck and gazed up at the towering volcano directly above them. This was not good. He could see a crown of clouds. It looked exactly like pictures of exploding volcanoes he'd seen. Was it exploding and nobody knew it? He watched the volcano off and on the whole way up, ready to warn everybody if something happened.

The ride up did not help his concern. There were perilous drop-offs all along the rutted, single-track, switch-back road, and the old driver, the oldest looking man he'd ever seen, kept falling asleep and having to be awakened by George before they went off into thin air. When the switch-back took Ethan to the outside, staring down the cliffs, he leaned hard against George, something he did not like doing. But George seemed to like it. He whistled merrily the whole way up.

Arriving at The Bottom, Ethan got more comfortable. These people wouldn't be here in this pretty little town if the volcano was about to explode. He could see the town was suspended somewhat precariously on the steep side of the volcano, and each house was painted a different color as though everyone in Saba had a strong desire to be different from everybody else.

...

As he stepped off the cart George found himself surrounded by women of all ages, white women. He never saw a black person on the island. The women wore broad straw hats, gaily wrapped with ribbon, long cotton skirts of a muted blue, white and red pattern, long sleeved blouses of varying colors, and some wore a patterned bodice.

Many of the women had large parrots on their shoulders. A panoply of green, blue, red, and yellow parrots greeted their arrival with raucous cries of warning to their owners, the squawking parrots then joining in a convivial welcome from the women. Everyone seemed delighted to see them.

The women were almost all blue eyed, but many eyes looked bleached, and some of the women appeared addled. Was this the product of inbreeding that'd gone on? With few people on the remote island George speculated to himself they had been inter-marrying for 200 years.

What he noticed about the faces of the women was that they were very weathered, even some of the younger ones. Life had to be very hard because of the poor, rocky soil and the constant struggle against a sea trying to bar them from accessing the rest of the world.

George's and Ethan's clothes were still wet. One woman said a large number of their visitors arrived with wet clothes having decided, as she jokingly put it, "To take their Saturday bath in the landing area surf. Next time let us know you're coming and we'll bring the soap."

George smiled. At least he was not alone in his mishap. He felt even better when dry clothes were produced from husbands' closets for them to wear while theirs were drying.

Though the island belonged to the Netherlands, all the women spoke good English, though with many words he found archaic. They said they were mostly descendants of English pirates who had used the island as a base in the eighteenth century because of its impregnable cliffs, and that the parrots had originally been brought by the pirates and were now the symbol of the island.

One of the prettier women grabbed him by the elbow, gave him a bold up and down appraisal, and said in a flirtatious manner, "There are few men here. They're all at sea."

Ahh, the women thought he was single. He had no accompanying wife, and several glanced at his left hand, which bore no wedding ring. He did nothing to discourage them in their belief and started kidding with the prettiest girls.

He and Ethan were invited to lunch in one of the larger houses, larger but very simple like all the others. The dining area, and indeed the whole house, was festooned with intricate white lace, lace curtains, lace table runners, lace doilies under just about everything. When he remarked on it he was told by one of the women with a wink, "When we can't have men we have lace. Saba lace is famous the world over."

Lunch consisted of fish, locally grown vegetables, and a large bottle of Schnapps. He spoke of his Hudson River Dutch ancestors and toasted Holland. One girl after another around the table matched him toast for toast. He was amazed by their capacity. It was joyous love and hilarity. Hugs for him. Kisses for him, most on the face, but several on the mouth. One woman plopped herself on his lap and had to be pulled off by the others. Had Ethan not been with him a few of them would probably have done more than kiss.

Ethan sat not far away with two middle-aged women, each with a very talkative parrot on her shoulder. One woman was Annie Farnsworth, who had introduced herself as the owner of the house. Annie's parrot was bright red and blue, complimenting the colors of her clothing. Perched on her shoulder the parrot was nibbling on Annie's earlobe in apparent loving fashion.

She remarked across to George, "Can't wear earrings. Sinbad always takes them off."

Sinbad seemed to like Ethan and went through a large array of words and comments looking directly at him, some quite obscene. George grinned to see Ethan laughing delightedly at the parrot, looking a bit round eyed at some of the words.

The two women asked Ethan about his voyage, his home, his family, but could not get him to talk. So they talked.

Annie told them that Saba was an unhappy island because most of the men were away eleven months of the year, coming back only around Christmas, wanderers of the sea much sought after because of their seafaring abilities, guiding long-line fishing boats far out into the Atlantic and tramp steamers all the way to Asia. She continued, "Everybody comes back at Christmas time and most everybody on the island has a birthday in August or September."

Ethan looked puzzled but George laughed.

Then the other woman turned to Ethan. "You should come back in a few years in the summer time. We make virile young men very happy in the summer. You're a pretty boy. We'll give you a very good time when you're older."

George whooped. "Ethan. They love you. You've got to come back here."

Ethan looked back and forth from George to the women, not understanding.

Before they left one woman asked Ethan what he wanted to be when he grew up. For once he talked, responding, "An engineer."

George's face lit up in a smile. Just what he had suggested on St. Martin.

Then Ethan paused, looking around, "Or maybe a sailor."

All the women laughed and one said, "Better not be a sailor because things happen when a sailor is away."

Ethan looked around at the women with a puzzled expression on his face and George let out an appreciative laugh, slapping his thigh.

They finally rollicked down the hill in the donkey cart, several women joining them, Annie's parrot crying sadly after Ethan. At the shore George and Ethan got into the dingy. The women waited for a break in the surf and propelled the dingy out, standing in water up to their shoulders. When Ethan turned around and waved goodbye he received a parting gift of kisses blown across the water.

George considered it a very good day indeed, mostly because he seemed to be finally getting through to Ethan. Whereas previously when he said something to Ethan it was often met with a look of suspicion, and whereas previously when he asked Ethan to do something it was often met with hesitation, which he took as doubt about his motives, for the last week or so, and particularly today, Ethan's responses had been more open and happier. Progress was finally being made toward a father-son relationship.

After dinner George told a story about parrots in honor of the parrots on Saba. "An ocean liner employed a magician to entertain guests. The magic show was in the Grand Salon, and in the Grand Salon the liner's captain kept a very smart parrot picked up during a visit to Saba. Seeing the same tricks over and over again on many voyages, the parrot had figured out how some of the tricks worked. He would waddle over and pull out a disappearing bouquet of flowers from under the table, or a card from the magician's sleeve, or scare the rabbit out from where it was hidden.

"A great storm eventually sank the ocean liner and the magician found to his disgust that he was sharing a life raft with the parrot. The parrot looked around, looked at the magician, looked around, looked at the magician, and finally said, 'All right. I give up. What did you do with the boat?'"

Both Johnson and Ethan laughed heartily, and George even harder, as usual drowning everyone else out with laughter at his own joke.

. . .

Ethan found the jokes to be one more reason to feel better about George. And there were many reasons when he considered it. George had never done anything to him except try and help him, to show him things. George obviously liked him a lot, totally different from his father.

He thought over the bad gossip he'd heard about George at the church parish hall. The old ladies said that George wasn't really Christian. But that couldn't be. They said prayers together every night. And they said George treated his wife badly. But he sure treated him well. The old ladies had to be wrong. There were some good things about George. He smiled over at George seated opposite him.

That didn't get around the memory of being hauled out of his home and George yanking him on the plane. But the fear caused by that memory was being crowded out by all the new Caribbean experiences. Still not comfortable, he decided to wait and watch. He remembered a movie where everything seemed normal. In the final reel it was all a scheme to get the hero's guard down. He was not going to let his guard down.

George had brought games aboard, and many nights they would play poker or Monopoly or Clue. The loser would have to do the dishes the next night, clean the head, or perform some other task. That night they played Monopoly and he won, accepting congratulations from George and Johnson at the outcome. Winning against George was great.

CHAPTER THIRTEEN

After Saba they tacked up to Antigua. The passage was rough. They short-
ened sail but were still heeled over so much that the lee rail was buried most
of the way.

Ethan didn't mind the roughness. He was starting to love *Rascal*.
Sometimes he felt he was riding the wind when *Rascal* plunged east through
the trade-wind as now. And sometimes he felt he was riding light.

He'd never seen light like this, fierce brilliance with almost physical
weight, blinding in reflection off the water, the immense white Caribbean
sunlight around him, embracing sea, sky, and the very air to the most distant
horizon. His dark thoughts had been like the heavy curtains keeping light
from his bedroom at home. Now the curtains were opening to light. How
could life be dark under this Caribbean light? He looked at the sky far above.
He was not only standing under the sky. He was standing inside himself looking up to light from his darkness.

He moved to the bow, almost skipping, not holding on despite the
steep pitch of the deck. He'd come to glory in the movement of *Rascal*. At
the bow, his back cradled by jib and forestay, he opened his mouth to catch
the spray and put his arms out to catch the wind. And the vigorous up
and down motion, freedom. The freedom he'd had wandering the woods at
home trying to avoid his father's hate, now magnified many times over by
the ocean.

He leaned over the rail and studied the varying patterns of bow wake
thrown out by *Rascal* as she breasted seas. Foam was being born and disappeared as it spread to the stern, looking like silver flower petals, evanescent
petals of light, vanishing without a trace, bubbles refracting all the colors of
the rainbow before joining together in opalescence. Happiness welled up in
him, more than he could remember feeling since her death.

Out further there was the intense ink-blue of the deep ocean streaked with the white ribbons of cresting waves. George had told him that the blue he saw was not the color of the water, rather a reflection of the sky, blue on a blue day, grayish on a gray day. This was a blue day. Nearer land George said the sailor saw a combination of sky reflection and bottom color. Aquamarine meant a coral sand bottom, brown meant a reef, black, sometimes even purple black, meant weed. Only by reading these colors accurately, and also reading the currents, could a sailor get into Caribbean harbors.

Ethan had already seen what happened when George didn't read the bottom correctly. In a harbor on St. Martin George had run *Rascal* aground perilously close to a foaming reef. Johnson had told him to steer clear. George had ignored Johnson's advice. When George ignored Johnson's advice, which wasn't often, trouble usually ensued. He had feared for *Rascal*.

Fortunately they were able to kedge off with no damage using the dingy and the aft anchor. This involved putting the anchor in the dingy, rowing the dingy out astern of *Rascal* and setting the anchor, winching in the anchor line from a jib winch at the stern the boat, and thus pulling *Rascal* backward off the reef.

Afterward George said sheepishly, "There are only two types of sailors that say they've never run aground. Those who never left port and those who are atrocious liars."

As they approached the coast of Antigua, a large island sloop came into sight with a launch tied up next to it. Men wearing uniforms were boarding the sloop from the launch.

Johnson shook his head and said, "Happen to me one time. Those be policemen lookin for contraband. When I be young, no know any better, I try smugglin liquor and cigarette up from Guadeloupe. English tax on Antigua high. French on Guadeloupe like der liquor and cigarette. Have low tax. So a lot of money to be made in smugglin from Guadeloupe.

"I was usin de oldest fishing boat I could find. Travel at night to avoid detection. And if I be detected I hope de police would think I just night fishing. Probably a rival smuggler tip off de police. Police launch appear where I never see one before. It be a dark, squally night. De police launch come out of big squall, no runnin light, race up to me. Policemen have gun in der hand pointing at me. Right away tie der boat to my boat. Want to inspect me.

"What I did was talk, talk, and more talk. I know some of de policemen. De' all stupid and fat, sit around on de dock all day jawing and pretendin de' be important. First, I talk about der family and mine. Then about fishin. Then about de weather. Anythin I could think of to keep them from comin aboard.

"Meanwhile my boat sinkin. When I saw de police launch comin alongside I pull de plug in de bilge. De sinkin was sort of slow cause de bilge hole small. But it invisible. My boat cover with canvass from gunnel to gunnel to hide all de contraband. Finally de stupid police recognize what goin on. De' panic as I know de' would. No good sailors. Fear that my sinkin boat take der launch down. De sea very rough. No have de courage to try and save my boat at de risk of der own. Just as I hope, they simply cut de lines holdin my boat.

"I remember standin in de stern of my boat, my arms crossed, just smilin at them. Down went my boat weighed by de heavy contraband. Down went all de evidence for my possible conviction. Down went many month in prison. De boat was no worth anythin anyway. And I was just transport for de contraband. No investment from me. So no great loss. De police very angry. Swore at me de whole way to St. Johns for trickin them. But have no choice but to take me ashore. Could no let me drown."

George said, "Marvelous story. Didn't they fine you or something when they got you to shore?"

"No. They embarrassed by de whole thing. In der report they say de' no see any other boat dat night on der patrol."

Holy cow. Like Robin Hood outwitting the Sheriff of Nottingham. He strode over to Johnson and shook his hand with both his hands, staring at him in wide-eyed awe.

...

Despite the rough (and slow) passage from Saba they arrived in the harbor of St. John's, Antigua, in time for Summer Carnival. This day George's daily story was about their rough passage.

"Last year I had a friend on board who would bring me cups of coffee from below while we were underway. The cups were always full no matter how rough it was. I could never figure out how he could keep the cups full. You both know how difficult it is to come up the companionway when it is rough. Finally I asked him. He said, 'It's easy. I take a big mouthful of the coffee before I come up the companionway. Then I spit it back in the cup when I get to the top.'"

Ethan scrunched his face in disgust and he gave out a loud, "Aagh."

The Antigua Summer Carnival celebrated the Antiguan emancipation from slavery, the end of July 1834. Riotous steel drum music blasted out everywhere. Other music groups featured fat men blowing tubas, thin men blowing trumpets, though sometimes the reverse. In the afternoon a parade through town with bands mounted on flatbed trucks blaring non-stop music, a discordant competition for which band could be loudest.

The stilt walkers astonished Ethan, many different groups, twelve, fifteen, even eighteen feet up, swaying and dancing provocatively to the bands' music with as much agility as the street dancers following the band trucks, the stilt walkers being given friendly heckling by people in second-story windows and giving back as good as they got, and all wearing long girlish gowns as though they were headed to the tall girl's ball, the color of their outfits depending upon the group to which they belonged. Johnson identified various stilt walkers as Moko Jumbie, Jumpa-ben, and Long Ghosts, based on their gowns.

They saw celebrants dressed in the wildest costumes. One group sported banana leaves and animal horns, nothing else. Some of the banana leaves kept falling off to the cheers of the crowd. Another group was dressed in Scottish kilts and performed a boisterous highland fling in the heat of the day. And some women wore intricate, multicolored, flouncy costumes that must have taken months to sew. Along the way spectators were wildly cheering their favorite group, most with beer cans in hand, and in some cases whiskey bottles, all held regularly to mouths between cheers, and they were flocking at various times to surrounding stands to buy food and carnival items.

George said had never been to Antiqua Carnival before. They watched for awhile, and George said, as much to himself as to Ethan and Johnson. "What we're seeing is Africa. This is Africa. Bunch of African niggers."

Johnson looked like he was going to say something but didn't.

George turned to Johnson, " I've always thought you Antiguans were the most dependable and civilized people in the Caribbean. But these people. They've thrown off civilization. Forgotten Christianity. Gone back to primitive African ancestry. Not one Christian cross in the lot. And look at those groups following the trucks. It's all tribal. Each group dresses alike and looks alike. Maybe they're all related like in African villages. Not throwing spears at each other. Instead it's insults and trying to drown each other out with their loud music. I've been to carnival in New Orleans. This is totally different."

George paused to watch a passing group of dancers. He shook his head and said, "I've seen a lot of Caribbean dancing. Nothing like this."

The group going by moved in ecstasy, wild, sexual, animalistic, primitive, bodies abandoned to strange backward and forward movements, arms thrown into the air, and cries in eerie guttural tongue. George said that it looked like newsreels he'd seen of natives dancing in the African bush. "That's exactly what we're seeing, Africa marching down the street."

Johnson said, "People no being African. De' just having fun."

George replied, "You're wrong. I've always said the Caribbean is really Africa covered with a thin veneer of colonial control. This proves it. The African nigger is coming out of hiding."

Johnson slowly walked over to him, stood only a foot away from him, and talked in a soft, matter of fact voice, "You think you a gentleman, right? No swear much."

George shrugged and tried to move away. Johnson moved with him, kept his face close to his. "Nigger de worse swear word mon can use. Worse dan any other swear word you know. Don't ever use it in front of de boy again. Don't ever use it in front of me again." The last was said with with definite menace.

George strode quickly away, saying nothing.

As evening came on George tried some of the powerful native rum. Slurring his words slightly, he grabbed Ethan's hand and took him to the dance platform, a raised area romantically lit by thousands of white fairy-lights dangling from poles. Locals were dancing with great exuberance, sliding in unison to the man's left with the Calypso rhythm, loudly kidding over and back to each other, laughing at the drunken antics of a few men who had chosen to fly solo across the floor.

Blacks were dancing together. So were whites, and there were black men with white women and white men with black women. One black woman was enormous, the largest woman Ethan had ever seen, and she twirled and swayed across the floor like a graceful elephant in the arms of a smallish white man.

George asked if he'd ever danced before. Ethan shook his head. "Well, Calypso is easy. This dance is the Merenque. Drag your foot along to the beat as though your right leg is broken. It's called the broken leg dance." He put Ethan in the woman's dance position and started leading him around the floor.

At first Ethan found himself stumbling, but started doing better and thinking dancing might be okay. Ethan could see Johnson watching closely from the side and frowning.

Johnson did not have to watch long as Ethan spotted a stand selling fireworks. That was it for the dancing. He asked George to buy fireworks, any fireworks, and got a large supply of Roman Candles. Local Antiguan boys were also buying Roman Candles.

One of the Antiguans suggested battle, and battle it was. Boys in the church yard next to the great St. John's Anglican Cathedral. Boys behind grave stones, bushes, corners of buildings, shooting Roman Candles at each other in disorganized pandemonium.

Ethan teamed with an Antiguan boy with very good aim. First two then five warriors on each side. His fellow warrior became the general for their gang of five. He knew the churchyard well. Fire splashing against obstacles, lighting the sky, every color of joy. Ethan had burn holes in his shirt. One boy had a slightly singed arm. But nothing more serious before the adults stepped in. He would remember that marvelous night as long as he lived, whooping with happiness as his team scored hits.

After the battle Ethan joined with his partner warrior, Joshua Greene, "Call me Josh," to have some ice cream. Ethan had a little money and treated in appreciation for Josh's accuracy and generalship.

Josh was fourteen but already had six brothers and sisters with one more on the way. He was the oldest so had a lot of responsibility, but said he didn't mind the responsibility as it was helping him grow up fast. He very much wanted to be an adult and help lead Antigua away from white control. He talked a lot about white control. Some of it he admitted was a repeat of what he heard from adult family members. But some was from his own observations.

His father was a local postman and got that sought-after job because his mother worked for a white woman whose husband was a colonial administrator. The woman had put in a good word for his father. "And dat how thing be run," Josh said. "De white control everythin and direct everythin. I goin to work to change dat."

The boys at home didn't have ambitions like that. They just seemed to be trying to get by, doing enough school work that their parents wouldn't punish them, and focusing on having fun. Josh impressed him. It would be great to set a goal to do something worthwhile like Josh.

Ethan never talked about his own family, didn't really say much of anything to Josh. But this didn't seem to matter. Josh treated him as his good friend, the first time another boy had befriended him in a very long time. In parting, Josh asked him to become his pen pal. Ethan replied an enthusiastic, "Gosh yes."

. . .

Before leaving St. Johns, Johnson insisted Ethan accompany him to see the statue of Prince Klass. George said he'd been there before but joined them anyway. The statue with its marble base was more than twenty feet tall, Klass impressively dressed in colonial costume with a plumed hat, his head thrown up to heaven, and blowing a conch shell to summon slaves to freedom.

Johnson addressed Ethan, "You see de good side of Antigua yesterday, a party. But you should also know somethin about de bad side. De bad side be plantation life." Johnson moved away for a moment, shaking his head in disgust. Addressing them again his face had taken on a fierce scowl, his nostrils flared in anger, the first time Ethan had seen Johnson anything but calm. Ethan backed away a half pace. "Conrad say, *'The yarns of seaman have a direct simplicity.'* Well, I be a seaman. I can keep it simple. I can say it in one word, *hell.* Plantation life was nothing but *hell.* A sin against God. The devil live on de plantation. De plantation owner join de devil. Beat slaves with no mercy, cut noses or cut off limb when slave disobey. Sometimes burn slave to death. Separate child from mother and sell de child off. Child belong to plantation owner. Not de mother. First present de' give der boy child on de plantation be small whip. De' all burnin in hell together.

"Now about Prince Klass. De worst thing dat ever happen in Antigua be de so call slave revolt of 1736. De white call it slave revolt. No true. It be murder.

"Happen 200 years ago and black Antigua people still mad about it. Whenever we have to deal with white Antiguan we think about it. I still be angry. One of my ancestor be burn to death." Johnson clenched his fists, the sinews on his arms standing out, and his face hardened. He spoke loudly and fast, unusual for Johnson.

"White Antiguan no admit de truth even today. Hide behind a false story. You ask a white mon in Antigua about it. He goin to say dat a revolt be planned by conspirin slave. Dat slave on some seventy plantation part of it. Dat de' intend to kill all de white. Intend to found de first African nation outside Africa. Maybe white Antiguan even believe dis nonsense they tell de lie so long."

Johnson looked at George and compressed his lips to a grim line, as though all whites were culprits. "All be hoax. Made up story. What really happen be de English panic. Three thousand or so white on de island, lot of women and children. 25,000 slave, way outnumber de white. Many slave revolt start on neighboring island. Condition for slave much harsher in de Caribbean then in de American South. English and French planter much crueler. Slave felt de choice revolt or die. De' revolt all around de Caribbean.

"English fear a revolt on Antigua would be next. Decide to scare de slave. Want to terrify de slave so much de' be obeyin for years. English pretend they find out about de slave revolt conspiracy. Slave named Klaas pick by de English as de alleged ring leader. De' choose Klass as de made-up ringleader because he well known in Antigua. He from de Ashanti people, supposedly be nobleman, and he also be obeah-man, dat be priest in de west Africa Yoruba religion. Would use him to make example to all de slave." Johnson bowed his head toward the statue as to a saint. "Antiguan later come to call him 'Prince Klass' because of his bravery.

"De English broke him on de wheel. Spreadeagled him on a wagon wheel. Like a crucifixion. Broke every bone in his body. But he no name other slave. So de English decide to kill leadin slave from each of seventy largest plantation in Antigua. Want to hit each plantation with fear. Kill eighty-seven in total. Seventy-seven burn at de stake and rest de' starve and then hang. Burn most because slave real afraid of burning as way to die. African believe that if you burn there no be after-life."

Johnson stood tall and focused on the face of the statue, Johnson's back straight, proud. "Black Antiguans put up dis statue in his memory. Big fight with de white to get de necessary permit. But we win. Now every year der be de big parade to de statue. We lay wreaths and flowers to thank him for his bravery."

George said quietly, "I guess the Antiguan plantation owners, last name Royall, were an exception. They were very good people. I have a cousin who went to Harvard Law School. Told me Harvard Law honors the Royalls as founders of the school back in 1817."

Johnson glared at George, his voice again loud. "*No* exception. Royalls have de biggest plantation in Antigua. Three hundred men and women living in hell. Brutal people like all de rest. Harvard Law a school founded for de white on de back of dying black men and women."

George responded, his chin thrust out more than usual, "You really have a chip on your shoulder."

"Maybe so. Maybe all black people have chip on der shoulder. Chip cut out of de black people by de whip on de plantation. What you say de Royalls an insult to all black. No plantation owner good. I quit another boat cause de owner start saying good thing about de plantation."

George shook his head and said nothing further.

...

Before leaving Antigua they sailed *Rascal* around the southern tip to show Ethan English Harbor. Ethan climbed over the extensive fortifications and found the cannons fascinating, rusted cannons still staring at the sea. He imagined himself standing there waiting for the French. He and his men would have blown them all up.

George had visited English Harbor before and told Ethan that from 1783 to 1787 Lord Nelson had been acting commander of English harbor, and commander of the entire West Indies English fleet out of the base of English Harbor. "At that time it was a pestilent place. Twenty-five to thirty percent of the soldiers and sailors died of yellow fever and bad rum. The officers knew enough to billet up there on that hill, Shirley Heights, away from the mosquitos. Below them their men were dying like flies in the harbor. They lost more men that way than they lost in all the fighting."

Johnson frowned and said, "A lot have to do with class and snobbery. Upper-class people always like to look down on black and lower-class white. Think de' be better than everybody else. Upper-class officers on Shirley Heights no want to have de enlisted men living up der with them. Would rather have der troops below dying than living safe if it meant living next to them."

George gave Johnson a decidedly unfriendly look, then continued, saying Nelson was a hero of his. He described Nelson in glowing terms, giving the details of his brave loss of an eye in taking the island of Corsica, an arm in a later battle, and his tactics and courage at the battle of Trafalgar. "Look hard at all of this, my boy. Remember what you see. This place is unique, unchanged from Napoleonic times. The only English Napoleonic-era harbor in the world still in active use. The fortifications, buildings, and docks are exactly what Nelson saw when he arrived in 1783. You're very lucky to be seeing what Nelson saw."

Johnson said, "I share Nelson name, but I tell you de' hate him in Antiqua. What he do at de battle of Trafalgar be later. What he do here no be good.

"When he arrive an elderly English Captain name Moutray be in charge. Everybody like him. He got a young wife, Mary Belle. Nelson force Moutray to hand over command to him. Try to seduce Mary Belle. Many think he successful. Captain Moutray take his wife back to England real quick.

"Next Nelson stop trade between de English islands and America, and all trade with de French islands. Do it on his own. Go beyond de law in stopping de tradin. Dis cause big loss for de English merchant here. Some go bankrupt. They sue and won. De Crown pay out lot of money because of what Nelson do.

"But worst for de Antiguans was dat Nelson treated them as dumb provincial. He state publicly, and many time, that there be no one in Antiqua worth talking to. He never willin to entertain de plantation owner at de fort here. And he never accept der invitation. Never even willin to make a social conversation with de various merchant and planter. In letters and communiques de' show you in de fort museum he call English Harbor, and all of Antiqua, '*That infernal place.*'

"Nelson get very sick here, so sick that he have a puncheon of rum ship on de frigate takin him back to England. De rum was to preserve his body in case he die along de way. De Antiguan feel dis be tremendous waste of good rum."

Ethan grinned. George didn't, and said scowling deeply at Johnson. "I can't expect an uneducated black to understand Nelson's accomplishments."

Johnson said, "You wrong. He be my namesake and I read everything written bout him." Turning to Ethan, "Der be a lesson here for you in Nelson." He stared hard at George. "People who fill themself up with der own ego often no have anything of themself left over to give to other in kindness."

George glared at Johnson, balled his fists, and moved toward him. Ethan thought he was going to hit Johnson or fire him or something. But he did nothing. Johnson turned his back and walked away ignoring George.

Lunch involved rowing into nearby Galleon Bay for a beach picnic. A grove of sea grapes circled the bay, their round dark-green leaves in striking contrast to the pale sand in which they grew, the trees escaping the sand on gnarled trunks twisted as though by the sand's heat. Johnson wandered down the beach smoking, and George explained that the sea grape rarely loses its leaves, so a message scratched on a sea grape leaf will remain for many, many years, almost like the initials some people carved on trees back home.

George grasped a large leaf, and with some ceremony, holding it so that Evan could see what he was doing, he scratched on it, *I love you*. " Your turn."

Ethan scratched his name. George sighed and shook his head.

George had bought Ethan a snorkel in St. Johns, and after their picnic at Galleon Bay, Ethan snorkeled for an hour in front of Galleon Beach. The beach was sheltered from the ocean by a quarter-mile long reef, a bathtub of warm water behind it. Only a few small waves were slopping over the coral to create pleasant forms and reflections on the water's still surface in invitation for a relaxing afternoon swim.

. . .

George sat on the shore watching, seated under the shade of a palm tree and thinking. He was still sorry Ethan hadn't come over to him during his excursions to the junior high playground in Niskayuna.

He thought back to the last time he had been there, just three weeks ago. That morning he'd gotten up, looked at his calendar, and found a hole in his busy afternoon schedule. Enough time to visit the playground. Then he checked the weather. Yes. It was going to be a nice day. The boys would be outdoors playing.

He'd gotten very happy, whistled happily to himself as he shaved and dressed, brought his happiness to Marge at the breakfast table with compliments about the hot cakes and the flowers she'd arranged all around the mansion, whistled his way happily down the broad front steps to the five-car garage, brought his happiness to his office, brought his happiness to the A&P where he went to replenish his supply of the Tootsie Rolls and Bazooka bubble gum the boys loved. Then in happiness he had driven over to Mohawk Junior High School.

He parked next to the playground in his usual spot and seated himself on the bonnet of the big Cadillac. For some time he just watched, waved to the boys as they ran past, swung his dangling legs in time to the running boys. The playground next to the school was the chosen venue for after-school play. Pickup games of football, baseball, sometimes soccer, and often boys just ran around letting out the energy bottled up during hours trapped in school rooms.

Normally fifteen to twenty played, occasionally more and rarely less, that sunny spring day about twenty-five. By now he knew them all by name. He smiled broadly, no better place in the world to be that afternoon. He called the boys over to distribute what he'd brought. And especially to talk.

What would his friends say if they knew he was spending afternoons with boys? They'd probably be appalled. But the hell with their opinions. No one understood how much he wanted a son. Not even Marge. When she couldn't get pregnant she should have agreed to adoption. Why didn't she? No good reason. Now no son ever. But at least he got to spend afternoons with boys.

When he had first started going to the playground his conversation with the boys was about what they were up to and their athletic prowess. He would urge them on.

"I watched you. You run very fast. Are you the fastest runner? Five pieces of bubble gum to the fastest runner." A short race would ensue, the boys yelling all the way.

And,

"You all look strong. Let's see everybody's muscles." The boys would roll up their sleeves and flex their muscles.

And,

"Can anyone here do a push up? How many can you do? Let's see." Bubble gum distribution for the most push ups.

As his visits to the playground continued over several years with a changing cast of boys, he had turned the conversation into more personal matters, at first innocuous.

"Anybody here like school?" Few yes answers to that.

"Anyone here like girls? What do you like about girls? Do any of you share a room with a brother? What's it like?"

Now the boys would speak to him about the most private matters in their lives. The trick, George had learned, was to clothe it all in kidding and jokes, and usually he had a number of new dirty jokes and stories he'd collected at the bar of his club. After telling these to many appreciative snickers, and some questions from boys less sexually educated, he would turn to them.

"Any of you got any jokes or stories today? Bubble gum for the best dirty story."

Some of the boys had come to trust him more than their own parents, telling him about their fears, their dreams, the sexual desires they were just starting to feel, vying with each other for his attention, telling him things they would never tell their parents.

Spending that day with the boys made him happy all over, laughing out loud, kicking his heels, throwing his arms wide in an airy embrace of them all. Sudden recognition came as he sat there on the beach. Those afternoons were a center of his life.

Coming back to his house that afternoon he'd felt disoriented. The real world lived at the playground. His great mansion existed as something artificial and unimportant.

He entered the front hall and looked around. No joy came to him from anything he saw. Marge looked like she had put on more weight. And those antique William & Mary benches in the front hall looked dated. Even the museum-quality stained-glass windows at the top of the front stairs, something of which he was usually very proud, seemed dull. Marge had probably forgotten again to have the servants wash them.

When he came home from an afternoon with the boys he often picked an argument with Marge. That night was no exception. "The dress you wore last night to the Clark's party was tawdry. We have to set the standards in this town. Nobody else does. You need to get your act together. I sure give you enough money for clothes."

Marge had responded with real anger, "Why is it that you pick these stupid arguments on days when you're so happy with me in the morning? I dread it when you're happy in the morning. All day long I know you're going to be ridiculous when you come home. The other day you were happy at breakfast. Complimented me on everything. Then you came home at night and lashed into me for a full twenty minutes. You attacked me every way from Sunday as a bad wife. And what was it about? I couldn't find your stupid special brand of French coffee at the store. So what. That Parisian coffee maker is ridiculous anyway. What's going on with all these arguments?"

He had glared at Marge and turned his back on her, not about to tell her the arguments weren't about her. They were about the pain he felt in leaving the boys of the afternoon.

. . .

As Ethan left the water he gave a startled yell. He'd barely escaped prowling gray-striped death. The fin of a ten foot Tiger Shark cut through the water, the shark cruising lazily over the exact section of reef he'd explored only minutes before. Three Jackfish preceded the shark hoping for morsels from the shark's jaw. Ethan's mouth went dry. Nausea gripped him and he froze motionless as though still in the water with the shark coming at him. The fin slowly disappeared around the end of the reef. The fear remained as he thought what could have happened. This was the closest he'd ever come to death.

George quickly told a joke. "Why is the ocean salty?" Then replied, "It's from the tears of sharks crying because they're not allowed to cuddle with humans."

He appreciated that George was trying to take his mind off the narrow escape. But he couldn't help thinking that had he not left the water when he did he would now be furnishing morsels to Jackfish. Cuddling with that shark would not have ended well.

And what would have happened if he had been eaten by the shark? Only Niskayuna boy to have ever been eaten by a shark. He imagined a banner headline in the Schenectady Gazette. *Local Boy Dies In Shark Attack.* Nobody in Niskayuna would have cared.

Johnson apologized to both Ethan and George, saying that in the Caribbean you never saw a large shark in shallow water behind a reef. "Teeth on de Tiger Shark be serrated and so can crush de shell of de sea turtle. De' chase de sea turtle. Maybe sea turtle bring de shark in. But I no see any turtle. De shark probably sick or injure and come in because it dying. God sea be full of life but also de dying."

Johnson promised it would never happen again. He would watch Ethan whenever he swam. Ethan believed him. He'd swim anywhere with Johnson holding watch.

CHAPTER FOURTEEN

Later that afternoon, back on *Rascal* anchored in Galleon Bay, Ethan was forward, looking at an old fort guarding the point on the starboard side. An immense bow loomed around the point, looking like that of the ocean liners pictured in magazines. Following the bow was a yacht larger than any boat Ethan had seen in the Caribbean, bigger even than the inter-island freighters.

George exclaimed with delight, "That's *Ariadne*. One of the largest private yachts in the world. She's over 200 feet long. Owned by the Biddlingtons of Philadelphia and Newport, Rhode Island. Among the richest families in America. If you have real money that isn't a bad way to spend it."

She looked marvelous, three decks with windows all around on the top two decks, twelve large portholes on the side facing him. Was each one a separate room? A large back deck with lots of white chairs and sofas, and a tender slung on davits from the stern that was so huge it looked like a yacht itself. His beloved *Rascal* suddenly appeared very small.

Ariadne motored very close to *Rascal* and dropped anchor. A lot of people were scurrying around. Many men dressed in white uniforms like he had seen in pictures of U.S. navy sailors. A few women also in white uniforms. And on the stern deck a plumpish woman with long blond hair, also dressed in white, and a tall man not in uniform. Instead a white shirt worn outside white pants. Boy, they must really like white. White yacht, white furniture, white tender, and everyone dressed in white.

George said, "That woman was pointed out to me in St. Thomas. She's a Biddlington. Owns *Ariadne*. Can't remember her first name."

The man and woman on *Adriana* were looking them over as well. In short order her tender was dropped and motored toward them, a sailor at the helm and another at the bow. As the launch rounded up to *Rascal* the sailor at the bow thrust out a long wooden pole with a notch on the end, and in the notch an envelope. Ethan raced across the deck and grabbed it.

It proved to be a formal invitation. Cocktails and hors d'oeuvres at 5:30 PM sharp. The invitation was issued only to him and George. No Johnson. He was sorry about that.

Ethan put on his best clothes and joined George who said he had put on his "show off" sailing attire, custom double-breasted blue blazer, white shirt, rep tie, fitted white pants, and hand-made rope-sole boating shoes. The tender arrived promptly at 5:30 PM with now three sailors aboard, one with apparently no other duty than to make sure they were comfortably seated.

The woman greeted Ethan and George at the top of *Adriane's* gangway. In addition to her white outfit she wore heavy gold bracelets on each wrist, a large gold necklace like a breastplate, and a substantial gold chain cinched around her waist. Ethan thought enough gold to sink her like a stone if she ever fell overboard.

She gave them a big hello, smiling at Ethan as much as at George, "My name is Mary Biddlington. Everyone calls me Mosey," and turning to Ethan, "Means you call me Mosey too, chum." She went on. "We don't have many visitors. I don't have much opportunity to talk to anyone. It's just Jean and me. So I'm always delighted to invite people with taste aboard." She was looking approvingly at George's nautical attire.

Ethan liked Mosey immediately. She was taller than his mother and her hair was a darker blond. And she certainly wasn't beautiful like his mother. Her face was long and kind of horsey with a large nose. And she wore a lot of makeup, which his mother never did, rouge, blue stuff under her eyes, and bright red lipstick spread above and below her thin lips, making her lips look larger than they really were. But she gave off a feeling of kindliness that was like his mother.

Mosey introduced her companion. "This is Jean Alois, my sailing buddy." She winked at Jean.

Jean said a few words of welcome in a strong French accent. He was much younger than Mosey and he was the handsomest man Ethan had ever seen. Taller than George, lithe looking versus the solidity of George and Johnson, curly black hair, black eyes in a face that caused Ethan to think of some of the swashbuckling heroes in the movies.

George introduced himself and Ethan. Ethan was relieved he wasn't introduce as the son of a good friend as George had done in the past. Rather George said, "Ethan's father is a member of my church. His mother died recently. I'm taking him along to get him away from the tragedy. He's a great kid, but you'll find he doesn't speak much after what he went through." George then said to Mosey, looking admiringly at her low-cut, flowing-white tropical dress with ruffled sleeves, "Paris, right. Dior?"

She gave him a nod and a warm smile.

Mosey escorted them to the commodious back deck and a man she said was her butler took drink orders. Ethan ordered a Coke, and when George ordered a Remy Martin and soda Mosey's face lit up. "That's what I drink. It's brandy for the sophistication of the French and soda so we don't get too French. Glad to see you don't guzzle rum like everybody else around these islands."

She offered Ethan and George a tour of *Ariadne*. George declined but both Mosey and George insisted Ethan go. And he was glad he went. He saw the five staterooms, the master suite gigantic in pink, gold leaf, and real mother of pearl, the main salon paneled in dark mahogany, the large galley (how different from *Rascal*), and the engine room, a cavernous area that looked a third the size of *Rascal*. He was particularly fascinated by the engine room.

Three quarters of an hour later when he returned to the aft deck there were hors d'oeuvres on the table and the butler was taking orders for another round of drinks. Mosey was slurring her words slightly. Had she been drinking all afternoon? He'd never seen hors d'oeuvres before and grabbed a handful. George shook his head, no, and said the polite thing is to take hors d'oeuvres one at a time. Ethan started to put the extras back. George admonished, "Keep those. You already touched them. One at a time from now on."

Mosey had been watching this exchange. She looked off in the distance and said softly, "Sometimes it's better to grow up not knowing about hors d'oeuvres."

Extensive conversation ensued between George and Mosey about the Caribbean, New York, opera, and other things. It turned out they knew some of the same people and had a common appreciation for art and the opera. This was all paced by refills of brandy and soda.

Mosey paused the conversation and studied George, then Ethan found her gaze on him. She sighed, paused again, and said, "George, drinking brandy and soda with you like this makes me feel you're an old friend. And Ethan's situation brings back many memories. So I'm going to tell you a story. It's a story I don't usually tell. But perhaps, Ethan, when you hear my story your troubles will seem a little less in comparison.

"About fifty years ago there was a girl from a very prominent family. She attended a leading New England boarding school. At the end of her senior year she got involved with a no-good lower-class boy. Definitely not husband material. She got pregnant. The scheme she came up with was to get herself away to a distant college and have the baby there, no one in the family the wiser.

"The family was not only prominent but also very strait-laced, very protective of their name. She feared with reason that if she brought scandal to the family they would throw her out into the cold.

"The college she chose was Mills College, near San Francisco. This choice caused an uproar. The women in the family had always gone to Vassar. But in the end she won.

"She had the baby in San Francisco, a girl. Put her in an orphanage under some important restrictions. In return for substantial annual contributions from her trust fund the orphanage was never to adopt out the girl. Also allow the mother to take her out of the orphanage for as long as the mother liked at times of her choosing.

"Starting when the child was five or so the mother took her to the summer house of the family for a month each summer. When friends asked about her the mother always said she was one of the orphans she had worked with while volunteering in California. The summer breaks went on each summer until the girl was fifteen. She came to think of the mother as her fairy godmother. Called her to herself "guardian angel." When she was six the mother married and had two more children. She was never allowed to play with them."

Mosey swirled her brandy and soda around the melting ice in her drink, took a large sip, really a gulp, and continued. "In case you haven't guessed by now, that little girl was me. The summer I turned fifteen I was at the big Newport house on my usual summer getaway. The woman who turned out to be my mother asked me to get some papers from her desk, a deed to some real estate.

"I didn't know what a deed looked like and rooted around in her desk. Couldn't find it. There was a little hidden drawer on the side of her desk that I knew about from playing in her room as a child. So I tried the drawer. At the bottom was my birth certificate.

"I charged down the stairs. Waved the birth certificate in her face. My mother broke down in tears. Confessed. Said how sorry she was. A big mistake. Then a lot of crap about loving me all along.

"At first I felt it was wonderful. Finally a mother. Tried for a year to behave as a dutiful daughter. Then I found out the whole family was in on it. My grandmother didn't much like the rest of the family. Whispered it to me at a family gathering.

"I was furious. The orphanage was terrible. I particularly remembered adoption days. I would sit there in my best dress and best smile. Everyone passed me by. Now I knew why. The family would rather have me rot in an orphanage than have their family name besmirched. No guardian angel, all devils.

"I was sent away to a New England boarding school. For obvious reasons they chose a different school than my mother attended. I could hardly wait until I reached my majority at eighteen. Then I could break the hell away from the whole bunch. A miracle occurred, a birthday miracle. My ninety-year-old grandmother died several days after my eighteenth birthday. In her will she bequeathed more than half of the family assets to me.

"I never knew why. Maybe it was a because of how the family treated me. Or maybe it was because at family gatherings I was the only one who spent time talking to her. The family contested the will. They lost. I ended up with the estate in Antibes, *Ariadne,* and much more. Could've taken the Newport house but didn't want to be vindictive. I've only seen the family once, at my mother's funeral. They were embarrassed to see me. I left early." Tears had formed in Mosey's eyes.

"Now I spend six months of the year in Antibes and six months in the Caribbean on *Ariadne*. Never married. Never trusted anyone enough. Every man was after my money. But I have good friends like Jean here."

Jean came over, put his arms around Mosey, giving her a comforting hug, and then a very long kiss on the mouth.

The butler announced dinner and Mosey brought the afternoon to a close. "Can't delay the servants." She ushered them back to the gangway with a friendly hand on Ethan's shoulder. Departure involved warm hugs all around.

Mosey was the first woman since his mother died who'd taken an interest him, the first to be kind to him. And when Mosey looked at him there was something of his mother in her gaze. Even though *Rascal* was his beloved new home he wished he could stay longer with Mosey. He boarded the tender in some sorrow.

...

On the tender trip back to *Rascal* George thought about his own upbringing. Really as bad as Mosey's.

People in town never suspected that hidden behind the high walls of the van Rosendahl estate, and behind the conspiracy of silence of his parents, he'd suffered a horrific childhood.

From the outside everything seemed normal, better than normal, in fact idyllic. As an only child of very rich parents he'd lived in luxury. Servants galore despite the depression, waiting on him hand and foot. Large estate acreage on which to sport (two tennis courts and a fifty foot long swimming pool). A compound on Lake George with sail and motor boats. More toys and other gifts than he knew what to do with. And his parent's social prominence had given him status with peers in his growing up years. That and all the toys and pool and tennis courts established him with other boys.

But behind the public facade he had been a veritable outcast in his own home, deprived of love, cut off from his parents and most other adults on a profound level, treated as totally unimportant, feeling he was isolated, alone, inadequate in his parents' eyes, tormented by beatings, all aspects of his life tightly controlled by his parents, and no freedom on his part to do anything on his own.

Even now at forty-four, motoring toward his lovely ketch across the beautiful waters of the Caribbean, he struggled with anger. For years he'd worked on his feelings about his parents, trying to find a way to accept their actions, trying not to hate them. He'd even seen a psychiatrist for awhile when he was in his thirties. No success. The same question kept coming. How could his father have been so unbelievably severe and distant? What had he done to deserve it? He'd never given his father any trouble. Yet his father punished him all the time for minor things or nothing at all.

His father preferred a razor strap for the beatings, beatings regular but often at unexpected times to increase his constant dread. Heavy footsteps would slowly approach the bedroom door. His father was prolonging the agony of his waiting for what he knew was coming. Then his father would flex the razor strap outside the door so he could hear it and fear more. Slowly the door would open, a big grin on his father's broad face. He remembered his father grinning the whole time he was administering the beatings. What was the grinning about?

He always cowered in the corner or tried to squirm under the bed, already crying in recognition of the pain to come. There was no escape.

His father would command him to the bed, licking his lips in anticipation. "Take down your pants. You've been a bad boy. We must punish bad boys." Or sometimes, "This is good for you. My father did it to me all the time." Then he would lash him, lash him, and lash him again, his grin if anything getting broader.

The beatings were always on his bottom and upper legs where no marks would be visible at school. His bottom and upper legs became criss crossed with welts, welts on top of welts, sometimes bleeding.

The beatings stopped when he was about fourteen. By then he had grown almost as tall as his father, and started to resist. But oft times in following years he observed his father looking at him with what he thought was regret that the beatings had stopped. George was sure his father missed the beatings.

His psychiatrist said of his father, "He was clearly a sadist, a very emotionally twisted man."

He sure agreed.

And as for his mother, how could she have allowed the beatings to occur? She had to know. Obviously she didn't care. All she cared about was her social position. As long as his treatment at home didn't get out, and her social standing wasn't jeopardized, what his father did was irrelevant to her.

Even worse than the beatings was the fact that neither one of them ever showed any interest in him. Did they even want him? Affection was nonexistent. He couldn't remember being hugged or kissed by either parent, ever.

Try as he might to rationalize their conduct he couldn't. It was as though in bringing him up they were trying to emulate the worst of Victorian family life. His father demanded he address him as "Sir." His father called his own father sir, so he made him do the same thing. Stupid nonsense. And every aspect of their relationship was unbelievably cold, detached, and formal.

Dinners were the worst. Every night his father would dress in black tie for dinner and they would sit, largely silent, at the great dining room table. He was not allowed to speak at the table or during most other times. It was always, *Be seen, not heard.* They seemed to believe that if one kept life polite and strict, emotions could be avoided.

His father said it over and over again, "A gentleman does not show emotion." An emotion never shown in the house was love.

One incident in particular stood out in his mind. When he was ten he escaped the house servants and joined four older boys. The boys were digging a cave in the steep side of a sandy hill near his house. Soft sand made the digging easy. Somewhat reluctantly the four older boys allowed him to play with them and set him to digging further into the back of what was already a hole ten feet into the hill. The boys went out looking for boards and logs to shore up the roof.

When the cave collapsed what saved him was the shovel. He was knocked flat but the shovel ended up under him in a way that formed a small air pocket near his mouth. The pressure on top of him was so great he couldn't even wiggle his fingers. And he used up most of the air in the air pocket yelling in terror.

The boys later told him he was very lucky. One boy was looking back at the cave when the collapse occurred. When they finally dug him out he was semi-conscious, his bladder and bowels had released, and he was vomiting sand. The boys helped him clear the sand clogging his nostrils and mouth, then quickly skedaddled in fear of the consequences of almost killing a younger boy.

He struggled home still dizzy and purposely placed himself on the antique Georgian settee in the middle of the expensively furnished drawing room. He wanted to gain his mother's immediate attention, to have her pity him, to have her comfort him and love him for the worst experience of his life. Tears streaked down the sand covering his face. The smell of the excrement on his legs overpowered the scent of his mother's prize roses displayed in vases on mantle and side tables.

When his mother entered a short time later she took one look, opened her mouth in horror, and let out a scream of anger. Hardly looking at him she started examining the settee for any damage, saying, *"Damn, damn, damn."* Each damn louder, and with the last damn looking at him with what he had thought was hate.

He tried to explain what had happened, tried to get her attention and sympathy, whimpering repeatedly, "I almost died. I almost died," tears pouring from his eyes.

She responded, "How dare you come into this room dressed like that. Is that excrement? You horrible boy. You probably ruined the settee. It's very valuable. The maids have just vacuumed. Now they're going to have to vacuum again. But you don't care, do you? All you think about is yourself. Go to your room until your father comes home."

When his father did come home, and heard about the dirt and excrement in the drawing room, he sent him to bed without dinner. Same for the second night. During these two days many beatings with the razor strap to the point where there was some serious bleeding. The blood stained things every time he sat down and his mother got angry all over again. When he tried to explain during following weeks what happened, neither parent was interested. They never knew as long as they lived that he almost died one Wednesday afternoon on a sandy hill near their home.

Both he and Mosey had grown up unloved, unappreciated, and unimportant in awful families.

CHAPTER FIFTEEN

George scowled his way through dinner that evening, patting his head occasionally. Over dessert he brightened somewhat and said to Ethan, "Tomorrow you will see a wonder of nature. We're going to Barbuda and the largest frigate bird nesting-colony in the Western Hemisphere."

But to Ethan Barbuda came to be more about thumb tacks than frigate birds.

The beat up to Barbuda from Antigua proved to be time consuming and difficult, a tough grind to windward. And the Barbuda anchorage was also difficult. *Rascal* set her anchor off an unprotected beach. Slop from ocean waves coming around both ends of the island rocked the boat vigorously from side to side on her anchor rode, a bobbing deck. Johnson said no good harbor existed on Barbuda and no calm anchorage.

The beach, however, was spectacular. Miles of distinctly pink-colored sand in each direction, the pink most pronounced where receding waves washed along the shore. It reminded Ethan of some shells he picked up where the pink of the shells came out when wetted.

Johnson confirmed his thoughts. "Barbuda have de longest pink sand beaches in de world. Little particle of red coral and pink shell make de pink. Red coral grow all around Barbuda on deep reef. Very valuable. Fortunate dat reef too deep for greedy people to steal easy."

Once ashore, the poverty assailed Ethan, by far the worst he'd seen. The 1,000 or so poor souls on Barbuda were scratching out a miserable existence on sandy soil unfriendly to crops. And without a decent harbor there was limited fishing. What fishing he observed involved launching small boats through heavy surf.

Hiking to Codrington, the largest village on Barbuda, he passed skeletal people wandering along in slow step, others sitting dejectedly on front stoops. And most of the dwellings were dilapidated shacks, often composed of driftwood.

Near Codrington was Codrington Lagoon, a large, brackish body of water. Thousands of frigate birds were perched on shore-side mango trees. George hired an oarsman to row them around the lagoon, getting not just a row from the oarsman but non-stop conversation, a scrawny man of about forty, all ribs and stringy muscles protruding from emaciated flesh, Abel Codrington.

"Yes. My last name Codrington. Just like de town. Many Codrington on de island. Sir Christopher Codrington come here 1624. Try to grow vegetable for de slave plantation on Antigua. Codrington vegetable no much good but he growed a mess of child with de slave girl. We count at least twenty-eight child. Probably much more. Most everybody round here descend from Codrington.

"Frigate bird just like Codrington. Come to Barbuda to be after de female. See dem birds in de tree blowing out der red pouch neath der chin? Look like red balloon. And all dat struttin around? De' de male. And dat loud drummin noise. Dat de male drummin on his pouch. Red pouch up to twelve inch long. De female floating way up der look for de biggest pouch, de biggest drumming. Come down and make babies. Big always attract de female." He chuckled to himself.

Ethan looked around at a magnificent display of nature in riotous creation. Every tree supported frigate birds with red pouches blown out and loud drumming, and thousands of females circling overhead picking their mate. Amazing.

Abel Codrington continued, "Frigate bird very special. Only sea bird who feather no shed water. No can land on de water. De' drown if land on de water. Feather fill with water and de' drown. So de' built to fly for months. Never stop. No land for months. Have long wing. Wing up to seven 'n half feet. And light body. Longest wing for weight of de body of any bird. Wing never have to move for long time. Float on de air current.

"But best is frigate bird be storm bird. Seek out big cloud. Fly into thunder storm. Ride wind current up thousand 'n thousand of feet so later can glide down without flappin der wing. Rest and sleep on der wing. No other bird fly de storm like frigate bird."

When they landed back at Codrington Village, Abel's wife, Mary, met them at the dock, all sharp angles and bones with a babe in arms and two more tugging at her frayed skirt. George gave Abel and his family thirty dollars. Their happiness was so great that on the way back to the dingy he said he wished he'd given them more. The standard fare for a trip around the lagoon was fifty cents.

A boat had pulled up next to *Rascal*, and as they rowed out, two rough-looking men were clambering around her deck, peering in the portholes. Johnson had locked her up tight so there was no entrance.

George yelled out in a belligerent voice, *"What* the hell do you think you're doing? Get your black nigger butts off of there. Fast. You want to get hurt?"

One of the men responded, "Just looking, mon. Like to look at nice boat. Dis a nice boat. Why you no calm down and give us a beer. We tell you about de island. Talk about you boat. No be mad. Like to talk to you. We just poor fisherman and no get to talk to people from other place."

Johnson said quietly to George, "De' no be fishermen," and Ethan could see no fishing gear in their boat. The men left *Rascal* not with any look of guilt but with truculent stares as though they'd been slighted and badly treated.

After dinner Ethan helped spread thumb tacks on the deck. This was standard practice on *Rascal* when they anchored in out-of-the way places. There were still pirates in the Caribbean.

Because of pirates most yachts sailing the Caribbean carried a gun, and George had brought an M-1 Carbine along. He placed the gun next to his bunk, and with the tacks on deck, everyone slept with their shoes on.

Ethan heard the first howl around 2:00 AM, followed by yelps in several different voices. George grabbed the M-1 and charged up the companionway. Ethan followed right behind, not wanting to miss anything. Half-way up George fired a warning shot through the companionway entrance, then hurried into the cockpit with the boy on his tail. Meanwhile Johnson had charged on deck through the forward hatch. Two men were hopping around on the tacks forward and another was in the process of clambering aboard, and directly in front of them in the cockpit was a fourth man. All were armed with new-looking machetes, their blades gleaming viciously in the light of the moon.

Faced with George's gun, the man in the cockpit threw aside his machete, sank to the cockpit floor, and raised his hands to the sky. The man closest to the bow had apparently turned aft at the sound of the rifle shot. He turn back forward toward Johnson and raised his machete for a blow. Johnson ducked under the machete and hit the man so hard on the side of the head that after teetering on the tacks for an instant the man fell overboard. The other man on deck near Johnson followed the first man with a quick dive overboard, and the man just coming aboard thought better of it and jumped back into a boat that was lying alongside.

All together in the cockpit, George, Johnson, and Ethan stood over the remaining man, still cowering on the cockpit floor, hands still raised in surrender.

George pointed his gun at the man's heart, his finger on the trigger, and growled, "What's your name?"

The man blurted out, his eyes wide with fear, "Collie Codrington."

"Any relation to Abel Codrington?"

"He my brother. Please. I be starvin. Never hurt nobody. Ask in town. I be good man. We no goin to hurt you. Just want you money. Please let me go." He had no spare flesh and did look like he might be starving.

George did not relent. Ethan recognized the man as one of the two stealing around *Rascal* the previous afternoon. He was sure George did, too. Without taking his gun off the man, George asked Johnson to call the police on the ship-to-shore.

Johnson responded, "Maybe no good idea. We goin to have to stay here while de' try and track down de men. Maybe a week. Maybe more. De' goin to hold us here until de' get de men so we can identify them. No let us leave. Impound *Rascal*. And I think Barbuda law same as Antigua law. Antigua law is we goin to have to come back here to trial. Have to testify or they goin to let them off. So even if we wait here for them to catch de men de' goin to let them off if we no come back."

George shook his head unhappily and snapped, "I won't be able to get back and I don't want to lose a week or more."

The boat of the robbers, three men back aboard, had moved off some distance. One of the men called out, "Think yo big mon wit you gun. Big mon hiding behind you gun. No so big. Let him go or I get my gun. Get my friends. Come back and kill you all."

George spun and fired the carbine without seeming to aim, hitting the man in the shoulder.

Wow. The shot was better than any cowboy in the movies. A snap shot.

George turned back to the man in the cockpit and shook his gun at him. "Get out of here and don't come back unless you want the same thing as your friend."

The man yelped his way across the deck tacks and swam off after his companions who had rowed some further distance away in great haste.

They all had an instant celebration of their escape, George slapping Johnson exuberantly and repeatedly on the back, very uncharacteristic of George. George then held up his hands and looked at them as though surprised at what they'd done. "Never had to put a gun on anyone before. Makes you understand the fear men have in war. My hands were shaking." He stared after the departing boat and continued, "That was a set-up. We were set up. Abel and Collie Codrington work together. Abel takes visitors out on the lagoon and talks a blue streak to hold them there as long as possible while Collie acts the Cain, stealing from their boat. Abel and Cain. What a pair. What happened was that when I gave Abel the thirty bucks he could see I was carrying a lot of money and the raid was organized. So much for Christian generosity."

Johnson nodded. "Many bad men on Barbuda. Partly government fault. England give nothin to Antigua and Antigua give nothin to Barbuda. Men are robbin here to stay alive. Maybe fortunate de' be so poor. If have more money would have bought shoes and not step on de tack."

"Well, they were rich enough to have new machetes," George said. "They're just too lazy to use them on their farms. Tried to farm *Rascal* for money instead. *Rascal* doesn't like to be farmed."

Ethan had been quiet throughout the celebration. After a time he asked, "Would they have killed me." He was far more scared of the men than he'd been on the Angeda Passage. Nature was one thing. Experience had taught him that people were much worse.

George put his arm around Ethan's shoulder in a comforting manner and answered, "Heck no. They just wanted to rob us. They wouldn't have killed us. They knew they'd hang if they did that."

Johnson added, "It all right, Ethan. No worry about it. Nothing happen. A mon should never worry about what never happen. Beside, we would no have let dem kill you."

George and Johnson went to the bow, Ethan assumed to get out of his hearing. But by straining he could hear what they said.

George started, "Cain was a killer in the Bible. I think he still is."

Johnson replied, "I could see de' had a lot of provision loaded in der boat. Intend to kill us, steal *Rascal*, dump our body off shore to de shark, then change de name and paint her different color. Probably take de boat to Guyana for sale. De' buy anything in Guyana. Same thing happen many time around de Caribbean since de war."

Ethan tensed, a cold knot of fear in his stomach, thinking of being thrown overboard to a shark like the one off Galley Beach. He determined to be brave and not show it. He wouldn't show how afraid he'd been. Throwing back his shoulders he marched over to George, took his hand, gave it a good shake, and said in a very loud voice, "Thank you for saving us."

George's face blossomed to a happy smile. This time his eyes crinkled at the corners along with the joyful expression on his mouth.

Then Ethan thanked Johnson, and shook his hand with equal fervor.

His fear dissipating Ethan exulted. That was something. Fighting real pirates. Not make believe like in the movies. Real pirates. They were a good team. No one was going to take them. He wished he'd had a gun. He would've shot them all. He pictured it. Bang, bang, bang. Shooting pirates. Boy. He sure would have liked the bullies back home had seen this. And even his father would have been impressed.

CHAPTER SIXTEEN

They set out early the next morning headed west, downwind to Montserrat, an eight hour or more passage. With the wind behind them, and in the lee of Barbuda, the boat was fairly stable for once. Ethan and Johnson were seated in the cockpit. George at the helm, whistling to himself and singing a little calypso now and then.

After what had happen in Barbuda, and because he trusted Johnson and was starting to trust George, Ethan decided he wanted to start talking more. He no longer felt isolated as he'd been at home. In Johnson and George he had people who were interested in him. He wanted them to know what happened when his mother died, to understand what he'd suffered. He turned to Johnson, "Do you want to hear about my mother? I didn't want to talk about her before."

Johnson said, "Sure. I be hopin you tell me what happen."

Ethan started, "I remember everything exactly. I should. I think about it all the time. It was terrible." Ethan then told the story of his mother's death in the kitchen, his father's hate, being kicked on the floor, and trying to explain. "I kept trying to tell my father what happened, that it wasn't my fault. I tried for weeks. When I'd start he would just shake his head and repeat that I killed my mother. I stopped trying." At this point Ethan was sobbing continuously. Johnson put his arm around his shoulder. "Awful story."

The sobbing let up and Ethan continued, "My father must have told everybody in town I killed my mother. During her funeral I got angry looks from all the people, and I even think from Father Smallwood. Same for people on the streets of town. And some of the boys at school started calling me, 'Mother killer.' Sometimes I could see my father looking at me as though he didn't know me. He didn't want to know me.

"I tried not to think all the time about what happened. Wasn't possible. I couldn't stop thinking about it. I kept seeing her when she died and hearing my father. All the bad stuff he kept saying to me. It was like one of those horror movies, reel after reel of horror movie. Then I started thinking I probably did kill my mother. I remember when I decided my father was right."

Johnson asked, "Is dat why you stop talking?"

Ethan looked out to sea, then turned back to Johnson. "Well. I didn't stop talking completely. Sometimes I'd say yes or no if someone asked me again and again and I'd have to answer. I don't know why I stopped talking. Everyone hated me so much. I felt what's the use of talking to them. And I kept remembering that when my mother died I didn't talk to neighbors. Maybe, I thought, I shouldn't talk any more if I couldn't talk to save my mother. I didn't deserve to be heard. I was just so sad. I just couldn't talk. I didn't want to talk. Nothing I had to say was worth anything to anyone. So why talk.

"It got really horrible. After school the bullies would wait for me, circle me, yell at me, 'Say something stupid,' or 'Say something, mother killer.' Then they would shove me. Boys on one side of the circle pushing me hard to the other side and then back again, like a soccer ball or something, laughing all the time, until finally I'd fall down and hurt my knees and hands, and probably rip my pants, which got me punished when I got home. I had no friends. My father was no friend. I was totally alone. I started to avoid people whenever I could. Just did my school work. That's all. Just be there. Nothing more. It's hard to describe what I felt like but it was like I was disappearing. There was some sort of weight on me pushing me down like vanishing into quicksand. The more I struggled the more the quicksand pulled me down. Sometimes when the 'bad times' came I imagined I'd already disappeared. I wasn't there anymore. I started thinking about killing myself. I even made plans. There was a railway bridge over the Mohawk River. I could jump off of with weights around my waist so I'd drown. I got a bunch of short pieces of lead pipe from a vacant lot down the street where people had been dumping stuff. Made a belt by putting a rope through the pieces of pipe so I could tie them around my waist. I called it my 'drowning belt.' Hid it in the woods. On days when the taunting was real bad, everyone calling 'mother killer,' I'd take the belt out, put it around my waist, and look at it. It felt good that I had a way to escape. One real bad day I took the belt to the bridge, went to the middle of the bridge and put the belt on. Teetered on the edge looking down. Couldn't do it."

Johnson said, "That's really, really bad. Why didn't you do it."

"Well as I was standing there I thought about what would happen if I wasn't around any more. I thought of each of the people I would make happy. It was a long list. I just didn't want to make the people happy who hated me." For the first time, Ethan smiled.

Throughout his telling of the story Johnson had gazed intently into his eyes, making him feel that to Johnson what he was saying was the most important thing ever heard, and at intervals Johnson had made clunking sounds and shaken his head in sympathy, and toward the end cried a little along with his crying.

Ethan expected that Johnson would try and talk him out of his belief that he had responsibility for his mother's death. He'd tried to talk himself out of it. Couldn't, so didn't think Johnson could.

Instead Johnson said, "Everybody do thing de' no like. Everybody think de' make mistake. A mon no let mistake stop his livin.

"My best friend growin up be Amos Tuttle. We do everythin together, especially fish together. We be seventeen. Our village have poor luck fishin for weeks. Village runnin out of food. We decide to bring in good catch and save de village. Took de fishin boat way out. It look stormy. We ignore it. We going to be big hero with our catch. Tremendous mistake as de weather get worse. Was almost a hurricane. Even have St. Elmo fire in de rigging. Never see dat before or since. Scary. Waves much bigger than you see in de Anegada passage. Some be thirty feet high. One giant wave crash over de boat and took Amos overboard. He be wearin a lifeline but somehow it broke. Goin overboard he must have hit his head on de boom or somethin. He lying face down in de water in his life jacket and only movin his arms and legs very little bit. I jump into de water holding the jib sheet and swam after him. De jib sheet pretty long but at de end I still thirty or forty feet from him. The waves so steep I could only see him when I was on de top of wave and he on de top of another wave. I panic. Afraid to let go of de jib sheet in de killer sea and go after him. Watch him appear at de top of a monster breakin wave, then vanish. Never saw him again. Pull myself back to de boat and start cryin because of the loss and me being a coward. Was rescue by a schooner de next day.

"For long time I think about it just like you thinkin about your mother death. Think that I might have save him like you think you might have save you mother. I always been very strong swimmer and Amos have life jacket. Talk myself into believin I could have save him just like you talk yourself into believin you could have save you mother. Finally, I decide to think what Amos would be wantin me to do. He no would like me to be all de time blamin myself. He would have want me to go on livin and be happy. I decide to treat what happen as just part of de good and de bad of life, just part of being alive on God earth, that it be wrong for me to let de bad take over my life.

"I know you mother want you to do what I did, to forget de past and go on livin. No be sad about de past. God put you here to be happy. You mother want you to be happy. And she want you to forgive youself for everything you think you do. A mon forgive himself. No let what happen in de past ruin his life.

"Whenever I see you mopin like you been doing I goin to remind you. Tell you forget it. Put it out of you mind. Dat's what you got to do. Dat what you mother want."

Johnson asked Ethan to start saying prayers about forgiveness, to pray to God to help him forgive himself, to pray to God to help him forget the past and move to a happy future. Ethan found himself following this prayer cycle. And when he thought about it he found forgiving and forgetting was beginning to get easier. All the new things in the Caribbean were crowding out his bad memories. It was like back home when he was feeling bad about something he'd been able to go to his mother and she would comfort him and take his mind off it. That's what the Caribbean was doing.

When George came off the helm he sat next to Ethan, patted his balding spot, and said with a happy smile, "I see the cat's given you back your tongue. That's just great. Really great. Are you liking the voyage?"

"Yes, I sure do. It's great."

"What do you like best?"

Ethan looked around *Rascal,* then the sea, smiling. "Everything. I love the sea, the waves, the fish, the dolphin, the birds. But best is *Rascal.* I love sailing with you and Johnson on *Rascal.* It's super." He then looked aside and said. "Really the best thing of all is being away from Niskayuna. Niskayuna is the worst."

George leaned closer, "Don't you miss your home sometimes?"

"Well, sometimes I miss my room. I have a special collection of rocks and other stuff I found in the woods."

"But don't you miss your father?"

Ethan's response was a small negative shake of his head.

"I'm sure your father misses you," George said. "You went through a terrible time. He understands that. Deep down, I'm sure he loves you."

Ethan turned his head away and gave a much stronger shake of his head. "My father wishes I was never born." Then he said in a loud, angry voice, "I hate him. He hurt my mother."

George took Ethan by the shoulders and forced him to look him in the eyes, speaking slowly and with emphasis. "You're here now on this boat. Forget home. Here everyone loves you. I love you. Even if your father doesn't love you, I love you. I promise you that. Forget the past. Just think about sailing *Rascal* and all the special things you're doing."

They sat silently for awhile. Then Ethan turned back to George. "Why did you take me from home?"

George's response was quick, as though he expected the question. "First, it was because I could see how unhappy you were. When I saw you at church it made me so sad. I thought that being away in the Caribbean you'd be much happier. Also, I could see you and your father weren't getting along."

"You can say that again."

"I thought if I separated you maybe your father would realize how much he loves you. That things would be better when you get together again.

"But mostly, it's because I don't have a son of my own." George leaned closer to him, his eyes misting, and said, "I thought that we might get to know each other real well sailing together on *Rascal*. Get to really like each other. And eventually you might come to look at me as your second father. You need a father who loves you."

This sounded great but no way did he want another father. One was bad enough. He held his tongue.

CHAPTER SEVENTEEN

Sailing downwind to Montserrat, out from under the lee of Barbuda, wind and swells increased greatly, and George set the sails in a way that was new to Ethan. The mainsail was let far out on one side of the boat and the jib let out similarly far out on the other side. George explained that this presented a wall of sail to the following wind and made *Rascal* go faster saying it was called, "Sailing wing and wing." It made steering challenging. *Rascal* was corkscrewing in the heavy following sea. George, and later Johnson when he took the helm, had to saw the helm violently back and forth to maintain course.

The corkscrewing was a different motion for Ethan. He stood with his feet wide apart, twisting his body from side to side and back and forth with the corkscrews of the boat, another game to play. His one stumble to the deck brought him to laughter.

Then trouble half-way to Montserrat. *Rascal's* steering cable parted, the vital cable between the helm, a steering wheel on *Rascal*, and the rudder. They had no replacement. *Rascal* without steerage turned abruptly into the wind, the sails flapping uselessly.

Johnson went over the side in the rough seas, attaching lines to each side of the rudder. The port line was led to a winch on the port side of the cockpit and the starboard line to a winch on the starboard side.

They continued to Montserrat with Johnson on the port winch and George on the starboard, winching the lines with all their might, steering *Rascal* by strength in a crooked path, trying to avoid yawing out of control.

It was very difficult and dangerous work because of the strengthening sea, breaking waves of eight to ten feet directly behind. *Rascal* surfed down the face of the waves, driven by the high wind, the waves threatening to poop

Rascal, threatening to bury her stern under a following sea, turn her on her side, and roll her over to capsize.

The boom was set out to starboard at a right angle to the boat and a preventer, a line, was tied to the boom and cleated starboard side forward. This was designed to prevent an unintentional jibe from crashing the boom to the port side in taking down the mast. When an unintentional jibe did happen—and it happened four times on the way to Montserrat—*Rascal* violently sought to turn to starboard, to come up into the wind. This wrenched the rudder over to starboard, and it became a tremendous feat of strength for Johnson on the port side to winch the rudder back straight so they could return to course.

Ethan's job when *Rascal* unintentionally jibed was to grab the mainsheet and and help force the main back over to starboard, assisting Johnson in his mighty efforts with the port rudder line. Working closely together, Johnson and Ethan were successful each time *Rascal* jibed, usually with George temporarily abandoning the starboard rudder line winch and joining Johnson to winch in the port rudder line.

An arduous six hours fighting the rudder, they cleared the south end of Montserrat and sailed into harbor. Ethan looked up. Above towered a conical volcano several thousand feet tall. Unlike the volcano at Saba that ascended in a series of cliffs broken by flatter areas, this volcano went up in a constant steep gradient. It looked like someone had taken a giant ice cream cone, turned it upside down, painted the sides with bright green foliage, then cut off the top in a perfect circle. One of his picture books at home showed a South Sea volcano like this, but not so precisely conical.

George arrived at their anchorage with bloody hands. Ethan arrived with profuse thanks from George and Johnson who said they would not have made it without Ethan's work on the main.

"Good work, mon," Johnson said.

"Everybody in town would have been proud of you," said George, grasping Ethan in a bear hug. Ethan grinned big and said, "Yah. Thanks." They really worked well together and he was part of it. He puffed his chest out, proud.

After anchoring Ethan joined Johnson rowing around the harbor to see if anyone had a replacement for their broken steerage cable. Fortune smiled.

They hailed a couple on a yacht that turned out to be going around the world. The couple just happened to have a spare steerage cable of the exact size and type needed. Johnson said it would probably have been impossible to find a replacement on Montserrat. The couple generously gave them the cable for free. They would pick up a replacement when they got to Panama.

George's joke that evening reflected the danger they had surmounted.

"A friend of mind back home has never sailed and asked me before this trip if sailboats sink often. I told him usually only once."

Nobody laughed, though they did have a serious shaking hands ceremony in celebration of arrival.

The next day they invited the around-the-world couple to lunch, middle aged, very English, looking alike in their pale graying hair, slightly over-weight stocky bodies, full faces with large English noses, smallish pale blue eyes, and alike in their too many worded ways of talking and constant finishing of each other's sentences, Harold and Mildred Smith. The boat they sailed, *Off Soundings*, a sloop, was about *Rascal's* size.

Their around-the-world sail turned out to be a memorial for their son, Lester. They said he'd been an outstanding sailor, had bought the sloop with the intention of going around the world, and was drowned trying to rescue another sailor off Cowes in a violent storm. According to Harold Smith, Lester's greatest dream was to sail around the world. All his money had gone into provisioning the sloop. They said he discussed his plans with them in great detail, and that when he died they'd each decided independently and simultaneously that their son would indeed sail around the world. He was with them.

They planned to take two years for the circumnavigation. Though they'd not previously done much sailing they'd bought many books and charts, had been studying them, and hoped to learn more along the way. Johnson looked over their sloop and made a number of suggestions to improve safety.

Later, alone with George and Ethan, Johnson made a sort of prayer about the Smiths. "They no know de danger. But der son does. Der son who be with them goin to sail der boat to a safe passage." Then said with confidence, "De' be on de holy mission. God goin to protect them." He turned to Ethan. "Remember dat, Ethan. When you followin God way, God goin to protect you."

Ethan answered with a serious, "I will."

George nodded, "One must always follow God's ways. I always do."

Johnson glanced over at him, opening his eyes wide and giving a small shake of his head.

Maybe it was being with proper English people that prompted George's lecture that evening. George sat him down, stood over him, and said, "I'm going to give you some important advice about how you can be a gentleman and have other people admire you. First rule is always stand tall. I notice sometimes you don't stand tall. A gentleman always stands tall. If you slump you look like you don't think much of yourself. And if you don't think much of yourself other people won't think much of you either. Stand tall and people back home will respect you. And always dress well. You see me always dressing well. They say clothes make a man and it's true. Most important, though, is the friends you pick. Pick your friends with care. Only friends who are rich or can help you in business. In the end it's all about appearances. You need to keep up appearances, the right friends, the right clothes, the right posture, appearances."

George was trying to be helpful, which he appreciated. But without any friends at all he didn't see how he could go about picking those who were rich. And what did appearances mean?

...

The next day en route to Nevis George was at the helm, as usual interspersing whistling between snatches of Calypso songs. His thoughts were about Ethan. He'd grown to love Ethan more than he believed most men ever loved their sons, and he'd been working hard on his plan to gain his trust and bring him under his loving control.

Always he was as attentive as possible, smiling at Ethan whenever he looked his way, trying to engage him in conversation about anything at all or nothing at all, pointing things out to him, congratulating him and thanking him for whatever he did, a number of times telling him that he loved him even if his father didn't. And he'd tried to be generous, buying him locally crafted gifts on each island to create a fabric of memories, buying more sweets than a thirteen-year-old should have. In shock he realized he'd been trying harder to bring Ethan to love him than he'd tried in courting Marge.

George felt some disappointment that his efforts weren't meeting with greater success. Ethan always thanked him politely for whatever he gave him, but never turned to him as a son would to a father, never with a hug, an embrace, or any other indication of more than friendship, and never seemed to understand his love for him. A man could go mad. Maybe it was just that Ethan was still too damaged to bond with anyone. But he could see that the boy was starting to bond with Johnson. Damn it. That should be him. He was going to have to warn Ethan about Johnson.

At this point he was well off course and Johnson, sitting in the cockpit near him, brought him back with a prompt.

George went back to daydreaming and fantasized about a future with Ethan. He brought to mind the time spent in Paris early in his marriage, picturing himself with Ethan in Paris, his arm around his shoulder, pointing out sites and the art treasures of the world. Then sophisticated restaurants with good conversation. They would eat at the restaurant where Moira Grayson had been chef. A suite to share at the Paris Ritz Hotel. After that, Venice. Dinner on the terrace of the Gritti Palace Hotel. He would show Ethan where Hemingway had stayed writing *Across The River And Into The Trees*. Afterward a gondola on the Grand Canal listening to romance sung in the quickening night. Another time Switzerland. Evan had never skied. A special dream was to rent a chalet in Zermatt and teach him skiing under the awe of the Matterhorn, then sitting together before the roaring fire exchanging stories of their day.

Ethan would lack for nothing—a fine New England prep school, then an Ivy League college, the best, then wealth, first partnership with him in his businesses, ownership at his and Marge's death.

His daydreams went to adoption of Ethan. Ethan's father didn't seem to care much about the boy. With all the blame he was heaping on Ethan for his wife's death maybe Fred would be glad to have him off his hands. Sure, Marge objected to adoption. But when she got to know Ethan things could change.

What if he offered something to Fred for the adoption? Money would be crude and rejected out of hand. But what could be accomplished if he arranged a substantial promotion for Fred with a bank in a distant city, giving Fred a way to leave the house in which his wife died, a house he must hate? Fred's excuse for leaving Ethan behind could be a desire to have him finish school, while distance would prevent his adoption of the boy from being known in the new town, shielding Fred from criticism in his new life. He would argue to Fred that he could give Ethan much more than he ever could. And from what he knew of Sarah, and her love for Ethan, he thought she would have wanted Ethan to have what he could provide. He understood Fred loved Sarah deeply. Maybe Fred would release Ethan because Sarah would have wanted him to have a better life. Fred seemed a weak man. Worth a try.

George looked forward at Ethan standing at the bow—tight red bathing suit, slender brown form, hair bleached white, sun around him, gathering in his hair, highlighting every part of his body.

At that point he had gotten well off course again, and Johnson again gave him a quiet reminder about the heading.

CHAPTER EIGHTEEN

Johnson often talked about the myriad creatures of the sea as blessings of God to earth. "Men be arrogant. Think de' superior because de' can reason and talk. But many creature reason what necessary for der life and speak to each other in way different from word. And look at all de thing de' can do that mon no can do. De' better than men in many way." He said one of his favorite quotes was from the Psalms.

"They that go to the sea in ships, that do business in great waters; these see the works of the Lord, and his wonders in the deep."

When some new and special ocean creature appeared he would exclaim, "Look, Ethan. Another of God's wonders in the deep," then he would say, and he always said it, "God be in all creatures. If you look closely you seein God."

Ethan already loved nature and now his love expanded to the Caribbean. At some point each day there seemed to be something new that nature brought, something new Johnson showed him. Ethan looked forward to it. It was always a moment of great joy.

He loved the birds. Johnson named the various birds they saw and told him the sailor can learn a lot from birds, from what kind of birds were visible and what were they doing. "If frigate bird be sitin up der then tuna, or perhaps bonito, schoolin below. De frigate bird waitin for de larger fish to drive de smaller fish to de surface. But if tern wheeling around and diving, with or without coverin flight of frigate bird, de fish below probably bait fish. De frigate bird cover de tern not so much to get bait fish themselve but to steal de bait fish from de tern after de tern catch de bait fish. Nature dress frigate bird in black like pirate. And they be pirate. Most of de fish de' eat stolen from other bird.

"I always watch de frigate bird. Like dat bad man Codrington say on Barbuda, frigate bird no mind de storm. Even like de storm. But you see them heading for shore, something real bad comin. Watch out. And if you see no frigate bird that de worst. Maybe hurricane comin.

"De small bird like de tern go to land every night. If a sailor lost all he have to do be to follow de small bird to find de shore."

Ethan's favorites were the pelicans. They rarely saw them far from land. Instead the pelicans flew over the reefs, usually in V formation like the wild geese at home, and sometimes only a few feet above the surface, gliding with their wings still as though the water was somehow supporting them. They reminded Ethan of the tight battle formations flown by World War II bombers in the movies. Then they became dive bombers, dive bombing the reefs from on high, exploding into the water, bringing swift death to fish below. Ethan watched them with fascination for long periods of time.

Throughout the voyage dolphin played surfing games at the bow. Johnson pointed out many different species— common dolphin, spotted dolphin, bottlenose dolphin, and striped dolphin. Ethan never tried to learn the differences. He liked them all. He would rush to the bow when they appeared, calling to them in greeting, waving his arms at them in the hope they'd come closer.

Occasionally, a dolphin would come very close and stare at him. It would slow down to maintain eye contact. A round, bright, black eye, expressionless but intelligent, trying to tell him something. Trying to say what joy it is to ride the waves together. Trying to say, we are brothers.

On the sail from Montserrat to Nevis they passed many turtles, and Johnson talked about them. They turned out to be a favorite of Johnson's. He loved all varieties—Green Turtles, happily bobbing and diving at the surface, bobbing and diving, bobbing and diving. Hawksbill Turtles, the speed demons of the turtle world. The bathtub huge, yellowish-plated Loggerhead Turtles. The Loggerheads were special, Johnson said, sometimes weighing up to 1,000 pounds, and they ate Portuguese Men-of-War. Johnson explained that he hated Portuguese Men-of-War. He was often badly stung bringing in fishing lines coated with their tentacles, and Loggerheads bravely ate the Portuguese Men-of-War, knowing to close their eyes, to pull their heads back as far as possible into their carapace, and then gulping them down, stinging tentacles included.

At Nevis Johnson took Ethan out in the dingy to a place where the water was about twelve feet deep. "Look down der. What you see?"

Through the crystal clear water Ethan saw several large green turtles lined up. The one at the head of the line was surrounded by thin, purple and gold, four inch long fish. They were darting at its shell and appeared to be feeding on something on the shell.

Johnson said, "De' be Wrasse fish, de clean-up crew for de turtle. Turtle swim slow and pick up algae and little sea creature on der shell. Wrasse fish eat all dat stuff off dem. Turtle know Wrasse fish be in dis place so come here to be cleaned. It de turtle-cleanin station."

Johnson paused, "It always remind me of men linin up for Saturday hair-cut, but more polite. No turtle jump ahead in de line like human. Better and more efficient than human."

Ethan watched the turtles for some time. Johnson was right. The Wrasse clean-up crew was much more efficient, completing their depilatory work much faster than a human haircut, helped by not having to engage in the lengthy banter between customer and barber that Ethan remembered as delaying haircuts back home.

When they returned to *Rascal* George called out to Ethan with a broad smile, "Having any fun yet?" a question George now asked several times a day. Ethan's response was always the same, a loud, "Yes."

When anchored Johnson went below to work on the engine and George took him aside for what turned out to be a "talk" not unlike his father's talks. This was about Johnson.

"You're getting too friendly with Johnson. Have you had any dealings with blacks back in Niskayuna?"

Ethan shook his head.

"Well blacks aren't to be trusted. They tell lies and give wrong informa-tion. Johnson is always telling you things, right?"

Ethan nodded.

A lot of it isn't true or isn't the whole story. It's not all his fault. Blacks are inferior intellectually, not as smart as we are, and they're immoral. You prob-ably don't know what immoral is. It means they do bad things God doesn't approve of and they don't even care that they are doing bad things. They like doing bad things. They're beneath a white person like you are, not as good.

Johnson is a fine sailor but you shouldn't make him your friend. A gentleman doesn't have a black man as his friend. If he does white people will shun him. You don't need that on top of everything else that people in Niskayuna are doing to you. You can be nice to Johnson. But on this boat he's a servant. One never gets close to servants. Understand?"

He said, "Yes," as that was what George wanted him to say. Then Ethan went to the bow to think about it. There had to be more to George's warning than another of his lectures about being a gentleman. Ethan remembered a movie, in fact many movies, where two men sought the same woman. The way George delivered his lecture reminded Ethan of a man lecturing a woman about a rival. A new thought. Did George see Johnson as a rival? Maybe. It looked exactly like he'd seen in the movies, even the way George's face clouded with dislike when he talked about Johnson. Did Johnson also see George as a rival? He saw no evidence, never from Johnson any criticism of George. He would have to be careful not to appear to like Johnson more than George. It meant hiding that he was coming to think of Johnson as a near father.

That evening at Nevis Ethan saw the green flash for the first time. It required an absolutely clear horizon, no clouds. The sun slid down the horizon, its lower edge disappearing beneath the purple rim of the sea, bright gold, then orange-red, shrinking moment by moment, then only a glowing orange fragment peeking above the horizon, and finally, for just an instant, the last rays of the sun flashed a bright grass-green.

Johnson said, "Green flash be miracle of God. Gift of God."

George agreed but gave the scientific explanation. "As the sun drops below the horizon the yellow and red light rays from the the sun can't bend enough to make it over the horizon. The blue light bends too much and is scattered in the atmosphere. Only the green light bends just right to throw a flash of green at the last disappearance of the sun."

George had brought a number of teen-age boy books abroad and Ethan had been going through them. That evening he said to Johnson that he'd gotten bored with them, and could he read the *Heart of Darkness* book Johnson had shown him?

Johnson said, "Well, as I say to you before, very difficult book. Many adult have trouble with it. But you smart. And maybe do you some good. You goin to find out about de evil dat many men have in dem. Show you dat all over de world people can do awful thing to other people like de people do to you in Niskayuna. You no alone.

"At de start of de book Conrad write about, 'Those who tackle a darkness.' You going to be tackling darkness when you read dis book. No story tell better de darkness of mankind, particularly white mankind. But black and white share de same with de darkness. De book remind me dat darkness is close to us all, all de time. Life sometime bring dark when you least expect it."

Ethan felt he'd already been tackling darkness for a very long time. No new darkness please. Still, he wanted to read the book.

"I give you de book but der be a way I want you to read it. Look at it like it be a puzzle. You like puzzle, right?"

Ethan nodded.

"De word and sentence in de book be puzzle for you to work out, and de whole book be puzzle. What you trying to find out no just what de word and de sentence mean but what Conrad intend. Dat de real puzzle.

"I goin to give you my dictionary. You need to go sentence by sentence, makin sure you understand everythin before you move to de next sentence. I goin to be here to help if you no understand somethin."

Ethan grabbed the book and started reading in the poor light of the cabin.

CHAPTER NINETEEN

Most days they anchored out, the docks in the harbors either being too flimsy to hold *Rascal* or occupied by fishing boats. At their next island, Saint Christopher (St. Kitts), they came into a small, almost landlocked bay near the central town of Basseterre. They anchored out and George said he had a surprise. Evening came on. The track of light from the westering sun shone on the ripple free water of the sheltered harbor, a bright path to the sun on a sea of glass. The sun smiled one last time and dipped to the place where sea and sky meet, the final rays painting the sky with cantaloupe orange, bright pink, and an eventual darkening red.

And with night, as though unwilling to allow the sun to deprive the world of light, light was taken up by the sea itself. The water around them went bright. George explained it was a bio-luminescent bay. Minuscule luminescent creatures had gathered to glow the water when disturbed.

Fish moved around *Rascal* with brilliant outline. Some fast, a flight of water comets. Some lazy, just watching the comets go by. Larger fish proclaimed exactly who they were and where they were going, with even their smallest fin movement flashing blue-white fire. Around the larger fish was the quicksilver of smaller fish glimmering here and there. George splashed his hand in the water and the cockpit came alight. Water lightening.

Ethan sat in the dingy at the stern for the better part of an hour, watching the luminescence play on his hands as he moved them slowly through the water, an enchanted being in shimmering light. Half awake, half dreaming, memories of his mother surfaced. He wished he could show her this.

The next morning they rowed into a broad beach on St. Kitts. The beach was littered with driftwood, scrounged by the sea from far and wide. "Can we build a fort?"

The challenge was taken up by George and Johnson. A competition developed to bring large pieces of driftwood to the fort site, then they worked together to raise walls and lay a precariously balanced roof. Finally the fort was completed to Ethan's satisfaction.

"You're the construction manager," George had said, and Ethan did give a few orders.

When it was completed he asked, "Can we sleep in the fort." George agreed despite the biting sand flies on the beach.

There were a lot of hermit crabs around, and Johnson showed Ethan how to organize a hermit crab race. A large circle was drawn on the sand. Then each one chose a hermit crab, their champion for the contest, and all three were deposited in the middle of the circle. The first crab that crossed out of the circle was the winner. They had many races. Ethan turned out to know his crabs, and George not so much, so it was George who lost the bet and had to clean the head the next day.

Later Ethan drew pictures on the sand and made sand sculptures. His attempt at Betsy was poor, though he did like the exaggerated breasts he drew. He thought his attempt at a village with roads and houses quite good.

He plopped down beside the drawings on his back and moved his arms in circles through the soft sand like he did making snow angels back home, for a time utterly happy.

Clouds to the west blocked the sunset and darkness swept up the sky. Ethan's dinner assignment was to collect kindling for the fire. Johnson appeared with lobsters from the reef and brought from *Rascal* blankets, utensils, plates, glasses, and other gear, everything they needed for a cookout and sleep over, including some brandy for George. All of Johnson's meals were good. But this was about the best, a wonderful dinner in a fort he helped construct on a deserted beach, three Robinson Crusoes together.

After dinner they sat around the fire, or reclined in George's case, the soft sand cradling his back. Conversation was desultory—how good a day it had been, where they were going tomorrow, the improving state of the weather, all of them watching the gleam of the fire find its way through the cracks in the fort to play light patterns on the beach. Ethan sat his hands around his knees, smiling to himself. This was a special evening, one of the most convivial evenings they'd shared.

Johnson interrupted everyone's reverie. "I almost drown today."

Ethan looked at Johnson in open-mouthed horror. George bolted upright and stared at Johnson.

"I was swimmin in a sandy place," Johnson said. "Just past de main reef. Crawling across de bottom be de biggest lobster I ever see. Maybe twenty-five pound. Maybe more. I pull back de rubber sling on my spear gun as far as it would go and hit de lobster in the middle of de back just where de claw come into de body. Should have kill him. Still alive. Lobster retreat into its hole in de coral. Retreat back-side first, claws waving at me. I try to pull him out with de rope on de spear. No luck. He holdin in der with de feelers on de side of his body, had set them hard against de coral, and de spear caught in de roof of his hole. Should have let him go. But want to show him to Ethan. So I dive down holding my breath to try and wrestle him out. Only about eight feet deep, not much over my head. I avoid his claw. These Caribbean lobsters no have much in de way of claw. I slip my left hand under him and grab his belly, and my right hand above him and grab his back. Start pulling hard. Big mistake. I no have purchase in de water and he still alive enough to jam himself further back in de hole. Both my hand under him and over him caught. I pull as hard as I could. Nothing. It de spear. I see de problem de spear. De spear jam into de roof of de hole in a way that de more I pull de more de spear jam. I be runnin out of air. Try to use my feet. Finally able to throw my right foot forward enough to knock de spear to de side. Then I make desperate pull with my last air and got free. Close call."

"You almost no have dinner tonight."

Ethan's face collapsed in distress, tears filling his eyes. He jumped up and ran over to Johnson, throwing his arms around him, Johnson comforting Ethan more than Ethan was comforting Johnson.

Johnson repeated what he's said in Barbuda, "No worry about what no happen. De Lord protect us. But no goin to stick my hand in de lobster hole again."

George frowned and shook his head, saying, "I was once buried in a sand cave without air. Nothing worse than no air." George gave Johnson a look of sympathy, the first regard for Johnson Ethan had seen from George in a long time.

Conversation lightened up and George took the opportunity to tell a pirate story, saying he wanted to get everyone's mind off what almost happened. "In the old days there were many pirates around St. Kitts. One day an old pirate was walking on the beach. Maybe this very beach. He had a peg leg, a hook for his right hand, and an eye patch on his left eye. He was obviously struggling in the beach sand with his peg leg. A young sailor came up to him and offered to help, an offer that was gratefully accepted by the pirate. They started talking. The young sailor asked the pirate how he lost his leg. The pirate said, 'Was knocked overboard in a storm and a shark got me leg before they could haul me back aboard.' Well, how did you lose the arm?' 'Saber,' said the pirate. 'Fight on the deck of an English frigate. I killed the Englishman. After the arm healed they put the hook on.' And what about the eye? 'Well, a seagull pooped in me eye.' The sailor, puzzled, asked, 'Can bird poop put out an eye?' The pirate answered, 'It can if it's the first day you have a hook for a right hand.'"

George laughed loudly and Ethan threw his head back and joined him, with Johnson also laughing. Ethan congratulated George on what he thought was his best joke yet. They rolled up in their blankets by the waning fire and had a good night sleep, except Ethan did have a nightmare about drowning.

. . .

After St. Kitts they sailed on to the island of Sint Eustatius ("Statia"), an English-speaking Dutch island that George said was known as the "Golden Rock" because in colonial times so much valuable cargo was funneled through its tax-free port, the principal trans-shipment port between Europe and the Americas. It was a fairly calm day for a change, and Ethan asked George if he could steer. George quickly agreed.

George started by teaching Ethan about helmsmanship. "A good helmsman turns the helm very little. Have you ever been with your father driving on an icy road?"

Ethan said he had.

"Maybe you noticed that on the ice your father corrected the direction of the car with only small, gradual movements of the steering wheel, never any quick turns. Now think of *Rascal* as slipping ahead on an icy surface. You correct the direction of *Rascal* with only small, gradual movements of the helm, never sharp movements.

"Also you need to learn to anticipate. When strong waves are hitting the starboard side as they are now each wave drives *Rascal* to port. You need to anticipate that, and just as the wave hits you need to turn slightly to starboard to meet the wave. Also you need to pay constant attention to the wind on the water. When a gust is coming it shows itself by black ripples on the surface. See that dark patch over there? That's wind coming. You can recognize wind a long way off. Just as the gust hits you need to turn up into the wind to keep the boat from being knocked down."

At first George had Ethan steer for specific visible points on the horizon, an island in the distance, or a headland. Then he taught him to steer by the compass in the binnacle. Ethan found this difficult but eventually got the hang of it.

Boy. This was really something. Steering *Rascal*. He felt like jumping up and down and yelling, but that would take him off course. Of all the things he'd done in his life this made him most proud. He stood taller and gave a commanding look around the boat, a captain's look. Master of a sailing vessel.

That day George also turned over to Ethan the job of keeping the ship's log, instructing Ethan to record distance traveled, course sailed, changes of watch, and sitings. In short order, Ethan was adding information on weather, wind direction and strength, islands visited, creatures seen, storms and squalls, and even noteworthy cloud formations. It became a complete diary of their voyage.

Later in the day on the way to Statia from St. Kitts Johnson asked Ethan how he was doing with *Heart of Darkness*. Johnson had been helping him, telling him about King Leopold and the plunder of the Belgian Congo, about the voyage Conrad took up the Congo, and the meaning of difficult words and sentences. "Do you like it?"

Ethan said, "Yes. It's much more interesting than the other books."

"I see you read forty page or so. What be missin in de book?

Ethan looked at him blankly.

"Look around you. What do we have in abundance? Light. Conrad completely suck light out of de book. Marlow was in de tropic as we are, right on de equator, and der be light everywhere. But none in de book. Conrad very skillful at bringin de reader into darkness in one of de most brilliant lit place in de world."

...

Arriving at Statia from St. Kitts, they ran into a major problem, fouling their anchor in more than seven fathoms of water (forty-two feet). They tried everything to raise it. Motored *Rascal* in circles around and around the anchor, pulling in every direction. Nothing. Finally Johnson dove down. The anchor was hooked onto a gigantic old ship's anchor, flukes more than ten feet across.

By winding the anchor line around three winches, all three of them grinding ferociously at the same time, they were able to raise the old anchor slightly from the bottom. Then George would motor *Rascal* toward the shore for ten feet or so until the anchor was again on the bottom. And by repeating this winching and dragging process for two hours the old anchor was finally pulled into shallow enough water so that Johnson could dive down and free *Rascal's* anchor.

Ethan accompanied George into the local village to announce the find. Great excitement. The harbor had been used by English warships during the Napoleonic War. The villagers were certain the anchor was a Napoleonic-era English anchor, which proved to be correct when they hauled it ashore.

As Ethan was standing in the village with George watching the retrieval of the anchor, they were approached by a stooped, very elderly woman who walked in slow step toward them leaning heavily on a cane. "I be Maggie Brown, everyone call me Mag, and I de official historian on Statia. I want to thank you from all of us for bringin in de anchor. Very special. We goin to mount it in de town square over der."

Mag's intense black eyes squinted at Ethan. "You remind me of my youngest at you age. He sure no as white as you." She cackled. "But he have de same look about him. You just getting ready for life. No know where life goin to take you. But de whole world waitin to be explored. You lucky."

She then addressed both Ethan and George and said, "I be ninety and have seen everythin."

She did look very old. Wrinkled, longish, nut-brown face, many teeth missing when she smiled, a pronounced limp, which explained the cane, sporting a jaunty, broad straw hat with a bright red cloth band matching the bright red lipstick that had been liberally and crookedly applied as though in the half light of dawn her aged mirror had made her miss the mark. Her clothing seemed to be chosen to divert attention from her age-diminished body, a garish multicolored calico skirt, a blazing red blouse, and semi high-heeled red shoes, the last a quite unique fashion statement from a ninety-year-old in the flat-shoe Caribbean.

George and Ethan leaned close to hear her low voice, at first listening patiently, but then fascinated. She drew Ethan in with her enthusiasm.

"Polio make me de historian of Statia. When I be fifteen de polio kept me in bed many month. Later I no could walk well because de polio paralyze my left leg. So I start readin a lot. One of my sister work as maid for de governor of de island. De governor have a big library with many history book. I have my sister steal book out at the end of de day for me to read overnight. Have to be brought back early morning so de gap of de missing book not be seen in de daylight. I stay up all night readin and sleep most of de day. Get to be very fast reader tryin to finish de book before morning.

"Now I try and read every book come on de island, specially history. Dat why my two husband leave me. No could stand that I know so much. No try to understand de word I use from de book. Common dumb seamen. Went off in der boat and good riddance. No could stand a woman bein smarter."

She turned to Ethan. "If you sailing round here you ought to know some of de history of de Caribbean. You bring in history with de anchor. You should know more about it."

Ethan said, "I'd like that."

"Okay." she said. "First Columbus. You know about Columbus, right?"

Ethan nodded.

"Well, what you teacher tell you probably wrong. De' probably call Columbus great man because of his voyages of discovery and make big deal out of him for discoverin de new world and all dat stuff. He did discover all de island in de Caribbean. But he really about killin and enslavin. Dat what his voyages be about. De Spaniard kill most all of de Indian on de larger island. De' take over Cuba, Puerto Rico, and Hispaniola. These be island populated by peaceful Arawak Indian. Indian no hurting anyone. Spanish leave few Arawak alive. De bloody Spaniards justify de killing by arguin dat de Indian no be human. Dat de' be some species of animal, humanoid but no human, so it all right to kill dem. De Spanish be the ones who no be human. A devil's excuse for murder.

"De Catholic Church no better. How could de' claim to believe in Jesus yet treat de Indian as a lower race and no human? To them de Indian be like cattle on de plain of Spain, to be treated as dumb animal, subject to Catholic Church will, only de Spanish treat der cattle better. With de hell Columbus bring to de Caribbean, people here wish he drown at sea with all his men. He claim to be serving God but serve de devil.

"I apologize for hating de Spanish so much. I have some Arawak blood and know what de' do. De' devastate every Caribbean island de' settle.

"Now let's talk about de Napoleonic War. Boys always like to hear about war."

Ethan nodded smiling.

"De Caribbean island be major objective of de British and de French during de Napoleonic war. Dat because de' then de richest island in de world with de sugarcane growing. In de Treaty of Paris in de 1760s France have a choice of either giving up der claim to Canada or der claim to Guadeloupe and Martinique. France choose Guadeloupe and Martinique. With de sugarcane de' worth more than all of Canada. Dat how valuable de Caribbean island be.

"Cause so valuable de English station der main battle fleet in de Caribbean. French, too. For awhile de English even put Lord Nelson in charge of der main port, English Harbor."

Ethan said, "We visited English Harbor and saw where Lord Nelson lived."

"Wonderful," Mag said. "English harbor very special place. Chosen by the English for der fleet because it be upwind from de French islands, the furthest upwind port in the central Caribbean. English Ship-of-de-Line swoop down on de French, kill tremendous amount of de French. At that time ship could no tack upwind very well. So de French be easily trapped by English ship dat move downwind on them. De French sitting duck. De' have no chance against an English fleet coming downwind on dem.

"Battles throughout de island," Mag said. "First an island be English, then French, then English again, and so on. Each change with blood all over de place. One island, St. Lucia, change from French to English and back again fourteen time. Some of de bloodiest battle of de Napoleonic War in de Caribbean. Stupid English and French kept attacking each other fort. Would charge uphill in clear terrain against gunfire from de fort. Tens of thousand killed by battles and yellow fever."

Mag asked, "You see Brimstone Hill Fortress on St. Kitts?"

Ethan answered, "Yes. We wandered around it the morning before we came over here."

Mag said, "De' call it de *Gibraltar of de West*. More than mile long. How could anyone want to charge uphill against dat fortress? But the French did it. Put 8,000 men against the fort for a month. Terrible slaughter."

Mag concluded, "Ethan, you part of all dis history. De anchor be waiting all dis time just for you. Want to bring you into our history. Our history be you history now."

For the rest of the voyage Ethan daydreamed regularly about being on Nelson's Man-of-War, bravely fighting the French, and dropping the very anchor he had helped to recover.

When Ethan parted from Mag she said, "We believe if you listen careful to the wind in our palm trees you can hear it call you name." They had moved to stand under the palm trees, spots of blurred sunlight sliding over their bodies.

"Can you hear de call, Ethan?"

A flurry of wind rustled the palm fonds. Ethan listened carefully, and did believe he heard something from the palm trees, his name, maybe.

"Listen for it wherever you are," Mag said. "You goin to hear de palm if you listen for dem. De' be calling you back to see you anchor."

When they caught up with Johnson, Ethan told him what he had learned from Mag, particularly about Christopher Columbus and the Arawaks.

Johnson said, "Conrad have it right. He write, '*The conquest of the earth, which mostly means taking it away from those who have a different color or a flatter nose, is not a pretty thing.*' Only he no say it strong enough. What done by white explorer and der follower be de total rejection of God."

. . .

A clear night gave George an opportunity to give Ethan an astronomy lesson, and it was a clear night in Statia harbor. Night was displaying each and every one of its brightest gems to him, a pre-moonrise sky like black velvet, reaching down to him, vying for his attention.

He'd taken an astronomy class at college, and throughout the voyage taught Ethan what he remembered, pointing out stars and constellations, sitting close to Ethan in the cockpit under the silent stars, under the humbling vastness of the Caribbean sky, enveloped by night, any distance between him and Ethan made insignificant, sweet shore breezes surrounding them with flowered land scents, the happiest time of the day for George.

Ethan participated with delight, fascinated by the stars, and he gave rapt attention to George as he carefully named each star and showed how to find it in its sheltering constellation.

Ethan asked, "Are the stars closer here. They sure look closer than at home."

He replied, "They do look closer. It's because there's no light from houses to get in the way."

Johnson said from the side, "No. It because God *is* closer on de sea."

George smiled and said, "Maybe so."

During the star-gazing lessons, when Ethan's attention was focused on stars, George would casually put his arm around Evan's shoulder or his hand on his knee, pointing out this or that, he thought exactly what one would do when instructing one's son. Ethan would eventually look around, shrug off his arm, and move away, just far enough to avoid contact. By Statia George could see that Ethan had already memorized most of the visible constellations and major stars.

That night George promised something special to Ethan, a meteor shower. The sky streaked and dazzled, lit up every minute or two with brilliant flashes, occasionally at intervals of less than a minute, looking like somebody standing in the constellation Perseus was throwing down fire balls.

George said, "Every meteor shower appears to come out of a particular part of the sky where a particular constellation is located. Showers are named after the constellations where they originate. This comes out of Perseus so is called the Perseid meteor shower."

A little while later Johnson said, "When I was de child de' tell me God is de jeweler of de heaven, and dat shooting star be his way of lettin people know dat he up der. Maybe some truth to dat."

CHAPTER TWENTY

Evening meant stories. When they were underway there was little talk other than discussion of sail-trim and course. George told Ethan that by tradition sailors talked little while underway.

All together in the cockpit at day's end, George made up for his earlier lack of conversation by talking, and talking a lot, chin thrust out, enjoying himself in the telling, not conversation with Johnson, but profuse talk directed at Ethan, George an entertainer, funny stories, often sexual jokes and stories Ethan thought were very dirty. After one dirty story George leaned close to him and said, "Come on. I tell you dirty stories and you don't tell me any. It's not fair. You can make one up if you want." He squirmed away.

George moved to sit next to him, real close, sort of leering at him.

"I bet you think a lot about sex? Boy's your age have a lot of sexual urges. You can tell me about it." Again he squirmed away and again George moved next to him.

"What about that girl you like. Was her name Betsy? I bet she's sexy. Tell me about her."

He said to George in an angry voice, "I don't want to talk to you," got up and walked to the bow, as far away as he could get. He didn't know any dirty stories and wasn't about to reveal to George the sexual thoughts he was increasingly having, especially about Betsy. George didn't try that again.

Many of the stories George told were about people in town. He would say, "Have I ever told you about?" And off he would go. These stories were uninteresting to Ethan. He didn't know the people. Also, many of the stories were about failures and missteps of his friends with George laughing about it, directly contrary to his mother's admonition never to belittle others. George turned out to be a thigh-slapper, regularly slapping his thigh at the conclusion of a story or joke, and sometimes Ethan's thigh. And sometimes Ethan found his own young teenager words coming back at him like wow, super, neat, and holy cripes, George trying to be a buddy.

Most interesting were George's stories about his family.

"My ancestor, Lord Killean van Rosendahl, bought an estate on the Hudson from the Mohicans in 1630 measuring twenty four miles by forty eight miles and the van Rosendahl family ran it for 200 years, becoming by 1840 one of the richest family in American history, a private fiefdom, almost a separate country within the U.S."

"My ancestor, Jacob van Rosendahl, used his wealth and connections to persuade the British he was a loyal Tory, talked his way into war planning, and smuggled documents to Washington in a full wig that always drew compliments from the very Torys and British he was deceiving."

"My father, Harold, donated a family estate outside Schenectady, "The Knolls," to the U.S. government as an initial location of the Manhattan Project when the U.S. government sought a site near Schenectady because of all of the atomic scientists working for GE in Schenectady."

Ethan knew the Knolls still operated as the "Knolls Atomic Power Laboratory" and his estimation of George went up a little because of the atomic bomb connection, even though the connection was remote.

The van Rosenthal stories piled up. Many of the stories were great, governors, senators, and generals as ancestors. But Ethan understood that this was George selling him on the van Rosendahl family. Was it really so great to be a van Rosendahl? George was the only example he had.

George also told him stories about his bad childhood. Ethan sensed that George was talking about this as a way to bring them closer in a shared memory of what they'd both endured. One evening when George talked about his beatings, the near death in the sand cave, Ethan went over and put his hand on George's shoulder. "I'm sorry you went through all that." But Ethan felt his experiences were his own, and what happened to George had nothing to do with what happened to him.

Ethan liked Johnson's stories better. Johnson started with Africa.

"My people be de descendents of de Igbo tribe of Nigeria, most Antiguans Ibo. It no good to be Igbo in plantation time. Plantation owner think de Igbo make de best slave, strong and dependable. And de Igbo no die so much from malaria and yellow fever on de plantation. So other tribe in Nigeria hunt down Igbo and sell dec into slavery."

In another conversation, Johnson said his home on Antigua was Freetown, and he felt privileged to be a citizen of Freetown. He talked a lot about life in Freetown, a community that he said was on the northeast, driest end of Antigua. "In de plantation time of Antigua nobody want de land der because de area have virtually no water. Escapin slaves hid in de caves near Freetown. Then with emancipation in 1834, former slave join de community."

"Life der be much like an African village. De' celebrate African way as much as de' remember dem. De white man way be rejected. Der be open worship of West African Yoruba religion saints in sight of de Methodist Church. Even de dialect de' speak der different from de rest of Antigua.

"De garden of Freetown be de sea. Freetown draw it strength from de sea. Little grow on de land. De best mariner and fisherman on Antigua from Freetown."

Many of Johnson's stories were about what it meant to live a life of the sea. Giant marlin and sharks caught by hand line from small fishing boats, hurricanes, men lost. But even more stories were about Johnson's family.

One evening, sitting in the cockpit, smoking a Gauloise with Ethan beside him, he fingered his cross and said, "When I be eighteen a beautiful, intelligent fourteen-year-old girl live in town name Rebecca. Everybody say she too young for me. But I love her and she love me. We steal a boat and escape to Green Island off Antigua. Then other island around Antigua. Live on fish and love. Finally families relent and we marry. Best thing I ever do."

There were many stories about Rebecca. Johnson was very proud of her. One story was that while he was away on a voyage a bad hurricane hit. "She save de younger boys by lashin them to stout trees, and then sent de older boys out to save other.

"Dat very dangerous. Tree crashin down and house bein swept away by de storm surge. I still amaze at how brave she be. How much she love God to send de older boys into killer hurricane on mission of God mercy.

"She give de boys de best education black children can get on Antigua, no as good as de education white child get." He scowled. "Antigua give better education to white than black to hold de black back. Rebecca give all de boy good Christian value. De sea-faring life of Freetown be hard. Build leaders. I think de' be leaders of Antigua one day."

Another time Johnson spoke about his fourth son, Nathan, who was Ethan's age. "Nathan older brother, Zachery, be attack by shark at de beach near our house. Shark mangled de leg. Nathan only eleven. He pull Zachery out of de water, have de presence of mind to rip up clothes, with de help of Zachery apply a tourniquet, then run for help. Save de leg."

At eleven he'd not helped his mother and never ran for help. He put his head down in despair.

Johnson said, "*Stop* that. You would do de same thing."

Ethan did not think so but was somewhat buoyed by Johnson's confidence.

At one point Johnson asked Ethan what he thought all his stories were about.

Ethan said, "Well, all your stories have been about the sea and your family."

Johnson, sitting next to Ethan, put a hand on his shoulder and turned him toward him, saying with a serious tone, "Yes. But somethin more. De' be about bein alive. Some people talk mystical mumbo jumbo about de purpose of life. Make de purpose of life very complicated. It simple. De purpose of life be to live. Jack London one my favorite author because he live life full. He write, '*Life that lives is life successful.*' Tolstoy write de same thing. '*If you want to be happy take what God has given us and live it with joy.*' When we feel joy we feelin de happiness God has in seein us livin de life He give us.

"God choose which persons He allow to live on his wonderful earth. He choose each person individually, one at a time. He choose you specially to live on his earth. And He want you, and each person He choose, to celebrate de life he be given." Johnson smiled broadly at Ethan, happily throwing his arms wide.

"Ethan, being alive de greatest gift you ever goin to get. God greatest gift to man be life. Be an insult to God not to accept de gift and enjoy everythin on earth. I tell you dis before. You need to put de past aside. Start livin again. Just enjoy bein here in de Caribbean. God want you to live. Try to no think about de past. Can you do that?"

Ethan said, "I'll try."

Johnson celebrated being alive each day. He was always making happy comments and laughing at what they were seeing and doing. Everything he did was done with enthusiasm, cheerful no matter how challenging the situation or how disagreeable the task, an exuberant presence on *Rascal*.

How glorious it would be to live life like Johnson.

One result of Johnson's sailing stories was that Ethan decided he wanted to be a mariner when he grew up. Over a period of a week or so he asked Johnson every question he could think of about the seafaring life. In his thoughts going to sleep, and in his daydreams, he saw himself steering ships in perilous waters, catching great fish, rescuing people from shipwrecks, (wouldn't it be great if he could rescue Betsy?), visiting all the lands of the earth. He felt greed for sailing adventures that would be his own.

Johnson sat him down in the cockpit one evening after dinner, drew contemplative drags on his Gauloises, and said, "You no have de right opinion about de life of de mariner. It no be interesting ports, nice shipmate, and fun adventure. Can be very dangerous. No because of de sea. But because of shipboard accident. De' happen all de time and kill and maim many sailor. Also, many shipmate get strange and sometime threatening on long voyage. Want to hurt other shipmate. But worst is de monotony. Der nothin to do for long period of time. You have to fight de monotony all de time. It can deaden you mind or make you little crazy. Joseph Conrad sail most of his early life and have it right. *There is nothing more enticing than the sea and there is nothing more enslaving than the sea.*"

Ethan said, "I don't care what Conrad says. I still want to sail all my life. It's the best thing I've ever done."

CHAPTER TWENTY ONE

After Statia they headed for Guadeloupe. The distance was too great to cover in one day and George decided to break it up by anchoring for the night at Long Island, a five mile long island near Antigua.

Ethan was reading *Heart of Darkness.* Johnson sat down next to him.

"I can see you're about two-third through. What do you think of the scene where the poor black dyin under de trees?"

Ethan replied,"Made me want to cry." Then he put his head down, looking away from Johnson, "Really. I did cry some."

"I cry too when I first read it. I cry because what happen der happen all over de Caribbean during slave day. I cry for de Caribbean. What I tell you about Prince Klass in Antigua just as bad as anythin dat went on in de Congo. At least in de Congo black who escape could go off into de bush. And in de American South de' could try and get North. In de Caribbean der be no escape anywhere. All slave island.

"De white in de Congo and them runnin de plantation here de same. Have total control to do whatever de' want to do. Der be no one tellin them no. De' could be as bad as they want, kill, rape, enslave and nobody would care. Or de' could be good. De fact dat so many choose bad rather than good show de evil waitin to come out of men if they allow it." He leaned close to Ethan. "Evil can jump out at any time unless we watch for it and make sure it no happen."

George said from the helm where he'd been listening, "I remember reading *Heart of Darkness.* The bad guy, was his name Kurtz, he was sent to the Congo as a missionary or something, supposed to try and change the barbaric customs of the natives. The book never explains how he sank to evil so fast. Not believable. Wouldn't happen to a Christian. A Christian wouldn't fall so far so fast. You shouldn't have given the book to Ethan. It'll just scare him."

Johnson said with a soft voice, "I disagree. With what Ethan go through with bad people I think it helps him to see others having to deal with evil. And de world be full of example where good Christian men suddenly descend to evil."

George thrust his head belligerently toward Johnson, eye to eye contact, trying to stare him down. Johnson stared back, unblinking, and George found himself straightening up and looked out to sea. He had come to dislike Johnson because Ethan was getting close to him and his dislike was becoming hate.

Entrance to the protected harbor on Long Island was tricky and involved twists and turns, a narrow passage through smoking, wave-crashed reefs. George had Johnson position himself at the bow, guiding him at the helm with hand signals, sometimes requiring him to make abrupt changes to port or starboard to avoid reefs that appeared ahead, barring their long coral teeth at *Rascal*, swirling brown-green and menacing. He nosed ahead at dead slow speed with waves sloshing on reefs on either side, often within yards of *Rascal*, finally made it through, and it was worth it—a very small anchorage area with water just deep enough for *Rascal's* keel, surrounded by a spectacular white coral-sand beach with nary a human footprint.

As they explored it was apparent nobody had been on the island for a very long time. And nobody could easily come onto the island while they were there as they were completely occupying the only safe anchorage. They owned the island. And they owned the lobsters on the reef. The reef had apparently not been fished in years. Johnson harvested three large lobsters in ten minutes, saying there were many more. Also he quickly dove up a mess of conch.

Johnson built a large fire on the beach. The shadows of night marched through the palm trees while Johnson prepared what he promised would be a Caribbean clambake, better than any New England clambake—just-caught lobster, conch stew, and various side dishes including an assortment of island vegetables Johnson had picked up in Statia while George and Ethan were talking to Mag, breadfruit, better than potatoes Johnson said, callaloo, the spinach of the Caribbean, chayote (sometimes called christophere), a pale squash, ackee, tasted like scrambled eggs, bloggoe, a type of banana that required cooking and was great with sugar for desert.

Normally at a lobster feast George found himself gorging as though trying to set the record for how much lobster a human being can consume at one sitting. Lobster was his favorite food. This night he consumed little and sat silently staring at his plate, taking lengthy pauses between bites. Johnson, who had laboriously prepared the meal, looked at him quizzically and asked if he was feeling all right. He waved off the question, walked down the beach, and plopped with his back against a palm tree.

Depression had been weighing on him all day. On the run to Long Island he'd said little, none of his usual banter, none of his usual enthusiasm for what they were seeing, no whistling or calypso songs.

He looked at the unforgiving silent moon. The cold light depressed him more than he was already depressed. He bowed his head, stared at his feet, and muttered to himself, his stomach roiling to the point of almost throwing up in reaction to what had happened.

Two days before while sailing into St. Kitts he'd had a revelation. It was a revelation that should have occurred much earlier. There was no hope for the relationship he wanted with Ethan. Johnson's stories and teachings were bringing a worshipful reaction from Ethan. Nothing like it for him. With him it was gratitude and good camaraderie, but no evidence Ethan was starting to look at him as a second father. Ethan was coming out of his withdrawal. But not coming out of it to be a son to him.

The reciprocal of his love for Ethan, the love of a son for a father, it was just not there. It was a fantasy. The whole dream of Ethan as his son had been a damn fantasy.

How could he have been so stupid for so long? He'd had a month of interaction with Ethan and seen no love. He should have known much earlier. He'd worked hard to get Ethan to open up to him like the boys on the junior high playing field, to get Ethan to let him into his life, his dreams and desires, from there an easy step to love. He'd failed completely. Maybe it was just that Ethan's relationship with his father was so bad he couldn't love any father figure. Friendship yes. Love no. And as for adoption, that was an absurd idea. His father would never consider adoption. He was a church-going man, and no matter how little he cared for Ethan he wouldn't be able to stand the criticism if he adopted out his only son.

With the revelation at St. Kitts had come a feeling of rejection. His love would never be returned. And rejection only intensified his feelings about Ethan, brought them to near desperation. During the days and nights on St. Kitts and Statia all he'd thought about was the boy. Lost hope of love had brought obsession.

Then there was what George sorrowfully called to himself the "language of the night." Looking over from his bunk each night he would see Ethan sleeping, his quiet breathing almost imperceptible, the sweet smell of his adolescence drifting through the cabin, his face open and unprotected, youth and beauty shining in the pale porthole light. He'd been gradually captured by the language of the night.

That's what caused last night, caused what happened. Rejection and then lying there night after night so close to Ethan. Damn it. It'd been horrible, beyond belief. When he went to bed in Statia the preceding night after the meteor shower, he'd watched Ethan undress and fall asleep, then himself half asleep the memory had forced itself upon him, not called by him but forced with evil intent.

Slumping in unhappiness against the palm tree he realized that it had been part of him all along. Somehow he'd kept it from rising to his conscious mind. It'd lain hidden and repressed, pushed out of sight where only an event like his obsession with Ethan could bring it forward. Last night it had burst from its dark hole and come to his bunk in celebration of its release with Ethan very much a part of it.

He was fourteen attending an exclusive summer camp in the Adirondacks. There were eight boys sleeping in Seneca Cabin. At lights out he'd gotten an erection. The thought had come to him that he should show it off. His announcement to the hushed cabin was that he had a surprise underneath his blanket. Would they come over and touch it? Several of the younger boys fell for it. When they came over to his bed he led their hands under the covers to fondle his erection. He'd enjoyed this immensely.

Last night the tentacles of this memory had invaded every part of his mind. He'd pictured Ethan as one of the boys in Seneca Camp fondling him. Tremendously exciting. He'd tried to push the memory back into the cesspool from which it emerged. It wouldn't go. His mind took him to Ethan's smooth round buttocks and the youthful manhood he'd glimpsed in the cabin. He became aroused. Then waking up he'd thought sexually about Ethan all day, continued to get aroused, on the voyage to Long Island he often had to turn away from Johnson and Ethan to hide his erection.

This was stupid. Ridiculous. He shook his head in disbelief. How the hell could the leading citizen of the town, a pillar of the church, a van Rosendahl no less, suddenly find himself with sexual desire for a young teenage boy, particularly one loved as a son. His mind was playing tricks, tricking him into thinking that he had a sexual attraction for young adolescents. No way. He always protected boys and tried to help them. Didn't he go out of his way to help that caddy at the club? And he certainly wasn't a homosexual. The whole thing was preposterous, probably coming from too many long watches. His mind had nothing to occupy itself so was pulling up a lot of garbage. Trust a boat on the high seas to bring to mind every evil thing that a man doesn't want to think about.

He determined that things would be better in the morning. Whenever sexual thoughts came about Ethan he would just force his mind to something else. Shouldn't be too difficult. He had great will power, just a passing infatuation. This would go away like infatuations he had with women in the past. Come morning he was going to get back to being like he was before. Ethan was not going to have his trip spoiled by something so idiotic.

CHAPTER TWENTY TWO

The next day they sailed on to Guadeloupe. George was no longer morose like he'd been the previous day. His usual joking and enthusiasms had returned.

Ethan sat in the cockpit trying to guess from the contours of oncoming waves whether they would break onto the deck. He'd made up many such games to play during the long ocean passages. Sometimes he would challenge the waves at the bow, going forward between waves and seeing if he could dash back fast enough to avoid getting wet. Balancing games, even trying to do handstands against the motion of the boat, not very successful. And many navigation games—-predicting from his calculations when they would be abreast a headland or island, or trying by dead reckoning of time and distance traveled to predict the actual distance traveled as measured by the log streamed behind *Rascal.* George had taught him simple navigation and with his love of math he spent hours playing navigation games.

What he liked to do best he could only do when it wasn't too wild. He'd perch on the bowsprit, holding firmly to the ratlines, and drag his legs in the water as *Rascal* dipped into the waves, spray flying gloriously around him, riding the waves and feeling their strength. Today he grasped the ratlines with one hand, raised an arm high in the air, and called out, "Yahoo." He was a bronco rider. George shouted to him from his position at the helm, "Ride em cowboy," and burst into cowboy song, *"Home, Home on the Range,"* and so on, for considerable time. Later Georg said, "Only boat in the Caribbean with a cowboy riding the ratlines," which brought a delighted laugh from Ethan.

Many days it was just reading. Everybody read during periods when they weren't on the helm and it wasn't too rough, and he had now just about finished *Heart of Darkness.* Intense activity only occurred on leaving a harbor, and in the evening when coming to anchor. The rest of the time was quiet.

Once in a while the quiet was interrupted by a call to activity from the helmsman, "Ready about. Hard-a-lee," when they were tacking east against the trade-wind, and "Prepare to jibe. Jibe-ho," when they were running west before the trade-wind, sailor's cries going back to the sixteenth century or earlier, but this was not often.

George said to Ethan, "Those that sail for only an hour or two on an ocean or lake see a lot of activity when the sailboat approaches or departs from land. They assume sailing is a high activity sport. On long ocean passages it isn't."

One thing he wondered about was why on the passages, and at other times for that matter, George and Johnson never talked about the things people talked about back home—Korea, the Cold War, politics, books, movies, music. The only stuff they ever talked about was sailing and islands. Ethan assumed that George was aware that Johnson knew a lot. Johnson was reading all the time, had told them that during layovers between voyages he studied many subjects, and he kept quoting books. Ethan assumed George didn't talk to Johnson about important things because of what George said on Nevis, that blacks aren't smart and know little. But the thought occurred that maybe George was afraid if they had such conversations Johnson would show he knew more than George did. Whatever it was, when Johnson quoted something, or said something based upon his studies, George would never discuss it, just look at Johnson skeptically.

As they were tacking to come up to Guadaloupe, still way out at sea, a batten flew out from its pocket on the luff (stern part) of the mainsail, the batten a thin two foot long piece of flexible wood essential to steady the mainsail. George said, "Damn. We need that."

Without hesitation Ethan dove over the side, retrieved the batten, and swam back to *Rascal*, which had immediately hove-to, turned into the wind with sails flapping to stop the boat. Johnson jumped over the side and helped Ethan back on board.

George white of face, grabbed him when he came aboard.

"What the hell were you doing? I could have lost you. It would kill me to lose you." A long, loving hug, tears springing from George's eyes. Then George stood there for a few minutes holding Ethan close.

"Promise me you will never, ever leave the boat again on the high seas."

Ethan promised, hung his head, and started to cry along with George. This was the first time he'd been chastised on *Rascal*. Some time passed with Ethan continuing to cry now seated in the cockpit.

George sat next to him and put a comforting arm around his shoulders. "That was stupid, but you were very brave. You were brave in the Anegada Passage. Now here you are brave again. Thank you for bringing back the batten, but no more jumping overboard for battens, understood? Battens jump out. Boys don't jump out."

Ethan nodded.

Johnson then said in a quiet voice, gazing intently into Ethan's eyes as he always did, fingering his cross, "In many place in de world boy can no become a mon until he show he brave. In part of Africa boy have to kill de lion. Here boy need to be brave in de sea to become a mon. You showin you brave in de sea."

Ethan gave them both his widest smile and said, "Thank you," looking each of them in the eyes for a long moment. Then his smile faded as he remembered that the only other time he'd done anything brave, and done it on his own, his escape on the Mohawk river, it had ended up in a vicious beating.

As they came closer to Guadaloupe, George said to Ethan, "I've been to Guadeloupe a number of times, a special place. They call it the butterfly island because of its butterfly shape. Two major volcanos form the wings of the butterfly and a narrow isthmus between forms the butterfly's body. Everything grows there. It's got some of the richest volcanic soil in the Caribbean. Very verdant. Look at the plants and trees when we're ashore. You won't see more different tropical trees, fruits, and vegetables anywhere in the Caribbean. I'll try and give you the names. Or maybe Johnson can."

They put in at Basse-Terre, the northernmost harbor on Guadeloupe, and cleared French customs including for Marie-Galante and Martinique, their next French ports-of-call, customs again an interminable process requiring sacrifice of a bottle of brandy. Right ahead La Grande Soufriere (big sulfur outlet) burst precipitously through a green mantle of tropical foliage to rise 5,000 feet in a series of bare volcanic slopes, its jagged crest capped by a tremendous mass of trade-wind clouds, the highest peak in the Windward and Leeward islands.

When Ethan heard it was an active volcano he went over and stood before George. "Please. Can't we climb it? Back in Niskayuna nobody lets me climb anything."

George agreed. Looking it up and down he said, "That's going to be one hell of a steep climb."

The next morning George said he hadn't slept the night before, that he was trying to work something out of his mind. "I couldn't," he said, shaking his head and looking very unhappy. "Maybe I can work it out with a hard climb."

They filled canteens, packed the lunches Johnson had prepared, and set off early as it was a long hike.

The path pulled them along for a mile or so through fairly level terrain with small farms on either side growing a great profusion of what Johnson said were most of the different vegetables and fruits of the Caribbean. Then the path showed its true colors. Having sucked in the traveler to tread its ways, it abruptly became very steep and narrow with branches poking them from either side as they trudged up. In many places steps were cut in the rock, Ethan thought by someone with very long legs as he sometimes had difficulty ascending from one step to the next. The slope of the volcano rose around them in pleated folds of impenetrable forest, then fell away in deep ravines. Looking back down the steep path Ethan felt if he wasn't careful he could easily tumble all the way back down to where the path had first pulled him upward.

Several times George begged a rest stop and abruptly sat, at one point saying, "I didn't know I was so out of shape." But he never gave up.

And while Ethan found it strenuous, the path eventually compensated for the cruel game it'd been playing. The whole Caribbean became visible to the north, myriad islands, shapes of bright green on deep blue sea, a mighty battle of clouds at the peaks with the losers streaming off downwind in great swirls, the sun bouncing off the ocean in a vibrating pattern from the great waves marching in from the east. They could even pick out Long Island, a green oblong against the larger green of Antiqua. Far below *Rascal* sat at anchor, a toy boat on a sun-glittered sea.

Two thirds of the way up the path decided to show them the geology of the volcano. It drew them into brown volcanic rocks, then brick red, old rose, yellow ochre, saw-toothed waves of lava on either side stained with brilliant colors. Around one bend the path startled Ethan with a group of pointy, sharply etched rocks looking like a band of Indians in full war paint ready to pounce, all red, black, and evil looking. Then higher still a great fissure in the side of the mountain fell away, perhaps 1,000 feet deep, where hot lava had poured on the land below in the last eruption. And even higher still there were cracks in the side of the mountain emitting grayish smoke. The strong sulfur oder made Ethan's eyes water.

All day the path surrounded, proceeded, and followed them with butterflies, butterflies even pursuing them to higher elevations as though they wanted to ensure they found their way. The number appeared to be in the millions. According to Johnson there must have been recent heavy rains. "Rain in de Caribbean bring butterfly in de Caribbean."

This was not a hatch of one species, Johnson said. "Usually only one specie hatch at de time. Nature protect against too many butterfly hatchin at de same time and havin to compete for food. Today look like all de kind hatch at once."

Ethan counted eighteen different species dancing around him, several tiny whites, three different yellows, one with black spots on its wings, two orange, one almost red, then several shades of blue, the largest a deep blue that seemed five inches across. He liked the big blues best.

When they rested beside the trail the butterflies gathered around them, floating to Ethan's yellow and red shirt as though they believed it was the great holy flower of the mountain, resting on his arms, shoulders, hands, even head. Ethan was festooned with butterflies. His eyes brightened in rapt observation as the creatures trembled and fluttered and seemingly vied for his attention with each one slowly flapping its wings to individually display its own full beauty.

Johnson commented he'd never seen anything like this before. Turning to the mountain as though addressing God on Mt. Sinai he loudly cried out, "Thank you, Lord, for all your beauty."

Ethan joined with a strong, "Thank you, Lord."

After hesitating a moment George said in a subdued voice, "Yes. Thank you, Lord."

When the path finally deposited them at the top (George was huffing and puffing from the steepness of the last stretch), Ethan stared across to the other side of the caldera, a distance of more than a mile, seeing lava scorched in shades of black and orange, looking fresh and non-eroded like the fires had only gone out yesterday. He edged gingerly to the rim and looked over. The chasm appeared to go directly down to the center of the earth. It had no bottom. Straight sides all the way. Deep shadow with smoke writhing below. A boulder sat by the side. With Johnson's help Ethan pushed it over the edge. One contact sounded not far below, then nothing. No sound. No bottom. A dark way to the center of the earth. This was really awesome.

But there was no bubbling lava. Ethan had hoped to see lava like in movies where an angry volcano terrifies the natives. His excitement was reignited when they ran into a Frenchman maintaining an observation post on the far rim of the crater. Using his limited French George was able to learn that the Frenchman was a scientist and was stationed at the rim because the volcano was emitting increasingly strong earthquakes, the earthquakes being an indication of a possible upcoming eruption, and that in the last 500 years Soufriere had erupted a number of times.

Ethan practically skipped down the mountain, telling George, "That was really great. We climbed a volcano nearly erupting. Bet no one in Niskayuna did that."

George said, "A lot of things on this trip people in Niskayuna haven't done. But you have."

As dusk settled, and they were finishing their journey, they chanced upon a large clearing where almost 300 people had gathered. All the people were dressed in white. The women had long, flowing white gowns. The men white pants and loose white shirts hanging down over their waists. Most people were black. But whites were sprinkled in. The center of the clearing held a high-banked bonfire.

Around the bonfire some twenty men and women were shuffling in slow step. Their eyes were opened abnormally wide. But Ethan didn't think they were seeing anything. They were all staring vacantly straight ahead, nobody blinking. Occasionally someone stumbled as though drunk. And once in a while one of the women loudly cried out something that sounded very strange and scary. The march was being carried forward by the slow cadence of large, deep sounding drums set up at the edge of the forest, and also the clatter of shaken gourds.

Johnson told them it was a Yoruba initiation ceremony. "People in America no know about de Yoruba religion. It de fifth largest religion in de world after Christian, Islam, Hindu, and Buddha. Be de religion of West Africa. And most of de people in Brazil, Central America, and de Caribbean practice some form of de Yoruba religion. Often de' practice Yoruba alongside Christianity. Even practice behind de scene in de American South like New Orleans. Many different name, many local name. Voodoo in Haiti and much of de Caribbean, Candomble in Brazil and de rest of Latin America, Santeria in Cuba. Confuses people. But all de same religion.

"My mother Yoruba before my father convert her to Christian. In der house de' have big cross on de wall. And in de corner a statue of Yoruba saint. Same in most other house in Freetown. My father okay with it. Jokes, 'You never know.'

"Yoruba religion be fatalistic religion. Believe that de thread of you life woven before you born. In Freetown people go to a Yoruba priestess. She be old hag. Try to find out which way de thread of der life lead, whether to marry, take trip, other thing. Through voodoo de priestess try to find which way de thread lead on big decision.

"God do make plan for every mon. And God make a thread weaving through his life. But God plan unknowable. No found by a Voodoo hag." He shook his head in disgust.

George looked around, "We'd better get out of here. Looks dangerous."

Johnson's replied, "No danger here. Dis be holy place. See all de small fire?"

About thirty small fires circled around the bonfire, all built in shallow pits. They could see offerings were spread around nearby fire pits including food, toys, piles of beads, pictures in frames, and sometimes bottles of liquor.

"Dem be family altar," Johnson said. "People leavin food and other thing by the fire for dem who be dead. If it toys be de child. De food left der goin to rot into de soil and nourish de holy earth. No stray dog goin to ever touch de food, even if de dog be starvin. De Yoruba saint protect de food. De' protect everythin in dis place. Nothing bad can happen to you here. Okay to watch."

Johnson continued and Ethan noticed he was speaking with a low voice as though they were in church. "Those people circling de fire being fed sacred plants to induce de trance. Through de trance de initiate tryin to join with de Yoruba saint, call saint Orishas in de Yoruba religion. De Yoruba initiate believe dat de Orisha spirit come into dem and direct der life. When de' join de Yoruba religion de' hope to be able to communicate with der own Orisha, find out what to do."

George said thoughtfully, "Odd notion to be invaded by a spirit."

Johnson appeared ready to reply. Instead just shook his head.

"Dis ceremony around de fire goin on until dawn. De drums goin to increase in tempo, calling de Orishas. Get more frantic. Create ecstasy in de initiate. Initiate goin to fall by de fire in deep trance. Orisha spirits goin to invade dem. Over and over again initiate goin to loudly call der own Orisha name. And de' goin to start yellin other thing in strange language. Yoruba think them word be prophecy from de Orishas. I hear de words many time. All gibberish."

With the heavy smoke the initiates appeared to be ghosts in their awkward movement around the fire, disembodied in their trances, parts of their bodies disappearing behind shifting curtains of white smoke as though already consumed by Orishas. Above them, the smoke was tendrilling in mysterious patterns through the low, overhanging tree branches, adding power and mysticism to a scene that brought a feeling of otherworldly presences and a belief that what they were seeing had been going on in West Africa for thousands of years, which Johnson said it had.

They walked back to the harbor in solemn step with moonlight scattering silver through the forest and eerie monochromatic light merging everything around them into a single shadow as though the Yoruba ceremony was accompanying them along their way. Nobody said anything and they went to bed with few words spoken.

They laid a course the next day for Saint-Francois on the other end of Guadeloupe. George appeared to be a little glum. The sea, however, was happy.

Some way out from Basse-Terre they were passed by a school of thousands of what Johnson said were short-finned pilot whales, the whales gamboling north across their path. Each was about fifteen feet long. Hours of whales, never deviating in direction for *Rascal* or anything else, diving under *Rascal* rather than going around. They had a purpose. A march of whales to some unknown objective.

This was a day when they trolled fishing lines. Johnson always put out fishing lines when he could, saying to Ethan there was something holy about fishing—-Christ had blessed it. Two fishermen, Peter and Andrew, were the first disciples Christ chose.

Ethan didn't need encouragement to love fishing. Fishing was the best. His parents had never taken him fishing. Now when lines were out he'd watch for hours, hoping for a bite, staring at the lines as they cut through the water, small wakes behind. A fish hooked, he'd rushed to the stern, balancing excitedly from one foot to the other, exclaiming at whatever Johnson hauled in, and even more gleeful if it was a smaller fish and Johnson handed him the line. The first fish he caught in his whole life was a small bonito. About the best thing that ever happened. He held it up on its line, admiring it, twisting it this way and that, and insisted they have it for dinner.

When they were sailing fast they usually only caught barracuda. They would be pulled onto *Rascal*, their jaws gaping, ready to bite. Johnson would bash them dead with a club on the aft deck and wash the blood over the side. It was always a struggle with the barracuda. The lines were not on reels, so pulling in a line was hard hand-over-hand work against the speed of *Rascal*. Ethan loved to eat barracuda, very meaty, his favorite fish. But Johnson wouldn't let them eat barracuda caught near shore. "Barracuda near shore eat de reef fish on de copper reefs and become poison."

When one very large barracuda was laboriously hauled aboard, more than five feet long, Ethan said to Johnson, "Do barracuda eat people? They look very dangerous."

Johnson said, "Lot of people fear to swim when Barracuda around. De' no should worry. Barracuda eat little fish. Only danger be if you wear something glittery, and de water no be clear, de barracuda may think de glitter thing a fish and try and bite it." George pointed to the shiny underwater watch he'd given Ethan. "If a barracuda swims up and asks you the time don't show him that."

Ethan laughed.

The dolphin fish were remarkable. Johnson said they have an ability to change color greater than any other fish or animal in the world. Ethan often saw them swimming close to the surface near *Rascal*, some four feet long, their spectacular dress clearly visible through the crystal water, never exactly the same color, a miracle of color, at times the palest azure, then phosphorescent green, then every shade of blue, electric blues, flashes of gold as they neared the surface, the sea outdoing in color the air with its parrots. The place to catch them was near the sea-bleached rafts of Sargasso Weed they passed. The dolphin fish hid there to wait for prey. Catching them was like catching sun. A series of great leaps with the fish turning from blue and green to gold as it felt the hook, a yellow-gold explosion rising repeatedly from the sea, sunbursts on their fishing lines.

Ethan found sorrow in catching dolphin fish. They were too beautiful to catch, one of the most beautiful things Ethan had ever seen. He said to Johnson, "I can see what you mean about God being in all creatures. Dolphin fish must be God's favorite."

Johnson agreed.

Once caught the dolphin fish changed color through a spectrum of inconceivable blues, greens, and yellows, as though showing the world what it was losing, then quickly turned to somber pearl-grey. Death could not be more visible. Ethan asked George to stop catching dolphin fish. He complied.

As usual they cleaned the fish they caught and threw the leavings over the stern. And as usual this provoked a shark feeding-frenzy. Two smallish Great White sharks, a bunch of Blacktip sharks, and an eight foot Bull shark, which Johnson said was as dangerous as the Great Whites, all roaring back and forth behind the boat. A large Mako shark exploded through the melee, grabbing a hunk of fish and leaping twenty feet into the air.

Johnson exclaimed joyfully, as though seeing a friend, "My favorite shark. De' swim up to fifty mile-per-hour and can jump thirty feet high. But de' can be man-eater. You get no chance when shark swim fifty mile-per-hour."

In the mid-afternoon Ethan returned *Heart Of Darkness* to Johnson. Johnson asked, "Did it scare you? It scare lot of people."

Ethan said, "It was not as scary as when my mother died and my father blamed me. That was for real. I kept reminding myself this was just make believe."

"I no think it would scare you. You brave boy."

Ethan gave him a happy smile.

"Would you like to talk some more about de book?"

"That'd be great."

"Let's talk first bout de characters. Did you see anyone in de book dat seem familiar. Who does de no-good chief of the central station remind you of?"

"My father."

"I thought you'd say dat."

Ethan said with enthusiasm, "And *you* are the good guy, Marlow."

"Thank you, but I no think I could get a steamship up the Congo river through all de peril Marlow face. What about de young Russian adventurer, de man on dat long odyssey through de jungle?"

Ethan said, "Is it me?"

"Yes. You may not know it, but you on a true odyssey across de Caribbean. Have you read *The Odyssey?*

"It was too long to read but our teacher had us read a summary."

"Well, think about dis voyage. You escape from you bad home is like Odysseus escape from burning Troy. And the adventure you having be real, no like *The Odyssey,* and many adventure just as good."

Ethan said, "Really?"

Johnson said, "Really."

An odyssey. He looked away for a moment, then back at Johnson. "Who's the person who gets real bad like Kurtz?"

"He no have appear yet. We hope he never appear. Now, what do you think be de heart of darkness in de book?"

"Africa. Or maybe Kurtz's heart."

"Good thought. Some people think de darkness be de devil. Conrad mention de devil fifteen time in de book. And de barbaric native woman, de native people with der horns, and maybe Kurtz himself, look like follower of de devil. But Conrad never tie what going on to de devil. It would be easy to do dat but he no do dat. He just focus on de darkness. He believe from his own life der be darkness in every mon.

"You notice the book both start and end in London in darkness, start in gathering darkness, end in complete darkness. What Conrad is saying is dat de darkness in not just in de Congo. It everywhere, including big city, everywhere mon is der be darkness to battle. According to Conrad de heart of darkness be de heart of every mon."

Ethan shuddered, looking a little scared.

"No need to fear. What Conrad leave out is dat Jesus come to man. Jesus say, '*I am the light of the world. Whoever follows me will never walk in darkness but will have the light of life.*' And der be moral teachin for those who no believe in Jesus. Blackness do exist in de heart of mon. But most mon successful in fightin it.

"De book do have one important lesson beyond how terrible white men can be to black. Do you think Kurtz was all bad?"

Ethan answered, "He did keep the natives from attacking. And when he died and said 'horror, horror' as his last words he seemed to be saying he shouldn't have done what he did."

"Exactly. Maybe no true for Hitler and Stalin, but most people who do bad also have somethin good about dem. When somebody do somethin bad to you, and de' will, de' already have back in your home town, always try and look for somethin good. It be der."

"I will, and thank you for the book and for explaining it to me. You were right. It's the best book I've ever read."

"Ethan. I proud of you for readin de book to de end. As I tell you, very difficult book even for adult. And remember, where we are in de Caribbean be light. De darkness in the book not going to come here. No worry about it."

Arriving off Saint-Francois they found a dangerous entrance. Waves were rolling directly into the harbor and jumping high over the sand bar at its mouth. Some did not break. But many broke steeply like beach waves, carrying the sound of their very audible crash, and spewing foam half-way to the shore. It looked very intimidating. They had to breast waves at other harbor entrances, the product of the blustery trade-winds this year, but nothing like this.

A discussion ensued as to whether to go elsewhere. Review of the charts showed no other harbors close by, and the alternative harbors farther away had no lighted entrance buoys so they would have difficulty entering at night, which was when they would arrive. Johnson studied the entrance carefully and told them he thought they could make it. He would try to run in on one of the waves between the breakers.

They took down the sails and proceeded under power to a point just outside the area where the waves were cresting. Waves rising and over-toppling ahead of them lifted *Rascal* almost eight feet as they passed under her keel. They sat there a long time waiting for the right moment. Finally Johnson gunned the engine. An incoming wave lifted *Rascal*, the wave breaking slightly under her stern, propelling her forward, tossing her down its face, surfing her forward at a speed that registered on the cockpit speed indicator as almost twelve knots an hour, by far the fastest Ethan had ever seen *Rascal* travel.

Johnson stood with calm concentration, moving the helm back and forth rapidly but delicately, trying to keep *Rascal* from yawing sideways, a death roll in the heavy surf, and trying to keep *Rascal* from burying her bow and pitchpoling end over end as she came down the steep front of the wave.

Finally they were through with Johnson commenting, "Worse than I thought it would be."

George thanked Johnson for getting them through, shaking his hand, the first time George had thanked Johnson for anything since the pirate encounter at Barbuda. Ethan was reminded of riding his sleigh down the steep hill behind his house, only this was much more exciting.

The Saint-Francois pier had a vacant slip allowing them to tie there for the night. Ethan set out a bowl of sugar water as he always did when they were at dock. The objective was the yellow birds of the Caribbean, wren sized, nectar eating, their breasts as bright yellow as any yellow Ethan had ever seen. Sometimes they came, sometimes they didn't. This time they came. First a single bird, bravely venturing into man's domain but timid in its approach as it gingerly advanced toward the bowl, a little way forward, then skittering back in momentary fear, then a little more forward, and so on until finally the bird received its reward for bravery, dipping its beak into the sugar water.

Other birds were observing. Ethan thought they monitored each other's success in food discovery. Less timid now that one had survived man's world, they approached the sugar water with resolve. Then more participants in the feast, then more, then more. Soon yellow birds were hopping all over the deck, talking delightedly to each other about finding sugar water, vying for the best position. A convention of sunshine chirping its way forward.

Ethan had never seen so many of these birds he loved so much. They moved toward the dish on mass, then for no apparent reason they would move off a bit, then back again, making a pulsating pattern of yellow on the deck he was sure was just to delight him. He threw his arms wide and loosed a delighted laugh, startling the birds.

They decided to lay over the next day at Saint-Francois so that Johnson could tune up the engine. They would need it working perfectly to break out to the open ocean through the heavy surf at harbor entrance. Johnson's work completed before noon, they went in to town and to the market.

Next to the market loomed a hill, largely denuded of vegetation, and upon it about twenty boys had congregated to fly kites. George went over with Ethan to see what the boys were up to, and discovered they were playing an island Creole game called "Coo-pay." At a signal from one of the boys, all would cut their kite strings and allow their kites to blow free. Then it was a race to see who could collect his kite and get back first to the starting point. The boys held up the start of play for a few minutes so that George could buy Ethan a kite from a nearby kite vendor. They played most of the afternoon with a new game starting after kites were collected from the prior game.

Ethan had a disadvantage over the local boys. While he was trying to figure out which way the wind would take his kite the local boys were already off and running. Experience counted. Also, some of the local boys turned out to be exceptional tree climbers. Many a kite ended up in a tree. Ethan boosted up his share of trees and had the scratches to prove it. Caribbean trees turned out to be a lot different from the apple trees back home.

Ethan never won but felt he'd done all right as he still had his kite at the finish. The kites of five of the local boys were irretrievably lost. What a great discovery. Language differences don't matter when you're having fun.

Back at the market Ethan found Johnson waiting for him. He needed to pee and Johnson sent him around a shed to find a spot. The man he came upon had his pants down and was moving vigorously on top of a woman. She had her red calico skirt up around her shoulders and was moaning.

Ethan retreated and told Johnson, "There's a man there hurting a woman."

Johnson spied around the corner and said, "Naw. De' just be makin love." He cocked his head and smiled at Ethan, "You know about makin love, right?"

Ethan cast his eyes down and said shyly, "Maybe a little."

"You father no tell you where baby come from, or de boy at school no talk about makin love to girl?"

"No. My father never talked to me about it and the boys at school never talk to me about anything."

"Well, you no know about de best part of bein alive. Go over der and piss. Come back to dis bench and we talk."

When Ethan returned Johnson asked, "You ever have an ejaculation, dat when de sperm, wet stuff, come out de end of you penis?"

Ethan felt himself blushing bright pink. "It might have happened the other night. I was dreaming about Betsy Sommers. I woke up and my penis was real hard and there was some wet stuff like you said."

Johnson said, "De' call dat a wet dream. Every mon have it. Means you becomin a mon. You should be proud you old enough to have a wet dream."

Ethan felt encouraged by this assurance as he hadn't known what to make of it.

"Now to de baby thing," Johnson said. "Woman have a slit between her leg so mon can make de baby. De mon penis get hard like you penis when you have de wet dream. Then de mon push his penis into de woman slit and move it back and forth. This cause de mon to ejaculate inside de woman." Johnson then explained how the sperm fertilized the woman's egg. "Now de good part. God want many baby. So he set up love makin as de most joyful thing a mon and woman can do on dis earth. It be a wonderful present from God to mon. When I make love to my Rebecca I feel God surround me with his love. He bringin me a little piece of his heaven.

"Okay. So now you know how to do it. But no just go and try and do it with any woman. Dat how some men get into terrible, terrible trouble. You need to wait for de right woman, someone you know real well and want to be with de rest of you life. If you wait de joy you goin to have in makin love to dat woman is de greatest joy you goin to have in you whole life."

. . .

George was definitely not having joy. What was going on? This was unbelievable. Ever since Long Island he'd awakened every morning with the hope that sexual desire for Ethan had disappeared. Watching Ethan dress in the morning, seeing his nakedness, his sexual desire had only intensified. He'd tried to keep projecting cheerfulness to Ethan. Difficult. Concern had taken over. Everything that made him civilized was being stripped away—intellectual conversations back home, the theater and opera, his role in town, even his Christian marriage, did they mean anything? Was it all just a thin veneer over lust for boys? God damnit. Couldn't be. But try as he might to control his desire, he hadn't succeeded. What could be worse than desiring a boy? Monstrous. It was driving him crazy. Stop thinking about Ethan. *Stop it!* He slapped himself twice on the side of the head, hard, saying aloud in a strong voice, *"Get the hell out."* Ethan, standing some distance away on the dock, looked at him with surprise.

But it didn't get out. That night he had an erotic dream about Ethan, he feared the first of many. It made him feel filthy inside and out. As soon as it was light enough to find and crawl back up the swimming ladder he dove overboard, scrubbing himself unmercifully with the salt water soap as though scrubbing his body would scrub his mind. Still shaken at breakfast the next morning, he doubled up on the special coffee he always prepared for himself. Then he set a precedent by insisting on brewing a third cup, slightly delaying their departure to the next island, Marie-Galante.

...

Leaving the Saint-Francois harbor was not as bad as entry, but difficult nonetheless. To secure maximum power they put up all their sails, and with a strong wind behind, and full power from the tuned-up engine, they succeeded in crashing through the breaking waves into the open ocean.

George had not been to Marie-Galante before. Johnson said it was a flat island with the chimneys of one hundred or more old sugar mills spread across the landscape, reminders of the the terrible slave plantations the French had run there.

"De French de cruelest," Johnson said..

Passing the southern tip of Guadeloupe on the way to Marie-Galante they entered the open sea. Waves ten to fifteen feet high were sweeping in from the port side across *Rascal's* course. George said to Ethan, "Waves are messengers. They're telling us about a big storm somewhere, probably off the African coast. Nothing between us and Africa. Storms push waves a long way.

"Are you aware that waves don't move?"

Ethan shook his head.

"Well they look like they're moving toward us, right? But they're not. It's an optical illusion. The water's just humping up and down in the same place. Did you ever shake out a bed sheet with your mother and watch the sheet billow up and down?"

Ethan nodded.

"That's how waves work. Think of the sea as a bed sheet. The wind is billowing the water but it's not moving it. Just going up and down like your mother's sheet."

Johnson leaned over and said, "Jack London have another example. Think of throwin de pebble into some pond. De ripple be a little wave and spread in de circle. If wave move water then der be de hole in de middle of de circle where you throw de pebble. No happen. Wave no move water."

As they came in sight of Marie-Galante George continued, "Waves bounce. You see those high cliffs over there?"

Ethan looked carefully at the cliffs and nodded.

"Look at what the waves are doing. They're hitting the cliff and bouncing back on top of de incoming waves. A double wave. Very dangerous for a boat. We're staying well off shore."

...

Ethan had moved forward, coiling lines on the port side. Johnson manning the helm, watched him. Ethan was clearly growing stronger physically. He was putting some real heft into tailing the lines. And he was getting stronger psychologically. When he came aboard the boy was almost absent in personality, turned inward so much that he completely ignored the world around him. Now he was interacting, talking without restraint, greeting people in the markets, exclaiming over new things,

His own boys' personalities had developed gradually as they grew older, there was a step-by-step progress to who they were and who they were going to be. With Ethan it was all coming in a rush. The man he was to be seemed to be practically erupting out of the boy, like a flying fish leaping from sea to shine in the sunlight. Johnson was fascinated. In his experience on Antigua he'd never had occasion to watch the progress of a damaged boy. Blacks never allowed boys to become this damaged.

What was Ethan going to be like when the voyage completed? Was he going to have a generous, outgoing nature, trying to help people, or was his trauma going to cause him to reject people, do nothing except for himself? And how would he use his obvious intelligence? Would he use it to gain advantage over people in revenge for what happened to him, or use it to better understand other people and the world around him? Worst of all, would he *never* fully come out of his protective shell, remain damaged all his life?

Johnson snubbed out his Gauloises and concluded that the progress was good. He would continue to do everything possible to help Ethan develop in the right way, but with what Ethan had gone through the outcome was still very unclear. There was no way to know which way the fish would fly.

CHAPTER TWENTY THREE

When they anchored in the harbor of Marie-Galante, Johnson pointed out a shark-processing station operating on the longest pier of the harbor. To Ethan the sad array of tail-hung sharks on the dock looked like dead men on a gibbet in a Western movie, and he didn't get happier when he learned it was being done for the sole purpose of harvesting shark fins. Johnson said to Ethan, "Rich men eat shark fin because de' think eatin them help in makin love to women. Dat stupid. And they order shark fin soup in restaurant, very expensive, showin off to der friend how rich de' be. All de rest of de shark you see der get thrown away. Many rich people like dat, waste de wonderful thing God put on earth." He glanced at George who responded with an angry frown.

Johnson continued, "You goin to be rich one day, Ethan. No waste what God give."

Ethan ginned and said, "I won't."

Later the three of them visited a small town near their anchorage and then walked some distance into the countryside. Simple houses were set along peaceful lanes shaded by flowering trees of many colors. Commerce was being conducted with old-fashioned, high-sided bullock-drawn carts, the produce of the fields going toward town in sleepy plod while highly piled loads of sugarcane went in the other direction to the few mills still in operation.

George remarked that the pastoral scene made him feel they had stepped back in time. "It looks like paintings of rural eighteenth-century France I saw in Paris museums."

There was a quiet about everything they'd not seen on any other island. The whole island was at rest.

Ethan noticed that they were not getting friendly greetings from inhabitants as was the custom on other islands. Numerous women passed walking toward town in clouds of bright red, orange, and blue garments, baskets on their heads or a large satchel in hand, small children being carried in slings or dragged along. The women gave them hard looks or looked away, refusing to acknowledge their presence. And he had not seen any other white people, even in town. Nonetheless the trudge ahead continued. George said he wanted to show him a sugar mill.

When they finally arrived at a working mill, the workers ignored them, did not invite them to see the process, and talked among themselves, staring furtively at them, unwelcoming glances. George said he was not going to be put off after the long hot walk, took Ethan's elbow, and started into the mill to explain the workings. Lounging against a fence was a group of young men and women, apparently without work and with nothing better to do, plainly angry at their presence judging by their hard looks.

One very thin woman, almost as tall as George, launched herself from the fence and strode boldly over to them, her face contorted with rage, said something loudly in the local patois, and spat at George's feet. George hunched his shoulders forward as though to hit her. The young men immediately came over, looking belligerent. George spun Ethan quickly around, and they retreated the way they came in, but not before George had grabbed a stalk of sugar cane for Ethan to suck on during the walk back.

After they'd proceeded some distance George asked Johnson, "What the hell's going on?"

Johnson apologized for not warning them, saying he didn't know that things had gotten so bad on Marie-Galante since his last visit. "Partly it about slavery. Remember I tell you de plantation here de worst. De people of Marie-Galante remember, too. In Anguilla de people very friendly as de' never have much slavery der. Here very different, and they remember. De' never like white people much on Marie-Galante. And they particularly hate de French. De' think de French take from de island and never give anythin back. During de war, and even after de war, de French and English take everything de' can out of de islands. Take de men and kill dem in de war. Take most of de food. And then after de war take what left. Now I think dat people here hate de French even more. People starvin. You see how thin everybody is? No fat people. Scarecrows."

He shook his head. "De' blame de French for de starvation. De' angry at you because de' think you French. No white come here but French. So de' think you French. De' no want French here."

George said that next time he'd wear an American flag.

They cut short their stay ashore because of the inhospitable atmosphere, and George took the opportunity to start his drinking early.

George's drinking had been part of the daily routine on *Rascal,* though not beginning so early. Each evening he'd pull out the bottle of brandy, usually Remy Martin, but he drank all brandies. He would ceremoniously announce, "I'll take the whip," and drink down a brandy and soda, sometimes slowly and sometimes fast.

Then again, "Better be whipped again," and then sometimes a third. He'd laugh about the whip. It had to do with a story George had heard somewhere about sailors on English Men-of-War being given brandy after a whipping.

After a few whips George would sometimes put his arm around Ethan as they sat in the cockpit, a friendly gesture of father to son. Ethan would eventually try and pull away. Johnson would often appear at these moments and stare sternly at George. George would then desist until the next time.

As afternoon progressed they realized that in their hurried departure from the island they'd forgotten to buy the denatured alcohol they needed for the cooking stove. No alcohol, no dinner. Johnson rowed in to secure the alcohol, something that would take quite a while as, once ashore, Johnson would have to walk to the general store in the next bay.

George had already had five or six whips. When Johnson rowed off, Ethan found himself quickly hustled below decks and seated on a bunk next to George with George's arm around his shoulders.

George turned to him, his face close to his, and said slowly and with a tender look in his eyes, "I love you Ethan. I love you very much. It's terrible what happened to you with your mother. I want to help you and love you. I want to take care of you for a long time. Do you love me?"

Ethan gave no answer and tried to squirm away.

"Please try and love me. If you love me I can help you. I can make everything bad go away. Just give me your love, and I promise everything bad will go away."

George paused, staring at him, and Ethan turned his body away. Love was how he felt about his mother. Not this. He liked George. He was one of the few adults who'd been kind to him. And he was drawn to the offer of love. No one had offered him love in a very long time. No one had embraced him and tried to comfort him for the loss of his mother.

He was abruptly pulled back to face George who started kissing him on the face, caressing his face, pressing his body against his, putting his hand on his bare legs and running it up and down. George was now pleading, "Please let me love you, Ethan. It will only be for a little while. Then I'll stop. I'll stop whenever you want. We can do things together. You'll like it. I promise."

This went on for some minutes. Ethan did not know how to react, did not know what was going on, went rigid, trying all the time to push away George's hands on his legs and body, and ducking his kisses. George started trying to loosen Ethan's pants.

Ethan shoved George away, bolted up, and said in a scared voice, "I don't want to do this any more. Please."

George stood too, grabbed Ethan by the arms in a powerful grip, and backed him against the companionway ladder. Then in a hoarse voice,

"I'm not going to hurt you. All I want to do is touch you. I couldn't hurt you. I love you. Just touching. Nothing more. We touch each other. I touch you and you touch me. Simple. Just relax. Sort of a game. You'll enjoy it."

George began stripping off Ethan's clothes. He unbuttoned Ethan's shorts and pulled them half way down while holding him pinned against the stairs. Ethan did not struggle much. Just kept saying, "Don't." George then grasped Ethan's shirt with his right hand and started pulling it over Ethan's head while starting to fondle his genitals with his left hand. With George's hands no longer gripping his body, Ethan lunged sideways, striped out of the shirt leaving it hanging in George's hands, rolled off the companionway ladder, raced to the bow and up the forward hatch, dove to safety off *Rascal,* and swam to the nearby beach where Johnson left the dingy.

· · ·

When Johnson returned to the beach he found Ethans sobbing, Ethan told him the story and showed him the red marks on his arms. Johnson rowed them back to *Rascal,* the oars creating one long explosion of water. Once aboard he grabbed George by the arm, threw him down to his knees on the deck, banging him hard against the cabin top and causing a loud cry of pain, then stood over him with his fists clenched debating whether to beat the hell out of him. Instead he dragged George forward out of reach of Ethan's hearing, again throwing him down to the deck, his voice choked with anger, spitting out each syllable, "I should turn you over to de police. What you did have very big criminal penalty in de islands, life in prison. I love to see you rot in prison."

George put up his hands in a gesture of supplication. "Please. I was drunk. I don't even remember what I did. I was just trying to be loving to him, to make up for the loss of his mother. Somehow something happened and I got carried away. I promise it will never happen again. I'll never touch him again. He's like a son to me. I could never hurt him."

Johnson stood over George, teeth bared like a wolf on its prey, growling like ready to rip him apart. "Being drunk no excuse. You just use de drink to hide behind so you could do what you want to him." Johnson paused and stepped back a half step, looking George up and down with disgust, shaking his head. "I no want Ethan to have to go back home, at least not yet. Home be terrible and he makin good progress here. Sendin him home now would be worse for him then keepin him on de boat with you. But I want you to understand what goin to happen if you touch Ethan again." Johnson again moved closer to George, his clenched fists close to his head. "I goin to beat you within an inch of you life. Maybe beat you to death. If you still alive I goin to turn you over to de police. Do you understand?"

George nodded.

Johnson said, "Say it."

"Yes. I understand that if I touch Ethan again I will be severely beaten and turned over to the police."

"Now go back and apologize to Ethan."

. . .

Ethan cringed as George shambled toward him with his head bowed down and tears in his eyes. "I did a terrible thing. I'm sorry. More than sorry. It was the worst. I don't really remember it. Too much alcohol. That's no excuse. I shouldn't have drunk so much. Drink makes you crazy. It makes you black out. It puts to sleep the part of the brain which keeps you from doing bad things. That part of me was asleep. It was as though somebody else was with you. Somebody else was there. It wasn't me. I love you, Ethan. I wouldn't ever hurt you.

"I'm never going to do anything like this again. I promise you. And I promised Johnson here."

Ethan did not understand it. Something seemed to be seriously wrong with George.

...

Late that night George slumped on the foredeck, again under the cold moon, and placed his back against the mast, hiding his face from Johnson and Ethan. He examined his hands, turned them over, held them up—brown, callused from sailing, a small cut on his right knuckle from a knock against the mast. These hands had tried to force Ethan into sex. He clamped his jaw together as hard as he could and clawed his hands so much that his nails were cutting into his palms, almost like when facing the dentist's drill he would claw his hands into his legs to create another center of pain to divert from the drill pain. This pain was much greater.

He felt like something inside him had cracked open, unbidden, spewing out the most loathsome thing imaginable.

He played what he remembered over and over in his mind. He knew he'd been drunk. But what had he intended? To rape Ethan? Did he really intend to rape Ethan? That could not be no matter how drunk he was. He loved Ethan.

He knew he wanted to have him naked, to touch Ethan and have him touch him. He remembered thinking Ethan might like it. He remembered thinking he wanted to control Ethan sexually. He needed to control Ethan sexually. His need for control had somehow merged with sex, needing to control a boy for sex. Be able to command him to do whatever sexual thing he wanted, no matter how sick. Would that have led to more than touching? Would he have moved on to penetration? Was he that perverted? " He moaned loudly.

It was bad enough to suddenly find he had homosexual desires. But a homosexual attack on a young teenager? This was the most unforgivable perversion in the world. The fact that he loved Ethan turned it into pure horror.

"God help me. God help me."

CHAPTER TWENTY FOUR

The next morning at breakfast, a sleepless night, George repeated the apology to Ethan. "I was drunk. I didn't know what I was doing."

Ethan turned his head away and tried to make sense of it. Couldn't. George had kept saying he loved him. Then he did the opposite, hurt his arms, tried to undress him, grabbed at his penis, played rough. What was going on? A complete change from the man who said he wanted to be his father, his buddy. Scary. Did drinking a lot of brandy make people that crazy? Or maybe it was something he'd done, though he couldn't think of anything.

All morning he stayed as far from George as possible, difficult on a small boat. It was an unhappy *Rascal* that headed off to the English island of Dominica, their next port-of-call.

Johnson said Dominica was the wildest and most mountainous island in the Windwards, and the most spectacular. He described it in great detail. Ethan remained subdued, looking at his feet while Johnson talked, lapsing into the silence of earlier in the voyage, afraid the "bad times" might be coming back.

By afternoon Ethan started to regain some interest in the world around him. He was standing near the bow. It was a magnificent sailing day. Fair trade-wind on the beam. Not too strong. The sun beat on him. He couldn't help but feel happiness started to creep in despite the night before.

Water erupted next to him on the starboard bow. The head of a great whale appeared. Slowly the whale rose to the surface, swimming lazily along next to them, not giving attention to their presence, then spouted vigorously, almost fifteen feet into the air, fishy smelling mist drifting down on him.

George raced below decks and appeared with the M-1. He walked to the rail as though in some sort of state, a kind of trance, his face expressionless, eyes looking neither left nor right, saying nothing. He abruptly shouldered the rifle and fired the full clip into the whale. Then he quickly reloaded and fired another clip into the whale. The whale let out a horrible low moan Ethan would always remember. It slowly sank beneath the surface trailing blood.

Tears formed in Ethan's eyes and ran down his cheeks.

Johnson strode over to George, grabbed the rifle out of his hands, and pushed him hard so he fell against the cabin top. "Very, very bad thing. De whale de greatest of God creature. If you have no reverence for de whale, you have no reverence for God."

George slunk back to the cockpit and sat with his head between his hands, gaze cast down to the cockpit floor, occasionally shaking his head as though trying to escape his thoughts.

. . .

Johnson regained the helm and lit a Gauloise, observing George and thinking about what had gone on. He became certain he knew. It had to be the devil. Things like the attack on Ethan and on the whale didn't occur without the devil being involved. Devil's work.

The devil had come aboard Rascal.

The devil had probably sunk his claws into George's soul way back in Niskayuna. George had brought it along. Now it had emerged, directing George's actions. From experience, Johnson knew that once the devil establishes itself inside a man it settles in.

Johnson decided then and there he needed to warn Ethan about the devil. He seated Ethan next to him by the helm where Ethan could hear him over wind and waves. Then talked loudly so George could also hear him.

"Sometimes a mon do somethin stupid and hurt himself or somebody else. Dat an accident. But when a mon do somethin bad on purpose, or do it because he angry or upset, then de devil involve. Most bad thing on earth done by de devil. John say in de Bible dat sin come from de devil. De devil be everywhere fightin God for de soul of people on earth. He de principal enemy of mon on earth. People need to fear de devil as much as de' love God. Does your minister at home warn about de devil in his sermon?"

"Never."

Johnson continued, "I think not. In de past minister warn people about de devil. But dat scare people off. People stop goin to church. People stop givin money to church. So de ministers stop talkin bout de devil, and hell, and damnation, and scary thing. Now der sermon be only about God and how to be good Christian."

He took a deep drag on the Gauloise, "Big mistake. De devil still be here whether de minister talk about him or no. De minister help de devil by no talkin about him. De devil cunnin. He able to do more evil when people no know he around. He like to hide dat it be he dat doin de bad thing. He let everybody think dat it people dat be doin de bad thing when really him.

"Many people do de devil work because de minister no remind em dat de devil exist. People forget dat de devil exist. A mon can't fight de devil if he no know de devil exist. And no defense being a good mon. De devil most like to enter a mon who think he be good mon. Easy for de devil to trap de mon into bad thing if de man no believe in de devil and think he be good mon." He glanced at George.

Ethan said, "The devil is scary."

"Yes. He feed on de darkness in men."

"Like in *Heart of Darkness?*"

"Right. Like in *Heart of Darkness*. I want you to pray to have God protect you from de devil. Each night in you prayer ask God to protect you from de devil and all his work."

Ethan said, "I promise." Then after a moment, "Can the devil get into boys?"

Johnson answered, "Yes. De devil can get into adult and de adult get a boy to do bad thing so the devil get into de boy, too. Dat why I want you to pray."

George was still sitting hunched in the cockpit. He scowled darkly at Johnson, and declared in a loud and self-assured voice, "I don't believe in the devil."

Johnson shook his head with a look of sorrow.

...

Dominica was as spectacular as Johnson had promised. In the approach the mountains looked different from other islands. The green of the foliage was so dark that it looked black in places, stark, forbidding, the mountains gobbling light from the shining sea and sky so that the island seemed in shadow even in the bright sunlight, and waves pounded savagely against cliffs all along the shore with a reverberating roar heard many miles off to warn visitors away. It looked to be a very unhappy and unwelcoming island. They anchored in the harbor of Roseau, the capital of Dominica, and when Ethan got ashore he found that even many of the birds were black.

Ethan got happier when they visited spectacularly lofty and boisterous waterfalls with pools below inviting diving from rocks and back-floating in forested luxury. He got happier still when he was told by a shopkeeper that there were real Indians on the island, Carib Indians. The shopkeeper explained that the Carib Indians had come up from South America 500 years ago, fiercely slaughtering the peaceful Arawak Indians who had been living on Dominica for more than 1,000 years, and that the Caribs had been cannibals. The shopkeeper added, "The word cannibal came from the word Carib."

"Real Indians! Cannibals! Please. Can we see them?"

George was not enthusiastic, but he talked to some people in authority and a trip to a Carib village was arranged.

First the three of them had a rough jeep ride. Then it turned out the path to the Carib village they had been told about was really a jungle trail. They had to constantly climb over rocks and fallen logs, and at one point had to steeply ascend 1,000 feet or more and then descend just as steeply. On either side of the trail were great walls of vegetation, an exuberant and overgrown mass of trunks, branches, leaves, and boughs in riotous obstruction of their progress, reaching out and trying to block their way, roots tripping them as they walked, low trees forcing them to bow down to nature. They ducked through tunnels of twisted branches painted green with moss and pushed aside predatory vines trying to ensnare them from above and below. Small streams sometimes ran down the middle of the trail, meaning detours through thick jungle growth. And one larger stream blocked their way and had to be waded with everyone's shoes held aloft.

Ethan had a strong feeling that nature on Dominica did not want man traveling through its primeval forest, at least not on the trail they hiked. The trail was deliberately making things difficult.

After two and one half hours they entered a hidden, tangled-green valley. Palm-fond roofed huts appeared, each set in orderly fashion in a way Ethan later learned had been carefully planned to bring cooling breezes into each hut while giving privacy to residents.

Striding briskly toward them as they entered the village was a man who introduced himself as the chief, Rala Aute, a commanding presence despite his small stature (shorter than Ethan). Well beyond middle-aged, compact in body, remarkably smooth, wrinkle-free round face, light tan complexion, and strikingly narrow slanted eyes. All the Caribs gathered around had the same slanted eyes.

Chief Aute was dressed in a collared white loose-fitting long-sleeved shirt, tightly fitting tan pants, polished calf-high boots, and on his head a narrow-brimmed store-bought straw hat. He spoke excellent English with a British accent and came up to them smiling. After the introductions he said, "We don't have many visitors and are always happy to show off what we've accomplished here." As they strolled around the village he continued, "What you see is pretty much how we lived in the old days. Same houses. Same food. We've chosen not to take the English ways.

"The real name of our people is Kalinago. Not Carib. That's the white man's name for us. And we call the island Waitikubuli, meaning 'Tall is her body,' because of the 5,000 foot mountain peaks.

"I am the shaman of the village as well as the chief, called a buyeis in Carib. Our religion derives much from the Mayan religion. We used to trade with the Mayans, many of the same gods. Our God of evil is called Hurican, Hurakan in the Mayan religion, and that's what the word Hurricane comes from. Like the Mayans, our worship involves the spirits that are in all things, wild things and humans, even inanimate things like trees. People like us who live close to nature know about the spirits. The American Indians knew about them. And the Shinto worshipers in Japan still know them. Christianity and Islam came out of the desert so forest spirits aren't included. Those religions deny their people knowledge of spirits that could help them."

He continued his lecture, showing them the various houses and a meeting hall where he said they had religious services.

"The Mayans believed the world was created by twin gods who drove out darkness and evil. We believe the same. Our twins are Tamosi and Pia, the

Mayans Itzam and Chebel. Through our religious practices we try to keep the darkness and evil from coming back. Each day we celebrate dawn as the triumph of light over darkness. Most Mayans have abandoned their old gods. We continue, and we believe we are keeping the darkness away not just from us but the whole world. We and a few Mayans we are the only ones left keeping the darkness away. If we didn't pray as we do the whole world would be enveloped in darkness and evil."

Ethan said, "Does that mean you are fighting darkness in people?"

"Yes, exactly, but also the whole world."

Wow. Something. Fighting with the darkness he'd experienced. How wonderful to run into these people.

The chief took them inside one of the larger house which he said was his own, simply furnished inside with cushions on the floor where the chief said they ate.

"The spirits of our ancestors are very important to us. They protect us. Until recently we kept the bones of ancestors under our houses for our protection. This house used to be loaded up with ancestor bones, some of them hundreds of years old. We used to keep them until the bones disintegrated."

Ethan shuddered. What would it be like at home if people kept the bones of ancestors in their homes? And what about his mother?

Chief Aute went on to state his conviction that the Kalinago way of life was better and more healthy than that of the rest of the island —no hard drink and no bad foods, and most important, no bad relationships among people.

"And the whole tribe decides things, everybody is equal. The rule that we live by is that no one is to cause offense to anyone else in the tribe. We have none of the competition and strife you see among Europeans and among blacks."

Ethan pictured Niskayuna operating that way. What a change it would be. Niskayuna sure was a long way behind the Caribs.

"Our medicine is better, too. We have over 200 herbs we use both as curatives and preventives. We were able to cure everything until the Europeans came and tried to kill us with their smallpox. Look around and see how well and content we are." He waved a hand to take in the people standing around, watching them. Ethan saw that like the chief, all the villagers, even the old people, appeared to be extremely healthy, and their faces were not wrinkled and careworn as were those in black villages Ethan had visited.

Chief Aute then took them to a hut where they kept artifacts of the past, including examples of the five foot tall longbows they'd used effectively against European invaders.

Ethan, fascinated by it all, asked what he had wanted to ask all along, "Were you cannibals?"

Chief Aute came right up to him, looked him over from head to foot, and said with a ghoulish grin, "We certainly were. And we particularly liked young boys. They're nice and tender, not tough like old people."

Ethan drew back, eyes wide.

The chief laughed, his slanted eyes closing in mirth. "In the old days we only ate a small part of a few of our enemies, a ritual offering to our gods. It was all ceremonial. The Europeans thought that was terrible. The Caribs thought the Europeans were two-faced as they ate body and blood in their religious ceremony.

"Things changed when the Spanish invaded, and later the French and English. We pretended to roast and eat prisoners, to tell the truth we actually did eat some." He said the last quietly looking away. "All we were trying to do was to scare them off. Didn't work. But we sure scared them."

Then he related an old tale, "In the 1600s a Spanish friar came to Dominica. We ate him, and then we all got sick. After that, the story goes, the Spanish put friar's clothing on their sailors before they came ashore on Dominica, just in case."

Another legend that the chief delighted in telling was that the Caribs found the Spanish stringy and grisly, as opposed to the French, who were rather delicious, and the English who tended to be rather tasteless. Chief Aute licked his lips, smiled broadly, and said, "Actually I always found the English to be quite tasty," looking Ethan up and down.

Chief Aute was laughing the whole time he told these stories, watching Ethan's reaction. Then he got serious, "We are very proud we were never conquered, the only Indians in the Caribbean that were never conquered. When the Spanish came the Caribs drove them out of all the Carib islands from Trinidad to Guadeloupe. Then the French and English came and tried to enslave us. We fought a guerrilla war with them on Dominica for 150 years.

Finally a truce, and in 1903 a large part of the island was permanently set aside for us as our country, our nation. We were never conquered. Where you stand has been an Indian nation for over 1,000 years."

At the end of their visit chief Aute chanted over a shell amulet and gave it to Ethan. "As long as you keep this you will have good luck."

Ethan thanked him profusely for the visit and the amulet, immediately put the amulet around his neck, and held it up to admire.

...

As they were starting to leave George found himself motioned aside by chief Aute, out of hearing of Ethan and Johnson. The chief talked with knitted brow and obvious great concern.

"I can sometimes sense things. That is why I am shaman. I can sense something with you. Something bad has come into you. Be very careful."

George, badly shaken, joined the others.

The last thing Chief Aute called to them as they started down the trail was, "Remember, we were never conquered."

On the way back George saw a shabbily dressed man selling the Sisserou parrots of Dominica. The man had confined a number, large birds, in primitive, brutally small wicker cages. Johnson went up to the man, stood with his face only inches from his, and said with an angry voice, "These bird very rare. It against de law to capture them. How can you put these beautiful bird in terrible small cage? It be an insult to God. You ought to be thrown in jail."

The man hung his head and said dejectedly, "My family be starvin."

Johnson walked away fuming, saying to George and Ethan, "No his fault. Fault of de English. De' no protect what God give them in de Caribbean, and de' let people starve. Take care of de poor in their English city but no give to poor here cause poor here be black."

George strode over to the man, and after some bargaining purchased all the parrots. George had Ethan set them free, which he could see made Ethan very happy, a small propitiation for his sins. Maybe God would notice.

Later he was standing alone by the quay waiting for Johnson to retrieve the oars for the dingy. Johnson always hid the oars when they came ashore to prevent the dingy from being stolen.

Ethan came up to him and said, "Thanks very much for taking me to the Caribs. I want you to know I'm very sorry for what happened to you at Marie-Galante. Maybe I shouldn't have told Johnson. I can see you are very sad."

Startled, he took Ethan by the shoulders, held his gaze, and said with as much sincerity as he could muster, "No, Ethan. Believe me, nothing is your fault. You did everything right. It was all my fault on Marie-Galane. I'm sorry I scared you. Stupid. It won't happen again. I want you to be very happy, Ethan. And I do love you despite what I did. Remember that okay."

Ethan said, " Yes. Okay," as it was what George wanted him to say, but doubted George loved him after what happened.

That night after diner, anchored in the harbor, George went to the bow and stood braced against the forestay, looking down at the water. Fish occasionally plopped at the surface, rising for night insects, and a soft warm wind was confusing the sea around *Rascal*, lapping small waves quietly against the bow. Then adding to the beauty, a low, brilliant evening star appeared in the west, casting a narrow silver path on the sea. A splendid backdrop for prayer, and pray George did.

As a member of the vestry he was used to saying repetitive prayers in church. But he'd never seriously prayed about anything until now. Over and over again he asked God to change his feelings about Ethan, to cleanse him of his desire, to forgive him for what he tried to do to Ethan. No relif. It was as though his prayers were being blocked. He had a conscious feeling that something had erected a barrier between him and God. Something was making it impossible for him to reach God in prayer. All his prayer was doing was to focus his mind more strongly on his obsession. Praying is useless. Damn. He'd find another way.

Johnson came toward the bow, working with his oil can on a halyard guide that kept sticking. George glanced at him, then looked at him hard, and became angry once again. Every time he thought about how Johnson had treated him at Marie-Galante it made him furious. Back home Johnson would be called an uppity nigger, or something worse. Where did he get off treating him like that. like a common criminal? So he'd made a mistake. But that wasn't the end of the world. Wasn't he doing everything he could to correct it—working with love and friendship to regain Ethan's trust, working hard to combat the desire. He could and would erase his mistake. Not the memory of Johnson's insolence.

He thought about getting rid of Johnson by simply abandoning the voyage—-take Ethan home and lay *Rascal* up in a safe harbor. But this would mean losing day-in, day-out contact with Ethan. He couldn't stand that. And to continue the voyage he needed Johnson. There was nobody readily available to replace him. To be with Ethan he was locked to *Rascal,* and *Rascal* meant Johnson. Besides, firing Johnson would devastate Ethan.

Also, what would happen if he immediately terminated the voyage? Ethan would undoubtedly tell his father about the kissing and undressing. On the other hand, if he continued the voyage, and never touched Ethan again, which he wouldn't do anyway, perhaps the incident would diminish in Ethan's mind.

He looked forward to firing Johnson at the end of the voyage, same deal as the black janitor he fired at the dealership. No severance pay, no reference letter, and for Johnson he committed to tracking down any place he sought work and advising against the employment, citing examples of Johnson's iniquity.

...

After Dominica the change became more apparent to Ethan. George became moody. Humorous stories virtually disappeared. Whistling and calypso songs were rare. Ethan missed that. Conversation between George and Johnson virtually ceased. Whereas previously there had been a limited amount of discussion about the islands and people they were visiting now it was only necessary talk. George gave Johnson formal orders in a military command voice, "Tack the boat. Change the foresail. Drop the anchor," and so on. Johnson would answer with a curt, "Yes, sir."

Ethan's haircuts also changed. It had always been George who cut his hair, usually singing to himself while he did so, and smiling all the time. Now Johnson took over. When Ethan's hair got long Johnson made no comment but sat him down in the stern and practiced the barbering skills he'd learned with six sons. George said nothing.

CHAPTER TWENTY FIVE

From Dominica they set course for Saint-Pierre, at the northern end of Martinique. Ethan, sitting at the bow watching the waves, thought about his days on *Rascal.* He'd now been aboard more than four weeks. Each day was the same. Each day was different. He'd become used to the rhythm of their time aboard, the slow swing from dawn to abrupt tropical dusk.

Mornings he'd get up early looking forward to the adventures of the day. The rays of the sun would fan upward from below the horizon, a blinding sun-rim appear, and suddenly it would be dawn, light for the whole world, the sun drawing its bottom from the sea with a distinct jerk, replacing the dull gray of early morning with the vibrant colors of the Caribbean. He would stare at everything emerging from the night, enthralled with the awakening world.

Breakfast was a specialty of Johnson's, prepared with a Gauloises nearby, and George would go through his ritual of preparing his special coffee in his own special way, patting his head occasionally as he watched the brewing process.

Johnson had taught Ethan simple cooking. So once in a while he was charged with breakfast duty. That was neat. Then the charts would be consulted, discussion ensue regarding courses and distances, the dingy brought in, the main hoisted by Johnson and usually reefed because of the strong winds, up anchor, and they were away, a glorious time for him each day when the wind would first strike *Rascal's* sails and the rustle of water would grow under her bow. The gentle straining of the sails, the hymn of wind in her rigging, the angle of the deck, all together gave him such a burst of happiness that he wanted to jump up and down and shout.

Later large or small jib would be set and mizzen raised depending upon conditions.

Lunch was taken underway, usually Johnson's excellent sandwiches, a beer or two for George, and Cokes for Johnson and for him. Johnson had taught him how to clean fish, and if they caught fish they would clean them together on the aft deck.

On reaching harbor, jib and mizzen were first lowered. Then they would luff up to the chosen anchorage site, utilizing the main alone, and Johnson would heave the anchor, all this followed by the swimming ladder over the side and a swim, everybody soaping off with salt-water soap, and then an expedition if there was a town or other site nearby to visit or supplies were needed. The engine was not dependable, so they rarely used it getting in and out of harbors.

Johnson prepared dinner, sometimes with him helping in the cooking, Johnson working miracles with the temperamental alcohol stove. Then the sunset, George taking a brandy and soda "whip" to salute one more in a lengthening series of fantastic Caribbean sunsets and he seeing something he'd never seen before living in a flat, wooded locale, the sun touching the horizon, gradually seeking shelter from the day below earth's edge, slowly withdrawing the warmth and light of life, the sea blushing in pink, gold, many soft colors in reflection of the sky, the colors fading into the darkening air. Wow.

Some evenings George would invite people on neighboring yachts to come over for a drink before dinner, or they'd be invited over to someone else's yacht as they'd been on *Ariadne*. Sea stories would be exchanged along with observations on places visited, and often as on *Ariadne* they would hear highly personal stories. George remarked, "Cruising on a boat for long periods is an isolated existence and makes people want to bare their soul."

Before dinner George would turn on the radio and surround the cockpit with the rhythms of the Caribbean, mostly calypso. At least in the early part of the voyage George would happily sing along, taking gulps of his brandy and soda between songs, and oft times directing his singing toward him, an audience of one.

After the dishes were done it was star gazing, games, or some limited reading in the poor light of the cabin. On many nights a camp fire on a beach with all of them sitting around, not saying much, but luxuriating in the fire's exclusion of the darkness. Then early to bed to get ready for the next big day of adventure.

This routine came to seem the norm, his past life the aberration. What he was doing now was all that mattered as if it had been this way always and always would be. Sometimes he was so immersed in his new life for such long periods that when memory of his past broke through it was like awakening and remembering a bad nightmare.

...

That afternoon they were ghosting along on the leeward side of Martinique, a hot day with few clouds, light wind and calms, the sun-track a searing reflection and this combining with a clear-sky sun to produce a lulling heat. Ethan had almost fallen asleep, his head lolling down, his eyes half-closed. *Rascal* was also almost asleep, her sails hanging limply in the stifling air.

Trade-winds had gathered on the windward side of Martinique, their combined force brought together to channel down a narrow valley on the leeward side of the island, funneled wind at over sixty miles an hour, revenge on any boat like *Rascal* trying to sneak around the leeward side of Martinique to avoid the heavy winds and mountainous waves on the windward side. No warning in gathering clouds as in the usual squall. Ferocious white wind without clouds. A white squall, the end of many a fine vessel and many a brave sailor.

Johnson saw it coming and yelled, "Watch out! Turn into the wind."

George reacted too slowly. *Rascal*, all sails set, was knocked flat by the gust. The stern half of main and mizzen plunged into the sea, and *Rascal's* keel rose nearly out of the water, lying on her side.

George was catapulted violently overboard, *Rascal* becoming a powerful slingshot to launch his body. In parting he managed to grab a jib sheet. Johnson had braced himself, seeing the squall coming, and grabbed Ethan as he flew past on his way to following George. Ethan called out to George, worried because he seemed to be floundering, then helped Johnson haul George back on board. The squall only lasted ten minutes. *Rascal* righted herself in stately fashion. She was a doughty vessel and no damage, but would have sunk had Johnson not battened down hatches and portholes as a caution when they came behind Martinique.

George thanked Ethan effusively for the rescue but turned to Johnson and said with a strained voice, "Was that deliberate? You could have warned me earlier. You trying to kill me for what happened at Marie-Galante, right?"

Johnson shook his head and walked away, then turned back, look hard at George. "If I wanted to kill you you'd be dead by now. Just stay away from Ethan."

Addressing Ethan, "White squall very rare here. White death. Devil's work. It be de devil playin with us."

Neither George nor Ethan responded. Just stood there for a few moments looking at Johnson before returning to ship tasks.

Approaching Saint-Pierre, they found that the main halyard had jammed at mast head, and they could not lower the main, probably the result of the knock-down. Ethan had become adept at boat tasks and was designated to go up the mast in the bosun's chair to free the halyard.

They hove-to, bringing *Rascal* head to wind, mast and boat rolling back and forth thirty degrees or more in the large swells, the mainsail slatting violently as the roll threw the sail from one side to the other. Ethan was placed in the small canvass seat of the bosun's chair and hauled up the main mast on the jib halyard. On the way up he had to hold on with both hands, and all his strength, fighting to keep from being whipped away from the mast by the roll only to crash back against the mast in the next roll. Finally at mast-head, it took some time to free the jammed halyard as he had to use one hand to hold on for dear life.

Success eventually achieved, the halyard freed, Ethan back on deck, Johnson said, "Ethan, well done. Even de best sailor have trouble doing dat with de boat rollin like dis."

George clapped him on the back. "One more time you were really brave. None of your friends back home would have even tried this."

Ethan asked, "You really think so?"

George and Johnson replied together, "Yes."

Ethan imagined the bullies falling from the mast and started humming to himself.

A several thousand foot steep-sloped volcano bulked green and menacing over Saint-Pierre, the volcano lying a close five miles beyond the town. Called Mount Pelee according to George, meaning "peeled"in French, because when first visited by the French in the 1600s all vegetation at the top had been peeled back by a recent eruption. George had been there before and told the story with obvious great relish, sitting across from Ethan in the cockpit and gathering his full attention. "You like volcanos. This is a great story about volcanos. In 1902 that town there was much larger" he pointed at Saint-Pierre, "The Paris of the Caribbean, beautiful homes, sophisticated people, a world-class opera, great wealth carried over from plantation days, and also great wealth brought over by aristocrats escaping the French Revolution.

"The volcano behind the town, Pelee, started rumbling and blowing ash into town. Nobody left. Can you imagine, a volcano right next to you belching ash and smoking like mad and you not leaving?" George shook his head.

" Stupid reason nobody left was politics. There were two political parties in town. The party of the planters was in power, the party of wealth. There was to be an election in two days. The planters' party felt that if people started leaving it would be the well-to-do who would leave first. They feared that there would not be enough wealthy people left in town to vote for them and they would lose the election. So they put out assurances that the volcano wasn't dangerous, article after article in all the papers, and also speeches. And they had soldiers block those people who still tried to leave. Wouldn't even let ships leave the harbor for fear of starting a panic. Over 30,000 people remained in town, and the harbor was full of ships.

"Well, what came wasn't lava. The planter's party had assumed that if there was an eruption it would be lava and the lava would be blocked by an intervening ridge. Instead there was a volcanic gas explosion, maybe the loudest bang ever heard by man. The explosion was forty times more powerful than the atomic bomb at Hiroshima. Think of it, forty times more powerful than Hiroshima. It blew the town off the face of the earth, even the stone buildings. Poison gas came down the mountain traveling at 100 miles an hour with a temperature of well over 1,000 degrees. Thirty thousand men women and children exploded. That compares to only 2,000 that died in Pompeii when Vesuvius erupted in Roman times.

Ethan's mouth gape open, "Exploded?"

George replied, "Yes, literally exploded. At over 1,000 degrees their blood exploded inside them. Their bodies exploded. And the sea boiled for twenty miles in every direction, killing fish and every other living thing. All of this took only three to five minutes.

"One guy escaped, a prisoner deep in the town jail. Cell had no ventilation so he didn't get the gas. But he did get the heat. He got badly burned. He managed to save himself by peeing on his shirt and wrapping it around his face so his lungs wouldn't burn. Same thing you'd have done, right Ethan?"

Ethan grinned and said, "Sure. Thought of it while you were talking."

George went on, "He lived to become an international celebrity. Toured around the world with Barnum & Bailey for years, showing off his burn scars and telling his story."

They wandered around the ruins of the opera house in Saint-Pierre, large and leveled to the ground, and saw the cell where the man who survived had been incarcerated.

George wanted to go to Fort-de-France, the capital, to visit the famous statue of Empress Josephine. Johnson was reluctant but finally joined them in an old jeep, driven by an old Frenchman, Ricard Tremont, over old and rough dirt roads. On the way they passed deserted plantation after deserted plantation, massive gray stone walls, most standing but some quelled by time, roofs fallen in, trees living in rooms previously occupied by wealthy planters, windows washed by slaves now poking out ferns and branches, doors and door frames rotting in the swift deterioration of the tropics, and also an array of imaginatively placed tin-can roofed shacks in each of the ruins, taking advantage of nooks and crannies in walls still standing.

Johnson remarked to Ethan, "Them shack be about de only thing black ever get from de plantation. Support for der shack. No much for all de blood that went into buildin de wall der shack lean on."

At certain places the road narrowed to one lane. If an approaching vehicle was driven by a white man, a fellow Frenchman, there would be an arrogant beep of the horn and Ricard would always back off, sometimes getting a "thank you," but often not. If it was a black man in the approaching vehicle Ricard always forged ahead.

Around a turn in a one-lane section of the road came a very black man driving a very dilapidated truck full of goats. The black man reversed his truck. The goats started bleating loud protests.

Maybe the bleats were due to the goats prior experience with the driver's backing abilities. Or maybe they knew how much rotgut he'd consumed. Ethan later smelled liquor on the driver's breath and observed his staggers. The fear of the goats was well founded. The driver backed his truck into a chasm-like roadside ditch, tipped the truck on its side, and scattered goats far and wide, populating a local farmer's fields with grazing goats chomping crops with delight.

Ricard felt responsible, and at his request they joined in a goat round-up. Ethan ran after a large nanny-goat. She turned and came to him like a friendly dog, trust in her eyes. Ethan became worried about the goats and asked George to find out where they were headed. To his relief it turned out the transport was from one pasture to another and not to slaughter. They hobbled the goats, and as they parted Ethan was sure his goat looked at him as though losing a friend.

They found Josephine posed regally on a pedestal higher than Ethan's head, positioned to look down on everyone and everything. Together they read the ornate bronze plaque below. Josephine had been born in Martinique to a renowned planter, the owner of a large plantation with 150 slaves. She'd first married a French aristocrat who was later guillotined, and then married Napoleon in 1796.

Johnson shook his head with evident disgust and said, "Hateful woman. Be de local slave revolt in Martinique in de 1790s followin de glorious lead of Toussaint L'Ouverture who free Haiti. France have enough. With de revolution in France de' abolish slavery in Martinique. Dat be 1794. After marry Napoleon, Josephine work on Napoleon for years to bring slavery back to Martinique. She work on him so her plantation-owner father and her father murderous friends could get back der slave.

"In 1802 she get her wish. Napoleon restore slavery to Martinique. Planter get der slave back. Burn some slave to create fear. Cut off limb of some other. Most brutal slavery in de Caribbean. Ethan, same evil in Josephine as de evil in King Leopold of Belgium dat Conrad wrote about in *Heart of Darkness*. Both of them no kill slave themself. But de' do worse from afar."

Johnson shook his fist at the statue as though Josephine was there in person. "Should have guillotine her. Statue put up by de planters to honor her and thank her. Terrible."

Ethan was wide eyed, the same anger Johnson showed when he described the killing of Prince Klass on Antigua, only this time Johnson kept glaring at George.

George said, outrage in his voice, "Stop glaring at me like that. I had nothing to do what happened two hundred years ago."

"You white people no have change in dat two hundred years. You be just as much a racist as de planters, maybe worse cause you know better."

George raised his arm as though intending to strike Johnson..

"Try dat and you find yourself on you back. De black mon plow dis dirt with his blood. I be happy to have you lie in de dirt and add some of you blood."

George backed away from Johnson.

Johnson said, "Why you bring Ethan all dis way if you no goin to be showin him what right and wrong? Terrible example for de boy to see a white mon dislikin black like you do."

"Johnson, mind your own business. That's an order. I do what I want to do."

Johnson turned away as though he hadn't heard.

On the way back to *Rascal*, bouncing up and down on the rutted road, Ethan thought about blacks and whites. He'd never thought much about it before.

George was trying to talk to Ricard, using a mixture of French and English. When whites were around, George always struck up a conversation. Yet when he dealt with blacks to buy supplies, or with the women on the islands who washed their clothes, or blacks on the docks, George never asked about their families, chatted about the weather, or described *Rascal's* voyage, no small talk. Conversation from George with blacks was always restricted. Same thing passing black people on the street. Just about all of them gave a friendly "Hello" or "Good day" or "Bon Jour." George would reply but never initiate the greeting.

Ethan was coming to feel differently about blacks. There was Johnson, of course, his new best friend. Also, most blacks he encountered smiled at him, greeted him on the street, talked to him in the stores, pointed things out, a far different experience from back home. Puzzling. Blacks in the Caribbean had been horribly treated by whites. Still most were very friendly. Different from whites in his very own home town—many still looking at him with reproach for his mother's death. George's lecture on Nevis about whites being better than blacks was clearly wrong.

Ethan spoke to Johnson about it when they returned to *Rascal*.

Johnson said, "George share de prejudice against black people of many white people, probably most though de' refuse to admit it. Deep down inside de' prejudiced but hide it from others and even from demself."

He sat down next to Ethan in the cockpit, took a puff on his Gauloise, and said, his voice slow and sort of sad, "You know how some people in you town treat you thinkin you kill you mother?"

"They hate me."

"Well, some white people treat black just like that, not all, but some, as though de black do somethin real bad, or goin to do somethin real bad. It be terrible thing to have white people look at you as though you be bad person. And de white people never blame demself for what de' doin. Long ago I memorize what Tolstoy write. *'I sit on a man's back, choking him and making him carry me, and yet assure myself and others that I am very sorry for him and wish to ease his lot by all possible means—except to get off his back.'* He be writin about de Russian noble sittin on de back of de serf but same thing, white mon on de back of de black mon."

Ethan put his hand on Johnson's arm and looked at him with understanding. As a black in a white world Johnson had to deal with things much like he'd had to deal with back home.

Later Ethan took out the football George had brought along and asked boys on a nearby beach if they wanted to play. One spoke some English and sides were chosen. None of the other boys had ever played football before. Soccer was their game, but they enthusiastically embraced the new sport, finding that getting around a defender in touch football was little different from getting around a defender in soccer. Passing was another matter—many interceptions, boys tumbling over each other in great muddles, arms and legs all over the place, great hilarity. Ethan found a popularity unknown at home as he was the only one who knew how to throw a pass.

How different from home. At home when there was football, or another game involving choosing sides, he'd stand with the other boys, hoping to be picked. Everybody would be chosen except him, and he'd be left with the other boys staring at him, snickering. He'd stopped trying to join other boys, avoided them. Not today, what a great afternoon. He went back to the boat skipping along and trying out his whistling.

...

The next day they left Saint-Pierre with the objective of cruising to Saint-Anne at the southern end of Martinique. A very slow passage, chasing stray winds under clouds in the wind shadow of Martinique. Often totally becalmed. When they finally got there it wasn't much of a place. They stayed aboard with Ethan practicing jumping off the spreaders, and that day he got up his courage and for the first time dove off the spreaders to the congratulations of George and Johnson, then a dinner of fish caught along the way and a few hands of poker.

Later George went to the foredeck and again slumped against the mast, this time a cloudy night so no moon haunting his troubles. He'd brought his brandy along. Sipped it slowly. It didn't help. He was in a cold sweat despite the heat of the evening. His mind flew around and around, seeking a weak spot, a crevice, an opening through which it might squeeze itself and escape the perversion. There was no exit. He'd been fighting, fighting, fighting against desire day and night for the better part of a week. No success. The obsession was getting worse every day, and days had a way of following days. How could this be? A hell of a fix. Something outside him must be causing this. This wasn't him. Something else. Damn difficult to lick. Discouragement was setting in. Under different circumstances he'd probably have sought the help of a psychologist or minister. Impossible here. He was strong. He determined to tough it through.

Rascal had always meant freedom, escape from the dullness of his hometown, from social responsibilities he'd shouldered because he was expected to do so, from buddies whose stories he'd heard too often, from a wife who looked at him with sorrow and puzzlement. Now on *Rascal* freedom had turned to imprisonment. God had imprisoned him with the object of his perversion to remind him every day of his iniquity. Had any man ever before been locked for two months on a twelve by thirty-eight foot floating platform with an adolescent boy he loved and desired, and without any possibility of doing anything about it? Had any psychiatrist ever studied a situation like this and the effect on a man? A psychiatrist would have a field day. If a psychiatrist called he could give first-hand testimony that the effect on a man was total devastation.

What had led to this? Clearly it wasn't aversion to women. When he first married he and Marge had sex almost every day. And until recently he'd conducted a sporadic affaire with an assistant at one of the dealerships. Can one like sex with women and at the same time have an attraction for a young teenage boy? Seemed to be the case.

Parents? Was it their fault? He muttered to himself. "They certainly never gave me any love. Made it impossible for me to love them." When he thought about it became clear. It was their total rejection and his response to that rejection. That's what caused it. Love that should have gone to them went instead to the boys around him. The love had to go somewhere. It went to boys. His parents were twisted and they twisted him.

He remembered a train set received for his tenth Christmas. As soon as he'd unwrapped it, and saw what it was, he focused not on how great it was to have a train set but on how he could install it in the basement and use it as a lure to bring boys down there. And in the basement he'd found he could get boys to do what he wanted. Not sex, but sometimes pants dropping, mutual examination, touching, dirty talk. Come summer the lure became the pool, the tennis courts, and all the toys, the same play as in the basement but even more unrestrained in the freedom of outdoors.

As he thought back on it the boys he invited were the boys he could control, and he'd discovered that by careful planning, and the right inducements, he could get most boys to do what he wanted. And how he remembered enjoying it. Controlling other boys gave him more pleasure than anything else he did in his youth.

That was how it was. Boys, not parents.

As he thought about it further he became convinced his parents also had a major role in repressing his sexual attraction for boys, keeping it buried until now, hiding it from him under the guise of his general liking for boys. His mother certainly scared the bejesus out of him when he was growing up.

He was twelve and invited a very attractive boy he liked very much to play with the train set. They had both dropped their pants and were examining each other's genitals. As they started to touch each other and get erections his mother burst in and caught them.

It was the only time in his life he'd seen her become emotional. She'd gone out of control, dragging him into a bathroom and attempting to "scrub" the dirt off while screaming, "Only twisted, sick, evil people do things like that. If you ever touch another boy you will burn in hell forever. I hope you burn in hell, you horrible boy. You're going to burn in the worst fires of hell. The very hottest fires of hell are for boys like you who touch other boys. And before you go to hell they'll put you in prison for the rest of your life. You hear me. If I told your father what you were doing he would beat you so badly you couldn't stand. Don't you ever touch another boy like that again as long as you live."

Dying young, his parents escaped having to acknowledge the thing they'd created. He wished he could confront them about it, and became angry at them one more time.

Well, it wasn't just them. He thought about life in town. The dealerships, the bank, the hotel, his club, his social position, even his position on the vestry, all had been handed him on a silver platter by his parents. He'd added little of his own. Instead he'd used it all to hide himself from himself. He acknowledged to himself, "I've packed my life with scurrying around town so I didn't have to think about what was hidden inside me. I was too afraid of what I'd find if I looked."

Then there was Marge. He began quietly talking to Marge. "I've been saying to myself I made a bad bargain marrying you, gave you position and wealth, got little in return. I blamed you for not producing a son. Railed at you for just about everything. But it's you that made the bad bargain." Then over and over again, "Forgive me, Marge."

He began talking louder to Marge. "The perversion was there all the time. Hidden in plain sight. What was I doing going to a playground to exchange dirty stories with young teenagers? Why did I always pick fights with you when I had to leave the boys? It was in plain sight. Damn it. I didn't see it. Kept me from loving you like I should have."

Again, "Forgive me. Forgive me," now so loud that Ethan looked forward to see what was up.

Marge made the right choice. She didn't want them to adopt a boy. Somehow she knew it wasn't a good idea, that his attraction to boys wasn't healthy. She was always smarter and more intuitive than he was. He'd just refused to give her credit.

Her intuition was certainly one-hundred-percent right about this voyage. Did she suspect he had an unconscious sexual desire for Ethan? He hadn't listened to her. Wouldn't listen as he wanted Ethan with him too much.

George got up from the deck vowing to write a long letter to Marge the next day, telling her he loved her, apologizing for his neglect in marriage, and promising to do better.

CHAPTER TWENTY SIX

They next day they plotted a course for St. Lucia, leaving very early in the morning. George said they needed to put in at St. Lucia so he could sign some papers his lawyer was sending down and get them notarized at the American consulate, and also mail a letter. The sea was waiting for them. Well off the southern tip of Martinique, too far out to run for shelter, they ran into a violent storm, nature announcing that the hurricane season was fast approaching.

The storm appeared suddenly, throwing up a towering line of dark clouds in the distance, rising ominously from ocean to sky. Moving fast, the clouds had already eaten up a quarter of the horizon. All went still as the storm approached, black and copper green and seething. A black wall. The end of the world. No thunder, no wind, no sound, just a few flickers of lightening from some hidden place. It was the stillness that made those on *Rascal* feel something sinister was poised behind the wall.

Then it was upon them, engulfed them. They got their sails down just in time as a few catspaws played over the boat as though tasting it for future consumption, and the first great raindrops smashed onto the deck. The full force of wind and rain struck together. It was as though wind and rain had been held up by a barrier and had burst through with hate. A full gale and more, steady wind of sixty miles an hour and gusts up to seventy miles an hour. The wind was so strong that *Rascal* heeled well over under bare poles. Stinging spray. Torrential rain that burst down in such amounts as to make breathing difficult. Ethan found that to breath he had to cup his hand over his mouth. And he was drenched immediately despite having quickly donned foul-weather gear.

Day dark as night. Lightening raged toward them, streaking and blazing as it advanced nearer and nearer, thunder detonating all around. The air smelled strongly of ozone. One brilliant bolt hit the top of the mast and came down to deck level on the lightening rod attached to the mast. St. Elmo's Fire flamed at mast head, mizzen mast head, and at the tips of the spreaders, steady discharges of blue-white light jumping many feet into the air, lightening of the earth trying to reach sisters and brothers in the heavens, otherworldly illumination bathing the entire boat. Johnson yelled to them not to touch anything metal and remained at the wheel, which fortunately was made of wood. George and Evan huddled in the cockpit, being careful not to touch anything, metal, wood, anything.

The storm ended abruptly. One minute it was pouring and the next minute the midday sun was out as though something had willed the storm to exist only for a set time.

Johnson announced, "Dat not be normal storm. Start too fast. End too fast. Only de second time I see St. Elmo's Fire. First time I tell you about, Ethan. My best friend, Amos Tuttle, he drown. St. Elmo's Fire de devil fire. De devil bring dat storm. Dis time God save us."

A cold chill ran down Ethan's spine as he imagined the devil near. On the other hand, the St. Elmo's fire was super. It looked like *Rascal* was shooting Roman Candles at the sky and the sky was shooting its lightening back, a celestial version of the Roman Candle battle in the churchyard on Antigua.

George said, "I told you before I don't believe in the devil. I still don't. St. Elmo's Fire is naturally occurring. It's not the devil."

Johnson said with great certainty, "You wrong. De devil here because you bring him." turned his back on George and started hoisting the sails back up.

They arrived at Castries, the capital of St. Lucia, late in the afternoon, anchored in the harbor, and wandered through town. Ethan felt Castries was by far the poorest Caribbean town they visited, other perhaps than Codrington on Barbuda. Few of the pretty houses seen on more northern islands, and the ramshackle tin-can-roofed hovels seemed smaller and dirtier than elsewhere, rag-dressed children pouring in and out in such numbers as to make it appear the smaller the living quarters the larger the family. Open sewers beside disintegrating streets did not flow as on other islands but sat stagnantly waiting for a strong, wash-away rain, the excrement plainly and individually displayed in the absence of water flow to break it down, the whole town permeated with putrefying stench. Even the public buildings were rundown, rust stains on outside walls and peeling paint on doors and window frames. Ethan felt sorrow for the people and asked George if he could do something.

George said, "Well, I'll give to the beggars. But it doesn't help much. Nothing is going to happen here unless the people get together and do it themselves. Remember Anguilla, St. Martin, and Antigua? How pretty the towns were? People worked together there and worked hard. Here it looks like people have been lazy about working to get things done. Just waiting for the English to do it and they're not about to do it."

Johnson nodded but said, "Colonial administration here lazy and incompetent. No all de people fault thing so bad. St. Lucia use by de English as place to hide away colonial official who are drunks or have other failure. People de' no can get rid of because of der family important in England."

The harbor was as bad as the town. In the broad view it was the most spectacular harbor Ethan had seen. Morne Fortune soared sharply upward dominating the harbor, a jungle mantled finger of earth reaching 2,500 feet into the air, and the shore was a riot of greens of every hue, folding around them to the harbor mouth, set off at intervals by yellow and red flowering tropical trees. Above trade-wind clouds danced shadows across the landscape to bring first one part of the landscape, then another, into the sun, and a rainbow played on a far mountain. It looked like a tropical paradise.

But when Ethan looked closer he saw something else. St. Lucia had apparently been using the harbor as the dumping ground for the detritus of the island for a long time. Listing island schooners were rotting at anchor. Beaches were littered with the carcasses of boats beyond floating, rusting oil cans, throw-outs from houses like sinks and refrigerators, what looked like thirty years worth of discarded tires, and many abandoned automobiles staining the clear water deep brown with their disintegration. And washing back and forth, pulling itself onto the shores, fouling the beaches, was so much oil-soaked debris and putrid, smelly garbage that when they returned from Castries that afternoon they decided not to take their usual evening swim, concluding that they would only get dirtier bathing in the harbor water.

The next morning George departed to sign his papers and mail his letter, and Ethan and Johnson went off to explore the island. Beyond the poverty, and the filth of its harbor, it was the most beautiful island Ethan had visited. They hiked part way up the spectacular Morne Fortune for a view over Castries and the entire Eastern part of the island, visited high waterfalls, and glens full of flowers.

On the way down they ran into a chain gang, twenty or more men, all black, dragging their beat-up bodies through the hot sun, the chains clanking on their ankles to give voice to their misery, white guards with gun and whip and happy faces as they prodded the blacks along. Johnson looked angrily at the procession. "You never see de white man in de chain gang. No even see many white men in jail. But if you a black man and you take some small thing, maybe you intend to give it back, you twenty year on de chain gang." He glowered at the guards. See de smile on all de white guard face?"

Ethan nodded.

"Dat because what they doin like overseer on a slave plantation. De' love dat." Johnson started following the procession, fury on his face. "White man sad der no more slavery. Miss de plantation. When de' can put de black mon in chain for crime like these guard doin de' get happy because de' treaten dem like on de plantation.

When you older you goin to hear a lot about discrimination and mistreatment of black. Discrimination another form of slavery. Never forget dat. Can't put black back in slave pen so they discriminate against them any way they can. Slavery still here for black."

One of the prisoners staggered and then fell to his knees, an older man. A guard went over to him, a broad smile on the guard's face, and whipped him twice, hard. Johnson strode over to the guard, his face contorted with rage, voice loud and menacing.

"You like dis right? Like to beat old black mon when he down. I remember you face. Better hide or leave de island. Have lot of friend on St. Lucia. De' be lookin for you. Beat you like you beat dis black man, only worse. De' be smilin' when de' do it like you be smilin. And de' be watchin' you all de time. You whip dis man again and de' kill you."

The guard pointed his gun at Johnson. Johnson pushed it aside as though he was used to having guns pointed at him. "You no goin' to shoot me. You hang. Like to see you hang."

The other guards surrounded Johnson, fists clenched, whips raised, and one gave him a strong shove.

Johnson stood his ground and pushed back at the man. Ethan thought there was going to be a fight as the men moved closer to Johnson.

Johnson said loudly, showing no fear, looking intently into the face of each man as though to memorize their faces, "You goin' to beat me up for tryin' to help an old man you whip while he down? Can't wait to tell police chief Randolph about it. He good friend of mine."

The guards dispersed, muttering, and lookin at Johnson with such hate that Ethan worried it would be Johnson who would have to watch himself.

Later Johnson had calmed down and they were sitting quietly on a deserted beach. Johnson was stroking his cross, and Ethan asked him about it.

Johnson shook his head as though recalling and smiled. "Well, dis cross save my life. Remember I tell you about sailing as mate on *Anna Maria*, de big schooner." Ethan nodded. "We were in Suriname picking up lumber for transport to de Virgin Islands and Antigua. A hurricane come north of us in de central Caribbean. We stuck in port. In de old days I drink a lot, a real lot. Started drinking when de hurricane come. Nothing else to do. Be in a bar in a bad part of Paramaribo and got in bar fight with de big Dutchman. So drunk I no remember afterward what it be about. Could see de Dutchman a good boxer, better than me, so I try to wrestle him. We rolling on de ground kicking and punching each other. He pull off my cross. Then he get away from me and stand up, pull a knife. I grab his knife arm with both hand but not before he knife me in de side. With my last strength I knock the knife from his hand on the corner of a table, slug him as hard as I can. His head hit de bar in fallin and he crumple to de floor. I reach for de knife intendin to stick it into him like he did me, maybe kill him. Lyin right next to de knife be de cross. Rebecca give me de cross just a week before. Be surprise for my birthday. She save up whole year to buy it. I look at de cross and look at de knife. Picked up de cross and leave. De cross saved me from murderin de man. If no cross I probably still be rottin in de Suriname jail. No more drinking after dat." Johnson kissed the cross and rolled up his shirt to show Ethan the scar from the knife wound. "Took a long time to heal."

Ethan got up, stood over Johnson with his hand on his shoulder, and said solemnly, "I'm very glad you're not in Suriname. You're my best friend."

Johnson gave him his broad mouthed smile. "So am I."

When they got back to the boat George was much happier, quietly whistling to himself and at one point singing a few snatches of *Maryann*. When some goat carcasses floated by he quipped, "Must have tried to soap-off in the harbor."

Ethan grinned at George, happy for the change. He'd gotten worried about him.

Despite the destitution of Castries, and maybe because of the beauty of the rest of the island, it was St. Lucia that focused Ethan's thoughts on the sounds, smells, and tastes he'd been enjoying in the Caribbean.

As they approached an island, St. Lucia being no exception, he would hear the poignant human-like bleating of baby goats calling for their mothers, not too different from babies calling for mothers back home. Once ashore there was a cacophony of tree frogs, shrilly protecting territory and seeking mates, village dogs barking at each other and at everything, and sometimes the song of the steel drum and music of the dance, happy people doing happy things. Then with night descending, the shore birds protested against the gathering darkness, and later, with darkness spreading over the water, distant human voices carried far across the still evening harbor, the human voices not protesting but welcoming the night, a time of peace and family. He was sure he would hear the islands the rest of his life.

Smells enveloped *Rascal* at evening rest in the protection of an island. Frangipani and other sweet tropical flowers released their powerful fragrance to the cooling evening shore breeze that spread down from the mountains, the flower-scent mixing with the ripe smell of the damp vegetation that had been discarded on the ground by surrounding foliage and fermented in rain and sun, and the combined scent seasoned by the piquant odor of spiced Caribbean cooking in village homes. He would breathe them in deeply, feeling them entering him.

And the tastes. They were the best. Fruits he'd never heard of. Mango and papaya, how he loved them, tastes of the sun. And the quenepa. It was a fruit the size of a small plum, pulpy, tasting like mango only more tart. The Puerto Ricans sought them out. On one island they visited grew a fifty foot tall quenepa tree in full fruit. Families had come in boats almost one hundred miles from Puerto Rico for the harvest. They told him that each summer there was a celebration in Ponce, Puerto Rico, to honor the quenepa.

Ethan honored the quenepa with absolute delight every time he put one in his mouth.

They left St. Lucia for St. Vincent on a beam reach. All the way going south from Antigua they'd been on a beam reach, trade-wind from the east on their port quarter, sometimes more a close reach when the wind moved more forward, sometimes more a broad reach when the wind was more aft, but always on the beam.

Rascal showed great grace in handling the large, open-ocean waves that came roaring at them from port that morning, a grace she'd not shown in attacking waves head on when they beat up the Anegada Passage. Starting in a wave trough lightly she would mount the steep face of an oncoming wave, then she would prance in wild foam over the crest as it broke roaring beneath her, thus exposing the far horizon hidden from view in the trough, then she would slide down the other side, always keeping the deck steady and making it easy work for the helmsman to stay on course, not even much spray except during occasional squalls.

The waves were immense, Johnson said there was probably a hurricane in the mid-Atlantic. When *Rascal* was lodged in a trough between waves, the next oncoming wall of water towered above them half or more the height of the mast, a daunting sight. And often the trough was so deep that wind was blocked. *Rascal* would pause with sails fluttering until the rise of the next wave brought the full force of the wind. Ethan loved it. He'd been watching the endless progression of waves, following their breaking passage under *Rascal's* keel. And he'd been watching the clouds, large cumulus clouds today turning on and off the sunlight as they passed overhead, a sky-based light switch. Johnson was at the helm and George was sitting in the cockpit opposite Ethan.

George had hunched down, head almost on his chest, occasionally patting his head, staring vacantly at nothing with his mouth slackly open as though in pain. He seemed to be looking inward rather than outward, and had been in this same unhappy position for the better part of an hour, this despite the fact that he'd been in a cheerful mood the evening before in St. Lucia.

The changes in George were now even more visible to Ethan, substantial changes since the confusing incident of the kisses and undressing a week or more ago at Marie-Gallante. George seemed to have gradually lost interest in everything, and had turned from being talkative to being somber and withdrawn for long periods of time. Previously he was always pointing things out to him, commenting on new things they saw, describing the next island they would visit, kidding him about winnings and losses in board games and poker. Now he was getting silent like he had, himself, been earlier, almost as if they'd changed places. This wasn't good.

He felt very grateful to George for bringing him to the Caribbean. His father was right, a great opportunity. The odd experience at Marie-Galante was probably a mistake, as George claimed. He still didn't understand it. Maybe just George drunk. He wasn't quite ready to reject George as a friend though it had reignited his fear of him. Mostly he was more than ever puzzled about how to react to him.

Sometimes George wanted to be a buddy, talking to him like he was another boy experiencing what he was experiencing. "See that? Isn't it great? Wow. Boy, this is wonderful. This really makes me happy. Does it make you happy?" And so on.

Other times he acted like a father—repeatedly telling him to stand tall, to write letters to his father, correcting his use of *I* and *me* and other grammar, giving him advice on life like being an engineer, subjecting him many times to the same lecture about dressing well and rich friends.

Johnson, on the other hand, seemed to want him to understand the world around him. While George in his buddy mode would point things out and exclaim, Johnson would patiently explain why things were as they were, which was definitely more interesting. Ethan felt himself much more drawn to knowledge than shared observation.

Once in a while, not often, Ethan compared Johnson and George. Johnson was always the same toward him, caring, attentive, helpful, trying to teach him. While George was caring there was something additional. Not just the kissing. The staring at him and touching all the time. Particularly he didn't like the way George watched him when he dressed and undressed. It made him uncomfortable and vaguely embarrassed. Sort of creepy.

...

Slumped across from Ethan, what George was trying to deal with was a new level of perversion. All his happiness of yesterday evening had disappeared.

Many nights now something monstrous brought him dreams of evil, taking his mind to various perverted things he could do with Ethan, assuring him that Ethan would like what he did, wanted what he wanted. He'd become certain this was coming from outside of him, yes, his own desire was there, but something else, preying on him, not part of who he was, invading against his will, out of his control. He felt it strongly. He'd taken courses in psychology. This was more than his id bringing hidden desires to the surface. More than a projection of his desires on something else. The other thing was definitely there. He shivered.

Some nights he struggled with it so long he hardly slept, and would awaken in horror from dream memories. Then last night it had brought the most depraved dream of all, a dream not just about Ethan but also about other boys.

It had started in Dominica. An adolescent was working in his father's shop, maybe a year younger than Ethan. The boy was striking with an unusual combination of very dark eyes and white-blond hair. He'd gotten on a ladder to get something down from a high shelf. George had noted his small, tight buttocks and saw his narrow waist, bared when the boy reached high for provisions. He couldn't take his gaze off him and found himself sweating with desire. In St. Lucia there had been a young black with a beautiful face and a lithe body covered with very little bathing suit. He'd stared to the point that the boy's parents grabbed the boy and shielded him, giving George dirty looks.

The pestilence was spreading. He could consciously feel it. He was on the way to damnation.

He'd not thought much about his soul before. Now he did. That nothing more serious happened with Ethan probably weighed in his favor, though the bible said don't covet your neighbor's wife. How would the Lord treat coveting your neighbor's son? Badly without doubt.

Reverend Smallwood at Christ Church was right. Original sin did exist. Man is full of sin whether he chooses to sin or not. He hadn't chosen to desire boys. Desire came from a dark hidden place, secreted in him, appearing against his will, and growing despite his strongest attempts to fight it.

And what did Smallwood say about it being difficult for a rich man to get into heaven? It had to be impossible for a rich man to get into heaven if on top of wealth he coveted adolescent boys. He'd been in a training course for hell ever since he started visiting boys on the playground. No doubt about it. He was going to hell unless he changed his ways. He vowed to redouble his efforts.

He raised his head and looked around. The beauty he always saw in the Caribbean seemed to be fading away. And the constant hard work of sailing and maintaining *Rascal,* work he always enjoyed, was becoming a burden.

CHAPTER TWENTY SEVEN

They anchored in St. Vincent at Young Island Cut, a much more protected harbor than the main harbor. Their plan was to stay at St. Vincent a number of days to try and get their engine fixed once and for all. Johnson knew a master mechanic there. The engine had only been working sporadically throughout the voyage despite much time spent by Johnson trying to fix it. Johnson had said in disgust, "Sailboats no like engines. Sailboats would rather sail." That seemed to be the case with *Rascal*.

Transport at Young Island Cut was horseback, not many wheeled vehicles anywhere on the island. George went off with some people he met at a beach bar and Johnson rented a horse for Ethan and one for himself. Most exciting, Ethan had never ridden.

The man who met them with the horses in the dusty sunlight of the stable yard was Henri Claire, who identified himself as the stable owner. Henri stepped toward them with an open smile and a welcoming handshake, a different looking man from other islanders Ethan had seen—very tall, very thin, features aquiline like a white man, chiseled chin, wide light brown eyes, not dark eyes like many, skin a light tan hue, not black. He had a pronounced French accent and looked them over with what Ethan took to be amusement.

First thing he said was to Johnson. "You're pretty black to have such a white son." Then he laughed uproariously. Johnson had been standing close to Ethan with a protective hand on his shoulder. Then Henri backed off, narrowed his eyes, and looked them over again. He said, "I was wrong. Now I see it. Johnson, you're Tonto, and this young man, Ethan is it, is going to be the Lone Ranger of Saint Vincent. From now on it's going to be Kemosabe or the Lone Ranger, right Tonto? No more Ethan. And Ethan, don't answer him if he tries to call you anything but Kemosabe or Lone Ranger." He laughed again and they joined in.

Henri said to Ethan, "You remind me a lot of a teenager who used come to me for confession, very blond like you. That's right. I was once a Catholic priest. The only black priest in that great cathedral of Saint Louis on Martinique. Quite an honor. But I screwed it up."

As Henri was watering the horses, getting saddles and tack from the barn, and going through paperwork, he told some of his story. He was obviously very well educated, spoke excellent English, and seemed to enjoy talking about his life.

"As you can tell, I'm not from the islands. Born and raised in Dakar, Senegal, on the West Coast of Africa. Do you know where Senegal is Kemosabe?"

Ethan said, "Yes. We studied Africa in geography class."

"I was orphaned in Dakar when I was ten. My parents died of cholera. There were a few relatives in a distant village. But I had no way of contacting them. So I wandered the streets of Dakar doing odd jobs and begging. Finally, I got a job catching the giant rats of Dakar, biggest rats in the world. They're all over, hundreds running around the stalls in the main market every day. The pay I got was about two American cents per rat."

Ethan asked, "What did you do with the rats?"

Henri said, "I turned them in at a government office." Then he cast his eyes down and said, "The truth is I often ate some when I was starving." Then looking up he said more brightly, "Of course, the corrupt bureaucrats were selling the rat flesh in the markets as bush meat so everyone was eating them.

"I lived in a discarded ship container. It stunk to high heaven. Right across from hellish Goree Island." He explained angrily that Goree Island was where slaves from up and down the West Coast of Africa were penned and then spit out to the horror of the Americas. "Up to 15 million slaves passed through the 'Door of No Return' on Goree island."

He shook his head and crossed himself. "Sometimes when the wind was right, lying in my hovel I was sure I heard the moans of the slaves who died on Goree Island. I was afraid to sleep."

He frowned and looked away as though remembering,. "The Catholic nuns found my hiding place and practically kidnapped me. Disciplined me to Catholicism. They were very harsh, somehow converted me into a priest, sent me to Martinique in robes far too hot for the islands, and with a lot of Catholic clap-trap far too strict for the islands. I soon discovered a lovely parishioner. She was ready to be converted in ways definitely not Catholic. That was the end of that."

Johnson asked Henri if he'd married the girl.

Henri smiled. Then he laughed. "Marry her. Hell, she almost got me killed. Joan Ramboir. Daughter of one of the leading families of Martinique, very beautiful and very, very white." He looked at Ethan, then Johnson, as though debating whether to go on. "Maybe this isn't good for young ears but it's a good story.

"Many days I would hear confessions, mostly blacks. My voice is distinctive, and whites would identify me in the confessional. Then they would go off to confess to a white priest. One of the only exceptions was Joan Ramboir. She sought me out. Then she would confess about her sexual desire for black men. About private things she was doing to herself thinking about black men. Outside the confessional she was constantly badgering me to meet, to help her abandon her sin and find God.

"I met her in the cathedral, figured one couldn't sin in a cathedral. But in hindsight I was already leaning the wrong way. I knew that Mondays the cathedral was generally deserted and that's when I had her join me. The organist chose that particular Monday to check the stops on the organ. Found us on the floor together right next to the high altar. Before I could get away the Ramboirs came down on the church seeking murder. A blood-thirsty lot. I ducked into a confessional and started taking confession. Thought they wouldn't look for me to break my vows by hearing confession drenched in sin as I was. Later I got up my courage, took some work clothes from a rack and a half empty garbage can, and walked past them, I'll tell you shaking in my boots. What I counted on was that as arrogant white men they had never really looked at me. I was a black in a cassock. Someone to ignore. Most blacks look alike to white men like that. They stopped me and asked where I was going. I put my head down and looked at my shoes in subservient fashion like most blacks do when accosted by whites, mumbled in the local patois that I was taking the garbage to a nearby ravine. They let me go. A friend snuck me over to St. Vincent in his boat that night."

Ethan asked, "Didn't the Ramboirs try to kill you in St. Vincent?"

"No," Henri said. "The English here don't like the French Catholics on Martinique. They protected me and still do.

"After I got here I went through agony for over a year, praying and trying to understand how I could have strayed so far. A dark time. Finally I realized that I couldn't do anything about it, if my soul was damned it was damned. I might as well enjoy life while I could. Perhaps God would think I'd already been punished enough for my sins with life on the streets of Dakar, and then having to undergo the rituals of the Catholic church.

"What I did was convert to a new religion. I call it the 'religion of self.' None of this Catholic mumbo jumbo. My new motto is, 'Its better to have than have not,' whatever the church may say. That's the way to live if you want to be happy."

Ethan had noticed that Henri's name was not only on the stable but also on the grocery store and many other businesses near Young Island Cut. The new religion must be paying off. Henri turned to Ethan and said to him with a serious expression on his face, "There's a moral to my story Kemosabe. That's why I told you. The story's about finding what I call your true life. Have you thought about what you want to be when you grow up?"

"Well I like math. Maybe an engineer."

"Sounds good but you're probably too young to decide just yet. Every once in a while you need to step aside from your life and decide what makes you happy. That's where your true life lies. Things will get in the way like the church did capturing me. Find a way to get around such things and always seek your true life. If you do you'll have a happy life. If you don't you'll hate your life." Henri came closer to Ethan and held his eyes. "This is serious stuff Kemosabe. Remember it. Okay?"

Ethan said, "Okay." This was interesting. Finding your true life, what made you happy. He didn't know what would make him happy but promised himself to think about it.

Ethan and Johnson having saddled Henri said to Johnson, "Take care of him, Tonto. Seeing him brought back all the memories. He looks so much like my favorite boy at the cathedral. Only white boy who didn't avoid my confessional. I felt like I was telling him what happened and giving him the advice on life I always wanted to, was never able to."

Johnson did take care of Ethan, teaching him to ride, and then riding all around the island. Henri had told Ethan that his horse, Buck Jones, was the stable's best. Ethan found he had little to do to guide Buck. Buck seemed to intuitively understand where he wanted him to go, only an occasional pull on the reins or kick on the flank. Riding Buck was almost as good as sailing *Rascal*. He loved Buck, frequently patted his shoulder to thank him for the ride, feeling the bunching of Buck's powerful muscles under his hand, and feeding him wild mangoes, apparently Buck's favorite. He pictured himself a cowboy, the real Lone Ranger, and daydreamed about having Buck as his very own horse.

Henri gave one warning. "Buck has learned to take the bit in his teeth when he wants to go somewhere and can be hard to stop."

They were riding toward a beach at a secluded bay. Buck took the bit in his teeth, galloped ahead with him hanging on for dear life, charged into the water, and swam across the bay. This happened every beach they came to. Buck loved to swim. At first Ethan panicked. Later he would stand in the saddle and call out, "Hi-yo Silver. Away," as Buck splashed happily along.

They rode up to Fort Charlotte, a large fort towering over Kingstown, the capital. Many canon and all pointing inland. Johnson explained they pointed inland because the greatest danger to the colony in the 1790s came from the Caribs in the interior, not the French fleet.

"Carib very brave, very good fighter, not afraid to die. Bloody long war here. Same war with Carib on many of de island." Ethan thought back to Chief Aute on Dominica with new respect.

...

The third day at St. Vincent Ethan was seated on the dock, looking into the water, counting a school of yellow tangs flashing by. Glancing up he was startled to see George sauntering toward him dressed in evening clothes, and this a hot sunny afternoon. George called out, "Surprise," grinning broadly, and came up to where Ethan was sitting.

"Niskayuna is important here. When the governor found out I was on island he did the gentlemanly thing. He's hosting a dinner party tonight in my honor."

Ethan laughed, "Come on. How'd you get invited?"

"You don't believe me? Actually one of my new best friend drinking buddies is the governor's adjunct. Managed to get me included and found me the clothes. I've always wondered whether that stiff-upper-lip English stuff gets abandoned in the colonies. I'm hoping so."

The best way to get to the governor's mansion was horseback and a horse was needed. George chose Buck Jones.

Henri, Ethan, and Johnson all warned, "Watch out. Old Buck hard to stop."

George paid no attention and rode off in his black-tie, already a little inebriated from a stay at a beach bar all afternoon.

The governor's mansion perched on a hill above lush Bartam Garden, the oldest botanical garden in the Caribbean, and was approached by broad stone steps. What happened next became legend on the island, and Ethan laughed every time he thought about it.

Buck decided he wanted to join the party. Bit in his teeth, up the steps he went in stately fashion, like a king entering his court, George sawing futilely on the reins, then through the elegantly dressed assembly with many cocktail glasses crashing to the floor in haste of avoidance, then up to the banquet table at about the same sauntering pace as a lord of the manor would use.

Buck commenced with the salad course. Buck was hungry and his table manners were atrocious. Fine china was tossed from the table to smash on the floor and food was scattered far and wide. Buck didn't care. He ate half the salad before George and some other men finally got him away from the buffet table. On the way out he left a smelly gift on the newly polished broad-beamed mahogany floor, saying, "I was here."

The governor was very pompous English. Also, he was very attached to his entertainments as he didn't have much else to do on the island. He was not amused by George or Buck Jones. *Rascal* was requested to depart the island.

This was the first time Ethan had seen George have a comeuppance. He felt a momentary joy recalling the evening on Marie-Galante, quickly replaced by shame for the joy as he remembered that the whole marvelous adventure was due to George. He had a lot to thank George for.

. . .

From St. Vincent they tracked further south through the Grenadine Islands (the "Grenadines"), taking their time, idling from island to island. What impressed Ethan most was the beaches. The Grenadines were a necklace of thirty-two high-palmed islands spreading across fifty miles to the south of St. Vincent in shallow, magically turquoise and blue water, each island, as though by plan, enshrined in pristine sand showing off every type and size of beautiful beach that a beautiful sea could produce—shining white coral sand, pink sand, golden sand, and on islands previously visited even red sand and black sand, waves of every size shallowing, deepening, lapping, crashing collecting, overbalancing, falling, collecting, overbalancing, falling, an endless procession, sometime tumultuous and sometimes benign.

Ethan was a well tanned fish on each beach. If waves were large he'd go out and attempt the body surfing George had taught him. If it was calm he'd don his snorkel and view the aquarium that was the Caribbean, floating hours at a time, lost in following Parrotfish, or maybe a large Grouper, or sometimes a school of Angelfish or Sargent Majors or Blue Tangs, following them through their colorful world of coral, twisting canyons decorated with both soft and hard coral of pink, yellow and mauve, orange-splashed antler coral, sea fans of deep purple, caves providing shadowed homes for unusual fish, and red coral far below, a changing tapestry of glorious colors woven in more beautiful pattern then any weaver had ever accomplished. What it must be like to be a fish living in such a magnificent home.

George had given Ethan a book cataloging the fish of the Caribbean and challenged Ethan to compile a compendium of all the different fish he saw. (His count eventually got up to almost one hundred). Sometimes he would just dive down and look up, viewing the golden orb of the sun shining through the water above, the light at the surface scattering and shattering over his face in the underwater world.

Two days into the Grenadines Ethan sat in the cockpit reading. George plopped down next to him and pressed his leg lightly against his, George's arm around his shoulders, his face close to his, and asked him what he was reading. Ethan looked up startled, but before he could squirm away Johnson appeared, hopping mad judging from the enraged threateningly look on his face. He yanked George to his feet.

George yelled, "What the hell you doing. We're just talking. Take your damn hands off me," thrusting chin out and clenching his fists threateningly as on Martinique, again seemingly ready to punch Johnson.

Johnson said very calmly, " I warn you what will happen if you no stay away. You want to get beaten up? Remember what I say. From now on talk from a distance."

They glared at each other as Ethan sat with his mouth open staring at them both and dreading another physical confrontation.

The next day while snorkeling Ethan ventured into an area with an underwater cliff populated by a colony of moray eels. He'd often swum near moray eels before, green heads protruding from crevices in the reefs, mouths gaping voraciously. They'd never bothered him and he'd lost fear, though seeing them out of their holes in dreadful slither along the bottom was sort of gross. This time a moray eel exploded out of its hole as he passed, lightening fast, a monster, at least five feet long and as wide as his thigh. In panic he thrust his right flipper at the eel. The eel grabbed the flipper in an unshakable grip and pulled him underwater toward its hole. He was going to drown.

His flipper was securely strapped to his ankle. Johnson always strapped them on tightly, making sure they wouldn't fall off. Now he struggled with his last breath and all his strength to unstrap the flipper. Just before he had to start breathing water he did so, rising to the surface sputtering and calling for help.

Both George and Johnson jumped in, Johnson getting there first. He stood on the beach and sobbed out what had happened. George strode over to him with his arms wide to give him a comforting embrace. Johnson put up a cautionary hand and gave George a threatening look. George backed off.

Johnson said, "You did well. Many would have let panic take over. They drown."

And George quipped, "Smart of you to give him the rubber flipper. Morays are going to think people are made of rubber, terrible to eat." Then he laughed. This was the first attempt at humor and first laugh from George in a long time.

Ethan appreciated George trying to comfort him. But he shuddered when he thought about it. He looked down at the foot that had been in the moray's mouth and went cold all over, picturing himself pulled into the hole, breathing water, feeling it fill his lungs, struggling vainly against dying. He'd been that close to drowning. Death only a few breaths away. But he hadn't died. As Johnson said he hadn't panicked. Just like Johnson in the lobster hole on Nevis. He'd found a way to survive. He could take care of himself.

It turned out to be quite a day. Late afternoon Ethan was standing in about four feet of water on another remote Grenadine beach and saw a shadow rapidly approach. Tentacles entwined around his legs and lower body. The octopus quickly realized that what it had captured was attached to something frighteningly large above the water, and streaked off in a protective cloud of ink. This all happened so fast that Ethan's reaction was surprise, not fear. Johnson said he was amazed. He'd never known an octopus to try to grab someone from a beach. Ethan felt special but he was not sure for what.

George jumped in with one of his stories, the first in some time. "Ethan, what do you think you're standing on?" They were standing on a beautiful white coral sand beach.

Ethan expected this was a trick question but answered anyway, "Sand."

George responded with evident delight, "You're mostly standing on poo. Yes, a little sand where waves have broken up the rocks. But mostly poo. Have you seen the parrot fish and some other fish pooing out what looks like sand?"

Ethan nodded.

"What's happening is the fish are chewing the coral to eat the algae on the coral and hidden creatures, and they are then pooing out the coral sand they've chewed off. Has been going on for millions of years. The pooed coral sand washes up to make white coral sand beaches. You can tell people back home that you swam all over the Caribbean on beaches made of poo," which brought a small chuckle from Ethan, a good attempt to divert attention from moray eels and octopus.

Many times in the Grenadines after swimming at whatever beach they were exploring Ethan would stretch out on his towel under a beach front palm tree, admiring the quivering reflections thrown on the green roof by nearby water, sun at play between palm fronds swaying to gentle breeze, shadows moving across his face, and small music from the fanning and fluttering of the tree, then higher—frigate birds floating in the blue, wings not moving, as though suspended by invisible lines from heaven. He'd feel afloat with the frigate birds in the brilliant air. Above care.

The only negative with resting under a palm tree after a swim was that George had a way of coming over and staring down at him, interrupting his reverie, not talking, just looking at him.

Johnson eventually put and end to it, "Leave him alone, George. You got to stay away from him for you own good."

George said, "I'm not bothering him. Mind your own business."

Johnson moved menacingly toward George. George adopted a pugilist's pose, fists out in from of him, and took a step toward Johnson. So fast Ethan wasn't sure he actually saw it, Johnson punched George in the stomach and he doubled over. "I'll get you for that," said George, still bent over and holding his side as he shambled away down the beach.

· · ·

This was the final straw. He'd never let another man cow him and he wasn't going to start now. A van Rosenthal being cowed by an uppity nigger. No way. His ancestors would be rolling in their graves. He thought again about firing Johnson, reaching the same conclusion as before. If he fired Johnson it would devastate Ethan and turn Ethan against him, something he couldn't endure. Was there another way to get rid of Johnson? Johnson had said he'd leave the boat if he started saying good things about the plantations. But if he did that now, after Marie-Galante, Johnson would probably smell a rat. Poison was also a near impossibility with Johnson preparing the food and Ethan serving it. And while he could lock Johnson below when he was repairing the engine, what would that get him? He decided to wait and watch. The opportunity would come. He had to prepare himself to act quickly, without scruple. Somehow he had to find a way to kill Johnson without Ethan knowing he'd done it.

· · ·

Sometimes in the Grenadines, and earlier too, they would sail a few hours into the night to cover distances. Johnson would leave the masthead and running lights on to attract flying fish. He told Ethan that flying fish flew blind at night and came to lights. If they were lucky, one or more flying fish would hit the sails or rigging and fall stunned to the deck. Flying fish for breakfast. Their wings were iridescent in marvelous colors when first aboard, then sadly fading to gray as they died.

That night in the Grenadines a flying fish leapt out of the darkness, hit Johnson square-on in the face with a loud smack as he stood at the helm. Johnson yelled. The fish fell to the deck where it was grabbed with delight by Ethan. Johnson shook his head in disbelief, complained that it stung (he had a small cut on his lip), and later said, "Only de best cooks use der face to catch breakfast." Johnson's "face fish" was next morning's breakfast. Delicious.

CHAPTER TWENTY EIGHT

Eventually they anchored off a high island in the Grenadines. George said it was owned by a wealthy Canadian, Reggie Foster.

Apparently one of George's buddies knew Reggie slightly from a real estate deal in Canada, and George and his buddies had stopped at Reggie's island the preceding summer.

George told Ethan that Reggie was an escapee, like Moira Grayson.

Oh no, not another one. Ethan felt dread.

"Reggie is sort of odd but was very nice to us last summer. Been down here some time, sort of hiding out. Told us he'd been ostracized by family and friends. A lot of people in Canada are after him for the collapse of one of his buildings. A whole bunch of lawsuits. He was a builder of low income housing. One of his buildings came crashing down in a heavy snow storm and killed seven people, women and children. Apparently investigators found that the construction was shoddy. The newspapers went wild, labelled him a murderer. He claimed to us that it was all the sub-contractor's fault. They cut corners. He had records to prove it. But he was afraid to produce the records because the subs were Mafia. You know what Mafia are, right?"

Ethan nodded.

"The Mafia supposedly already made one attempt on his life, driving a heavy truck into his car up in Canada, putting him in the hospital. He's trapped between lawsuits and Mafia with no way out."

They rowed into the beach below Reggie's house and found a rope on a post with a sign saying: *"Pull Me."* The rope went up the path to the house perched on a high cliff overlooking the ocean.

George pulled the rope. A bell tinkled faintly far above. Several donkeys came down the path toward them, donkeys that appeared to have been trained to descend the path at the sound of the bell. George helped Ethan on his donkey, his hands lingering on his buttocks.

Johnson called out, "Watch dat!"

George's hands came away as though he was touching fire and Ethan saw George turn and look at Johnson with what he thought was hate.

Going up George and Ethan had to wrap their arms around the donkey's necks as the path was dangerously steep. Johnson stayed behind closely monitoring their ascent. On the way up, Ethan noticed a heavily armed guard hiding in the woods by the path, giving some credence to the story about the Mafia.

What looked large from below was gigantic upon arrival. A great ocean-front balcony stretched almost one hundred feet around the side of the house. On the balcony strode the owner, a smallish, florid-faced man with a midday drink in hand. He had on knee socks, carefully pressed khaki shorts and shirt, and a pith helmet, looking like pictures Ethan had seen of white hunters in Africa.

He came toward them with a glower, lips compressed, looking like he wanted to attack someone, didn't welcome them, just acknowledged their presence with a nod. Ethan never saw him smile the whole time he was there. Just various stages of scowls.

Reggie had apparently not had anyone to talk to (or complain to) for a long time because he immediately let loose a profanity-laced diatribe about everything. Anger at the Canadian government, anger at business associates who betrayed him, anger at a deserting wife, and at his children who wouldn't talk to him. At one point Reggie cursed God for giving him the life he had. He seemed most angry at God.

Drinking started in earnest. Shotguns came out. Ethan found himself ignored. The game with the guns was to shoot the pelicans. A great reef spread below the house. Pelicans were riding the trade-wind over the house to take fish on the reef.

Both men turned out to be good with shotguns, even with the drinking. The kills were many, each one marked by congratulations and a substantial toast from never empty glasses. One pelican was hit and managed to flop to the far end of the balcony. Ethan went over. The pelican was on its chest, facing him, wings extended as though still in flight, shotgun pellet wounds along its right side. The pelican raised its head slightly and looked at him. Ethan didn't see fear or pain. Rather he felt the pelican was looking at him in the belief that he was the one who shot it. After a few minutes the head went down, and he watched the blood drain out of its broken body as it died, his favorite bird the pelican.

Ethan marched over to the two men. Stood between them and pushed their guns to each side. Said loudly, *"No more.* The birds have done nothing to you!"

The men stopped but Reggie's face went red, contorting in rage. He slowly moved his gun over in Ethan's direction. "Damn insolent pup. Nobody interferes with me in my own home."

The Canadian was going to shoot him.

George said, "No!" pushed Reggie's gun away, stood up, grabbed Ethan, and hurried down the path.

Back on *Rascal* George sat Ethan down and told him in a loving way how scared he'd been for him, that what he did was extremely dangerous, he could have been killed. "Reggie has changed since my last visit. His loneliness and guilt are driving him mad. He's gotten frighteningly unstable. I never should have brought you there."

But Ethan felt he had gained new respect from George because of his bravery. Whereas previously George had called him "boy"and referred to him in conversations with others as "the boy," now he addressed him as "young man" or sometimes "Mr. Ethan."

Johnson later said to Ethan, "You do right. Mon have to do what right. Mon have to stand up for what right".

Ethan replied, "Yes. It's what a man has to do," and he stood proud.

The next day they left Reggie's island to cruise further into the Grenadines. It was Ethan's fourteenth birthday, August 14th, a double fourteen as Johnson pointed out. Johnson said, "You born under a sun sign, Leo, why de Caribbean make you it friend." Then he gave him a professional sailor's knife like the one he wore that Ethan had long admired. Wow. A really nifty knife. Ethan thanked him profusely.

George had forgotten his birthday but quickly fished out a hundred dollar bill that Ethan accepted with great pleasure. He tried to thank George just as profusely as Johnson. This was followed by a lobster dinner and a birthday cake, both of which Ethan ate with gusto. He could never figure out how Johnson baked the cake without him knowing about it.

He said to them both, "Having a birthday on *Rascal* is the best," then hesitated and said, "Or maybe the second best."

George responded, "I'd love to hear about that other birthday, Mr. Ethan. Why don't you tell us about it."

Ethan's face went sad. "Okay. It was with my mother." He looked first at George and then at Johnson.

George said, "Go on."

Ethan said, "Well, it was my eighth birthday, August 14, 1945. I was sort of stupid then and didn't understand things that were going on. But what happened was great, especially because I didn't understand what was going on.

"My mother gave me a birthday party and invited some boys from the neighborhood that I played with. She always baked great birthday cakes like Johnson's cake, and she gave me the neat baseball mitt I wanted. I think my parents put me to bed at my usual time, around 9:00 PM.

"Anyway, before I got to sleep my father came charging in. I could see he was very excited about something. He said, 'We're going to the city. Come in your PJ's.' I was really surprised. I was never allowed out of the house in P.J.s. Then driving the car into the city was strange. With gas rationing we never used the car except to go to church or in a real emergency like when I fell from the tree. Then the strangest thing. We picked up a hitchhiker, a sailor. My father always said never, ever pick up a hitch hiker. Nobody told me what was going on. But my father and mother were excited so I got excited. I thought maybe they planned a birthday surprise.

"When we got to the city it looked like people were celebrating my birthday with the biggest party I'd ever seen. The whole city was there. People were hugging, men and women kissing. I didn't think they even knew each other. There was a band playing and people were dancing. I remember my mother dancing up and down, laughing like I'd never heard her before. This was on the main street of Schenectady. I thought this was the best birthday party any boy ever had. And when I think back on my mother it is her dancing and laughing that night that I try and remember.

"I felt like a real moron when after an hour or so my parents finally told me it wasn't about my birthday. It was about the defeat of Japan. World War

II had ended. And on my birthday, August 14th. Then I remember getting real happy. What a great present to have on your birthday."

George said, "Wonderful story, young man. Not many people bring peace to the whole world by having a birthday. The whole world thanks you."

Ethan replied, "You're welcome," and grinned from ear to ear.

George said, "I never asked you about your name. Did Ethan come from someone in your family?"

Ethan replied, "Ethan Allen was one of my mother's ancestors."

George said, "A very brave man with his Green Mountain Boys. No wonder you're so brave." Ethan hung his head shyly with a happy smile.

. . .

The next morning Johnson was at the helm, a Gauloise hanging from the corner of his mouth, watching George as he moved slowly and heavily around the deck, looking like everything was a burden. George had somehow shrunken. Didn't stand as tall. Voice not as loud. No longer raised his chin to talk down to him. More serious drinking. Even a tot of brandy at lunch. This didn't seem to affect his functioning on the boat. But when George was at the helm, he tried to stay close. George was clearly having trouble.

When he'd first seen Ethan with George he'd felt something wasn't right. Once in Freetown there'd been a white man in a large house on Non Such Bay who had molested two Freetown boys. One of the families was a member of Johnson's church. Good Christians, they eventually forgave the predator. He would have liked to emulate them but couldn't. George continued to cast lustful glances at Ethan.

The former owner of *Rascal* had treated him as a sailing companion and the professional he was, deferring to him on matters related to sailing. George instead treated him as a servant, asking him to fetch for him. Sometimes ignoring his sailing advice, usually to their detriment. It especially rankled that George had never asked to meet his family, despite bringing *Rascal* to Antigua the last three years running, and despite having Ethan aboard this trip. Then there was George's unapologetic racism. Johnson had long ago concluded that one of the worst things was for a wealthy man, leader of his community like George, to be racist as it excused everyone around them to be racist.

Johnson had considered quitting after sailing with George the previous year. That he had not was due to pay well above what was available elsewhere. One of his sons had medical needs.

Antiguans learned hundreds of years ago how to conceal from whites their anger at the discrimination, the slights, the forced subservience. He was an excellent practitioner of this discipline. So George didn't know that for almost two weeks he'd been planning to kill him.

He wasn't motivated by the attack on Ethan. While the attack was bad, Ethan was not harmed, and he thought he could protect Ethan from here on out. Rather it was what the attack portended. He was absolutely certain the devil would direct George to further molestations. He'd seen how hard George stared at adolescent boys on Dominica, Martinique, and St. Lucia. Repeat molestations were the norm. After the white man on Non Such Bay had molested the two boys, he'd gone on to attack other boys before being arrested. Among the devils of the land, molesters of boys took the high seats next to the evil one, and they kept at it. George had to be stopped.

But could he kill George? God gave him six sons. So maybe He wanted him to be a protector of boys. And God made it so easy, made it so easy here on *Rascal*. Maybe this meant God wanted him to do it. All it would take was a simple maneuver—run *Rascal* downwind with the heavy trade-wind behind her, do a jibe and not warn George, knock him overboard. George often stood in the cockpit taking sightings, not noticing things around him, and with the full weigh of the jibing boom crashing across the deck, accelerated by the roaring trade-wind, George would not only be knocked overboard but probably knocked overboard unconscious. Then he would be a little slow getting back to him. George was not a strong swimmer. He couldn't stay afloat very long even if conscious. Unintentional jibes happened all the time. Everyone would think it was an accident with the trade-wind blowing this strongly. Losing someone overboard was common in the Caribbean. And Ethan would never suspect what really happened.

Johnson had been mulling it over and over and over, hashing and rehashing, thinking about the methodology but mostly about whether he as a Christian could justify killing another human being. If he was going to do it today was the perfect day. The wind was howling and coming from almost directly behind *Rascal* so only a small movement of the helm was necessary to start a jibe. And two new islands had appeared on the horizon, prompting George to stand by the binnacle doing sightings, paying no attention whatsoever to the sails.

Johnson stood resolute, waiting for the right moment to start the turn, his hands clenching the helm, knuckles white from the strength of his grip, steeling his resolve, thinking of the boys he would be saving. He looked over his shoulder for the hard gust that would slam the boom across. Two hundred yards to the stern it appeared. The water was boiling black with wind. Approaching fast. He tensed his body, gritted his teeth, narrowed his eyes to slits, avoiding looking directly at George. Then the gust was upon *Rascal*, jumping on his back and whistling around him. His arms pulled the helm over to start the turn. Now the wind was directly behind Rascal, now a little bit to the lee, only a fraction more and Bang, it would all be over.

He couldn't do it. His arms wouldn't turn further. Frozen in place.

How could he kill another human being? All his life he'd protected life. And he'd tried to live God's commandments. *Thou shall not kill.* But didn't exceptions exist? What about Hitler? Wouldn't Jesus have approved killing Hitler to save Jewish children? And if that killing was somehow acceptable, wouldn't Jesus have approved killing Hitler if Hitler was promoting the molestation of Jewish children?

It went dark. The sun vanished. He looked up. A black cloud had descended over the boat, quite different from the few gossamer-white trade-wind clouds floating past. Where had that come from? There were no storms around. He felt a jolt of fear. The devil. Waiting for him. Hoping he'd kill George. Hoping it could attach itself to his soul just as now attached to George's. Ready to haunt him with the murder the rest of his life, to take him to hell. Johnson shuddered and yanked his hands off the helm as though they'd been scalded. With no one steering, Rascal quickly turned into the wind. George stared back at him. He shook himself and retook control of the boat. This was a battle between God and the devil for George's soul. He wasn't going to step in.

As he considered further, he was surprised to find that he actually had some sympathy for George. Every night he could hear George writhing in his bunk, sometimes crying out in what sounded like anguish. He was sure the devil was working on George, visiting him repeatedly. The devil had drawn George into sin. Now the devil was tormenting George for the sin, trying to get him to sin more, and not waiting for hell but punishing him here on earth. He could see George was trying to fight against his perversion. Give him credit for that.

Maybe he should talk to George and warn him, tell him that the devil was visiting him. That would be the Christian thing to do. But did he want to be Christian regarding George? And George would never accept the devil's presence anyway.

The worrisome thing was the other boys. In the Bible the Lord casts out demons. Maybe if he prayed to Him he would do so again. He decided to try, not praying for George but praying the Lord would confront the devil and protect boys from George. And he also vowed to redouble his watch on George to bar anything further happening to Ethan. The voyage would only last a couple of weeks more. Then he would quit with great delight.

He left the helm very satisfied. In one watch he'd moved all the way from almost killing a man to thinking about prayer. Not bad.

. . .

They lazed through the lower Grenadines, working south toward the island of Grenada, stopping at Bequia, Tobago Cays, Mayreau, Union Island, and many other idyllic islands and cays, seeing little inter-island traffic except for the occasional fishing boat, and giving Ethan opportunity to be in the water a good part of each day, a series of major explorations of the reefs of the Grenadines. Ethan added more new fish to his fish compendium during this week than in all the previous weeks of the voyage combined. Many days *Rascal* was the only work of man in a universe of sea.

One day they sailed mostly in shoal water, radiant light all around, the sails only needing to open to fill the world with joy. Ethan was hoisted to the spreaders to be on the lookout for coral heads, brain coral that sometimes grew as much as thirty feet up from the bottom to rest two feet under the surface in the path of unwary sailors. George told Ethan the brain corals were named "nigger heads" because their spherical configurations resembled a large head and the coral on their surface looked like the crinkly hair on a curly haired black man. Johnson was behind George so George missed the disgusted look Johnson gave him.

Later in the day Johnson stood on the stern deck looking out. He threw his arms open as if trying to capture the wind, capture the whole sea world to his breast, to hug it to him. Breaking out his broadest, open-mouthed grin he proclaimed from the Bible, *"This is the day the Lord has made. Let us rejoice and be glad in it."*

Sitting on the spreaders, Ethan was indeed glad. It was a blast. Happiness welled up. Had his life ever been this good? From his roost he could see fish of every color, rainbow painted friends from his reef explorations. They were darting though the shallow water to decorate the coral, fluttering like marine butterflies, and occasionally a shark, barracuda, or ray cruising along between the reefs, and even a few turtles in flopping progress. It was with a sense of loss that he came down from the mast at day's end. Then he realized he'd not thought about his mother all day. Guilt swept over him. How could a day pass without him thinking about what he did to his mother?

. . .

Leaving the Grenadines *Rascal* stopped at Carriacou to secure supplies, an island just north of the island of Grenada. In the market the stalls were decorated with colorful island cloth and piled high with produce and household items. Fish and meat were separately displayed on what looked like very clean counters. All the stalls sat in neat rows with little signs designating what kind of merchandise was being sold, a very orderly market.

An elderly black woman toting a large bundle passed Ethan. Ethan offered to help her, an offer gratefully accepted, and he carried the bundle to her donkey cart at the edge of the market. This was the second time he had done this in a market, and both George and Johnson commented on his good deed.

At the far end of the market a small stall was manned by a very black woman dressed entirely in white. Even her straw hat was painted white, the color of death. She looked to be about fifty, grossly fat, with dead-white hair, natural or dyed, that hung down straight to below her waist. She was selling amulets, charms, and grotesque small clay statues, and appeared to be doing a good business.

Johnson said she was a voodoo woman. When he heard this Ethan wanted to meet her, and when they went over to her stall she proved willing to talk. She said her name was Nour Devron and explained that what she was selling was a very necessary part of life on the island of Grenada and surrounding islands.

"Der many bad spirit here, some brought over from Africa. Most left by de French and de English. De' enslave Grenada 200 year, leave many evil thing behind. One of de worst Lou-Garou. He be werewolf that can shed his skin, can fly, and can pass through a house keyhole seeking de blood of de victim. De little statues you see der protect de home against Lou-Garou. Even worse be La-Ja-Bless. La-Ja-Bless be de she devil with beautiful, sexy figure.

"She wear long dress to hide de fact dat one of her foot be cloven. Other foot normal. She seduce married men dat stay out late at night. La-Ja-Bless get married mon interested. Lead him to a precipice, or a dangerous place by de sea, or sometimes she come on de boat. She lift de wide, floppy brim of her hat. Show her skull head and eyes of fire. Dat frighten de man so much he jump off de precipice or off de boat into de sea.

"Around here when married man die in de sea or from a fall we know he not bein faithful. La-Ja-Bless took him. Amulets you see protect against La-Ja-Bless."

Ethan noticed that many men around them were wearing the voodoo woman's amulets. He wondered whether this meant they were straying from their wives and wanted protection while they strayed.

Nour Devron stopped talking, stared intently at George for more than a minute, and pulled a very different looking amulet from a hidden drawer beneath her display case. The amulet looked very old, appeared to be made from silver and ebony, and was incised with what looked like hieroglyphics. She insisted that George buy it and said the price was one hundred dollars.

"You need dis. Will protect you from de dark thing. Very special amulet. Come from Egypt. De only one in de world. You have to have dis to protect you. You in danger. You in big danger. Please, please buy de amulet to protect you. I want to protect you. I like to give you de amulet for free to protect you. But I no can. I pay a lot of money for de amulet." She told him over and over again he needed it and it would protect him. Growing increasing loud in her insistence she eventually drew a small crowd of onlookers.

George said, "No," repeatedly, that he was not going to pay one hundred dollars for a voodoo amulet.

Eventually he stomped away. Nour Devron shrugged, hesitated, looked up at the sky, and then like a Caribbean banshee called after George at the top of her lungs, "Let it be on your head." At the same time she was rubbing her hands together in a hand-washing motion much as Pontius Pilate must have used in casting Jesus to his death.

George slowly trudged back to the boat, looking burdened, as though the shadow he was pulling behind him had great weight in the tropical heat.

Ethan eventually said, "She sure was angry you didn't buy that amulet."

George replied, "She thinks I need protection. Maybe I do. But I'm not about to have a voodoo woman try and protect me."

Back at the dock Ethan studied the spectacular, green hill-nestled harbor of Carriacou and gave casual attention to the wind-wrinkles on the translucent water around the dock and to schools of brightly colored fish hiding under the dock to escape larger fish and sea birds, passing time while waiting for Johnson to finishing buying new docking lines in the nearby marine store. A bare flagpole stood next to the dock.

George interrupted his thoughts. "Want to see how you can use shadows to tell time and find compass directions?"

Ethan said, "Sure."

"Okay," George said. "Look at the shadow next to the flagpole. See how it's gradually getting smaller and moving counter-clockwise? Let me know when the shadow is at its smallest."

Ethan watched carefully and reported when he thought the shadow had stopped shrinking.

George said, "Now it's twelve noon." This was confirmed by the twelve noon peal of a church bell in town. "Now look at the direction the shadow is pointing. That's true north.

"It doesn't have to be noon to use shadows. You can tell approximate time and direction at any point in the day from shadows. A sailor never needs a watch or a compass when he has his boat at dock or anchored in a still harbor. All he has to do is to look at the shadow from his mast. And, Mr. Ethan, you can do this back home if you ever get lost. Just find a tree without leaves, maybe a dead tree, and look at the shadow. It will tell you time and direction."

Ethan thanked George, telling him he knew just the tree in the woods behind his house.

...

After spending the morning in Carriacou they sailed to Sauteurs Bay, Grenada. George's depression had become so great, not helped by the voodoo woman at Carriacou, that he felt like walking off *Rascal*, walking off into the enveloping blue, have the air and sea take him away, punishment for his sins and escape from his pain. He was making no progress. It was worse. The desire was part of him, beyond addiction, relentless. He'd tried to discipline himself not to watch Ethan dressing and undressing. Something was forcing him to glance over, entrapping him, and he always got aroused.

As they sailed toward Grenada he found himself perched on the rail, perched with crossed arms, not holding on, sitting there in despair. He didn't remember going there. He never sat on the rail, always sat in the safety of the cockpit. Now sitting on the rail he found himself moving backward and forward with the motion of *Rascal*. One little backward lean and he'd be gone. A little backward. The least backward. The slightest backward. That would end it.

How simple it would be. All he had to do was ignore any life-saving ring thrown to him, and in these rough seas by the time Johnson and Ethan jibed *Rascal* around and came back for him he'd be lost. It took all of his determination to fight the lean.

When he looked up Ethan was staring at him with a very worried frown on his face. George looked away.

A hole in the clouds and he felt the full power of God's light beating down upon him, assaulting him without mercy. There was no mercy. He stopped teetering and started thinking about death.

He'd never thought much about death. The death of a friend or relative was a relatively rare occurrence. A funeral brought church platitudes that gave no meaning to death or dying that he could discern. Did it matter if he died now? He must inevitably die anyway. Who would grieve him more than church rituals required? Would any part of him be carried forward in the minds of anyone? Marge? With his neglect he'd already brought her so much grief that grief from his death would only add slightly. Ethan? He hoped so.

Then there was him. Death ended everything. It was nothingness. They would fold him into the earth. No longer would life keep him from the soil. He would become the soil. Did he really want that? His life suffocated forever in earth and darkness? Eternal darkness?

Not realizing that now he was talking out loud, "Aren't there things in life which can still bring me happiness? But really are there?"

Ethan looked over at him and he focused on Ethan, admiring his beauty, more beautiful than ever. Then with a determined voice, "Not today!"

He left the rail feeling he just couldn't deal with it anymore. Death, perversion, staggering concepts. He'd no experience thinking through such things. Here he was sitting in the blazing sunshine of the spectacular Caribbean and thinking about death and perversion. As exhausted as he had ever been in his life, he went below decks to lie down until his watch was called.

As they anchored in Sauteurs Bay the waning moon swam up as a small sliver from the ocean, showing them they were off a broad beach and next to a large sailboat of some sort. Sunrise revealed the most spectacular sailboat Ethan had seen. It was a sloop, about sixty feet long, all brightwork, no paint from stem to stern, just glistening wood with beautiful graining covered with many coats of varnish, the sides of the boat alive with light reflected from the rippling sea.

Johnson said, "Dat *Cocoban,* one of de most famous sailboat in de Caribbean. Own by Malcolm Fitz Gibbons. He de richest mon in de Caribbean. *Cocoban* name after all de coconut and banana plantation he own. No think he expect to own any of it. His mother was de black mistress of old Harry Fitz Gibbons. Harry divorce his wife and live with Malcolm mother, but never marry her. When he die his will give everything to Malcolm and his mother. Big fight with de white heirs. For once de black win. Mother die. Malcolm get everythin and carry on de business. A smart businessman. Not only own many plantation but he took over all de processin of Grenada spice, very profitable. Grenada call de spice island. Many valuable spice grow here."

George entered the conversation pointing out a high cliff near the beach. "Sauters means 'jump' in French. The bay was named Sauteurs because many hundred Caribs jumped off the cliff rather than become slaves. Jumping points exist all over the islands where Caribs killed themselves to avoid slavery." He paused and looked thoughtful. "Sometimes death does make sense."

Shortly after dawn a crew of about thirty men appeared on the beach along with a string of about the same number of horses. The men quickly attached ropes to *Cocoban* and pulled her into the shallows using the horses and muscle power, solid wood and very heavy, a struggle. They tipped her on her side as they were pulling her in so her bottom was exposed, and started scrubbing the bottom to remove algae and barnacles. George, Johnson, and Ethan rowed in to watch more closely. In the late morning a light-skinned black man strode down from the back of the beach wearing jodhpurs, riding boots, a white shirt, and a planter's hat. Johnson told them he was Malcolm Fitz Gibbons.

Malcolm motioned them over and introductions were made. He said he careened *Cocoban* like this every six months to clean the bottom. "I give de local village a couple of keg of rum and it get done in one long day. De' like der rum."

He asked if they'd had lunch, and when George said no, Malcolm said, "Well, come on up to my house for lunch. Normally we have company for lunch. Not today. And I always like to extend courtesy to visiting yachtsmen. Maybe need de courtesy in return sometime." He smiled, a nice warm smile.

Ethan liked him right off the bat. Malcolm might be the richest man in the Caribbean but nothing showed in his friendly welcome. And he didn't look the part. His eyes were small and set close together, lips too thick and protruding, and skin badly blotched with patches of pink interspersed with dark brown. An ugly man to be so rich.

Horses were saddled. After an hour's ride through coconut groves and banana plantations they arrived at a sprawling white mansion surrounded by broad balconies sited on a hill with extensive views across the island. Getting off their horses, the first thing Malcolm did was apologize that the house hadn't been painted recently. And he continued to apologize their whole time there—that the lovely Caribbean-style furnishings, which looked new, were not what they should be, that the meal, which was excellent, was not better, that the wine, which George said came from an outstanding vineyard and an outstanding year, might be inadequate because of travel damage in shipment from France. It was all very strange.

Malcolm's wife did not sit with them, though an additional place was set. She hovered in the background almost like a servant, pretty, very black. He

never introduced her but he eventually pointed to her and said, "Dat my wife."
Again very strange.

Most of the meal was taken with sailing talk. George recounted their
voyage and Malcolm recounted various sailing adventures. At the end of the
meal Malcolm said they were gelding some colts that afternoon, and would
they like to watch. He addressed this invitation particularly to Ethan. Ethan
asked what that was. Malcolm explained.

Ethan said, "Gosh. That sounds great." Was he making a big mistake?

Three colts had been gelded before Malcolm turned to Ethan. "Would
you like to do the next one." Ethan hesitated. Malcolm said, "Come on. Every
boy have to do it. It part of boy becoming a mon around here."

Ethan had observed the process. The farm hands would tie the colt,
trip it down with ropes so it lay protesting on its back, then one of them
would swiftly pull the balls away from the body using a strong twist, providing room for the slash of the gelding knife, this followed by a heartrend-
ing scream and the cauterizing iron. Ethan approached his colt, pulled and
twisted mightily on the balls, watched the gelding knife do its work, and
heard the scream, a far louder scream than from the other horses. He felt like
crying but didn't. Instead he swore to himself that he'd never do anything
like that again.

Riding back to *Rascal* Ethan said to Johnson, "That was weird. The richest man in the Caribbean and he seemed shy."

Johnson said, "No shy. Embarrassed. He embarrassed to be black when
around white men. No think he good enough, or what he have good enough.
De white in de Caribbean try and make sure black feel dat way. You see
him apologizin all de time like he think you and George better than him
despite him bein so rich. Many mulatto in de Caribbean like dat. Apologize
to de white for der blackness and to de black for der whiteness. Because of
Harry Fitz Gibbons, Malcolm caught between bein black and bein white. No
a happy mon."

Ethan turned in his saddle and studied everything around, workers harvesting coconuts in a grove to the left, to the right bananas dangling in profusion. The skinny dun colored horse beneath him moved in a heavy trot, and
as they ascended a hill the sea beckoned in the distance, shimmering in late
afternoon light. Everything new, different, wonderful, and he was living it all.

Had he ever felt so alive before? He doubted it. It was as though he was experiencing life for the first time. He'd never thought about what it meant to be alive. At home he wasn't living. Summer there would have only brought more sadness, getting worse, getting darker. Here he was out of that, seeing exciting things, amazing things every day, a whole new world. He pulled fragrant air deeply into his lungs. *He was alive.*

CHAPTER TWENTY NINE

The next day they scooted around the northwest corner of Grenada and George had them anchor in a broad bay near several plantations, Duquesne Bay. He said he intended to show Ethan spice cultivation on the plantations the following day. Their anchorage was in the protected lee of the island but Johnson said they couldn't anchor close-in because of shoaling. They ended up anchoring so far out that it seemed to George they were anchored in the open ocean.

After dinner he went forward and stood clutching the forestay, fighting the pain. He couldn't take it anymore. Each day had become more difficult than the last. Monstrous things were coming to him in the night, ever darker things. Last night he'd left a nightmare in stark terror and cried out, "Lord, Lord." Then more loudly, "I've lost my soul." When awake he'd found Ethan standing by his bunk, asking if he was okay. He wasn't. For more than three weeks he'd been destroying himself, his mind chasing itself around, trying to find a way out of his perversity, flailing itself, the torment continuing and growing. He'd gone over everything so many times his mind was numb, unable to think clearly anymore. He feared for his sanity. And even more he feared what he would do if he got Ethan alone. He had been thinking about it for weeks and was sure he would rape him. His desire had grown so great that all restrain would be whipped aside if he got him alone.

He had to end this voyage and fast.

Dragging himself back to the cockpit he announced in a strained voice, "Tomorrow we head back north."

He gave Ethan and Johnson no explanation of why a change from the original plan to sail all the way south to Trinidad. Just told them he was in a hurry to get north and end the voyage, and that to get back quickly they would bypass most of the islands they'd visited on the way south, instead sail long passages day and night without stop.

Ethan's head bowed in unhappiness. George could see he was near tears. He took his arm and made him sit down in the cockpit, standing over him.

"Mr. Ethan, you knew voyage had to end. You've know that all along. Are you worrying about going home?"

Ethan gave a small nod.

"Don't worry. Everything will be fine. You're different than when you came aboard. Quite different. Aren't you aware of that?"

Ethan said, "Yes," in a soft voice with his head still lowered.

"You're a tough guy now. An ocean sailor. No boys back home are going to want to bother you. No people are going to bother you. None of them have done what you've done. They're going to respect you. And I promise you if anyone isn't nice to you just tell me and I'll take care of them."

Johnson said, "You no longer a boy. You be mon now. Almost grow up. What back der boy stuff. A mon can handle it."

George continued, "And as for your father, I'm going to give your father a good talking to when I get back."

. . .

Ethan listened carefully to George and Johnson's words. He did feel different, and as he thought about it, he was feeling differently about his mother's death. Back home the pain was so great that it felt like a physical wound. The longer he stayed in town the greater the pain, constantly reopening the memory, constantly forcing himself to go over each and every detail of her death, then go over it again and again, punishing himself.

It reminded him of when he cut his leg a year ago. It was a bad cut, and he'd picked at the scab and picked at it, preventing it from healing. That's what he had been doing with his mother's death, picking and picking at the wound. It would never have healed back there.

The Caribbean had changed things. Now her death was just a bad part of his life. And he felt that the bad part was passing. All along Johnson had been preaching he should forgive himself and was always saying, "Forget it," when he was moping. He could never forget it. But finally he could think about her death without that terrible guilt feeling. He found himself accepting what Johnson said —that her death was just something to get over, and that bad experiences in life are balanced by good ones. Wasn't he having a wonderful time every day in the Caribbean? He wasn't going to let his mother's death ruin his life anymore. He would try and be the man Johnson wanted him to be.

A smiled, then a much broader smile, and he started humming. George and Johnson looked at him in astonishment.

...

What happened next began at sunset. Johnson later decided that it was George's change of plans to turn north that provoked nature, that's what caused nature to reach out a tentacled arm and try and pull *Rascal* into the depths below. Nature was angry at *Rascal* for not continuing her joyful dance south with the Caribbean.

Johnson watched the ocean go flat calm as the sun set, eerie in trade-wind latitudes, a breathless stillness. Off in the distance to the west multiple thunder storms were lighting the horizon with mammoth displays of lightening. They were far south, and a blanket of warm air had been pulled up from the jungles of Guyana and Venezuela. They were all perspiring copiously. Heat shimmered on the water, the air too close, heavy with moisture, a strange, sticky heat unlike anything they'd experienced on the voyage.

Johnson went to his bunk uneasy, sleeping fitfully, feeling something wasn't right, getting up repeatedly and looking around the horizon from the forward hatch, difficult to see anything as it was a black night. He heard George and Ethan go to their bunks and go fast asleep, except for occasional tormented sounds from George, now a regular part of each night.

When he saw it he yelled at the top of his lungs, *"Get up! Leave you clothes! Hurry! We got to get out of here!"*

George and Ethan bolted top-side. Bearing down on them, less than a mile away through the near darkness, a gigantic waterspout. It looked to be more than half-a-mile wide.

The anchor was weighed faster than ever before, fortunately coming up freely, and the engine started immediately, again fortuitously. Rascal rammed ahead at full speed in desperate attempt to escape.

As the water spout approached where they'd been anchored, now not much more than a few hundred yards off, its violence was transmitted to the air and water. Johnson at the helm found his face stung by the spume whipping off the sides of the waterspout and spiky waves churned up, leaping onto *Rascal's* stern though he tried by violent movement of the helm to avoid them, swamping into the cockpit, pouring vast amounts of water below decks though the open companionway hatch, the hull quickly filling to a point where water was sloshing back and forth between the bunks and *Rascal* was in danger of foundering. George had quickly lashed himself and Ethan to cleats in the cockpit using the jib sheets and Johnson held onto the helm with all his strength as waves broke across his back. One last, gigantic sneaker wave roared into him just as he took one hand off the helm to rub the salt water out of his eyes. He grasped the helm with the one hand still on the helm, horizontal to the deck and several feet above it in the wave but all his strength wasn't a match for the strength of the wave. Finger by finger his grip slipped and he was pulled overboard. The waterspout roared past, voicing rage at having missed them.

Johnson treaded water as best he could in the tumultuous sea, waves crashing over him and making it difficult to breath. Between waves he watched George speed the boat away, disappearing in the storm. He look around. His first thought was to swim to shore. In the continuing rain and mist he realized he didn't know the direction to shore but thought he could find it. He treaded water a few minutes more, thinking, and started swimming through the gloom after the boat. It was far more risky then swimming to shore but he couldn't leave Ethan alone on the boat with George. He smiled to himself. If I die it is for Ethan.

At first the swimming was not too difficult. He was a strong swimmer. What was difficult was maintaining the proper angle to the initial course of the boat. All he had to go on was the direction of the waves. The boat had moved off with the waves hitting the starboard side slightly towards the bow and he followed that course using the direction of the waves as his guide, though he was constantly getting knocked off course as waves crashed over him. After an hour he felt his arms getting tired, though he'd stopped every once in awhile to tread water and rest. And he was starting to feel a little nauseated from water he was swallowing in the wild sea. He peered through the mist from the top of a wave. He could see little over half a mile. Nothing.

The boat couldn't have gotten too far. The water in the bilge would seep into the engine room and flood the diesel. But with no boat he was starting to have doubts. Had he guessed wrong? He believed he'd figure out George's plan to kill him. George would gradually, imperceptibly to Ethan, altered course to either left or right. That way when George went back for him, and looked for him in the sector behind the boat, George could be assured he wouldn't find him. And it would appear to Ethan that George was doing a conscientious and thorough search.

He'd made a bet George had turned right and had been pursuing a course somewhat to right of the angle at which the boat had left him. Right handed people normally turn right and George was right handed. Or had George been smart enough to turn left against his right handedness? Johnson set off swimming to the left, at right angles to his present course, more slowly now. He swam for half an hour. Nothing. He stopped, treading water and thinking. George was smart, but he was also arrogant, and he had shown he didn't think a black was intelligent enough to figure things out. He was right the first time. George turned to starboard. The swim back to where he had been was hard to the point of near exhaustion. He had to swim back the same half hour at the same pace to be able to return to the vicinity of where he'd been when he detoured left. Continuing the original course he was running out of strength and time. He buoyed himself thinking of Rebecca and his boys waiting for him. He pictured them standing on the water ahead their arms outstretched in welcome. Then he had a separate picture of George exulting when he couldn't be found. He was not going to let George win. He was not going to let George have his way with Ethan. More determined than ever he swam on counting strokes, ten more strokes, then ten more strokes. Ten strokes for Rebecca, then ten stokes for each of his boys, then ten strokes for Ethan, and then repeat it all, how many times could he do this?

No more. He could go no further. Rebecca was no longer urging him on through the mist. The boys and Ethan had disappeared. He was alone. He slowly treaded water. The waves were breaking over him and pushing him down. It was increasingly difficult to struggle up for breath, legs now as tired as arms, trying to cough out the water entering his lungs. He gasped out to God, "Thank you for everything you've given me," and he made one last scan of the horizon. Miracle, there it was in the far distance, just getting ready to sail. Could he make it. Maybe.

. . .

When Johnson went overboard George raced below, turned on the bilge pump, and took the helm. Ethan shouted at him, "We've got to go back for Johnson. Turn around." When George did nothing Ethan grabbed the helm and tried to turn the boat. George shook him off.

"We can't go back now. We'll sink if we don't get away from these waves. We'll go back when it calms down a bit." After some time, still going away from Johnson and the worst waves, there were two coughs from the engine and the engine died. They wallowed there, rocking back and forth in the still tumultuous seas.

Ethan went up to George, tears in his eyes. "We've got to start searching for him and not wait any longer. He may be drowning. Can't we sail back for him or restart the engine?"

George said in a dismissive way, "We're too waterlogged to sail until we clear the below-decks of water. And the engine won't start under water. We're going to have to hope a passing fisherman picks him up. It will take a long time to empty the boat of all that water."

. . .

For the next hours Ethan found himself varying his time between checking the level of the below-decks water and standing on the stern gazing out, watching for Johnson though the obscurity. Several times he burst into tears and wailed, "We can't lose him. We can't," as though his cries could bring Johnson back. Glancing at George he would occasionally see George smiling broadly. Did George hate Johnson so much he wanted him to die like that?

It took George almost three hours to agree to sail back for Johnson, and it went so slowly. He'd never seen George make sail so slowly. Ethan yelled at him, "We've got to hurry. We may be too late already." George continued to move slowly saying, "We have to go very carefully with so much water still on board."

Ethan looked up and saw a distant splash through the gloom. A dolphin? Didn't move like a dolphin and was coming directly toward them. He hardly dared hope it was Johnson, and then it was Johnson. George's face went white under his tan. He stared in stony silence at the approaching swimmer as though his stare might hold him back. Johnson was swimming very slowly, tiredly, stopping repeatedly. Ethan threw out a life ring and put down the swimming ladder while George stood sourly at his side. Johnson appeared to have barely enough strength to come up the ladder, and then in one violent, fluid motion threw George hard into the cockpit, standing over him.

"Nice try but you too stupid to pull it off." Then Johnson collapsed on the other side of the cockpit, breathing heavily, his face lined with an exhaustion Ethan had never seen in him before.

After a time Johnson raised his head and said to Ethan,

"Knew I be dead if no see you in de few minute. Den I see you. What kept me goin be determine no let George kill me and determine to see you." Johnson took Ethan by the shoulders and held him close. "Would miss you a lot."

Ethan gave Johnson a big hug back and stepped back from him, imagining what it must have been like swimming all that time looking for the boat. He couldn't think about it, wouldn't think about it, too scary. Then he looked across at George, seeing him with new eyes. George had definitely changed into Kurtz. He was going to avoid him as much possible.

Later Ethan asked Johnson, "How did you see the waterspout coming? It was pitch dark."

"Be de miracle. I look out from de forward hatch real early. One of de giant thunderstorm move very close but nothin else visible. I start to drop back to my bunk. Some sort of movement catch my eye. Be some livin thing behind de gloom. I could no see what and stare and stare.

"Suddenly it break into de clear. De most evil thing I ever see, coming right at us, towering, black as pitch, trying to swallow us up. Some waterspout not too dangerous. This no normal water spout. Be a true tornado. If it pass any closer would have sunk us, and nobody would see us go down way out here." Then in a very loud and certain voice he said, "Dat be de devil tryin to take us down to hell." Throwing up his hands, face to the sky, staring upward as though seeing God, and with an even louder voice, "Thank you Lord. Thank you Jesus."

George was limping around the deck in obvious pain and scowled at the mention of the devil, turning away. Ethan looked fearfully around, imagining the devil might reappear.

They stayed at anchor the whole next day. It took many hours for the bilge pump to empty the final water from below decks. Bunks were soaked, and water got into everything in drawers under bunks, and even into the hanging locker. *Rascal* became a clothes dryer, her normally neat appearance hidden under an array of bed clothes, towels and garments hung over booms and railings, and clothes-clipped to the rigging as far up as they could reach. Midway in the day George ordered Johnson over the side in rough seas to scape the barnacles and small sea growth off the bottom to speed progress north, a difficult and somewhat dangerous job. Johnson complied but said to George, "You tryin to kill me again?"

CHAPTER THIRTY

The way back north was fast. With the advance of the seasons the trade-wind had moved more southeast, surfing *Rascal* down waves at almost eight knots an hour much of the time. *Rascal* was dashing.

Ethan played a major part in their progress, taking a regular trick at the helm and steering a very straight course despite the tumultuous trade-wind seas.

Johnson said to him, "People no realize that Sir Walter Scott knew sailing. Scott write, *'He is the best sailor who can steer within the fewest points of the wind.'* You sailing de wind just right."

Ethan beamed and gave him a thumbs up.

Often he was the one who noted a sail had to be adjusted, the jib pulled in to end the slight luff, the main let out to luff point, adjustments to gain maximum sailing efficiency, adjustments he did without help, working the winches and the sheets without anyone tailing. He was proud he'd gotten strong enough to grind the jib winches by himself. After several days of this George said, "You're getting to be as good a sailor as I am."

He smiled to himself. He was already a *better* sailor than George. Not as strong, but he read the wind better, navigated better, and knew when sails had to be adjusted before George. He started correcting George at the helm. "You're getting too high to starboard. We're luffing too much," or "Where you're heading is going to get us too close to those reefs. Turn more to port."

George eventually quipped, "Mighty uppity, young man. But I like it. Keep it up," and he always smiled at Ethan, or laughed, when Ethan gave him sailing directions. But no talk between George and Johnson. George looked at Johnson with the hate more plain than ever, giving him loud and brisk orders. Johnson did what was requested but never replied to George, no more "Yes sirs," never even looked at him, shunning him as though he did carry the evil of the devil.

As they sailed north Ethan felt *Rascal* was communicating with him. Somehow she was telling him what to do to sail her at her best. And she was also communicating the unimportance of his problems back home, sailing him away from them, leaving them behind just like she left behind the dangerous reefs he helped navigate around. He now believed that all along *Rascal* had been working to save him. He loved *Rascal* more each day.

To gain time on the journey north they often made passages at night as George had decreed, watches four hours on and four hours off all night and all the next day. Ethan shared watches with Johnson, something Johnson insisted upon. They had to keep careful lookout for whales sleeping on the surface at night and had several near misses, Johnson saying collisions with whales at night were the leading cause of boat sinkings in the Caribbean. And nobody had much sleep. When sails needed to be adjusted or changed the off-watch often had to be called up to provide assistance. Ethan got to repeatedly use the in-the-dark bowline tying skills he'd learned in the Virgin Islands.

Sailing long passages at night was traveling in another world. Ethan was full of wonder at what they were seeing. For reasons Johnson couldn't explain, there was much more luminescence in the water than normal. Blue-white fire lit the breaking crests of the large waves rolling toward *Rascal* and the foam tossed by the bow swashed bright eddies along each side of the boat all the way to the stern and beyond.

Light also from a vast night sky, drawing him in, inviting him to awe. When George was giving his astronomy lessons from the anchored boat, the sky appeared to be very close. Underway it seemed much closer. They were sailing in a giant bowl of stars, *Rascal* and all aboard captured in a brimming pool of starlight from horizon to horizon, the stars descending as a curtain of light into the ocean without an island in sight, hanging so low he felt he could almost touch them. The light from starlight and luminescence together was so bright they could nearly read charts in the cockpit.

He scrunched his eyes nearly closed. Sky and sea merged as the shimmering light below joined the sparkling light above. There was a magic space where sky and sea grew together. Light above and light below became one.

Rascal was sailing in light somewhere between the sea and sky. No. She was flying through light.

. . .

George did relent on their long passages when they got to the Isles des Saintes archipelago, a spectacular group of islands off the east coast of Guadeloupe with some of the prettiest beaches in the Caribbean, islands populated by French fishing folk. George had not visited the islands before and *Rascal* had bypassed them on the way south. He agreed they could stay two nights to rest up, saying he wanted to see where in 1782 the English destroyed the French fleet that had blockaded Yorktown in the American Revolutionary War, the Battle of the Saintes.

The first night they anchored close to a small island unpopulated except by pigs, lots of pigs. People on neighboring islands had apparently been feeding them from boats. They had learned to swim out to the occasional anchored boat and beg, startling to be anchored and find pigs in the water next to you.

The next morning two pigs swam out to Rascal, and Ethan gave them most of his breakfast—eggs, fresh-caught fish, some bread. They had soft mouths and seemed to like the eggs best. Ethan laughed and laughed. a breakfast with swimming pigs.

After breakfast with the pigs still swimming around, George muttered, "I never shot a pig before."

As he got up to go aft for the M-1, Johnson put a hand on his shoulder and muscled him back down, George landing on the hard cockpit seat with a loud thump.

George's face crumpled in anger. "Take your damn hands off me. What the hell do you think you're doing? This is *my* boat. You're just a damn paid hand. I'll do what I want on *Rascal*."

Johnson responded in a quiet voice, "Every pig belong to family. You no see de notches on der ear? Kill them and de family lose what de' dependin on, maybe even starve de family."

From George in an equally quiet voice, "Keep this up and you're going to get killed like I shot the man on Barbuda, self-defense to protect myself from your attacks. A white colonial jury will buy it if I pay enough money to the right people. A black attacking a white and you won't be there to tell your side of the story. I won't fail the next time."

Johnson still quiet and absolutely convincing said, "Try it and you goin to die."

George said, "Not likely," compressing his lips, his eyes hard.

Ethan felt utter dread. One of them would kill the other. He'd hoped it would get better. It was getting worse. What had been a voyage to show him everything, Johnson's words, had turned dark, George's hate stronger than what he experienced himself in Niskayuna. He doubted George could best Johnson and vowed to help Johnson any way he could. But he couldn't think of anything to do. Why didn't Johnson take the gun and throw it overboard? Maybe there was still a danger of pirates. He looked out at the pigs still swimming by the stern, going cold all over thinking George might shoot Johnson like he was trying to shoot the pigs.

. . .

After a number of hard all-night slogs, including again the Anegada passage (not so bad on a beam reach and with much calmer weather), George brought the boat to Virgin Gorda in the Virgin Islands. On his visit to Virgin Gorda the previous year the beautiful Rennie Black had welcomed him to her house, brought in two girlfriends to boot, then had entertained him and his two sailing buddies for two days of pure hedonism—non-stop riotous sex and drinking. Rennie's husband was often away.

Maybe an opportunity to break, or at least diminish, his desire for Ethan? He'd tried everything else to no avail. Could losing himself in the arms of a passionate woman be the answer? He didn't know, but he was willing to try. Getting on the ship-to-shore George found that Rennie was available, and that her husband was away yet again.

They anchored in a windswept bay, palm trees leaning over a beach litter with coconuts, the brilliant sapphire of the bay meeting an almost blinding expanse of white sand. Above a large pink house spread balconies around to give varying views of the ocean, with a glass cupola shining out from above its center.

Usually George would tell Ethan beforehand about the people they would be visiting, not this time. All he said was that it was a "free-living family." But then he went on to say, "That cupola you see there is above an amazing room, octagonal and no windows. All the light comes from multi-colored spots shining down from the glass ceiling mixing with multi-colored spots shinning up through the glass floor. Lights are programmed to music. The owners can program the lights and the music for whatever mood or activity they have in mind. The intent is to make you lose yourself, and it's pretty effective."

...

Johnson knew quite a lot about the room, but said nothing. He'd heard that the couple was being investigated by the authorities because they'd been inviting local youths to the house, giving them alcohol and drugs in the party room, and taking advantage of them. He'd also heard the investigation was going slowly because the couple was a major donor to local charities and hosted lavish entertainments for local government officials. Everyone said they were very wealthy. The way they were spreading money around the island proved it. A rumor was floating around that the couple had come from Ohio and been kicked out because they were running a free-love commune with young people involved. No secrets existed in the Caribbean, at least when it came to wealthy white people.

...

As they landed the dingy an attractive blond woman came running out of the house with arms wide in welcome for George. George's response was hesitant. Ethan could see he was not his usual confident self, and not nearly as effusive in returning the woman's greeting as she was in delivering it. She hurried back up to the house, calling George to follow. George took a number of steps after her, paused, looked around, shook his head, then proceeded to the house.

The woman had two teenage daughters. Melissa was fourteen and Jessica was fifteen. Ethan stepped out of the dingy and started talking to them, trying to get them to like him, trying to charm them like he'd seen guys do in the movies. He told some of George's jokes, eliciting giggles, and stories from his sail about pirates and the like, getting rapt attention. They seemed delighted with him. In Niskayuna girls avoided him like he had the plague or something. And here were two very pretty girls with long blond hair, fantastic, him and two pretty girls. They grabbed his arm and hurried him to The Baths, a geological wonder in the next bay. He followed along very willingly.

Giant, light-gray granite boulders, many as big as a small house, were piled on top of each other for a mile along a spectacular white beach. Some of the boulders advanced a considerable distance into the water, creating homes for myriad brightly colored fish, and others balanced into the sky producing structures as high as fifty feet tall. All were situated as though purposely to create an irresistible impetus to explore, a magic castle of boulders and sand and sea with a host of interconnected caves. Many caves were accessible only by knee-crawls through narrow openings. Others fronting the ocean required a swimming entrance through the shallow, aquamarine water. All caves were lit by brilliant shafts of sunlight that with great ingenuity had wedged itself through small cracks between boulders resting above. In the sea caves the shafts of sunlight were reflected by barely perceptible ripples to create dancing light shows on the walls.

Ethan had never seen anything like it. The girls darted ahead of him, leading the way, smiling back at him, beckoning him. Both had long legs exposed below very skimpy bathing suits. And their breasts weren't hidden much either, breasts that looked bigger than Betsy's. This was something.

In and out of the caves and around the boulders they led him, sometimes hiding from him, sometimes chasing him, sometimes putting their arms around him and hugging him. Finally they brought him to a very hidden cave and some mats on the ground that looked like they'd been stolen off chaise lounges.

Jessica said, "This our special place. When we really like a boy we bring him here."

They sat on the mats and motioned him to sit between them. Jessica had her arm around his shoulder and Mellisa had her hand on one of his legs.

Jessica asked, "Do you have a girlfriend?"

Ethan responded, "I like Betsy Sommers. But she's not my girlfriend. I never asked her to be my girlfriend."

"Can we be your girlfriends?"

Ethan responded with a happy smile. "Gosh, Yes."

Both girls started to kiss him, turning his head to meet the lips of first one and then the other. "Which one of us kisses better?" Melissa asked. This required much kissing from both sides.

Ethan finally said, "I've never kissed a girl before so I don't know."

Jessica said, "Have you heard of French kissing?"

When he said no he found himself sticking his tongue into each girl's mouth and playing a little dance with their tongues. He also found himself with a strong erection.

He was embarrassed and tried to hide it with his hands.

But the girls had noticed, and between French kisses Jessica said, "Can we touch it. You can touch us if we can touch you."

Ethan said, "Holy cow. You'll really let me touch you down there?"

Both girls nodded. Ethan raced the girls in taking off bathing suits.

"What do you want me to do."

Jessica said, "First, kiss our breasts." He planted a cautious kiss on one of Jessica's breasts.

"More," Jessica said. "Suck them. I like that best. Do them both. Now do Melissa."

At this point his erection was so hard it hurt.

"Now touch us," Jessica said. "Down here." She guided his hand down to the blond hair between her legs. "Put your finger in. Do both of us together. Move you finger up and down, faster."

Both girls were writhing. At the same time Jessica was stroking his penis up and down. It was excruciating. He arched his back and groaned as he ejaculated. At almost the same time, the two girls' bodies shook under his hands, and Jessica let out a small scream.

This was better than Johnson said, amazing, the greatest thing ever. He *loved* it. He loved Jessica and Melissa. He looked over at them, their full breasts, the area between their legs, and felt himself getting another erection.

Jessica was staring at it. "Do you want to do it again? We can show you some things that are even better."

He remembered Johnson's warning. Wasn't he darn close to doing what Jonson said not to do. What would he tell Johnson when Johnson asked him about the girls? He shouldn't be doing this. A feeling of guilt and some embarrassment took over. He shook his head and said mournfully, "I've got to get back. Got a lot of work on the boat."

When he stood up to put on his bathing suit, the naked girls wrapped around him, kissing him and foundling him, trying to get him to lie back down.

"No. No. I can't do this. Stop. Don't do that. I've got to go." He finally pulled away, slipped on his bathing suit, and gave each girl a long parting kiss. Boy was it hard to leave. Both girls had tears in their eyes.

Disoriented by what happened, his mind going every which way, the whole thing unreal, he missed the main path back to *Rascal.* The obscure path he ascended led to a meadow some distance from the house. The meadow was carpeted with soft grasses, as soft as a bed, and perfumed by abundant flowers in neighboring trees, an isolated little paradise.

George appeared at the other end of the meadow, stumbling slightly and glanced around in unfocused gaze. He looked like he'd had too much to drink. George never waved but came slowly at him across the meadow with strange fits and starts, repeated hesitations, step by step as though struggling against something holding him back, as though he didn't want to be there. Getting up to him George said nothing, no greeting, just looked him up and down as though he'd never seen him before. No emotion showed on his face, not grim, not happy, blank, expressionless, just the eyes staring intently at him. George put a hand on his shoulder, paused, and studied his face with concentration, then let out a peculiar strangled sound.

Ethan looked down. George had an erection. He struggled mightily and broke George's grip. But George took him down with a football tackle, turned him over on his stomach, pinned him with his weight, and mounted him, pulling his bathing suit down around his ankles and then pulling down his own pants. One of George's hands moved to the middle of his back holding him down, and the other slowly run up and down his legs, over his body, stroked his behind, and finally reached under him and fondled and pulled on his penis, George all the while panting and making occasional mew like sounds. Both of George's hands moved to his shoulders, and Ethan felt George's penis pressing hard against his anus, seeking entry. George was now panting more loudly. Ethan screamed "Help" at the top of his lungs, though despairing. No one would hear his cry from the isolated meadow.

Then a flash of memory. His muscles knew what to do. He reached quickly around George's pinning arms, did the same pulling and twisting he'd done on the colt in Grenada, only harder on George. The result was the same. An anguished scream.

George leaped up holding his balls, face contorted in pain, bellowed out, "God damn it, I think you ruined me."

A call came from Jessica coming up the path Ethan had ascended. They barely got themselves clothed when Jessica burst from the underbrush, out of breath. "Is everything all right? I heard yelling. I wanted to say goodbye again."

Ethan answered, "Just a misunderstanding," grabbed her hand and hurried them both down the path, not even looking back at George.

Ethan stayed only a short while with the girls, saying a final goodbye, kissing them repeatedly, again very hard to leave, then headed back to *Rascal* on the main path. Halfway along George leaped from behind a tree and grabbed him. Ethan struggled, this time to no avail.

George said, "Calm down. I'm not going to hurt you. I was drunk, really drunk. Rennie Black had me drinking all day. That's no excuse. I'm terribly, terribly sorry. It's the most horrible thing I've ever done. The worst thing in my whole life." He had been crying and his eyes were still full of tears. George wiped tears from his eyes with the back of his hand. "I didn't want to do it. I couldn't help myself. I've been fighting it since Marie-Galante. It's like I have a disease. Something takes over and makes me attack you. It wasn't the real me in the meadow. Something else. Maybe you saw how hard I struggled not to come over to you. I fought against it all the way across the meadow."

Ethan continued to try and pull away.

" I love you. I never want to hurt you. I think of you as a son."

Ethan stopped struggling. It was no use. He avoided looking at George, very afraid, trembling, wondering what George might do next. This was just like Kurtz in *Heart of Darkness*. Hidden underneath all George's nice talk during the voyage he was a very bad man. His fear of George at the start of the voyage was right on. Ethan said in a thin, scared voice, still looking away, "Johnson isn't going to like this."

George's face darkened, clouded with menace, eyes hard and scary, lips curled. He gripped Ethan tighter, pulled his face to his, and said with slow emphasis, "I can't have this getting back to Niskayuna. If you told Johnson I'd have to kill him. Do you *understand me.* If you tell him I'm going to *kill* him. I talked about killing him the other day with the pigs. Now I'll do it. Can't have him going to the authorities. He threatened me with the authorities if I tried to attack you again. Damn his insolent hide. You saw me shoot the man in Barbuda and the whale. It'll be easy for me to shoot Johnson the same way. Don't make me.

"And don't you tell *anyone* either. If you tell people in Niskayuna they're not going to believe you anyway. I'm the most important man in town. It's not your fault what people in town think of you. But if you tell people they'll add liar to the bad things they already think about you."

Ethan ran back to *Rascal* as fast as he could go.

Johnson looked him up and down as he rowed him out to *Rascal.* "What happen to you? You look like somethin bad happen."

Ethan replied, "Nothing."

Johnson said, "You sure you no want to tell me? Maybe I can help."

Ethan shook his head and once aboard retreated to *Rascal's* bow.

When George arrived he went quickly to the sail locker where the gun was stored, his legs bowed wide apart as he walked, in obvious pain. Ethan smiled to himself at what he'd accomplished and felt some of his fear disappear. Gun in hand George met Ethan's gaze with a hard stare, then announced loudly that he'd heard pirates were around. He kept the gun next to him at dinner, a silent meal, for the first time no grace, neither George nor Ethan saying anything about the day, and Johnson looking quizzically at first one, then the other. When George went to bed that night there were no prayers, again a first. George put the gun on the floor next to his bunk as he had in Barbuda and looked pointedly over at him.

Ethan struggled against sleep, difficult with all that happened that day. George snored across from him. Had enough time passed? He wished he had a glow-in-the-dark watch like George's. It felt like it'd been hours, but had it? He sat up in bed as quietly as possible, slowly folded the covers away from his legs so no noise of brushing fabric, put his left foot down silently on the cabin floor, and raised himself from sitting position to stand.

In the dim light from the portholes, he could see George was sleeping on his back, covers pulled down, his right arm dangling so his fingers were only an inch or so above the gun. Ethan tried to breathe shallowly and noiselessly while moving one foot at a time slowly across the intervening space. Then a careful crouch to reach the gun.

George's snoring caught and Ethan froze. Then it resumed.

He was still too far away and inched forward in his crouch, reaching out and touching the gun, putting one hand on either side of where George's hand dangled. Ever so slowly he slipped his fingers under the gun. The gun barrel felt cold to his right hand and he had difficulty getting his left hand under the stock. Then he pulled the gun back gradually toward him, raising it slightly off the floor so it wouldn't make a scraping noise. It turned out to be much heavier than he'd anticipated. Because of the awkwardness of his crouch position, and the weight of the gun, the gun somehow brushed George's fingers as he pulled it away from the bunk.

George bolted upright. Had he really been asleep? Ethan was quicker, the gun directed at George's chest, and a loud yell to Johnson. He didn't feel fear. Determination. He wasn't going to let George kill Johnson.

Johnson was there in seconds.

Ethan talked to him very fast in an excited voice, "George tried to attack me again. I grabbed his balls like the horses on Grenada. He said he'd kill you if I told you."

Johnson took the gun from Ethan, and with a roar of rage slugged George hard on the side of his head, then again on the mouth, then twice fast in the stomach, knocking against the back of his bunk where he cowered as far away from Johnson as possible. Johnson grabbed him by the legs and pulled him closer, beating him more around the head and stomach, once very deliberately in the already injured balls which caused George to scream loudly for some time. George was retching all over the bunk, his mouth and nose bleeding freely, the blood mixing with vomit. At one point he passed out. Johnson shook him awake and shouted at him, "I told you what I do to you if you touch Ethan again. And de police in St. Thomas goin to put you away forever." Then he punched George in the stomach again brining on more retching.

George cowered further back in his bunk, groaning, sometimes loudly, shoulders caved, eyes staring at nothing, a very red swelling rising on the side of his face, both eyes blackening, blood running down his chin and dripping on the bunk. He put a hand to his mouth and lisped out, "Damn it. You knocked some teeth out," and then put his hand to his side, "My ribs are broken." He said this with resignation, acceptance, not belligerence.

After some time George looked up, wiped the blood from his mouth, and addressed Ethan rather than Johnson. George's voice was shaky and pleading, unlike any voice Ethan had heard from him before. "I love you. I was just trying to scare you into not telling." He sighed and wiped more blood from his mouth. "What I said to you on the path, it's true. Something is making me attack you. I can't help it. It's not me doing it. A thing outside me takes charge. I've tried everything to get rid of the dark thing that's gotten into in me. It's stronger than I am. I've fought it every hour of every day these last weeks. Now this horrible afternoon. I wish I'd told you long ago about what I'm fighting. I'm glad you finally know.

"Johnson here keeps talking about the devil. I know the Bible talks about devils in people. I just don't believe in the devil. But some dark thing has certainly gotten into me. It makes me do what I don't want to do. More than anything else in the world I didn't want to do what I did.

"It's all my parents' fault. I told you about the terrible way they treated me. Well, they treated me so badly they made me into a man who attacks boys, that's how bad it was. They made me into what I am."

Johnson came closer and glared down at George, his fists still balled. "You wrong. It *is* de devil. All you people try and blame something in psychology for what you do. Try to escape blame by blaming something else or somebody else. Not your fault you say. Your parent fault. Well it *is you* fault and de devil you take in you. De devil invent psychology to hide that it really him causin de psychology problem."

He turned away and then turned back with a grimace, "Few week ago I intend to kill you cause of what you become. Probably should have." Ethan's mouth dropped open. George's eyes went wide.

"Yes, it true. Have a good plan to do it. Nobody know I kill you. No could do it. Afraid de devil that in you would come into me if I kill you.

"Right now I feel like going back to killin you. Could shoot you right here and throw you overboard to de sharks. Gettin hung for killin you might be a fair trade. Might do it still."

Johnson said all this in a considered, non-threatening, matter-of-fact way, as though simply reporting what he would probably do. The gun hung over his right arm, pointed in George's direction.

George looked fearfully at Johnson and raised his hands as in surrender. Ethan wondered if Johnson would tie George up until they got to St. Thomas, or maybe just shoot him like the Germans sometimes did with prisoners in movies. George plainly expected to be tied or shot.

Instead, Johnson moved to the other bunk and sat down, apparently thinking. After many minutes he rose, shook his head unhappily, and came over to George.

"It very difficult for me to have anythin more to do with you. Almost impossible with what you do, dis attack and you tryin to kill me earlier. Even bein Christian I no want to help you. I search to see if I have any Christian feelin toward you and no be der anymore. You drive it out. You deserve whatever the police do to you in St. Thomas.

But I worry about somethin. What if de court no convict you? May happen. De' slow to convict white mon. De' may let you off as Ethan stop both attack. And de' may no convict you for tryin to kill me, treat it as de accident. What will happen if de' let you off? You goin to go on and attack other boy. I sure of it. De devil take you soul. De devil make you attack other boy. I fight de devil wherever he be. No want de devil to win dis time or any other time. So I goin to suggest somethin. Understand, this is to defeat de devil and save other boy. Not to save you. You no worth savin. De devil can take you to hell for all I care.

I know very special woman, stronger Christian than I be. She might be able to get rid of what you have. Happen she live on de next island. Don't know whether she goin to see you when I tell her de terrible thing you do. Should I contact her?

George responded, "I need all the help I can get."

Okay. I goin to try to arrange it. No forget I have de gun. No try and escape de boat."

...

In the early afternoon they anchored in a shallow bay on St. John's island. The white coral-sand bottom was reflected through serene blue water as rippling aquamarine light. Ethan watched the play of light through the water for some time.

"This be a manta ray hangout," Johnson said, "Come every afternoon."

Sure enough, in the late afternoon giant rays started to jump, some with wing spreads of more than fifteen feet, black shadows racing across the bay, then freeing themselves from the grasp of mother sea, launching in bursts from one side of the bay to the other, Ethan thought five or six feet in the air, landing absolutely flat with loud reports that could be heard for miles, exuberant spray. The rays repeated and repeated, bang, bang, bang, freeing themselves from parasitic sucker fish attached to their underbellies, the sucker fish breaking free and swimming frantically to catch up with their hosts, ugly eel-like creatures, some as long as three feet.

Johnson said, "Sucker fish de worse fish in de ocean. Good for nothing. Suck de blood out of de poor fish de' attached to."

George had been closely watching the efforts of the rays while holding an ice pack to the side of his head and breathing shallowly with his bound fractured ribs. He mused quietly, "Would that it were so easy to get off what's attached to me."

...

At dinner Johnson told George the meeting was set and said to Ethan, "You don't have to come with us tonight. It could get very scary."

Ethan replied, "I'll be okay." He wanted to see whatever Johnson had in store for George.

George peered at Ethan through his blackened eyes, "Whatever happens tonight, or in the future, I want you to know I've taken care of you. Maybe you noticed on St. Lucia I was happier for awhile?"

Ethan said, "Yah. You seemed much happier."

"That's because while I was there I signed papers my lawyer sent down. I've set up a trust for you. The trust will pay the cost of your prep school, college, and graduate school, the finest in America, whatever schools you want to go to. Also, it gives you substantial funds for the rest of your life. You'll never have to worry about money."

Ethan's jumped up and grabbed George's hand in a strong handshake. "Holy cow. That's really great. My father told me he wasn't going to send me to college. He didn't want to spend any money on me."

Heart of Darkness. Good in bad men. He stared at George feeling maybe he wasn't as bad as he'd thought.

...

Johnson led the two of them up a well-used path from the beach to a medium-sized whitewashed building. The interior was laid out as a church with pews for perhaps sixty people. An impressive white cross was mounted on the far wall, and on the side walls and back wall were large pictures of blacks, deep hollowed holes for eyes, bodies writhing in some sort of ecstasy, arms twisting toward the ceiling, fiendish grins on their faces.

No altar was visible. Rather a low circular stone platform positioned in front of the cross with a fire burning at its center. The flame was constant while they were there though George never saw any evidence of fuel.

A strikingly beautiful woman stood next to the platform, tall, at least six feet, lustrous tan skin, eyes a pale green, features more caucasian than negroid, black hair down to her waist, and dressed in a flowing white garment similar to that of the voodoo woman on Carriacou.

Her voice was soft and melodic with little evidence of Caribbean dialect. She said to George, "I've been looking forward to meeting you. My name is Lucretia. I'm both an ordained Christian minister and a priestess of the Yoruba religion. In the Yoruba religion I'm called an Iyalawo or 'Mother of Secrets.' My good friend, Johnson, has told me of your problem. I can't promise I can solve it. But if you do as I ask we may make make some progress."

George said, "I'll do anything."

Lucretia said, "I have come to believe there is truly only one God, however man in his ignorance and tribalism has chosen to treat him as many. The Yoruba region has a single Godhead as does the Christian religion, and many saints as does the Christian religion. What I'm going to do is to focus together the strengths of these two religions. We are going to do a Christian exorcism aided by knowledge gained over more than 2,000 years of Yoruba practice in

Africa. First, I want you to drink this potion. It's bitter but it will bring you to a state where I can communicate with what's inside you."

George drank as instructed. Very quickly the fire started dancing on the walls where no fire existed and the priestess started shimmering in magical movement. Her voice became hypnotic.

She chanted for over an hour, interspersing what he assumed was a West African language between periods of Christian ritual. For the West African portions she faced the fire, her voice going up and down an eerie musical scale, shrilly calling out at times the names Oludumare, Shango, and Orun, all the while lifting her arms up in writhing movements like the figures pictured on the building's walls. For the Christian portions she faced the cross, sometimes standing, sometimes kneeling, sometimes with her forehead pressed against the floor. At certain points she came over to where she had him kneeling and made the sign of the cross on his forehead, his chin, and his breast.

The Christian ritual had many passages from the Bible, readings about satan being cast from heaven and Jesus exorcising demons, then the invocation of a long litany of saints, culminated by her facing him and chanting,

"I command you, unclean spirit, whoever you are, along with all your minions now attacking this servant of God, by the mysteries of the incarnation, passion, resurrection, and ascension of our Lord Christ, by the descent of the Holy Spirit, by the coming of our Lord for judgement, by the Lord's grant to the Holy Apostles the power to tramp devils underfoot and the authority to say, 'Depart, you devils,' that you obey me, I who am a minister of God, that you do my bidding, and that in doing my bidding you shall not be emboldened to harm in any way this creature of God, or the bystanders."

She then lifted him from his kneeling position, took his arm, and led him in slow step around the fire six times counterclockwise, all the while chanting in West African language and again invoking the Yoruba gods.

Her next instruction was for him to kneel in front of the fire. She put a silver bucket next to him, turned to the cross, bowed low, turned back to him, put her hand on his forehead, and said in a loud voice, "I cast you out unclean spirit, along with every satanic power of the enemy, every specter from hell, and all your companions, in the name of our Lord Jesus Christ. Begone and stay far from this creature of God for it is He who commands you, He who flung you headlong from the heights of heaven into the depths of hell. He who now throws you back into hell."

She then took his hands in hers, made the sign of the cross over them, and said an invocation in West African. "Now," she said, "Place both hands in the fire palm down." He did so and felt no pain. Her arms again writhed toward the heavens. She chanted in West African and cried out, "Oludumare, god of all, by your power to preserve man on the holy path to eternal life, expel from this man the dark spirits, Aloguns of no name, that have invaded the sacred center of his life. Force the evil presence from this man as you have protected us from evil and from misdirected ways throughout all time. Through his hands held in worship in your holy fire draw the evil spirits from their hidden place within him and send them through the sacred flames into the dwelling place of eternal evil from which they came." She put her hands in the fire and held his.

"Dark spirits, Aloguns of no name, spirits of evil and of all iniquities of man, we link our hands to command you to our will. Hear us and obey. Never return to this man. Never again torment him with your fiendish enticements. By the powers of Oludumare, Shango, Orun, and all the Yoruba saints, I order you to leave this man forever."

The fire flared up and George started shaking violently, then ever more violently, his head jerking, snapping back and forth uncontrollably, foam on his lips, yelling bizarre words at the top of his lungs and making deep grunting animal sounds that seemed to come from something inside him, then one scream after another. His stomach exploded, great pain like his bowels were being pulled through his throat. Vomit rose up in him as hot fire. He half rose and screamed again as he threw up into the silver bucket, his mouth burning. Collapsing on his side, he rocked on the floor, hands cradling his stomach, moaning. Momentarily the bucket glowed.

Abruptly it came to an end. The priestess spread her arms wide and called out in a loud voice to them and all she'd summoned, "Now we will be quiet."

George had to be helped up, and he stumbled and almost fell as they left the church. Johnson and Ethan practically carried him back to *Rascal* and to bed, all in silence.

The next morning he woke up very early, long before anyone else, and first looked at his hands. There was not a mark on them though they'd been in the fire for what seemed like many minutes. Then he looked over at Ethan lying half naked, the covers around his ankles. His vision of Ethan was obscured as though he was looking at him through swirling smoke. Maybe it was the continuing effect of the potion. But when he looked elsewhere in the cabin he could see objects clearly. Something clouded his eyes as he viewed Ethan in his nakedness.

The obscurity around Ethan started to dance in odd, fractionated, refracted patterns similar to the dusky light through the trees at the Yoruba ceremony on Guadeloupe. Motes of orange flashed like remembrances of the fire of the previous evening. And something was writhing the obscurity like the arm-raised movement of the Yoruba priestess. This was crazy. Was this dawn reflecting through the portholes or something more? He stared at Ethan for several minutes, looking intently at every part of his exposed body, and felt no desire.

He was saved.

He leapt from his bunk and started to dress to go and greet God's morning with thanks for being saved.

The light in the cabin flickered. Pain shot up from where his hands had been in the fire, and a sound invaded his ears, growing, growing, a sound like no sound he'd ever heard, terrible in his head. Something was trying to burrow into his mind. He could feel it. First, an excruciating pain in one part of his head, then another. With each burst evil thoughts of Ethan flooded in. What had been expelled was attempting to force its way back in, trying one part of his mind after another, looking for an opening.

He turned so as not to look at Ethan naked, dashed up the companion-way, went to the foredeck and fell to his knees, holding his burning hands to God in heaven. He would not give in.

For the better part of an hour he swayed on his knees in torment, back and forth, saying every Christian prayer he could think of, even prayers from his childhood. "Now I lay me down to sleep." And promises to God. "Please, dear God, protect me from my desire for Ethan. I will devote all my worldly possessions to good works and the glory of your name." And later, "Allow me to escape this evil and I will dedicate the rest of my life to preaching your word to the world." He repeated these and other promises over and over again. And he tried to remember the incantations of the priestess. "Cast out the devil from me, Jesus. Take from me the devil and all his minions."

He was winning. Now when thoughts of Ethan tried to push into his mind he was able to force himself away to focus on other things—God, activities at home, sailing, anything. He gritted his teeth with the effort, his body tense as though in combat, sweat pouring from his face and body.

Gradually the pain lessened. The discomfort in his hands diminished. He looked up to greet the morning, just in time to see Ethan appear on deck for a morning swim.

Naked.

Ethan strode toward him and looked around the ocean with a beautiful smile, a young sea-god viewing his domaine, the new sun lighting every part of his lithe body, then he arced over the side in a graceful dive. George stared and all was lost. The sound roared back into his head. What had been chased out reentered his mind and soul. He started shaking badly. The pain was so great he grasped his head with both hands to keep it from exploding, tears streaming down his face. "God help me." The devil, or whatever it was, was back. He screamed even more loudly than he had the night before when the thing left him.

Ethan came out of the water and hurried toward him. He waved him away.

At breakfast George sat looking down, not eating, bandages on his hands to add to his bandages from the beating. Johnson asked if it was any better. He replied, "Maybe." He didn't want to disappoint Ethan, who was seated next to Johnson. Either the devil was too strong or what he had was more than a devil. His despair deepened.

CHAPTER THIRTY ONE

They were already into the start of hurricane season. *Rascal* needed a safe place to hide. The next day they took her to Hurricane Hole, at the far end of St. John's island.

On the way over Ethan thought about the last two days, the attack, the gun, the priestess, and especially the girls. He grinned thinking about the girls. It'd been truly amazing, unbelievable. How could he think about his problems back home when this kind of thing was going on? Heck, the old problems didn't matter a hill of beans. And somewhere along the way he'd lost the left-hand-counting habit.

At Hurricane Hole they secured *Rascal* among the mangoes. Johnson said a mango bay was the best place during a hurricane as mango trees deaden the forces of hurricane waves and wind. Other yachts were already grouped there. Everybody would be watching out for each other's boat during the hurricane season.

Johnson reserved horses. There was no motorized transport on St. John's. They needed to ride the length of the island to Cruz Bay,, thence take a ferry to the end of St. Thomas at Redhook, thence transport into Charlotte Amelie.

The morning of their departure for Cruz Bay, George said nothing at breakfast, ate nothing, sat staring down blankly at his plate, hardly glancing at Johnson and Ethan. Ethan had heard him muttering to himself all the way over to Hurricane Hole. And last night, anchored in Hurricane Hole, he heard him pacing the deck for hours.

George downed several tots of brandy at breakfast, something new. And for the first time he didn't go through his morning coffee-brewing ritual. He suddenly looked at them both and said, "I'm a bad man."

He did not explain but muttered several times more in a low voice, "I'm a bad man," sipping more brandy all the while and shaking his head.

Just before they left *Rascal*, George looked up, appeared to think for a moment, and disappeared below. He came up with the ship's log and presented it to Ethan, emotion in his voice.

"Don't ever forget me. Don't ever forget *Rascal*."

Ethan, equally emotional said, "I'll never forget." He gave George's hand a strong shake as he had many times before at the end of a sailing passage.

. . .

They loaded two pack horses with their clothing and other gatherings from the boat, put their personal items into their saddle bags, and rode off, Johnson having strapped the M-1 onto the back of his saddle and making sure George knew it was there. George insisted on taking the lead, saying he'd ridden the trail before. He swayed occasionally in the saddle and was still muttering to himself. Also, he swore occasionally as the motion of the horse jostled his broken ribs and other damage from the beating. Ethan followed George, and Johnson took up the rear with the pack horses.

The trail commenced along the beach, then rose sharply through dense undergrowth. The Caribbean day dawned splendid, sparkling, glistening, humidity lower than normal in the Caribbean, the sky a deep and marvelous blue dotted with small trade-wind clouds moving merrily west to fetch against the mountains.

George focused on the world around him. With his many visits to the Caribbean he found the countryside familiar to the point of being uninteresting. Today he felt he needed to experience everything. He distinctly heard the soft creak of his saddle and the saddles of the horses behind as they ascended the steep trail, the huff of protest his horse made as it pulled up the sharper inclines, hoofs on the stones, the sound deadened by the thickly intertwined surrounding foliage, an occasional whinny from Ethan's horse, a talker. The sun streamed through gaps in the tunnel of trees creating differently shaped puddles of light around him as he passed under one kind of tree and then another.

He knew something of the plant life on the islands and saw around him samples of almost every species that grew in the Caribbean. He studied them individually as though he had not seen them before. The whole island was a gigantic botanical garden, a botanical paradise. The Garden of Eden could not have been more beautiful.

By the beach he saw Sea Grapes, bravely fighting salt and sand for their place in the sun, then Soursop growing on small trees a little farther inland, ugly green spiky fruit the size of a large apple. He found them bitter. In dry, rocky places along the trail Aloe was spiking upward as though trying to escape the hard soil. In better soil grew large clumps of Yellow Bells, bright yellow trumpet-shaped flowers resting at the top of thin olive green branches, bursts of sunshine, a native flower of the Virgin Islands and a favorite.

Bougainvilleas and Hibiscus flaunted their bright colors at random places where least expected, trying to surprise him, wild Papaya everywhere, in many places small, pink-tinted flowers that did not give him their name but were garlanded in the prettiest swirling vines imaginable, thrusting out at him to be admired. Pushing into the trail were the feathery leaves of the rapaciously spreading Tamarind, an ugly tree trying to take over everything, twisting and tangling in search for sun. But the Heart Leaf wouldn't let it in, green hearts in rows lining the path. Nature's heart was larger than man's. There must be some reason.

Then the light, George did not think he'd ever seen such light, bouncing off foliage, creeping into hidden dark crevices, sun-dappling maize-colored rocks along the trail, and an occasional blue flash from the sea piercing the foliage and setting a counterpoint to the colors along the way, everything illuminated as though especially for him and in a way he felt he'd not experienced before.

Ahead by the trail appeared a Stinking Toe tree at least a hundred feet tall, the tallest species of tree in the Caribbean, a yellow-bellied sap sucker at work on the trunk, fluttering, a brown-winged familiar. He knew sap suckers flew long ocean distances to St. John specifically to poke the bark of the St. John's Stinking Toe trees. This sap sucker was signing its presence with its own special pattern of holes on the bark. The fruit of the Stinking Toe Tree hung down like old men's toes, toes released from tired shoes to spread happily in the sun. He remembered the taste, sort of dry but good.. Also the smell, when you broke one open the smell really was old men's toes. He had to eat them without breathing through his nose. You were eating old men's toes.

He focused even more intently, noticing the very veining of leaves, the small bright – green frogs croaking shrilly to protect their chosen territory, insects of various sorts including a type of broad-backed beetle that looked like it was made of solid gold, and foliage by trail side quivering in the rush of flower sweet air, all an exquisite joy.

Each detail of the world around him stood out separately, new, different, beautiful.

They were now at a higher point. His horse was still huffing the slope and Ethan's still talking its whinny. The whole dazzling blue, shimmering Caribbean opened before them to the north. He could see Jost Van Dyke with its beautiful White Beach. And Tortola, was the "White Witch of Tortola" still shooting out the windows of neighbors?

Ahead was a glen of magic. White Cedar trees had dropped their flowers to carpet the ground, dressing the green shadows below the trees in bright white carpet to duplicate the cloud of white flowers held to the sky by branches above, and around him appeared thousands of pale butterflies, floating slowly in the still air beneath the trees, snow above, snow below, snow all around him, a Caribbean snow storm.

How special was the world. For the first time in weeks, he was feeling alive. He looked at his hands on the reins, felt the pace of the horse moving his legs gently back and forth, and all the terrors of recent weeks seemed to diminish.

Through the underbrush he could see shining bark, vibrant browns and grays in glistening patterns. Then the trees themselves, at least twenty in the grove, most were forty to fifty feet tall, his favorite tree, the Bay Rum tree. He used St. John's Bay Rum every day at home as his aftershave lotion, the best bay rum in the world.

In the far trees a harvest was taking place. Pulleys had been attached high up and youngsters were being strapped into harnesses and pulled up thirty feet or more. They were then pushing off from the main trunk with their legs, swinging to the outer branches, and cutting twigs with ten or fifteen leaves attached. The newly emerging leaves at the tips of branches were what was distilled into bay rum. The youngsters were dropping their leaves to women who were waiting with baskets below, likely their mothers. He knew the leaves would be hauled to St. John Bay Rum Distillery, a converted sugarcane mill not far away.

The three of them watched for awhile. It looked very dangerous, the youngsters occasionally crashing back to the main trunk from branch tips after they'd harvested the leaves, giving joyous whoops of warning during their flight.

The bay rum broke his reverie, took his thoughts back to Niskayuna. He pictured himself sitting in his favorite barber chair with Joe, a good barber and a great guy, applying bay rum to his face. And in the next barber chair, sitting with a barber's cape around his neck, one of his buddies was talking to him. "I understand you took the Carpenter boy on a sailing trip to the Caribbean. Do anything interesting?" Maybe the interesting thing was he'd spent some time in jail because of his attempts on Ethan, though he figured with a good lawyer, and spreading enough money around, he would probably beat it. No one observed the attempts, and Ethan might not want to testify to put him in jail.

Then there was Marge. He'd not called her in two weeks, though he ordinarily reported in at least once a week. She would ask for a detailed accounting of the trip. He couldn't tell her what was really going on, so no phone call. God, he'd given Marge a terrible life. Now this, what a mess, what a mess he'd made of it.

Could he even make love to Marge again? In the party room of the house on Virgin Gorda he'd tried to make love to Rennie Black, tried repeatedly with Rennie getting angrier and angrier with each failed attempt. He knew the problem. He loved Ethan too much.

Even if he could make love with Marge he suspected she would sense something terrible had happened, that intuition of hers. Could he live with Marge day in and day out, pretending as if nothing had happened, live a lie? Maybe he could lie enough to hide what happened from his buddies, and even Ethan's father. Ethan's father didn't seem to love Ethan enough to care. But Marge? She would want to find out why he'd changed and might look up Ethan to find out, then what?

Also there was the question of his future role in town. It'd been worrying him for weeks. Could he even live in town anymore? Could he continue to let people think he was a moral person, a leader of the community, go to church, run the businesses, and behave like other men, civilized men, men without perversions?

It was one thing to live in town before when he didn't know he was leading a false life. It was going to be quite a different kettle of fish now that he knew. He couldn't picture himself walking down the main street in his old, bon-vivant way and greeting people in the shops with his back slapping and smiles, or going to the club and playing a round of golf with all the banter and kidding on the course and later in the men's bar, or going to vestry meetings and discussing matters of God.

He would be leading such an immoral life of pretense he might just fall apart, or even confess. Wouldn't people be able to look at him and know he was carrying something terrible inside? In a recent nightmare everyone he knew had turned on him, were pointing at him and calling him disgusting names. That was what it might be like, and most frightening, something drove him to attack Ethan despite his love for Ethan. Wouldn't it be the same back home? Wouldn't it drive him to attack other young adolescent boys in town?

Sure life was beautiful, but to what end? Certainly not for him life as it was in the past, not for him a normal life, not for him being a normal person.

Then there was the end of daily contact with Ethan. How could he stand it? The pain was already bad being with him each day with no way to get close to him. It would only grow worse living in the same town, knowing he was there and not being with him. He couldn't even imagine how bad it would be.

George turned in his saddle and addressed Ethan. "Please forgive me for everything".

Ethan stared at him.

The trail had leveled out. They were on the south side of the mountains now where daily trade-wind showers had dumped substantial moisture. The trail grew narrower and more difficult. Large boulders to snake around, small streams to ford, and at a high point a washout had occurred from recent heavy rains, soil and rock had slid onto the trail from the inland, right side, leaving a narrow passage to the left. And further to the left was a substantial fall off, almost perpendicular, down at least 500 feet to boulders, then the ocean, a spectacular spot. To the south, the green mass of St. Croix bulked in the distance, great rollers, sweeping unimpeded from Africa, were crashing below in wild spray, and in the near distance a tangle of sea birds pirouetted and dove over a school of some kind of fish.

George paused his horse and turned it slightly toward the ocean. For several long minutes he stared out, turning his head slowly, taking in ever part of the broad vista, then he looked back once at Ethan. Suddenly some of the soil under his horse's forefeet gave way. George heard Ethan's warning but did nothing. More soil gave way. He felt the horse sliding away beneath him over the edge. It screamed with fear. He was falling. He is falling. Nothing.

. . .

The horse and George both hit the boulders hard. The horse somersaulted and propelled George some distance into the ocean. Johnson and Ethan finally managed to find a way down the precipitous slope and pulled George's body out of the water, difficult in the heavy surf, the dead horse lying on the rocks beside them. There was a big gash on George's head but they couldn't tell if he'd died from a head injury or drowned, maybe both.

Johnson propped the body against a rock in a sitting position and straightened his clothing in unspoken recognition of George's normally very neat attire. George's head slumped forward, a sad reminder of the many times in recent weeks that he'd sat in the cockpit with his head similarly bowed.

Ethan was in shock. This was the second person who'd died right in front of him. He was weeping steadily, his lower lip quivering in anguish. He sobbed, "How could this have happened. We never should have let him ride. We knew he might fall off. We knew he'd been drinking."

The sorrow of his mother's death had returned, and with the second death something more, a strong fear of death. His left hand returned to the thumb-finger exercise and he was doing it rapidly.

They got back on their horses and rode to Cruz Bay, Ethan crying at intervals and repeating that they shouldn't have let George ride, and Johnson trying to comfort him.

At Cruz Bay they had to track down the sole constable on the island, finding him at home where he was taking what was apparently his usual afternoon nap. After they woke him he told them he would dispatch a team to George and that they would have to report the death at the main police station at Government House in St. Thomas. So they crossed by ferry to Redhook, took a taxi to the police station, and filled in a report with the help of some very sympathetic police personnel.

Afterward Johnson took him to a bench in a lovely park near Government House. Someone with great taste had sited the bench so that it looked down an avenue of royal palms, the most impressive palms Ethan had seen. It reminded him of the cathedral he'd visited the year before in Albany. Light through the palm trees touched the kindness on Johnson's face.

He repeated what he'd said over and over again. "We never should have let him ride."

Johnson deposited his half-smoked Gauloises on the bench next to him and placed a strong hand on his shoulder, his brow knit in concentration. He brought his face close to his, looking intently into his eyes, never wavering, the seriousness of his gaze projecting the importance of what he was saying.

"Each mon responsible for his own life. I be. You be. George be. You mon now. You responsible like every mon. And through God each mon also responsible for his own death. It may seem chance that George die when he do. Or maybe we could have talk him out of ridin, though I doubt it. But it George life, good or bad, and that determine when God decide to take him. In George case, I believe God take him because George want to die. Maybe he could no stand any more what he be, sorry for what he be. Or maybe he fear I turn him over to de police like I promise. But I think somethin else. I think he die to protect you and other boy from himself. He no want to live knowin he might attack you again or might attack other boy. God and de devil be wrestlin for George soul. If he die to protect boys, maybe God win a little. Maybe his time in hell be less." Johnson took a pull on his Gualoises and put it back on the bench.

"Because it God that make de decision on when someone die we need to accept it. No can argue with God. Real mon accept what God decide. You no responsible for when God choose to take you mother. You no responsible for George death. Mon get sad but realize God bring death as natural part of life. Accept it. Dat what your mother and George want."

He paused, then grasped Ethan's arm and brought him even closer. "George and you mother de' die. But you live. You carry der live with you. Dat what you need to think about. Der life carry on through you life. Der spirit inside you. Always with you. Whatever you do de' be part of it. If you live a good life de' be livin it with you. De' be very proud."

Over the next half hour Johnson repeated this message many times, and in many different ways, making sure Ethan understood.

Johnson lit another cigarette, his first cigarette still burning on the bench next to him. "You have two people die in front of you now. You afraid of dyin youself? You afraid of death?"

Ethan hung his head and started to cry.

Johnson threw his hands up as though preaching. "No should ever worry about death. Be silly to worry about death. When de time come for you to die, you goin to die. No can be help. A real mon no afraid of death. Death can no separate you from God love. The Bible say, *'Death, where is your sting?'* Mean death is nothin. A real mon no waste time thinkin about dying. A real mon thinkin about livin."

Johnson went on, "What God want, Ethan, is for you to choose life, not think about death. Life be beautiful. You no see in de Caribbean dat life be beautiful? No feel de power of life all around you?"

The last two months—adventures on *Rascal,* the islands, beaches, the sea, and now the girls, "Yes," he answered in a soft voice.

"One of God greatest miracle be just being alive. I tell you dat before. Think about it every day. You be alive. You be smart. You can do anythin. De whole world der for you. Dat a big gift. Look at me, Ethan. Stop lookin away. I want you to do what I do. Every day when you wake up I want you to say to youself, 'I'm alive.' Say it in a loud voice and thank God for de wonderful thing to be alive."

Johnson turned aside to light a third Gauloises, two now burning on the bench next to him. He stared ahead, occasionally turning his head upward to blow smoke into the still air, fingering his cross with his left hand.

After several minutes Johnson put down his latest Gauloises, fingered his cross again, and once more fixed his intense gaze on him. "I want to talk to you about one other thing. A mon think about his future. I want to talk to you about you future. It my last chance to talk to you about it. We no be together much longer."

Ethan started sniffling.

Johnson responded with a sharp, "Stop that! Now that I have gotten to know you I be certain der be a marvelous life waitin for you. In the Bible John say, '*I came that you may have life and have it abundantly.*' God have a plan for you, Ethan, a plan for an abundant life. Dat certain. I be certain of it."

He spoke more slowly, "It all be up to you. As you grow older it be up to you to find de plan God have for you. You need to look for de plan, Ethan. God have set aside a special plan just for you. For you alone. It waitin just for you. You must look for it and find it. The man on St. Vincent talk about findin a true life, say you should find what make you happy and live it. Dat right. But to find you true life God has to be part of it.

"Findin God plan easy. Just keep listenin for de word of God. Isaiah say in de Bible, '*When you turn to the right or when you turn to the left, your ears shall hear a word behind you, saying, This is the way, walk it.*' Ethan, you going to hear de word of God leadin you. At some point you goin to hear de word of God showin you de way. Keep callin out for Him, Ethan. In Jeremiah God say, '*Call me and I will answer.*' And Matthew say, '*Search and you will find, the door will be opened for you.*'

"You may find you plan early in you life. But if you no find it early no give up. Keep prayin to God and keep listenin for de word of God. Step by step and day by day, at exactly de right time in you life and at exactly the right place in you life, God goin to guide you. You goin to find God plan and it goin to be a wonderful plan. I be positive."

Johnson turned his head to take another long drag, this time blowing smoke out his nostrils. Turning back he said, "And listen to me. Dis be important. What goin to happen if you no follow you own special plan, the plan God have for you? I tell you. Then you goin to be livin de plan of someone else. You goin to spend all de day of you life on de end of a string someone else pull. Just like a puppet for them. Dat a terrible life. A puppet all you life. You no want to be puppet, right?"

He said, "No."

Johnson grasped Ethan firmly by both shoulders, turned him so they faced each other on the bench, and again spoke slowly. "We've gone through a *lot* together, you and me. De sea bond people together. We shipmate forever. *Rascal* make us shipmate forever. And shipmate never break der promise to other shipmate. *Do you understand?* Shipmate never break any promise to each other."

Ethan nodded, staring intently into Johnson's eyes.

"I want you to promise that you do de thing I talk to you about dis afternoon. No forget. You goin to remember to look for God plan and follow it?"

Ethan nodded and whispered, "Yes."

"And promise me that you goin to stop thinkin so much about death. Dat past. Forget it. Think about life. God goin to bless you with a good life. Dat what you think about. Okay?"

Ethan gave a strong, "I promise."

Then Johnson repeated one more time, "And never, ever let anyone make you der puppet."

Ethan looked around at the patterns of bright sunshine filtering through the magnificent Royal Palms, studied the banked purple, orange, and pink bougainvillea and the bright red hibiscus growing in profusion on either side of the path, and the colorful houses grouped at the far end. He turned his attention back to Johnson. Johnson's face was suffused with the great love he had for him. Yes, Johnson was right. It *was* good to be alive.

Ethans thoughts turned to the voyage, all the marvelous and scary things he'd experienced. He could see that throughout the voyage he'd progressed step by step to find the future Johnson talked about. He didn't know yet what his future and true life would be. But he felt he would find it. Hope and happiness had gradually replaced the darkness. A new world had opened up. How'd that happened? Certainly Johnson and *Rascal.* But wasn't he part of it, too? Wasn't his future a reflection of who he was, inside him all along, just waiting for him, a loving gift of his mother? Maybe. Maybe he'd traveled far to discover what was already there. Wasn't that something?

As they were walking to their hotel Johnson made one further request. "You can stop dat left-hand counting now."

Ethan said, "I already have."

The next day Ethan's father arrived in St. Thomas to take him home. Right off the bat his father said to him, "I missed you. I've not been a very good father. I just loved your mother too much. I'll try and do better. Let's have a fresh start." And he smiled at him.

He couldn't remember the last time his father had smiled at him. He smiled back.

Johnson joined them at the airport for their departure. Ethan was doing his best to hold back tears, miserable at leaving Johnson.

Johnson took his hands in his and said, his voice choking, "No goodbye, Ethan. Never goodbye. You part of me and I part of you forever. We no leave each other. We always together in our heart and soul. Understand?"

Ethan nodded, starting to sob.

"What you do on *Rascal* make me real proud. I proud to know you, Ethan. Very proud. You very special mon. May de good Lord bless you and keep you always. I sure He will."

Johnson embraced Ethan in his strong arms. Tears were running down Johnson's cheeks as well as Ethan's.

The Caribbean had taken them where it wanted, woven its magic around Ethan's soul, wrested him from evil through the faith of one of its own, and willed him to the future.

The Caribbean had its way.

EPILOGUE

Ethan kept in touch with Johnson and became close to his family. Johnson's wife was as special as he had said she was. One of Johnson's sons became a senior official in the Antiguan government. One became a much-respected doctor. One became the minister of one of the largest churches in Antigua, bringing to the substantial congregation the love of God that Johnson had taught him. Another became a businessman specializing in fish products. The youngest went to Nigeria as a missionary, returning to the land from which his Igbo ancestors had been stolen. He built his church in the north, struggling with Islam for men's souls. The son Ethan's age carried on Johnson's hatred of white treatment of blacks, becoming a leading crusader for equal rights in England.

The traumas Ethan had experienced, and Johnson's ministrations, strengthened him to follow God's plan. He avoided becoming a puppet, breaking out from an architectural firm where he had started his career, becoming a very successful naval architect in his own right, designing among other things the beautiful wooden, and later fiberglass, sailing yachts of the Hinkley Boat Works of Southwest Harbor, Maine.

The fifty-foot yawl he came to own he christened *Rascal*. He kept it in New England in the summer and English Harbor, Antigua, in the winter, raced it successfully in many yacht races including the Bermuda race, but mostly sailed it around the Caribbean, showing his two sons places of remembrance. At Galley Beach he looked for the "I Love You" sea grape leaf, impossible to find as many new sea grape trees had sprung up, but the bitter-sweet memories were there. In Statia his sons joined him in admiring "his" anchor, proudly displayed by the village in its main square. In Martinique, the blacks had beheaded the hated statue of Marie Antoinette, guillotining in stone what they couldn't guillotine in the flesh.

And always he visited Johnson.

Ethan's father never remarried. He and Ethan eventually reached an accommodation, not love, but a respectful tolerance, which is why Ethan was surprised at the depth of his grief when his father died prematurely of an aneurysm when Ethan was away at graduate school.

When Johnson was ninety-two Ethan received a call saying that he was dying. He dropped everything and hurried to his bedside. Johnson was still alert but failing rapidly.

Ethan took his hand, his eyes tearing, and looked deep into Johnson's now clouded eyes. "You made me. Everything I am is due to you. *Rascal* and what you gave me mean more than anything else I've ever had. You truly gave me life. I love you."

He had to lean close to hear Johnson's response. "I love you too. Always have since I first met you. Remember our conversation about death?"

Ethan nodded.

"Well, I goin to find out if death do have a sting. I'll let you know. Listen for me in de wind as you sail you *Rascal*."

The End

Made in the USA
Monee, IL
09 September 2023

42344918R00173